LADY DRAGON

D Jordan Redhawk

Bella
BOOKS
2015

First Bella Books Edition 2015

Editor: Ruth Stanley
Cover Designer: Linda Callaghan

ISBN: 978-1-59493-438-4

Other Books by D Jordan Redhawk

Broken Trails
Orphan Maker
Lichii Ba'Cho
Tiopa Ki Lakota
Freya's Tears

Sanguire Series
The Strange Path
Beloved Lady Mistress
Inner Sanctuary

Dedication

Anna Trinity Redhawk—I couldn't have done this without your unconditional love and support. Thank you for always being there!

About the Author

D Jordan Redhawk lives in Portland, Oregon where she works in the hospitality industry. (But don't make the mistake of thinking she's hospitable.) Her household consists of her wife of twenty-seven years, three crazy cats and a white buffalo Beanie Buddy named Roam.

For more information on D Jordan Redhawk, visit her website: *http://www.djordanredhawk.com*

Acknowledgments

Man, you are good.

Yeah, I'm talking to you. *You!* The person holding this book in hot little hands and reading these words. You, the reader!

You've waited so long for the final book of the Sanguire series...That speaks of sheer patience and dedication right there! Not many writers can boast having a readership that does such things. A lot of folks with less gumption would have forgotten the Sanguire by now, moved on to better and shinier things. You must have really liked the previous books to still be here.

Thank you for waiting all these years for this last installment.

Thank you for the occasional random emails asking for information.

Thank you for being you!

I'd also like to acknowledge a couple of other folks while I'm at it. Anita Pawlowski, Shawn Cady and Anna Redhawk were my first readers. They've waited a lot longer to see this final product, having begun sending me feedback in the dark ages of 2006! Troopers, each of 'em!

Added to that list is Susan Jacobsen. To support a friend after a horrific car accident, I offered a character auction. Susan was the winner. Talk about patience! She's had to wait three years to see her character reach print! Susan, you're awesome! My apologies for the delayed gratification! I hope the Jake you see in these pages is one of which you can be proud!

All right. I'm done. Well? Don't let me stop you! Turn the page! Get started!

CAST OF CHARACTERS

The Davis Group

Father James Castillo–board of directors–European

Chano–board of directors–American Indian

Jenna "Whiskey" Davis–**Ninsumgal**, president of The Davis Group–American

Dikeledi–board of directors–African

Reynhard Dorst–**Sañur Gasum**, board of directors–European

Margaurethe O'Toole–**Ki'an Gasan**, CEO of The Davis Group–European

Valmont Strauss–**Sublugal Sañar**, board of directors–African-European

Phineas Blackwell–Whiskey's chauffeur, cousin of Margaurethe O'Toole

Susan "Jake" Jacobsen–**Zi Agada**, Whiskey's primary bodyguard–European

Sasha Kopecki–**Ugula Aga'us**, Captain of Whiskey's personal guard–European

Sithathor–Whiskey's chambermaid–Indian

Wahca–Whiskey's maternal grandmother–American Indian

Zica–Whiskey's maternal aunt–American Indian

Whiskey's Pack

Alphonse–brother to Zebediah–American

Chaniya–daughter of Dikeledi–African

Daniel Gleirscher–Whiskey's personal physician–German

Whiskey's Pack (cont.)

Nupa Olowan–nephew of Chano–American Indian

Zebediah–brother to Alphonse–American

The *Agrun Nam*

Lionel Bentoncourt–**Nam Lugal**, chairman

Aiden Cassadie–**Sabra Sañar**, Diplomat

Bertrada Nijmege–**Aga Maskim Sañar**, Judiciary of the High Court

Samuel McCall–**Maskim Sañar**, Judiciary of the Low Court

Ernst Rosenberg–**Sa'kan Sañar**, Master of Treasury

Elisibet Vasillas–**Ninsumgal** of the European Sanguire, assassinated by Valmont in 1629

Nahib–former **Nam Lugal**, brutally executed by *Ninsumgal* Elisibet Vasillas in 1629

Francesca Bentoncourt–Lionel Bentoncourt's wife

Orlaith O'Toole–*Ki'an Gasan* Margaurethe O'Toole's mother

Tireachan O'Toole–*Ki'an Gasan* Margaurethe O'Toole's father

Baltje–*Nam Lugal* Bentoncourt's aide

Alfred Basco–**Saggina**, European Sanguire magistrate to the Portland area

A glossary of terms is located at the end of the book.

CHAPTER ONE

The day was still new with promise. Indirect sunlight brought out the reddish highlights of Margaurethe O'Toole's shoulder-length mahogany hair. Though slight of form, she was tall, giving her a waif-like appearance. Today she wore a black business suit designed to offset this perceived delicacy. Deep-set emerald eyes scanned her surroundings as her mind did the same. She felt the presence of the two *aga'usi* before she saw them flanking the double doors leading into the executive offices. She nodded her approval with a smile.

"Good morning, *Ki'an Gasan* Margaurethe." A guard opened one door.

"Good morning, Peiter. Thank you. Is Father Castillo still here?"

"Yes, *Ki'an Gasan*. And *Sublugal Sañar* Valmont is also in audience with the *Ninsumgal*."

Margaurethe let that information pass without comment as she slipped into the office sitting room. Regardless of what had transpired three months ago, she didn't trust Valmont. In light of his involvement in her rescue from the hands of the Sanguire assassin, she'd been willing to ease her negative opinion of him…until she'd heard of his confession during her absence. He'd had designs on kidnapping Whiskey and spiriting her away to Europe. Margaurethe's discovery of his original traitorous intentions toward Whiskey hadn't facilitated confidence. That he still served as an advisor was a point of contention between her and Whiskey.

The Human executive assistant smiled as she stood. She skirted the monstrosity of a reception desk, a stalwart symbol of final defense protecting Whiskey from the uninitiated petitioner. "They're in her office, *Ki'an Gasan*. Would you like me to make you tea?"

"Thank you, Helen. That would be lovely." The assistant went one way and Margaurethe the other. She paused at Whiskey's door, the tendrils of her mind reaching out until it brushed against a number of essences and sensations on the other side. The only one that mattered was the aroma of roses, blood and a slight hint of water. The aroma grew stronger as Whiskey noted Margaurethe's mental contact and strengthened it. With a polite tap at the door, Margaurethe opened it and stepped inside.

The interior was standard as far as offices went. Whiskey was the president of The Davis Group, and money hadn't been spared to fill the office with expensive furniture. Her desk alone was a work of art with engraved carvings that had taken artisans months of toil to complete. Dark wooden shelves held tomes and scrolls from all the ages. The only incongruent piece was an ancient scarred writing table made of pine pushed against the wall behind the desk.

Two of the occupants rose as Margaurethe entered. "No, don't get up," she said, waving both Father James Castillo and Whiskey Davis into their seats. They both ignored her. Valmont, ever the annoyance, didn't even make the attempt, a sardonic grin lighting his dark face. Margaurethe refused to react to his impertinence though she felt an irrational tickle of aggravation at his petty behavior. Instead, she experienced satisfaction at the sight of the fourth person in the room standing behind Whiskey—a personal bodyguard that Margaurethe had hired immediately after the kidnapping and assassination fiasco three months ago. She smiled a greeting to everyone, even Valmont, taking Whiskey's offered hand and coming around the desk. Bending in for a kiss, she suddenly wished they were alone. "I hope I'm not interrupting anything."

"Not a thing." Whiskey wore black cargo pants and a white button-up shirt. The sleeves were partially rolled up her forearms, revealing the twining tails of two dragons on her right arm. A delicate golden locket rested in the hollow at the base of her throat. Her light blond hair hung straight past her shoulders. She'd tied back the sides, leaving the back loose, and long bangs framed her oval face. The only other jewelry she wore was a signet ring on her left middle finger, the large onyx stone carved with the likeness of a scorpion. It was the sigil of her house, one she'd researched extensively before deciding upon. Margaurethe remained uncertain as to how the *Agrun Nam* would react to it when they arrived, providing they knew much of scorpions to begin with. Scorpions were solitary hunters, vicious and poisonous, apt to sting first and investigate later. That Valmont had heartily approved of the design hadn't eased Margaurethe's mind.

"Actually, I was just preparing to leave." Castillo hadn't returned to his seat. He was shorter than Margaurethe, though of similar stature. His dark brown hair was wavy and hung to his shoulders and a neatly trimmed beard graced his face. Margaurethe had never seen him wearing anything but the cassock and collar of his order. An ornate Gothic-style cross around his neck was his only jewelry. "I've about bored My *Gasan* to tears with ancient history."

"He's not lying." Whiskey rolled her eyes.

"I should hope not. He's a priest." Margaurethe smiled. "He'd hardly set a proper example for his flock if he had difficulty speaking the truth." Having ignored Valmont for as long as politely possible, she finally did more than glance at him. He looked as dusty brown as ever, both in clothing and skin color. His hair was an elaborate mop of dreadlocks, and a goatee circled his sardonic lips. "And how are you this morning, Valmont?"

His eyes widened in a parody of surprise. "Why I'm spectacular, *Ki'an Gasan* Margaurethe. So kind of you to ask."

With effort, the smile remained on Margaurethe's face. Her duties to Valmont complete, she turned back to Castillo. "Actually, Father, I was wondering if perhaps we could speak a moment."

"Certainly, *Ki'an Gasan*. I've nothing scheduled until this afternoon."

Whiskey raised an inquisitive eyebrow, and Margaurethe smiled reassurance. She felt the featherlight touch of her lover's mind, meeting it with her own. The connection lasted only a moment before Whiskey lifted their entwined hands to kiss Margaurethe's knuckles.

Again Margaurethe wished they were alone. The past three months had seen many issues settled between them. Margaurethe didn't know if it was her view of Whiskey that had changed, or that Whiskey had indeed grown into her capabilities. She didn't care. What mattered was that something fundamental had altered between them after Whiskey had put down the assassin, Andri. An emotional stumbling block within Margaurethe had disappeared and she no longer spent vast hours worrying for her lover's safety. She glanced over Whiskey's shoulder at the personal bodyguard standing silently in the corner. *That probably doesn't hurt, either.*

With some effort Margaurethe released Whiskey and stepped toward the door. Castillo preceded her, opened the door and bowed farewell to Whiskey, gesturing Margaurethe to lead the way.

Margaurethe's last vision was Valmont hastening to his feet to give a formal bow and a jaunty wink. She couldn't help the sour turn of her lips as Castillo closed the door behind them. "That man is irrepressible."

"Perhaps." Castillo smiled at the executive secretary hustling toward them. "But he teaches Whiskey things neither of us can."

Margaurethe *hmphed*. She graciously accepted the cup of tea Helen brought, accepting apologies for its lateness and expressing her own for having to rush away. She took the cup with her as she led the way toward the executive dining room.

The room was empty, as expected for a Sunday morning. Most of the management staff that resided on property were either sleeping in or enjoying their breakfasts in the resident lounge on the fifteenth floor. If it weren't for the impending arrival of the *Agrun Nam* she and Whiskey would still be abed as well.

She took Castillo to a table in the back, far enough away from the entrance and kitchen access doors to keep from being overheard should someone enter. No one would be on duty in the kitchen today anyway. If the *Agrun Nam* chose to remain on property, they could utilize the resident lounge like everyone else. Besides, a welcome reception with plenty of food had been planned for later this evening. She put the never-ending to-do list out of her mind. "I'll get right to it, Father. You work closely with Whiskey. How is she?"

If he thought her question odd, he didn't say so. "She's doing well. She's yet to be stumped by any of her lessons. Quick to think on her feet. Her critical reasoning is growing by leaps and bounds, and she's surpassed me in math and sciences. Which reminds me, you'll need to find a tutor for her in those areas."

A frown creased Margaurethe's face. "That's not what I meant."

Castillo studied her, as if gauging his response. Just as Margaurethe prepared to demand an answer, he spoke. "She's in pain. A friend under her protection has died, the love of her life was seriously endangered, she killed an elder in her first formal adult duel, and at least one of her mortal enemies will be arriving this afternoon to live within her defenses."

Margaurethe sat back, the words slapping her with their bluntness.

"But this is nothing new to you, *Ki'an Gasan*."

"I know. But I'm too close." Margaurethe stared into her tea, not finding answers. "She hides things from me."

"She doesn't want to hurt you."

Her lips thinned. "It's not me who's hurting."

Castillo leaned forward. "Perhaps not, but it's the only way she knows to protect you."

Margaurethe tilted her head, eyes sharp. "Are you her confessor as well as her advisor?"

"She's not a member of my church, I can hardly be her confessor. Besides, I'm not currently active." He smiled and relaxed in his chair. "But I do what I can."

He had certainly become cockier over time. The longer he worked as one of Whiskey's advisors, the more he settled into the position. Margaurethe rather enjoyed their early days when she could browbeat him to keep him in line. It was obvious his time with Valmont had sullied him. Or perhaps it was all that time he'd spent with Whiskey's pack of younglings before they'd come to live here. Shepherding that particular flock had to have influenced some attitude changes.

He seemed aware he had displeased her for the smile left his face. "My apologies for being flippant, *Ki'an Gasan*. I realize you care deeply for Whiskey. We all do."

Somewhat mollified, she wiped the dour expression from her face. "Do you think she's coping well? Is she in any danger?"

Castillo's gaze swept away as he considered the question. "I believe she's coping as well as she can. Her mechanisms always veer toward stuffing it down and being alone. She's spent years in foster care or on the streets. You don't survive that with your heart on your sleeve." He focused on Margaurethe once more. "But she's grown considerably on an emotional level since her walk along the Strange Path. You didn't know her before—I can see a radical difference in her behavior and thought patterns. I think as long as we're all available for her, she'll be fine."

She couldn't help but notice his inflection. "All of us? Including Valmont, I suppose?"

His face was unreadable. "Yes, *Sublugal Sañar* Valmont was included in that statement."

"Whatever did he do to impress you, Father?" Margaurethe shook her head. "He has done nothing but lie about his intentions for months, exposing Whiskey to risks for his entertainment, not arguing with her when she pulled that idiotic stunt to rescue me. Do you know he even swore noninterference with Andri so she could fight him herself?" she said, referring to the most recent incident involving an elusive assassin that had come very near to succeeding at killing Whiskey.

"Yes, I'm aware of the situation. But he told the truth, Margaurethe. He confessed his traitorous activities to his ruler, and swore fealty a second time. He's been nothing but the epitome of an advisor and friend since." Castillo's gaze reflected an odd haunting look. "He's paid for his original sin a thousand times over. Isn't it time to let him start anew?"

She narrowed her eyes. "Are you speaking of Valmont or yourself?"

His brow cleared, a smile quirking his lips. "That didn't answer my question."

"And I notice that you didn't answer mine." Before he could respond she waved the topic away, changing the subject. "So you're of the opinion that Whiskey is doing fine as far as her emotional welfare is concerned?"

"As well as can be expected under the circumstances. It's good that she's had the time to work through her thoughts and feelings before the *Agrun Nam* arrives. Speaking of which," he cocked his head, "what time should I be at the airport?"

Margaurethe sighed. "Their plane should land at two thirty this afternoon." She rolled her eyes. "Their assorted personnel began arriving three days ago and are in the process of setting up residence as we speak. They've had hundreds of deliveries, cases of documents, personal effects, and the like. Thank you for suggesting bomb dogs. While they haven't found anything, the added assurance eases my mind."

"You're most welcome."

"You'll be available to attend the soiree this evening?"

He bowed his head in agreement. "Of course. I look forward to it."

"I'm glad someone is, Father. Other than Reynhard, the rest of us will be biting our nails to the quick."

* * *

Whiskey watched the door close behind Margaurethe and Castillo with mixed emotions. *I wish the* Agrun Nam *were already here and gone.*

"I believe that's my cue to depart as well."

She looked at Valmont who had remained standing. "You'd better be here tonight. If I have to suffer through this, so do you."

Valmont affected injury as he held a hand to his chest. "I would never leave you to the tender mercies of the *Agrun Nam* alone. Besides, Aiden can be such a bore. You'll need at least one person to talk to that isn't interested in etiquette. How droll." His lips quirked into a smile at her laugh. "I'll be here with bells on. Five o'clock?"

"Yes. Margaurethe says they'll be here around three this afternoon. That should give them time to get settled before the reception." She pushed to her feet and came around the desk. "What are the chances of you getting dressed up for the occasion?"

He snorted at her, taking her offered hand. "Slim to none, I'd say. My days as a dandy have long passed, *My Gasan.*"

Her smile was a sad one, the melancholy brought on by memories of political receptions past when a much younger Valmont had delighted in the color and splendor of a new outfit. The recollections weren't hers; they belonged to Elisibet Vasillas, the Sweet Butcher of the European Sanguire. Most of those memories were brutal and unwanted, but occasionally Whiskey uncovered gems of pleasure. It was odd how she missed the Valmont of old though she'd never met him. She shook his hand. "Maybe so, but does it really take you seven hours to prepare?"

Valmont laughed, releasing her. "I've been discovered!" He glanced past Whiskey at the woman posted behind the desk. "Jake, help me out here."

Whiskey turned to regard the bodyguard who had been her constant companion for almost three months. She had the same height and coloring as Whiskey, though her hair was prematurely graying and her eyes were hazel. She appeared to be in her late twenties, but Whiskey knew her to be over five hundred thirty years old.

Jake raised an elegant eyebrow at Valmont. "That's not in my job description, *Sublugal Sañar* Valmont."

Valmont grumbled with little heat, a grin still teasing the corners of his mouth. "Since I've been thrown under the bus by your protector, I'll take my leave. I may come early to welcome your guests." He stepped backward, bowing low as he went. The obeisance usually annoyed Whiskey, which is why he did it.

"Until this afternoon or evening, My *Ninsumgal*."

Whiskey pointed at him, warning in her tone. "Count on it." Once he was gone, her humor melted away. She drifted toward the window, staring out at the park across the street and the river beyond.

Soon the person responsible for the two assassination attempts against her would arrive. She'd demanded that the *Agrun Nam* send three representatives to her and had no doubt that the man would be among them. At least she knew it was a man—the only woman on the council was Bertrada Nijmege, and her goal was to kill Whiskey herself. Whiskey blew out a breath, knowing that Nijmege would probably be one of the representatives too. The *Agrun Nam* had spent months attempting to retrieve Whiskey and bring her to Europe. That had failed, which left Nijmege no other choice but to come to her. Arms crossed, Whiskey leaned one shoulder against the window frame. Her stomach twisted, a light reminder of the forthcoming emotional turmoil she'd have to endure as she met people who actively wanted her death. *Why did I ask them here again? Oh, yeah. To make things right.* That was a laugh.

"You should move away from the window, *Ninsumgal*. You're making a target of yourself."

Whiskey looked at her bodyguard. Jake's skin was of a lighter hue than hers, but from far enough away that detail wasn't noticeable. Reynhard Dorst, Whiskey's security advisor, had recommended Susan "Jake" Jacobsen for this position just after Margaurethe's kidnapping and rescue, citing that at the very least Jake could double for Whiskey from a passable distance. To that end, Jake had moved forward to mimic Whiskey's stance, facing her. She did that a lot. It was almost annoying in a younger sibling sort of way. "Are you ready for tonight?"

"Of course, *Ninsumgal*. I've read all the dossiers that *Sañur Gasum* Dorst has given me. I also receive updated reports regarding the movements of *Agrun Nam* personnel in this and the neighboring building." She tapped the tiny wireless radio bud in her ear.

Leaning her temple against the frame, Whiskey studied Jake. "Does Reynhard foresee any trouble?"

"At this sort of function? Doubtful." Jake stared out the window beside her, eyes scanning every pedestrian, every vehicle passing on the street below. "Whomever has threatened you works alone until he contracts an assassin. He'll use the reception tonight to gauge the situation—check security, judge the general feel of the people in attendance. He'll be looking for potential allies and connections. So far he's been meticulous in his planning, so it's doubtful he'll suddenly decide to throw caution to the winds and personally attack you, especially in a public place. He remains secretive to capitalize on your demise; he needs to be officially disassociated from your death."

Whiskey grinned, turning so her back was against the window frame. "Good. Then you can take the night off."

Jake smiled, a glint of humor sparking in her eyes as she continued to search for danger. When in a room full of people, she portrayed studious attention or bristled with danger. Only when Whiskey was alone with her did she loosen up, though she never forgot her duty. "Not likely, *Ninsumgal*."

"Don't you get tired of it? Following me around, day in and day out? Never getting to cut loose?"

"No, My *Gasan*, I don't. This is what I enjoy doing." Her smile widened at Whiskey's scoff of disbelief. "Besides, where else can I get an opportunity to practice my Setswana?"

Whiskey laughed at the reference to the language spoken by Chaniya, the African youngling who had attached herself to Whiskey's entourage. Whiskey's pack had become a conglomeration as racially mixed as her board of directors. Whiskey was the youngest of them, the oldest being Daniel at a venerable fifty years of age, and members represented a cross-section of American, European, African and American Indian peoples. Chaniya had come aboard months ago when her mother had been sent to negotiate with The Davis Group. She'd stayed because her mother, Dikeledi, had joined the corporate board. Chaniya had tutored both Whiskey and Jake in Setswana slang, teaching them vulgar words that Whiskey could never use in her business conversations with Dikeledi.

Using her shoulders, she pushed away from the window frame and returned to her desk. A current photo of Betrada Nijmege looked back at her from the computer monitor. The years hadn't been kind. Two deep lines bisected her brow, lines that were mere hints in Elisibet's memories. Coupled with a sharp beak of a nose, the effect was one of a bird of prey, ever vigilant, ever seeking some hapless rodent upon which to dine. And Whiskey was the rat.

Whiskey leaned across the desk, propping her chin on one hand as the other played across the leather texture of the blotter. As she studied the image, her fingers tingled. It took a moment before she realized that she no longer caressed the blotter, instead reaching through the paper and leather with her gift, touching the wood beneath. After months of disappointment, not knowing what psychic talent would manifest once she reached maturity, it had come as a shock to discover she was *Gidimam Kissane Lá*, a fabled Ghost Walker. That gift had saved her life more than once, and she'd become skilled in its use. These days it was as common as breathing. She jerked her fingers away from the surface of the desk and the tingling sensation stopped.

A glance over her shoulder showed Jake back in position behind her, staring out the window. That was the good thing about Jake; despite being constantly underfoot, her presence rarely impinged on Whiskey's senses. It wasn't that she was invisible, or that Whiskey had simply become accustomed to her constant attendance. Something about Jake made her blend into the background until she was needed. So far she hadn't been.

Whiskey knew that was going to change very soon.

CHAPTER TWO

The cavalcade consisted of several nondescript sedans full of security personnel and adjutants conspicuously surrounding two limousines. Lionel Bentoncourt looked out the tinted limo window as they neared downtown Portland, examining the cityscape. Beside him, his wife, Francesca, held his hand. Father Castillo shared the seat across from the Bentoncourts with Bertrada Nijmege.

For a mere thirty minutes, it had been a long and tedious trip, brimming with Nijmege's fuming and fury. Bentoncourt had no illusions regarding her opinion of this summons; hard put to be oblivious when all Nijmege had done for weeks was to complain in any ear, sympathetic or not. Even her ally on the *Agrun Nam* had gotten tired of the rants. That was probably why Samuel McCall had chosen the second limousine for this trip from the airport. Whether or not he had received a better deal remained to be seen. Dorst was in that car, and there was little doubt that the conversation would be flippantly outrageous.

Bentoncourt's gaze flickered to the man across from him. Castillo's expression was pleasant and neutral despite the cloud of anger surrounding his seating companion. He had a level head and a professional demeanor, both excellent qualities for an advisor to a young *ninsumgal*. Jenna Davis had enjoyed very good fortune since her discovery. Bentoncourt was certain Castillo was rabidly devoted, as *Ki'an Gasan* O'Toole and Reynhard Dorst no doubt were. He made note to have someone double-check Castillo's file. Perhaps there was something more at work than an ambitious youngling making himself indispensable to a new ruler. It wouldn't be the first time the Human church had scrabbled for wealth and power and this priest followed their religion. Still, Castillo didn't set off any of Bentoncourt's alarm bells. Whatever he was drawn to didn't seem to be money. It wouldn't hurt to have more information on all of *Ninsumgal* Davis's advisors, however.

"How much longer?"

Castillo glanced out the window to get his bearings, ignoring Nijmege's rude tone. "No more than fifteen minutes, *Aga Maskim Sañar* Nijmege. If you look west, you can see our buildings—the white ones to the left of the tall brick."

Bentoncourt allowed himself to be distracted by the view, finding the building in question as the driver took them over one of many bridges spanning the Willamette River. The Davis Group sat near the edge of the water that cut through the center of Portland. A large expanse of grass, apparently a public park, ran along the river's length, forming a natural amphitheater of greenery before it.

"It's rather oddly shaped," Francesca observed from beside him.

"It used to be a hotel, *Gasan* Bentoncourt. The majority of the business offices are there, but the upper floors have been rebuilt as a series of residences. The building to the left has been renovated for your residences and offices, and behind the brick on the other side is another building that's being refurbished to provide production and shipping facilities."

"And where does Jenna Davis reside?" Nijmege's muddy-brown eyes sharply studied the structure.

"Our *Ninsumgal* lives in the penthouse of the main building."

Bentoncourt smothered a grin at the priest's inflection. Leave it to him to remind all of them why they were here and who was truly in charge.

Nijmege grumped but didn't rise to the bait, surprising him. She'd been less than subtle about her opinions of Davis. Bentoncourt considered Castillo's status, realizing why she didn't seek to disavow the *Ninsumgal's* place to the priest. He was an underling and beneath her notice. If Nijmege made her beliefs known it would be to her peers or Davis herself.

The limousine pulled into downtown traffic. The streets were busy as the residents enjoyed their Sunday afternoon. It seemed the city had an extensive transit system, evidenced by the number of people loitering around partially enclosed bus shelters. The sun hadn't gone down, but buildings towering above blocked off direct sunlight. There seemed to be trees everywhere and a full half of them were lit up. "It's still some time until Christmas."

Castillo gave him a quizzical look and followed his gesture. He smiled. "Ah, yes. Several downtown businesses leave the lights up year round. It makes the area easier on the eye."

"I've heard there are some wonderful old churches located downtown. Aren't there, Father?" Francesca said.

"Yes, there are, *Gasan*." Castillo listed some locations. "As a matter of fact, there's one about six blocks up that street. If you'd like, I'd be more than happy to give you a tour once you've settled in."

Francesca squeezed her husband's hand. "That would be splendid, Father. Perhaps you could fill me in on the history here, as well? I'm woefully ignorant of doings here in the New Country."

Bentoncourt's wife scented and gathered facts by second nature. He knew she was beginning the hunt. Before the night was complete, she'd be able to tell him everything she'd gleaned from the individuals she so politely pumped for information. "It's hardly the 'New Country' anymore, my dear." His voice was fond as he raised her hand to his lips.

She blushed, letting him cast her as the not-too-bright wife of a high official. They both knew different, as did anyone familiar with them.

"I'd be honored to answer any questions you might have, *Gasan* Bentoncourt."

Beside the priest, Nijmege gave a discourteous snort. Bentoncourt felt a trickle of pleasure as Castillo ignored the insult. Yes, this young Sanguire made a wonderful advisor to *Ninsumgal* Davis.

The limousine changed direction, turning into a driveway and drawing his attention back outside. They pulled onto a wide front apron, the sedans before them moving to the right lane so the limos would stop directly before the main doors on the left. Leaving the engine running, the driver exited. He did not yet open the door, however, waiting for the other vehicles to release the main force of *Agrun Nam* security. Once guards were in place and given the go-ahead, the driver opened the door.

"Welcome to The Davis Group, *Nam Lugal* Bentoncourt, *Aga Maskim Sañar* Nijmege, *Gasan* Bentoncourt," the driver said, a cheerful Irish lilt to his voice as he bowed.

Castillo gestured for them to exit first.

Bentoncourt climbed out of the limousine, taking his wife's hand and assisting her. "Thank you."

The others had disembarked their limo and were herded toward the front entrance by the stark black-and-white apparition of Reynhard Dorst. He had on the same type of clothes he'd worn months ago when he'd delivered Davis's "invitation"— black leather from head to toe with various archaic spikes and studs and zippers in the strangest of places. His pale head was bald save for three jet-black mohawks that spiked over it.

Aiden Cassadie appeared amused, his brown eyes dancing on his handsome face. As ever, he was elegantly dressed—this time in a three-piece business suit of black, a royal blue handkerchief peeking from his breast pocket. Bentoncourt was surprised Cassadie hadn't worn a tuxedo the way he'd been on about the trip. As ever, Ernst Rosenberg was implacable, no indication of his feelings about their travel companion evident on his angelic face. The youngest member of the *Agrun Nam*, Samuel McCall, had a disgruntled expression. Since Dorst had turned up alive and well, McCall had been most interested in the Sweet Butcher's spy. A thirty-minute trip had been apparently more than enough time for young McCall to get his fill of Dorst's brand of humor.

Dorst gave an obsequious bow, his leather trench coat swirling about him. "Please accept my utmost apologies that I cannot spend more time in such an august gathering," he intoned, the delight in his black eyes and a slight mocking lilt in his voice belying his words. "But I'm called away to business forthwith."

"Off to crawl among your webs, are you?" Nijmege muttered.

Bentoncourt gave her a sharp look.

Dorst's visage shifted into sorrow, an expression that didn't meet his eyes. "I'm wounded, *Aga Maskim Sañar*. Surely you don't believe I'd wish to be anywhere else but in your extraordinary presence?"

Considering Nijmege was the most discernible threat to Davis, Bentoncourt was certain Dorst wanted to keep constant tabs on her. Regardless of her feelings about Davis, however, they all needed to remember this was a fact-finding and diplomatic mission, not a bar brawl. Before she could respond to Dorst's jibe, he stepped forward. "My apologies, Reynhard. We're all tired from our trip." He mentally reached out to touch Nijmege's mind, the sensation and smell of autumn leaves filling his mind.

She accepted his correction, lips twisting into a barely passable smile. "Yes, of course."

The expression on Dorst's face indicated he was aware Nijmege hadn't truly apologized. His grin was infectious as he bowed once more. "I'll see you all this evening at the reception." With that he turned, his coat whirling at his ankles, and stalked off toward a ramp presumably leading down to the parking garage.

"And how was your ride?" Cassadie asked Bentoncourt, eyes twinkling. "Not nearly as interesting as mine, I'd wager."

"No doubt." Bentoncourt affected a mild tone.

"If the esteemed *Agrun Nam* will follow me." Castillo led them toward a pair of doormen who opened the double glass doors.

Bentoncourt took his wife's arm and followed Castillo inside, the rest of the council trailing behind.

The lobby of the office complex was elegant. Buttery Italian marble spanned the floor, accented with strips of malachite and gold. An octagonal mosaic in the entry held a stylized motif. He ruminated over it a moment before realizing it was a scorpion, stinger poised to strike the person entering. Interesting. He noted inviting couches and chairs of yellows and greens perched upon burgundy rugs. Overhead, a dome of opaque glass hung from golden chains, the soft glow it gave off not noticeable in the light of day. To the right of the doors, a teak desk with a marble counter spanned that side of the lobby. On the left was what appeared to be a coffee kiosk, currently closed. And hanging above the attentive security posted across from the doors was a portrait.

Nijmege cursed in Bulgarian.

A sullen and gaunt Elisibet slouched on a stool. Her light blond hair, streaked with black, flowed loosely about her shoulders. She wore mirrored sunglasses, blocking the vision of her eyes. Her lips held a familiar sardonic twist, and Bentoncourt's heart thumped in dread. This had to be a portrait of Jenna Davis, not a reconstruction of the Sweet Butcher. Was this the image of Mahar's prophecy? Was this young woman truly as hard as the painting indicated? She wore a black camisole, the baggy pants ripped and torn to reveal black cloth beneath. One dirty boot, laces dangling, sat cocked on a rung of the stool. Her hands rested easily between her widespread legs. Here the artist had gone a step further than a simple portrait. A tattoo ran up her right arm, twin dragons of green and red slithering along her skin. Taking poetic license, the artist had painted them sliding from her flesh, as if escaping the bonds of skin and ink, to twine about each other and her.

"Interesting work, isn't it?" a humorous voice asked.

"Illuminating." Bentoncourt dropped his gaze from the unsettling scene. "*Sublugal Sañar* Valmont, it's good to see you again."

If anything, Valmont's grin widened. He bowed graciously, a hand over his breast. "And you, of course, *Nam Lugal* Bentoncourt." His gaze swept past Bentoncourt. "Bertrada! I've so missed you these last three months."

Behind him, Bentoncourt felt Nijmege bristle. Here was something of interest. Valmont had apparently been in contact with her since Davis had appeared in Seattle. Valmont's arrival on the scene made much more sense in light of that fact. Nijmege had brought him in to further her goals. *That certainly hadn't worked in her favor, had it?* Apparently unable to find something to say that wouldn't bring up incriminating questions, Nijmege remained silent. Bentoncourt let the painting draw his attention. "It holds an eerie likeness to Elisibet. Who's the artist?"

Feigning somberness, Valmont regarded the artwork. "Unfortunately, the artist is dead. Perhaps you knew him?" He turned back to the newcomers. "Rufus Barrett, the Human assassin who attempted to kill my liege before she made it through the *Ñíri Kurám.*" He seemed to be trying to surprise some sort of response out of them.

Bentoncourt gazed calmly into questioning brown eyes. "I've not had the misfortune."

Valmont winked and let the moment go. "My dear *Agrun Nam.*" His voice rose to address them all. "I have been charged to welcome you to your new home." He bowed low, making the mannerism more an insult than respect for their status.

Bentoncourt almost heard Nijmege's teeth grinding together. "Thank you, Valmont. It's been a long journey. Perhaps you could direct us to our rooms so that we may refresh ourselves."

"Certainly."

Castillo, who had been speaking to the security at the desk, returned. His smile was a bit more open, and he carried a handful of folders. He handed one to each councilor. "The location of your suites and offices are inside, as well as rooming assignments for the staff you've brought along. Any last-minute additions will need to speak to our security here to arrange lodging. You'll find layouts for both buildings, a security procedural standard and emergency response instructions."

"Security procedural standards?" Francesca echoed, peering past her husband's shoulder at the paperwork inside.

"Yes." Valmont interrupted Castillo before he could respond. "It's primarily a list of areas to be avoided if you wish to remain in the *Ninsumgal's* good graces."

A fleeting expression of irritation crossed Castillo's face. "As well as the location of security desks, how to get your keys replaced if necessary, who to call for questions and repairs, and who is allowed in the more secure areas of your residences."

"How thoughtful," Francesca murmured.

"The doors are electronically locked. You'll see a key card in your packet. That will get you into most areas. Your residence and personal offices also have a keypad. Reynhard has included the current combination and suggests you change it immediately. Instructions are in the green envelope." Castillo looked past the *Agrun Nam* to the other people drifting in with luggage and boxes. "Your people will find their keys and information packets inside their rooms."

"And when will we meet our most humble host?" Nijmege asked, a feral smile on her face.

Valmont opened his mouth to respond, but Castillo took a quick step forward and inserted himself between the verbal combatants. "Your presence is requested this evening at five, *Aga Maskim Sañar. Ki'an Gasan* Margaurethe has arranged an informal gathering to be located in the ballroom downstairs in the lower levels of this building. *Ninsumgal* Davis requests you, your spouses and consorts, and personal aides in attendance."

Bentoncourt looked over his companions. Rosenberg remained solemn. McCall seemed put out, as if he wasn't sure whether he should be offended for Nijmege's sake or irritated with the professionalism being shown.

Cassadie winked at Bentoncourt and stepped forward. "Please tender our gracious thanks to Ms. Davis." He nodded to Castillo. "Speaking for myself, I'll be overjoyed to finally meet her."

The others remembered their manners and mumbled some sort of acceptance. Valmont's lopsided grin indicated exactly what he thought of their graciousness. "If you'll follow me." Castillo waved his hand to the right. "Elevators are over here, and I have aides waiting on the third floor to escort you to your quarters."

Bentoncourt trailed the priest, his wife taking over the packet of paperwork. She extracted the rooming list. "I'll give this to Baltje," she said, referring to his chief aide. "He can get everyone situated."

She disappeared from his side as he entered the elevator and admired the warm teak-paneled interior. Once his companions joined him the doors closed, revealing a mirrored surface. As his gaze traveled over the other *sanari*, he wondered exactly what they were in for.

* * *

Samuel McCall studied downtown Portland from his open living room window. Unlike his peers he'd been to America, but it had been over a hundred fifty years ago. He had never been this far west before. Green hills loomed close, dark pine trees giving way to cleared areas where homes and businesses had been built into the hillside.

Behind him, he listened to the intense search conducted by his assistant and a handful of *Agrun Nam* guard. They had the latest in snoop detection devices with them, sweeping his quarters for any nasty little surprises left behind by Dorst. So far, the hunt had turned up nothing. Either Davis had held Dorst back from his natural inclination, or the spy had found some toy that was far more sophisticated than that which anyone else had experienced. Considering the scanty reports on Davis, he felt his chances were actually good for the former. She didn't appear to be cutthroat, unlike her predecessor. Dorst seemed completely infatuated with her too. Would he disobey her honorable yet ridiculous order to not bug private dwellings?

"Nothing, *Sañar*."

Apparently, he wouldn't. He looked at his assistant. "Check my offices. Follow that up with everyone else's quarters."

"Yes, *Sañar*." The woman spun around, gathering up the security team with a gesture, an economy of movement more suited to a covert operations team leader than a mere aide.

"I'll see you in the audience hall at the proper time."

"Yes, *Sañar*."

Returning his gaze to the city, he barely heard the gentle *snick* of the door closing behind them.

The inevitable had happened. He was trapped in the house that Davis built. His plans to overtake the *Agrun Nam* and assume the throne were in shambles. What to do? What to do? Hiring another assassin would be redundant. The Human had failed because he'd been Human, the Sanguire because he'd held a bizarre sense of honor. Would McCall have time to locate anyone at this late stage? Word of the Sweet Butcher's return had flown far and wide. The rumors facilitated his opportunity to locate some disaffected person willing to kill her, but getting an assassin through the strict security would be another matter. It was too late for such measures. He shouldn't have waited so long to make the second attempt. That decision hobbled him now.

He let out a frustrated breath. The air was cool but nowhere near as chill as back home. There, the first snows were on the horizon, the mountainous landscape around the palace soon to be in keeping with one of those silly holiday cards of which Humans were so fond. This climate was akin to his birthplace on the Scottish coast. All he needed were cliffs and the ocean churning in the dark to feel at home.

Only one option remained open: to fully support Nijmege in deed as well as word. He knew the *Agrun Nam* would sign a treaty with Davis, regardless of Nijmege's arguments. A larger, more powerful ruler than the Sweet Butcher had ever dreamed of being would dilute their control over the European Sanguire. Losing that control wouldn't cripple the *Agrun Nam*, but it would put to waste the plans he'd set in motion a century ago. Disbanding the *Agrun Nam* and taking the European throne would be three times as difficult if they had the global resources of The Davis Group from which to draw. Nijmege, though fanatical in her desire to kill Davis, was too emotional. He hated to back her, knowing that the wrong statement or action from any quarter could send her into a fit of fury. Any thought of revenge would filter through a red haze of emotion, no doubt rendering her all but useless in the ultimate goal. But what other choice did he have?

He closed the window of his temporary home, turning his back on the city. A clock on the wall indicated the hour with a soft chime. The clock was ticking, faster and faster; soon there would be no time left to plan, to achieve his goal.

Shaking off annoyance, he headed for his bedchamber to dress for the evening's function.

CHAPTER THREE

Unbeknownst to her new guests, Whiskey watched their entrance from the primary security complex on the lobby level, mere meters from where they'd walked into the lobby. Racks of video monitors adorned one side of the room, one of which she'd taken over for her voyeurism. Four security personnel sat along the bank of displays, monitoring the comings and goings of this and the adjoining buildings in a constant hum of radio chatter. As the *Agrun Nam* passed the guard post en route to their temporary homes, Whiskey paused to study a three-ring binder for instructions. Entering two keystrokes on the computer keyboard changed the view, and she observed them enter an elevator. Castillo remained behind until the doors closed, letting the *Agrun Nam* continue with their assigned escorts. Entering another keyboard command, she switched to the camera inside the elevator.

A number of office chairs had been rolled into the surveillance room, though most remained empty. Chano, an elderly American Indian occupied one, his aged hand clutching his fetish-bestrewed walking stick as he peered at the monitor with avid curiosity. He wore what passed for business casual for his people—loose-fitting jeans, hand-made leather boots laced over the calves, and a long-sleeved wool shirt of grass green. His hair held the wispiness associated with advanced age, his sharp eyes contrasting the perception.

Beside him sat the newest addition to The Davis Group's board of directors. In stark contrast, Dikeledi, the African Sanguire ambassador, was young and strong. Her back was ramrod straight. When she stood, she towered over everyone else on the board, even Dorst. She wore a simple dress of bright yellows and reds, a matching kerchief holding her hair. Though still a relative unknown, Whiskey had been impressed with her abilities to negotiate an agreement between the corporation and her countrymen. Dikeledi seemed as fierce as her daughter, Chaniya, something that Whiskey respected.

Margaurethe stood behind Whiskey, a delicate hand upon her shoulder. Ever in the background was Jake, silently watching even when allies and security surrounded Whiskey.

Valmont strolled into the room with Dorst. "That would have been much more entertaining if the priest hadn't intervened." Valmont tossed himself carelessly into a chair, winking at Dikeledi. He craned his neck to see the monitor. "I had hopes of Bertrada saying something snide."

Whiskey smirked but gave him a slight disapproving glance. "Bloodshed in the lobby on their first day doesn't give me warm snugglies. It's probably just as well."

"Whatever." Valmont shrugged away her words.

"How was the trip from the airport?" Chano asked, his voice the sound of gravel.

Dorst, who had remained standing by the door, swept forward. "It was most enjoyable, sir, though *Sa'kan Sañar* Rosenberg was his usual stoic self. Most of the conversation was between *Sabra Sañar* Cassadie and myself." He paused, pursing his lips in a thoughtful frown. "*Maskim Sañar* McCall hardly spoke a word, though his sour expressions served to illuminate much."

"Like what?" Whiskey turned her attention to Dorst. McCall was a wild card, having been appointed to the *Agrun Nam* after Elisibet's death. She had no ancient memories of him or his family to draw upon. All she knew was what his dossier held and that he'd sided with Nijmege in her plans to deal with Whiskey.

"He's not a happy man."

Valmont snorted. "I should hope not. I doubt any of them are pleased with this turn of events."

Dorst shook his head, mohawks waving with the motion. "It's more than that. Yet he keeps his counsel, cards close to the chest. I wouldn't want to play poker with him."

Margaurethe frowned. "Ernst has always done the same."

"True. Yet, Rosenberg has a known history, a well-documented one regarding his voting. He has always seemed an honorable and thoughtful man."

"And this Samuel McCall doesn't?" Dikeledi asked, arching an elegant eyebrow. She'd only been on the board for two months, but was fully informed regarding the threats against Whiskey's life. While she'd yet to develop real loyalty toward Whiskey, she at least understood the political ramifications should The Davis Group president be murdered before her people saw any benefit to the agreements they'd signed.

Dorst waggled his hand in a seesaw motion. "His voting record indicates he's willing to do the proper thing, however, most of his decisions indirectly benefit him by increasing his power."

"Imagine that." Valmont's voice held a measure of sarcastic wonder.

Chano grunted. "Sounds like a true politician."

"Did anyone bother to explain why all five of them showed up?" Margaurethe focused on Dorst, who tittered in response.

"Oh, my, yes! That did come up in my discussion with Aiden." His expression morphed into the sly conspirator as he leaned forward, dropping the volume of his voice to complete the effect. "Apparently this is a gesture of goodwill toward My *Gasan*. They wished to show her their…'support,' if you will, for her business endeavors. Aiden and Lionel will be returning home in three days to carry on governing their people."

"Leaving two snakes and an unknown element to talk terms?" Chano snorted.

Dikeledi nodded, an imperious motion that was echoed in her rich voice. "This 'support' seems quite useless."

"But not unexpected," Dorst added with an enigmatic smile.

Whiskey watched the monitor. McCall and Rosenberg had long since left the elevator. With another glance at the instruction sheet, Whiskey switched the camera view to the twelfth floor of the neighboring building, focusing on McCall being directed by house staff to his apartment. At Dorst's request, Margaurethe had purposely put McCall and Nijmege on different floors. It seemed McCall wasn't at all pleased about sharing his floor with Rosenberg though they were each in different wings. Irritation glowed on his young face. At the door to his quarters, he snapped something over his shoulder to his escort, chasing the woman away. He opened the envelope from his packet, plugged in his password and utilized the keycard. Three of his staff preceded him before he disappeared from Whiskey's view.

She regretted not having security cameras or microphones inside the residences. Dorst and Valmont had both argued for them. Even without the Padre's disapproving frown, she knew better. If this was to work, the *Agrun Nam* had to feel safe in their temporary apartments. Their personal security officers would probably do full sweeps to ensure their privacy anyway. She hoped it would raise their opinion of her if they found nothing out of the ordinary.

With nothing further to watch, she instructed the monitor to return to its programming and leaned back in her chair, turning toward her advisors. Margaurethe moved away, settling a hip on the edge of the console beside her. Another knock on the door heralded Castillo's arrival.

"That's one less thing to worry about." He wiped imaginary sweat from his brow. "Your guests will soon be comfortably ensconced in their suites, My *Ninsumgal*."

"Thanks, Padre. Now sit down. You know when you hover it gives me a headache."

He grinned and took a chair.

"We've heard Reynhard's report," Margaurethe said. "What of yours?"

Castillo stroked his beard. "As I expected, *Nam Lugal* Bentoncourt and *Gasan* Francesca were pleasant and professional. Regardless of the circumstances, I think they both believe what they're doing is necessary."

Valmont nodded. "And Bertrada? Does she feel the same?"

The priest grimaced. "You know as well as I." He gave Whiskey a serious look. "I highly recommend you keep Valmont separated from Nijmege. It wouldn't take much for those two to fall to blows."

"No doubt," Margaurethe murmured.

Whiskey saw Valmont's indignant expression and waved her finger at him, shaking her head. "No, don't act innocent. You showed up here two hours early just for this. You know as well as I do how you enjoy goading your enemies."

His face melted into a rueful grin and he relaxed back into his chair. "Guilty as charged."

She couldn't help but smile at his unrepentant manner. Behind her, she felt Margaurethe's displeasure and shrugged it off. Her lover's problems with Valmont were based upon their shared violent history. It would take more than a few months for them to satisfactorily work out their differences. Knowing how Margaurethe felt, it would take decades or more for that to happen. She marveled for a moment at the thought, noting how her perceptions from a short Human lifespan to a much longer Sanguire one now came so easily, before reaching out with her mind to soothe Margaurethe's annoyance.

Castillo continued his report. "In any case, Nijmege will be trouble, as expected. She's of the obvious opinion that you are not who you claim to be."

Dorst's melodic tones cut into the conversation. "How odd. It rather defeats the purpose, doesn't it?"

"How so?" Dikeledi asked.

He gave an effete wave of a fine-boned hand. "If My *Ninsumgal* is not who she claims, then how can the esteemed Nijmege reasonably attain her goal of revenge? Yet, she seems to believe you are who you say you are, My *Gasan*. Else why plot with McCall against you?"

"No one said she has to make sense." Valmont snorted. "She's become a vicious and irrational woman since Nahib died."

A vision of Nahib's execution flashed before Whiskey's vision, his once strong body nothing more than pieces of raw meat after Elisibet's punishment. "Small wonder." Before Whiskey could succumb to melancholy, she forced herself to remember that she was not the Sweet Butcher of the past, regardless of the vivid memories that plagued her.

Margaurethe lightly touched Whiskey's mind before speaking. "Do you have an idea when Nijmege will act?"

Dorst's face became a caricature of disappointment. "Regrettably, no, *Ki'an Gasan*. Though I doubt she'll be too swift to make an attempt. She'll wish to settle in, become familiar with her new environs before moving forward with her plans."

"Appoint me your champion." Valmont sat forward in his chair.

Margaurethe made her opinion known with a derisive scoff. Ever the observer, Castillo merely raised an eyebrow as Dorst turned to gaze at Valmont. Dikeledi pursed her lips in puzzlement, and Chano merely grunted as if he'd heard a tired argument one too many times.

Whiskey glanced sharply at Valmont, not expecting him to make public a demand she had already refused in private. The ambivalence was odd. Valmont had been Defender when he broke his original oath of fealty to Elisibet. Though Whiskey trusted him with her life now, she couldn't get over a sense of dread at the thought of appointing him to the position again. It smacked of tempting the Fates, begging them not to set the same story in motion.

Valmont continued speaking, bolstered by her lack of immediate refusal. "If I'm your champion, it would sway others from making a challenge. Certainly Bertrada will think twice before doing so."

"And what's to stop her from doing something to circumvent such a challenge? She's hardly any more honorable than you are." Margaurethe's words were spoken with distaste. "I haven't forgotten that the two of you have colluded before."

The hopeful expression on Valmont's face faltered, and his jaw set in familiar anger. He lowered his chin, rising to glare at Margaurethe. She, in turn, braced her feet as she prepared for an attack.

Castillo and Whiskey also stood. She felt the air crackle between her lover and her friend. Much as she wanted to use her mind to separate them, she knew they had to make the decision to obey her. Nevertheless, she remained poised to interrupt any physical or mental bloodshed.

"Stop that!" Chano barked in a voice that sounded young and strong. "I've no patience at my age for your temper tantrums."

Margaurethe's face reddened. Whiskey felt both fury and shame coming through their bond. Valmont glared at her, jaw twitching as he ground his teeth. After a slight pause, he lifted his chin in concession. Margaurethe accepted the motion and the two potential skirmishers backed down from one another in slow increments. The crisis past, Whiskey ordered them both to sit, daring them to disobey her. Valmont dropped bonelessly into his chair, a hint of his usual sarcastic self in his faint grin. Margaurethe lifted her chin in concession and took Whiskey's discarded seat.

Whiskey returned to the topic at hand. "We've discussed this before, Valmont. This isn't the European Sanguire. I'm not the ruler of a nation. I'm the president of a corporation. Business and industry leaders don't need champions." He grimaced, looking away, and her heart went out to him. "Realize, however, that if I ever have cause to appoint a defender, you're first on my list of applicants." She felt Margaurethe's hackles go up, but a quick caress of her mind stopped a verbal argument. No doubt she'd hear all about the vagaries of that insanity before the night was through. So be it. There were other things to worry about right now. "So. Tonight. What should I expect?" She took Margaurethe's previous position—hip perched on the edge of the counter, arms crossed over her chest.

"Ass-kissing and backstabbing," Valmont said.

"Hardly helpful." Whiskey grimaced. "I was hoping for something a little more specific."

He waved a vague apology, still miffed at her rejection.

"If I may, My *Ninsumgal*?" Dorst awaited a nod of permission before speaking. "You'll have little to fear from the lesser aides and attendants of the *Agrun Nam*, though I'm sure everyone will be under orders to be watchful for any weakness that can be exploited." He brought an elegant finger up to tap his lower lip in thought. "As for the *sanari* themselves, I doubt there will be any immediate action. Aiden Cassadie is quite pleasant, and Ernst Rosenberg reticent. If trouble comes from any quarter, I believe it will be from Bertrada Nijmege."

Castillo nodded. "I agree, though I don't believe she'll act overtly. As Reynhard said earlier, she'll wait until she's more comfortable before taking steps to achieve her goal."

That covered all but one. Whiskey tilted her head. "And Lionel?"

Castillo smiled. "At this time, I think he'll be a valuable ally. He has ever been open-minded regarding your return."

"As has been my opinion," Dorst agreed. "When I investigated the *Agrun Nam* at your order, I found Lionel Bentoncourt to be a staunch and honorable man. He believes that you're here to lead our people, and will gladly assist in any way possible."

"Until he changes his mind," Margaurethe said.

Whiskey ignored the comment, knowing that Margaurethe's distrust of the European Sanguire leadership was as deeply rooted as her hatred for Valmont.

"As for Samuel McCall…" Dorst's shoulders hunched in a shrug. "I'm afraid to say that I have no honest clue. He's enigmatic, rarely prone to discussing his views except inside council chambers. His behavior in the limousine indicates he'll cause no trouble today." He cocked his head. "In fact, I believe young Samuel is the more level-headed. He'll no doubt keep Nijmege in check for a time."

"Then I guess there's nothing more to discuss here." Whiskey glanced up at the monitor that automatically flickered through various camera views.

"If you will excuse me, My *Ninsumgal*, I'll be on my way." Dorst bowed.

"Of course, Reynhard. Will you be there tonight?"

He grinned, his gaunt face twisting into a death's head visage. She wondered if he knew what he looked like, then decided he did. He was *Gúnnumu Bargún*, a shape-shifter, and one of the more powerful ones known. "I may or may not, My *Gasan*."

"I understand." If her chief spy were present, she wouldn't know it without mentally scanning for him.

As Dorst bowed himself out of the room, the others stood, this informal meeting unofficially called to a close.

"I'll see you this evening, Whiskey."

She took Castillo's hand with a smile. "I didn't think you'd miss it. I can tell you're itching to interview everybody."

He grinned. "Am I that transparent?"

"Just a bit," Valmont said dryly. He stood a bit stiff after her public refusal but no less loyal as he bowed. "Until this evening."

Whiskey watched everyone but Margaurethe and Jake leave.

As she turned back toward the row of monitors, a phone rang. One of the guards answered. After a brief back-and-forth, he hung up. "*Ninsumgal?*"

"Yes?"

"The security desk in the lobby requests *Ki'an Gasan* Margaurethe's presence. She has a visitor."

"Thank you." Curious, Whiskey returned to the notebook of camera instructions. She called up the view of the lobby, seeing a diminutive woman calmly seated on a divan. Alarm bells went off in her head. The woman was familiar, but she couldn't quite place her. Beside her, Margaurethe gasped in recognition. "Who is it?"

Emerald eyes stared blankly at her. "It's my mother."

* * *

What in God's name is Mother doing here?

Margaurethe's heels clicked upon the marble floor as she strode down the corridor of the security complex. It had taken some doing, but Whiskey had agreed to remain in the office instead of escorting Margaurethe to the lobby. She probably had the security cameras trained on both women right now. Reminded of her invisible audience, Margaurethe hid her expression of concern behind a mask of pleasantness. It wouldn't do to give her mother the satisfaction of knowing this unexpected visit unsettled her. As if Margaurethe hadn't enough problems today, what with the *Agrun Nam's* arrival.

At least her father hadn't made an appearance.

Pushing trepidation away at that idea, she exited into the lobby. The elevators were to her right, and she turned in that direction. One of the *aga'gída* silently joined her, an unwelcome but necessary companion considering the tensions and guests on the premises. As she rounded the corner, she passed the long reception desk. One of the attendants subtly nodded to his left. An unexpected feeling of pleasure jolted through Margaurethe as she saw her mother rising from a couch, at odds with the annoyance of her unannounced visit. It had been some time since they had seen one another. *How long? Thirty-five years? Thirty-six?* "Stay back," she ordered the guard. "I'll be fine."

"Yes, *Ki'an Gasan.*" He drifted away from her side to stand at the security desk and keep distant vigil.

Bracing herself, Margaurethe smiled and stepped forward. "Mother! What a surprise."

"I'm certain it is." Orlaith O'Toole was a smaller-boned version of Margaurethe, slightly shorter but similar in most other respects. It was obvious to anyone that the women were related, sharing thick reddish brown hair and delicate facial features. Orlaith's mother had been born near the Black Sea, imparting on her daughter and granddaughter the Mediterranean skin tones they shared. They could almost pass for sisters due to their Sanguire heritage's slow aging process, yet Orlaith was a full two centuries older than her daughter. She took Margaurethe into her arms. Their embrace was quick, yet strong; not a token hug between potential enemies. It eased Margaurethe's mind. There'd been no love lost between the Sweet Butcher and her parents. Hopefully, her mother would see Whiskey for who she was now and not see Elisibet's memory.

"How did you know where to find me?" She urged Orlaith to sit with her on a couch.

A shadow crossed the older woman's eyes. "Rumors have run rampant of Elisibet's return." She took Margaurethe's hands in hers. "I received a letter from your father telling me the specifics. With the *Agrun Nam* coming to North America lock, stock and barrel, it seemed a logical choice to follow." Her eyes, blue-gray compared to her daughter's green, flickered to the portrait hanging above them, her lips thinning. "I had no doubt I'd find you here."

Margaurethe looked at the painting. She had insisted on putting it there to throw off the *Agrun Nam*, knowing they would see Elisibet in Whiskey's sullen, street-tough appearance. Apparently, her plan had worked too well, backfiring as Orlaith assumed the same thing. "You don't know her, Mother." She squeezed the hands in hers. "It's not as it seems."

"Really?" Orlaith gave her a cool appraisal. "Does she even know what you went through? Does she care?"

Flushing, Margaurethe dropped her gaze at the reminder. How was it that her mother knew exactly what to say to trouble her? Margaurethe angrily shook away the shame and loss she had held at bay for so long, looking up. "She's not the same. She's not Elisibet."

"She doesn't know." Orlaith sighed, lips pursed as she tightly gripped Margaurethe's hands.

Margaurethe frowned. "Not exactly. I haven't told her." No, she hadn't spoken of it, but Whiskey was aware of the painful emotions of that time for Margaurethe, had felt the soulless despair she'd suffered. How could Margaurethe explain to her mother the unique bond she and Whiskey shared? Very few Sanguire seemed aware of the deep, abiding mental bond that Whiskey could induce between them. To voice it could reveal a strength to her enemies. Like it or not, Margaurethe knew Orlaith still ranked among them.

"Why? Will she see it as a weakness? Will she decide you're not worth the effort, throw you aside for someone else?"

The words weren't nearly as damaging as the almost hopeful gleam in Orlaith's eyes. Margaurethe tucked her chin, pushing her mother's hands away. "No. She's not that way. She'll feel guilty for something she didn't cause."

Orlaith studied her. "If she didn't cause it, she has nothing to feel guilty for."

Margaurethe's chuckle was humorless. "You don't know Whiskey."

"Whiskey." Orlaith looked back to the portrait. "Is that her name or her alcohol of choice?"

"It's her nickname. Her true name is Jenna Davis."

"Intriguing. She doesn't look all that dissimilar from her portrait at the old palace."

"Her eyes are different." Margaurethe blushed at Orlaith's calculating attention, cursing her inability to remain calm and serene in the woman's presence. To override the sensation, she forced herself to explain. "They're dark brown, almost black. This painting doesn't show them."

"Hmmm."

Margaurethe brushed nonexistent lint from her skirt, unable to keep from prattling. As she spoke, her Irish accent became more pronounced, indicating her level of nervousness. "The tattoos are real, though, and she's gained some weight now that she's eating regularly. She was living on the streets when Father Castillo found and reported her to the *Agrun Nam*. She's dyed her hair back to its original color—" She stopped speaking, her tongue seeming to cleave to the roof of her mouth. Distantly, she felt Whiskey soothing her. Her lover didn't interfere with the private moment, didn't do more than let Margaurethe know she was there, available if necessary. Tranquility washed through her as frayed nerves and emotional history faded to a dull ache.

Orlaith frowned and sat back as she watched the transformation. "She's with you now?"

Margaurethe sat straighter. "Yes and no. She's watching through security cameras." She indicated their location with a subtle flick of her hand. "She can see I'm upset and is here for me."

Her distaste obvious, Orlaith shot a glare at the indicated camera. "I suppose the advanced technology available will be a boon to her. She can spy anywhere she desires."

A flash of anger shot through Margaurethe. "That's not what she's doing, Mother."

"Oh?" A refined eyebrow rose in question. "Tireachan wrote me a letter. He says she has Elisibet's memories. Who's to say what else she may hold?"

Warning bells went off in Margaurethe's mind. "How does Father know that?"

"Just because we weren't at court during her reign doesn't mean we don't still have connections. Your father has heard the same rumors as I. He went to Bertrada to see what he could ascertain."

A flash of anger coursed hot and clean through the remainder of Margaurethe's childhood emotions. She shot to her feet, startling her guard into taking a step forward. With a quick wave, she halted him. "Bertrada Nijmege has the soul of a dung heap," she said, pleased to note she kept control of her voice. It would hardly do to scream such things at the top of her lungs.

"Margaurethe—"

"No!" She took another step back as her mother stood. "You know nothing. You don't know Whiskey. You don't know the obstacles she's had to overcome or understand her true nature. Instead you listen to a vicious woman who infects the air around her with her vile poison."

Orlaith dipped her chin, her eyes steeling. "Then you'd best get me an audience with this woman." She jerked a rude thumb at the portrait. "I can only make decisions on the information I have. You say she's so different from the Sweet Butcher who, I might add, nearly destroyed you. Let me see it."

As quick as the anger formed, it faded, replaced by grudging respect. A slow smile crossed her face, obviously easing the security personnel's minds. They relaxed their stances, though not their vigil. "You always could play me well."

"It's the benefit of being a mother. Someday you may know the same skill."

"All you had to do was ask."

Orlaith's lips twisted into an echoing grin. "As protective as you are of her? Do you really think you'd have granted my request?"

Margaurethe examined her. During Elisibet's time, her parents had made their intentions quite public as far as Elisibet was concerned. They hated the ruler for taking their daughter against their will, subverting her sweet innocence to the decadence of the European court and Elisibet's bed. Margaurethe remembered how Elisibet's death had all but destroyed her until word of Mahar the Oracle's prophecy reached her ears. Her parents had protected her from the Purge at no little expense. She knew how they would feel about Whiskey. "No. I wouldn't have."

"And now?"

She looked around the lobby, not seeing the rich elegance of the décor or the seemingly placid security posted there. A featherlight touch reminded her of Whiskey's vestal presence. Whatever happened, her lover wouldn't forsake her. Perhaps seeing Whiskey's true nature would begin to heal the vicious wounds caused by Elisibet's callous actions. "I'd like to ask you to a small get-together this evening, Mother." Margaurethe acted as if she'd always had the intention to invite her. "Are you staying in the city?"

Orlaith smiled, subtly raising her chin. "Actually, I took a taxi from the airport. I've yet to check into my hotel."

Margaurethe took her mother's arm in hers and began walking them toward the security desk. "We've plenty of room. Let's get you situated here, and I'll show you around."

CHAPTER FOUR

Whiskey entered the sitting room from the direction of her apartment, tugging at the cuff of her silk shirt. She disliked cuffs but knew rolling up the sleeves would wrinkle the material. Sithathor would have a cow over the issue. Better to suffer the discomfort than her chambermaid's annoyance. To vex Sithathor resulted in fewer desserts offered at mealtimes. A glance at the clock told her she had less than an hour before the reception. She wasn't looking forward to it. Even when interacting with pompous asses who deserved the deportment, she didn't feel comfortable with the royalty act. Occasionally she received some mischievous satisfaction and a little bit of pleasure at making some idiot fall over backward, but the whole genuflection thing embarrassed her.

Jake followed, closing the connecting door behind her. She strode across the sitting room to take up her normal post near the front door, a deadly shadow.

Whiskey threw herself onto one of the couches. The long narrow room held a combination of tasteful and comfortable furniture. Margaurethe had tried to install furnishings appropriate to Whiskey's rank, failing to consider that Whiskey and her rambunctious pack of young Sanguire were all less than fifty years of age. At least half of their spare time was spent loitering here with Whiskey, playing video games on the big-screen television or music on the state-of-the-art stereo system. It had taken two impromptu wrestling sessions between Zebediah and Chaniya before Margaurethe had saved the French provincial chairs from future abuse, replacing them with cheaper and more modern materials.

Whiskey's gaze strayed out the glass doors separating her from the balcony, knowing that she suffered an attack of nerves. Her first official meeting with the *Agrun Nam* was imminent and the unknown gnawed at her gut. She remembered her first encounter with Valmont, the sudden fear and anger that had nearly overwhelmed her when he'd finally gained an audience. Those emotions weren't hers, they'd belonged to Elisibet. Watching the *Agrun Nam* arrive had caused an echo of that fury. She'd almost eviscerated Valmont when they'd met face-to-face, would these distant emotions for the *Agrun Nam* cause similar reactions? Or would she be able to control herself and leave the European Sanguire with a positive impression of her?

Up until now, the idea of being the reputed *Ninsumgal* of the European Sanguire hadn't been too difficult to swallow. After she'd gotten over the initial confusion of the *Ñíri Kurám* and heeded the bizarre memories of another life, it was easy. Besides, she'd been focused on business and dealing with other nations, not governance. Today she would meet the five people responsible for keeping their government in action since Elisibet Vasillas's assassination four hundred years ago. The only conversation she'd had with them was the video link she'd set up three months ago, demanding their attendance. This time, she would be in the same room with some very powerful people, at least two of who wanted her dead—one on a very personal level.

Unable to sit still, Whiskey stood. She paused at the stereo, turning it on and jacking up the volume. The sounds of hard-core death metal filled the room. She strolled to the French doors and stepped onto the balcony, the strains of electric guitar, and Jake, of course, following behind.

The terrace was now enclosed by glass, yet another indication that the situation had changed. After the second assassination attempt by the shape-shifter imitating her valet, Margaurethe had insisted on upgrading security. Dorst had assigned Jake, and Margaurethe had put up bulletproof glass around the balcony. Whiskey didn't know whether to feel protected or caged. Terracotta containers held several varieties of plants, the smell of loam and growing things enhancing the sensation of being outside. It remained an enclosure, however, a sign that she would never be free again.

Moving to the edge, she looked out over the Willamette River. Shards of reflected streetlights sparkled back at her. Trees across the river had begun to change, indicating that winter wouldn't be long in coming to the City of Roses. She peered at the traffic sixteen floors below. From here she saw the front drive where the *Agrun Nam* had arrived, all five of them. *Gesture of support, my ass.* Frowning, she caught sight of Jake standing nearby, making herself visible to throw off potential snipers. "You don't have to do that, you know." Whiskey rapped a knuckle against the glass protecting her. "I'm safe here."

Jake grinned, tapping the barrier herself. "Maybe so, *Ninsumgal*, but if there's enough confusion from a distance, it'll help if anyone makes it past the perimeter."

Meaning an assassin might go for Jake first in the chaos. Knowing another person would die because of her didn't make Whiskey feel better. She stifled a flash of anger at her sense of weakness, returning her gaze to the eastern half of the city. Castillo had said that she had every reason to feel helpless. Anybody with half a brain felt that way when swimming in a pool of sharks. Valmont had agreed. One of the *Agrun Nam* had hired two assassins, and another had made it plain she wanted to rend Whiskey to pieces with her bare hands. At least Whiskey had begun to settle into the role of leadership when dealing with other governments. This quagmire of Elisibet's memories and emotions made things so much harder with the Europeans.

The song faded, opening to another. This one was heavy with bass, one she had heard at the underage club in Seattle many times when she lived on the streets. Whiskey stepped away from the glass, gliding into the sitting room. She needed to center herself and nothing did that better than riding the music. Closing her eyes, she ignored her shadow on the balcony and gave up the trepidation of the unknown, the frustration of trying to be someone she didn't feel. She let them go and sank into the bass and drum, dancing, moving in a way she hadn't done since this whole mess had started.

One song faded into another and then again as Whiskey lost herself. No pressure, no expectations, only the sound and the release as she reconnected with her spirit. Her soul, starved for the attention, reveled in the experience. As the music wound to an end, she slowed. Her eyes still closed, she felt Jake, who had remained out on the balcony to lend her some semblance of privacy, and realized someone else had entered. A lazy smile graced Whiskey's lips. "Hi." She opened her eyes to observe Margaurethe leaning against the wall by the stereo. The next song began, its strains muted as Margaurethe had adjusted the volume.

"Hi, yourself." Margaurethe walked to her. "How are you doing?"

"Much better. I didn't know how badly I needed that."

Margaurethe stopped just out of reach, studying Whiskey with an amused expression. "You look marvelous. That outfit does you justice."

Whiskey looked down at her clothes. "Really?" She wore black slacks flared at the bottom where solid motorcycle boots covered her feet. Her silk shirt was a splash of color, a royal blue, shimmering in the lamplight. Somehow, she'd rolled the cuffs up to her forearms while dancing, revealing the twining dragon scales on her right wrist and a thick silver bracelet on her left. Internally, she winced, her gaze flickering behind her as if expecting Sithathor to be waving a nettled finger at her. "Isn't it a bit much? I mean, they're probably expecting something a little more frilly or professional."

A chuckle brought her gaze back to Margaurethe. "I doubt I could get you into anything frilly." She stepped closer, adjusting Whiskey's collar. "Besides, we don't want to give them what they expect. The longer we keep them off balance, the easier our task will be." Her hands stilled, resting lightly against the silk above Whiskey's breasts. "Their first impression of you must be one of danger, of uncertainty."

Whiskey conceded the point with a grin, though she didn't feel particularly dangerous. "I've missed you." She wrapped her arms around Margaurethe's slim waist. It was a measure of how relaxed she'd become in Jake's presence that the bodyguard didn't even cross her mind.

"I know." Margaurethe leaned against her. "I've missed you too."

"And it's only going to get worse." Now that the *Agrun Nam* had arrived, the amount of work would triple. They both knew it and both dreaded their diminishing time together.

"We've got decades together, *m'cara*. Centuries. As soon as everything settles down, you and I will go on a very long, very expensive vacation."

"I'll hold you to that." Whiskey kissed her nose.

Margaurethe smiled. "But first, we need to get through tonight."

Sobering, Whiskey peered into Margaurethe's eyes. "How did it go with your mother?" She watched ire flash across Margaurethe's face. "That bad, huh?"

"We have always had our differences."

"No surprise." Whiskey well knew the dispute between the O'Tooles and their daughter. Elisibet had many memories of dealing with the acrimonious parents. Rather than having centuries to spend with their daughter, the O'Tooles had lost her to Elisibet's bed by the time she'd reached twenty-five. The Sweet Butcher, showing a surprising measure of restraint, had banned them from court to avoid the overwhelming temptation of executing them. The only thing that had kept them alive was their blood link to the woman she had loved. "I'm guessing you didn't patch things up with them...afterward."

Margaurethe glanced away, covering her discomfort by checking the clock on the wall. "No. After Elisibet...afterward, when I came out of my fugue, I was too focused on Mahar's

Prophecy. Mother and Father were unimpressed." She drew a deep breath, her expression changing as she put away the dusty pains of her past. "It's time."

Whiskey's heart thumped with sudden adrenaline, not pursuing the topic. This wasn't a conversation to be had with witnesses and just before meeting a nest of vipers. She sighed, giving her lover another squeeze, and released her. "I'm not ready, but I doubt I ever will be."

"You'll do fine, love. I have every faith in you."

"You ready to go, Jake?"

Hearing her name, Jake entered from the balcony, firmly securing the door behind her. "Of course, *Ninsumgal*."

Whiskey felt the gentle caress of Margaurethe's mind and opened herself to it, basking in the familiar woodsmoke and mulled wine. What trickle of dread still remained within her heart melted into nothingness as they walked together, Jake trailing them to the door. They paused long enough for Whiskey to don her leather jacket, Margaurethe pulling her long blond hair from beneath the collar.

Whiskey donned sunglasses as they exited the apartment. Four of her personal guard, the *aga'gída*, stood at attention in the corridor. She acknowledged them with a nod and a smile, amazed that she didn't blush. Though her insides trembled, Margaurethe's mental and physical touch grounded her as she entered the waiting elevator.

* * *

Whiskey held Margaurethe's hand in the crook of her arm as the small crowd marched along the back hall toward the banquet kitchen. Three guards led the way and four trailed behind. Gone were the days when Whiskey could run around the service areas of the building with impunity. The Sanguire assassin three months ago had changed all of that. All members of the board had agreed that Whiskey's safety was much more nebulous with the *Agrun Nam* in residence. Whiskey hadn't argued the point but wondered if the extra fuss would ever feel comfortable. Rather than go through the kitchen, they slipped out into the southeast corner of the foyer. A black drape had been hung across the hall here, hiding her from the view of her political guests in the main foyer. A set of double doors to her right led into the ballroom, but she was directed toward a single door on her left. She heard muffled chamber music beyond the curtain as her guards whisked her into a small room and closed the door. Jake locked it from the inside.

The room had been transformed from a standard conference room to a cozy lounge. One corner held a conversation area with several plush leather armchairs. Teak occasional tables gleamed beneath lamplight. A buffet stretched along one wall, filled with food and an impromptu wet bar. Whiskey's stomach reminded her she was hungry, though the thought of eating made her queasy. A large television screen had been spliced into the security feed, its high definition display divided into six scenes, each showing different aspects of the ballroom and foyer.

Whiskey turned in a slow circle. "Wow."

"You like?" Margaurethe smiled. She took two glasses from the stack on the buffet.

"It's nice. My home away from home tonight?"

"Something like that. Consider it your private audience hall."

The clink of ice hitting glass drew Whiskey's attention. She joined Margaurethe as her lover poured a can of soda. "Nothing a little harder?" She took her sunglasses off, laying them on the table.

Smiling, Margaurethe handed her the drink. "Not yet. You don't want to lose your edge. Not tonight."

Whiskey feigned discontent. "Too true." She took the glass and turned away, circling the room. Jake stood at the door, eyes fixed on the monitor as Whiskey joined her. Her guests sprinkled the foyer, enjoying the two bars that had been set up near the ballroom entrance. Waitstaff filtered through the crowd, offering hors d'oeuvres and champagne. A four-piece orchestra played in one corner.

Scanning the people, she saw only three *sanari* present. Lionel Bentoncourt escorted his wife, Ernst Rosenberg stood alone and Bertrada Nijmege spoke with Margaurethe's mother. Whiskey's heart thumped. Compared to dealing with the *Agrun Nam*, the idea of meeting Orlaith O'Toole made her palms sweat. She gulped half her soda, the bubbles painful as she swallowed the carbonation. Margaurethe was right. If Whiskey drank any alcohol, she'd be hard put not to drown herself in an abortive attempt to flee the inevitable meeting. Teeth clamped together at the thought of it. She considered lessons learned, both from her time on the streets and those from Elisibet. *Get it over with now.* Running away, letting fear stop her only made her more vulnerable. She closed her eyes. "Jake, give me your radio."

Hazel eyes regarded her with a hint of surprise. Jake didn't argue the point, quickly unplugging the wireless earplug and handing the item over.

With the earplug missing, Whiskey heard the chatter of her *aga'gída* as they patrolled the ballroom and foyer. At a lull in their conversation, she pushed the transmit button. "Um, this is Whiskey Davis."

Though probably surprised, the shift supervisor didn't waste time in responding. "Yes, *Ninsumgal*. How may I serve you?"

Whiskey looked at the television, noting all the guards almost standing at attention. Good God, this was almost as bad as showing up unannounced in their quarters or something. "I was wondering if someone could please escort *Gasan* Orlaith O'Toole to…my location?" Surprise rolled off Margaurethe as the supervisor agreed. "Thank you." She handed the radio back to Jake.

"Whiskey."

She took a bracing breath. On the screen one of the guards moved away from her post and approached Margaurethe's mother.

"Are you sure about this?" Margaurethe asked.

"Hell no," she answered honestly. "But I'm more nervous of her than the others. If I don't get this out of the way, I might puke or something."

Orlaith appeared surprised at the request, Nijmege disgruntled. She made her apologies, sharp eyes looking about for the cameras as she allowed the *aga'us* to escort her.

Margaurethe gently rubbed her back. "You'll do fine. Don't be kind to her on my account. We've had our differences of opinion as far as Elisibet is concerned."

"I remember."

Jake, radio reconnected to the plug in her ear, brought her microphone up to her mouth. She murmured approval and unlocked the door behind her. Margaurethe stepped away as the door opened.

A slender woman stood beside the stern young security guard beside her.

"My *Ninsumgal*, may I present *Gasan* Orlaith O'Toole," Jake intoned.

"Thank you." Whiskey glanced at the escort, searching for a name. "And thank you, Jalila."

Surprised at the recognition, a hint of pleasure caressed the guard's face. She stepped aside with a bow, gesturing Orlaith into the room.

Once Orlaith had entered, Jake closed and locked the door, her attention securely fixed on Whiskey's guest. Past warred with present as a flash of Elisibet's memory superimposed itself over the woman standing before her. A younger Orlaith, livid with fury, demanded the release of her daughter from court; a tall ruddy man with woad tattoos on his face standing behind his diminutive wife. Margaurethe hadn't been present, too young to easily stand up against her parents' wishes. Elisibet had taken control of the situation, sending the O'Tooles away with threats of dire consequences should they ever return.

The past faded. Orlaith's gaze was level, her face showing no indication of the hatred she must feel. Whiskey cast around for something to say. Should she apologize for Elisibet, insist she was nothing like the Sweet Butcher, beg for forgiveness she didn't deserve or need? Maybe she should promise to do better than the previous *ninsumgal*, to treat Margaurethe with the love, nurturing and respect she deserved. The tableau was all encompassing, not even Margaurethe attempting to break it as they stared at one another. Whiskey's eyes narrowed as several moments passed with neither speaking. To do any of those things would show vulnerability. Whether she liked it or not, the Sanguire were hunters; weakness in prey resulted in death. The mistake Elisibet had made was going over the top to prove her strength.

She stepped forward, holding out her hand. "*Gasan* O'Toole, I'm glad to finally meet you. Welcome to my home."

A slim eyebrow rose, Orlaith's only hint of surprise. Another moment passed as she considered a response. She slowly took the offered hand. "Thank you, Miss Davis."

Margaurethe finally found her voice and growled a warning. "Mother."

"No, she's right." Whiskey raised her hand to forestall Margaurethe's argument. "She's not a member of the corporation and the European Sanguire aren't yet members either. Unless a contract is negotiated she has no reason to call me by that title." She stepped back, gesturing at the chairs. "Won't you sit down? Can I get you something to drink?"

Orlaith's mouth twitched in a slow smile. "The future High *Ninsumgal* offering to serve me? How novel." She swept the room with a prideful gaze. "Wine, if you have it."

Whiskey nodded and went to the bar, passing Margaurethe. She saw seething anger just below the surface. With a gentle caress of her mind, she quelled Margaurethe's not quite murderous desire. Finding a bottle of some sort of wine, she rummaged around for a corkscrew. Ideally, she'd be able to pull off the sophisticated routine to impress Orlaith. Chances were much better, however, that her lack of aristocratic training would shine through to illuminate the idiot she truly was.

Margaurethe sensed her uncertainty. She joined Whiskey and uncorked the bottle with an economy of movement. With a tight grin and a wink, she poured the wine, handing the glass to her.

Mouthing the words "thank you," Whiskey took a slow breath and approached the seated Orlaith. Once the glass was accepted, Whiskey sat in a chair beside her guest. She watched Orlaith go through the long process of sampling the wine—smelling, swishing it in the glass, taking a small sip to test. Seemed a ridiculous way to drink the stuff. It must have met with her acceptance as an expression of grudging approval crossed her face. "Not bad. Do you have any clue what it is?"

Whiskey felt blood rising to her face. "No, I don't. I don't have much experience with wine."

"Or anything else, no doubt." The words were spoken smoothly yet were meant to lance through her.

It worked on Margaurethe, who started forward, a scowl on her face. Whiskey shot her a glare. This was not about the two of them; it was about Whiskey and Orlaith. Margaurethe couldn't protect her here. The warning glance wasn't lost on Orlaith, who watched everything over the rim of her glass. "Neither did Elisibet when she came to power," Whiskey reminded her visitor. "And neither did you when you were my age."

"I did not have the world as my plaything."

"And I do?" Whiskey smiled. "I'm not the monster you expect me to be. That person died several hundred years ago." She didn't follow up with "and good riddance," but her tone implied it.

Orlaith set her glass down, giving her full attention to Whiskey. "Did she? Yet, here you sit, pretending to be an innocent. How can that be when you have Elisibet's memories?"

"The Sweet Butcher's crimes were her own. Valmont and the *Agrun Nam* saw that she was punished for them." Whiskey lowered her voice. "What I remember are the multitude of her mistakes."

Changing the subject, Orlaith said, "What are your intentions toward my daughter?"

Whiskey's mind galloped to catch up. "Intentions?"

"Yes, intentions. Do you plan on keeping her by your side? Treating her as a loving partner? Acknowledging her as your soul mate, or whatever the current claptrap calls it?"

"I love her." Whiskey frowned. "I would never hurt her."

"Oh?" Orlaith arched her eyebrows. "Like you didn't hurt her before?"

"Mother!"

A spark of anger flared within Whiskey. "Margaurethe, this is between the two of us." She leaned forward in her chair, staring intently at Orlaith. "I know Elisibet hurt her, shredded her to the core. She loved Margaurethe fiercely but couldn't see through her own cruelty and bloodlust to treat Margaurethe as she deserved. I'm not going to make that mistake."

"Really?" The tone indicated how much Orlaith believed her. She set the half-full wineglass upon the table and rose. "You weren't there in the aftermath when her father and I protected her from the Purge and herself."

The words reminded Whiskey of her bond with Margaurethe, reminded her of the crippling pain her lover had suffered when Elisibet had died. Margaurethe had explained that she'd been catatonic. To this day Margaurethe still didn't know how much time she'd spent in the state; the emotions ran too deep, were too incapacitating for her to remember. Did she attempt to take her life after Elisibet's assassination? The sickening memory of Margaurethe's emotions of that time softened Whiskey's anger, and she remained seated. "No, I wasn't. I don't even know if my parents had been born by then. I certainly wasn't."

Orlaith sniffed, a gesture reminiscent of Margaurethe when she was at her most peeved at Valmont. It was meant to convey disdain but failed as humor flowed through Whiskey. Standing, she allowed a smile. "My hope is that eventually you and I will come to terms. Margaurethe is free to come or go as she pleases; she's not a prisoner here. I don't plan on keeping her as a consort, either." Both of them showed surprise at that statement, a hint of hurt coloring Margaurethe's mental touch. Whiskey's grin widened. "No, if anything, Margaurethe will be my partner, my equal in all things. I want to marry her."

Two pairs of eyes stared at her, and she felt a tickle of pleasure at stupefying both of them.

CHAPTER FIVE

Nijmege frowned as security whisked Orlaith away. The pair disappeared past a black curtain draped across a hallway. No doubt, Davis had a sitting room somewhere nearby. Lips pursed in distaste, Nijmege sipped at her wine, scanning the room for conversation.

Bentoncourt and his frill of a wife had cornered an unfamiliar aide—probably one of Davis's people. Francesca had her arm through the poor sap's, beguiling him with her charms as her husband pumped the man for information. Nijmege wondered how long it would be before Francesca's true nature was exposed. That wide-eyed innocence was the biggest sham since the alleged death of Christ. It would take time for word of it to spread. Bentoncourt would have an inside track on everything until then.

Rosenberg stood near the orchestra, solemnly, looking more like a Greek statue than a living man. His heavy-lidded eyes remained at half-mast, giving the uninitiated the impression that his attention remained on the small orchestra in the corner. In reality, he cataloged everything within sight, noting conversations, subtle nuances of body language, and watching who spoke with whom. It would be interesting to hear his version of the evening's events. She toyed with the idea of drawing him into an exchange but decided to wait. She'd much rather hear his opinions of Davis after she made an appearance.

Continuing her study, she noted Cassadie with some chippy on his arm. How did the womanizer find them so quickly? Nijmege often wondered if her fellow councilor had access to an underground Sanguire escort service. It seemed he never attended a public function without a woman accompanying him. Aside from a handful of favorites, they were rarely the same women either. She stifled a groan as Cassadie caught her eye. He grinned, said something to this evening's companion and patted her hand. Then he blithely transferred her to one of his aides and headed for Nijmege. *Marvelous.*

"Bertrada! You look radiant this evening." He took her hand and brushed the back of her knuckles with his lips, ignoring her grimace.

Reclaiming the appendage she glared at him, finding his infectious grin as irritating as ever. "Hello, Aiden. Tell me, where do you find all the nubile females for these things? I haven't seen that one before."

He dimpled, white teeth flashing as he turned to regard his latest conquest. "You might see her more often. She's extremely enjoyable company."

"I'm sure," Nijmege said, voice dry.

As usual, he refused to be baited. "So, tell me. What do you think of all this?"

"It's a farce. We've gone to all the trouble to arrive here, and for no good reason. We're facing a monstrous political backlash when our people realize we're actually following through with this charade. She's not who she says she is."

"I doubt we have that much to worry about, diplomatically." His expression edged into slyness and he winked. "You can't say she's not the spitting image. Especially with that portrait in the main entry."

Nijmege snorted, looking away. "We've only seen a painting, a handful of photos and a fifteen-minute digital transmission."

She glanced at him. "Tell me, how many Humans have you seen over the centuries who have looked similar to others? How many times have you come across someone you thought you knew, only to realize that person had been dead eighty years, and this was his doppelganger?"

Cassadie bowed his head in humorous concession. "Very true. However, the doppelganger usually cannot stand up to intense scrutiny. Davis has."

"Hardly." She tossed her thick hair over her shoulder. "The only intense scrutiny she's supposedly stood up to is a pathetic traitor who'd do anything to redeem himself and a heart-broken woman who wants her lover returned."

"Such a callous view. It must be difficult to wake up in the morning if that's how you see the world."

"Don't you dare turn this around on me, Aiden." Nijmege dropped her chin. It forced her to peer up at him past her eyebrows as he stood a half-foot taller. "The reality is that we've been duped. Davis is Sanguire but she's not the *Ninsumgal* reborn. She's a pawn in O'Toole's plan for revenge against us."

His expression was one of forced cheer and disbelief. "And what of her memories? We've all been in contact with her through post. I don't know about you, but there have been several things she's written me that she couldn't possibly know unless her claim is true."

"Fed to her by Valmont and O'Toole, no doubt."

They stared at one another for a moment, the music washing over them. Cassadie's face faded into unnatural seriousness, a look he rarely expressed outside of council chambers. "Bertrada, you protest too much. It's common knowledge among us of your true intentions. You argue against Davis's true existence, yet you plan to exact a revenge that cannot be hers."

Her mouth dropped open. She hadn't been openly accused since that disastrous emergency meeting Bentoncourt had called just after the Sanguire assassin had kidnapped Margaurethe. She'd tried to downplay her desires since, but enough time hadn't passed.

Cassadie continued speaking. "If what you say is true, then you cannot avenge Nahib by killing her. If she is whom she says, you still cannot, for she isn't Elisibet. She's her own person, not even born of the same bloodline." The gaze he gave her was thick with sympathy, and she mentally recoiled from him. "You're basing everything on a false assumption. You either have no chance at revenge or you kill an innocent. Which will it be?" Nijmege ground her teeth together. "Leave me."

He stayed a moment longer, torn between wanting to reach past her anger and allowing her the privacy she desired. She wondered which he would do, and how she would respond. Right now, the thought of ripping his throat out preyed heavy on her mind. The last thing she wanted from any of the *Agrun Nam* was pity. Oh, poor Bertrada, forever doomed to be in charge of the judicial branch of their government, forever doomed to not achieve the justice she so richly desired.

He drew himself upright, taking a bracing breath in the process. Slowly, the familiar pleasantness washed over his face, returning him to his normal appearance. "My apologies." He bowed. "It's not my place to interfere in your personal affairs."

Nijmege refused to respond, not wanting to scream her anger at him for his presumptions.

"Until tomorrow then." He drifted away to return to his latest conquest.

She turned away from his receding back, taking a fierce swallow of her wine. If Cassadie was attempting to reason with her regarding her vengeance then Bentoncourt was involved. The two were tied at the hip on many issues. Did Rosenberg follow their lead? Her glass empty she handed it off to a waiter, using the movement to scan the room. Rosenberg remained stoic in his place. She could hope he hadn't noticed the altercation but doubted such was the case. Her aquiline features narrowed further in response to her dark thoughts. She wished McCall would arrive.

As if her thoughts had called him, the elevators opened to reveal McCall. A young man dressed in black and maroon announced his arrival. Conversation stopped a fraction of a moment at the introduction before continuing. McCall spotted her and gave her a solemn nod of greeting as he moved closer.

Behind him, a handful of his aides and security filtered in, dispersing to mingle with the others.

Nijmege couldn't help but be impressed at O'Toole's attention to detail. There hadn't been heralds or liveried servants for two centuries, yet here they were. The security officers—her mind whispered the phrase "*aga'gída*" and she grimaced—wore solid black, the only spot of color a shoulder patch with the scorpion design. The waitstaff's attire was predominantly maroon with touches of black; and the multiple clerks, assistants and other pencil-pushers wore their own clothing, accented with black and maroon armbands. At least there was no doubt who served Davis in this growing mass of people.

Nijmege accepted two glasses of wine from a waiter. "I wondered if you'd make it." She handed one to McCall upon his arrival.

"I wouldn't pass this up for the world." He lifted his glass in a toast. "To distant enemies, may they come near enough to taste their blood."

"To distant enemies." She raised the glass to her lips.

He scanned the room, eyes calculating. "Quite the turnout. I don't see your pet, Valmont, anywhere."

Nijmege sniffed in disdain. "He's Davis's pet, not mine. And you'll notice you don't see Dorst or the priest, either."

"Probably waiting for a show of solidarity."

"Or Dorst is already here." The thought unsettled her. She began a serious study of the people she knew on sight, wondering if the spy would be able to pull off a subterfuge under close scrutiny. It was rude to mentally scan strangers and minor acquaintances, especially in political situations as this. She felt McCall's mental touch, amused that he seemed as nervous about her veracity as she of his. Once they ascertained they were indeed who they were supposed to be, they relaxed, reserving their wariness for those outside their immediate circle. Instead she pondered Cassadie's words, ignoring the dull throb of anger. "Aiden had an interesting thing to say."

"Really?" McCall glanced at the man being discussed. "Gods, another one. Where does he get them?"

"Jealous?"

He snorted. "Hardly. I'm surprised he keeps his mind on international affairs. Do you think all of his ambassadorial abilities run toward bedding world leaders?"

Nijmege's mouth twitched. "Someone had to take Elisibet's place in that arena."

"With Davis here, perhaps she'll reclaim her diplomatic crown."

A bubble of irritation popped her idle response before it could be voiced. They had to focus, especially now that they were deep within enemy territory. "Aiden has accused me of continuing with my intentions regarding Davis."

That got McCall's attention. He gave her a sharp look, brow furrowed. "What did he say?"

"He said I couldn't have it both ways, that he knew I didn't believe Davis wasn't who she claimed. Aiden is under the assumption that I plan to kill Davis for what Elisibet did to Nahib."

"It's to be expected, I suppose, considering the manner in which you were outed several months ago." McCall scanned their surroundings. "You think it came from Lionel?"

"Oh, very, very much." Nijmege sipped her wine.

"Yet, here we are, minutes from meeting the young *ninsumgal*." He studied his drink in thought. "We may have to change our plans."

"I won't miss my chance, Samuel. I'm too close."

"We can always muck up the negotiations. The *Agrun Nam* has to be in unanimous agreement to accept terms like this."

Her laugh was bitter. "You're so naïve, Samuel. We'll sit in that session for years if we lock horns. No new business will be begun; no old business will be concluded. What will happen to the people we're supposed to rule in that time?"

He looked away with a sigh. "Are you suggesting voting in favor?"

"What choice do we have?"

His eyes grew distant in thought.

"Once we've submitted to her control, my hands are tied. To challenge the *ninsumgal* is tantamount to treason against the realm. I may as well just lay down and die now."

"We're looking at a business merger, not a governmental one," McCall pointed out. "It might not equate to the same thing."

Nijmege scoffed. "Do you think that any treaty we sign with The Davis Group won't have that stipulation in the contract?"

"What if she challenges you?"

Nijmege stopped and blinked.

McCall grinned. "If she challenges you to judicial combat, you'll have free reign to do as you please. Certainly, you're more experienced with blades than she is; she's a child! You've centuries of experience."

She listened with half an ear, running through the European legal complexities. Her responsibilities within their justice system gave her a wealth of information. It could work. All she had to do was incite Davis to call the challenge. "What if she's appointed a Defender?"

"If we move fast enough, it may be moot." He touched her arm, strengthening their mental connection in the process. "Think about it. Who would she appoint, if anyone? Valmont the Traitor?" McCall laughed at the absurdity. "She says she has Elisibet's memories. She'd be a fool to put Valmont back into the same position he held when he assassinated the Sweet Butcher." He regarded the crowded foyer. "She'd never appoint Dorst or that silly little priest. The only people left are the old Indian and their newest member, Ambassador Dikeledi. Do you think the esteemed ambassador would accept the honor when she's so new to her position?"

Good God, it really could work. Frustration and anger faded away in light of the first real hope Nijmege had felt in months. It was almost finished. Soon her revenge would be complete, Nahib's death avenged, as it should have been so long ago—by her hand, and no one else's.

"*Maskim Sañar* McCall, Bertrada."

Nijmege forced her mind back to her surroundings, finding a grim Orlaith O'Toole beside her. She tamped down her elation, setting aside the barely formed thoughts and plans until she could give them more attention.

McCall formally bowed. "*Gasan* O'Toole, it's a pleasure to see you here. I had no idea you were invited."

She smiled a greeting. "I wasn't. I'm a gatecrasher."

"I see you've survived your first audience," Nijmege said.

"Yes. It was…intriguing, to say the least."

"Do tell," McCall said, his interest obvious.

Before Orlaith could regale them of her meeting with Davis, the dulcet sound of a bell rang through the foyer. Everyone in the room paused in their conversations, their eyes drawn toward the double doors that opened. The herald stood there, calling out in a clear voice, "Hear me! Hear me! Be welcome! It is my joyful privilege and duty to announce *Ninsumgal* Whiskey Davis of The Davis Group. Enter and be welcome!"

CHAPTER SIX

Two *aga'usi* and Jake escorted Whiskey and Margaurethe from the private sitting room. In the corridor, she heard her guests still mingling in the crowded foyer beyond the black drape. Another pair of *aga'usi* had taken up positions at the double doors across the corridor, crowding the short expanse of hall. Unlike Whiskey's *Baruñal* ceremony several months ago, there was no need to loiter in the hallway. After a brief check on the radio, Jake ordered the door to the ballroom opened and ushered Whiskey and Margaurethe inside.

The room was smaller than the stately dinner affairs Whiskey had suffered in the past. One of the benefits of taking over a former hotel with banquet facilities was the use of the temporary walls built into the design. Since the guest list was only three hundred names long, the ballroom had been divided in half to accommodate the lesser number. Several tall cabaret and small cocktail tables were scattered about the room, each draped with black linen and lit by glowing burgundy tea lights. The walls held prominent tapestries bearing the colors and sigils of each

Agrun Nam member's house. Central to the room, two gorgeous buffets curved on either side of an ice sculpture. Whiskey raised an eyebrow at the crystalline scorpion adorning the center of the table. Margaurethe had argued for weeks against her choice of sigil, but certainly wasn't shy in rubbing Whiskey's political enemies' noses in it when given half a chance.

The *aga'gída*, her royal guard, stood at all the doors, each wearing a baldric of black, maroon and silver. She overheard frantic discussions from the service aisle as the staff made last-minute announcements. A handful of servers put final touches on the buffet, and bartenders manned the portable bars ensconced in two corners of the room.

A low riser with a single chair and a side table sat at one end of the room. Hanging floor to ceiling behind it was the black and maroon banner with her stylized sigil, the silver threads glinting as air from a ceiling vent caused the material to shift. Though the overhead lights had been lowered to give a relaxed ambience, they also made the spotlight on the stage that much more striking. Whiskey frowned. Margaurethe hadn't been able to sway the board of directors to introduce a formal throne into this reception, but she'd done everything else possible to create the illusion of royalty. She'd claimed it would put the *Agrun Nam* off their game if Whiskey were introduced in a manner that suggested she ruled them. Whiskey thought it would put them off in a completely different way. There was such a thing as overkill. It behooved her to keep the European *sanari* on their toes for as long as possible, but the line between pomp and insult was very fine. She wouldn't be able to get away with removing the seat entirely, but… "Jake."

"Yes, *Ninsumgal*."

Whiskey pointed at the stage. "Find another chair like that. I think there's one in the foyer, over by the restrooms. I want it placed on the stage, too."

"Of course, *Ninsumgal*."

As Jake spoke into her microphone, Margaurethe gave Whiskey a wary look. "What are you doing?"

Whiskey smiled, patting Margaurethe's arm where it hooked through hers. "What I told your mother I was doing. You're my

equal in all things, *minn'ast*." She felt Margaurethe stiffen, and
her smile widened. "And if I have to suffer under a hot spotlight,
so do you."

A flurry at one of the doors interrupted Margaurethe's
attempt to debate the issue. A matching chair was hustled into
the room and placed on the stage. One of the *aga'usi* had the
foresight to snag a server, and a pot of hot water and a teacup
soon sat beside the bottled water on the side table.

"Much better, don't you think?"

Margaurethe tried to scowl but failed. She leaned over to
kiss Whiskey's cheek. "It looks fine. Thank you."

Unable to stall any longer, Whiskey allowed herself to be
escorted to the stage. She waited for Margaurethe to choose a
chair, suddenly not sure on which side she was supposed to sit.
There were so many rules and regulations about etiquette that
she still hadn't gotten them all straight and Elisibet's memories
didn't always play out when she needed them. Her woefully poor
knowledge of protocol perforated her confidence, deflating her.
She swallowed hard as her nerves reminded her that she was
moments away from meeting the *Agrun Nam*. Even if Elisibet's
memories were playing hide-and-seek, the emotions of betrayal
and anger burned hot in Whiskey's abdomen. Margaurethe sat
in the left chair, and Whiskey settled in the remaining one with
relief.

"My *Ninsumgal*?"

Whiskey darted a look over her shoulder. Jake had taken up
position at her right shoulder. Two other *aga'usi* were stationed
at either rear corner of the stage and two stood on the ground
level before it. Jake raised her eyebrows in question, one finger
to the earbud she wore. Her professional calm did much to ease
Whiskey's sudden attack of jitters. "Yeah, okay. I'm as ready as
I'll ever be."

Margaurethe reached across the space separating them
to take her hand, giving it a squeeze before releasing it. Jake
murmured into her microphone and all the guards in the room
suddenly seemed more alert. The door nearest the foyer was
pushed open, and Whiskey heard the clear voice of the herald.
"Hear me! Hear me! Be welcome! It is my joyful privilege

and duty to announce *Ninsumgal* Whiskey Davis of The Davis Group. Enter and be welcome!"

The sudden hush in the foyer didn't last long as guests filtered into the room. When people of social status entered, the herald called out their names and ranks, just like in a bad movie. At least two-thirds of the visitors had been here before when Whiskey honored other visiting delegations. There might have been a hitch or two in step and speech as they noticed the stage and unusual seating arrangements, but they quickly overcame their surprise. Free food and drink was a universal balm regardless of station. It was just her imagination that all she heard was the blood pumping in her ears and the gentle creak of her leather jacket when she shifted in her chair. She cursed silently to herself as she realized her sunglasses were still in the sitting room. Too late for that particular crutch now.

At least a third of the guests bowed to her as they drew near, heads tilted to reveal their throats. It wasn't lost on Whiskey that they were all Sanguire and all wore her colors. Others nodded or smiled in greeting—delegation members and their support staff who had previously met with the board of directors, Human employees of The Davis Group, and local Sanguire and *kizarusi* who'd had the privilege of attending functions here before. Those that did neither were the *Agrun Nam* and their personnel. She thought it interesting that many of the latter looked to their *sanari* for a hint of proper procedure. They wanted to follow the protocol set by their peers, but weren't sure they should.

Whiskey straightened in her chair and lowered her chin, giving them all a good look at her. This was what they had come for, to verify who she was and who she would be. She always sympathized with animals in zoo exhibits during these functions, now more than ever. No doubt they thought her an animal, clad as she was in biker jacket and boots. It wasn't the first impression she'd wanted to give to Orlaith O'Toole, but Margaurethe was right. Whiskey's rough appearance would give her an added edge of protection for a short while, at least until the *Agrun Nam* ascertained she truly wasn't Elisibet. Margaurethe indicated her approval of the stern pose by caressing Whiskey's

mind, leaving the smell of mulled wine and woodsmoke in its
wake to drift across her senses.

Whiskey's gaze swept across the strangers and she picked
out the *Agrun Nam*, locking eyes with each in turn. Bentoncourt
appeared reserved as always, his true feelings hidden behind a
mask of calm. Next to him stood his wife who avidly examined
Whiskey in return. Rosenberg hovered along the rear wall,
standing tall under Whiskey's scrutiny. Both McCall and
Orlaith O'Toole appeared unimpressed and bored with the
proceedings. As expected, Nijmege glared back, tucking her
chin in firm defiance.

It was Cassadie who broke from the rest. He glided forward,
stopping at the base of the dais so as not to alarm the guards,
and bowed. "It's a pleasure to finally meet you, Ms. Davis. Aiden
Cassadie at your service."

"It's a pleasure to finally meet you as well, Aiden. I'd like
to welcome the *Agrun Nam* to my home." She lifted her voice
and the attendees quieted, allowing her words to permeate the
room. "Please, enjoy yourselves. We're here to get to know one
another better as we'll all be working closely together." She
gestured to the orchestra that had used the break to move their
instruments inside the room. They began to play again and the
hushed buzz of conversation became louder to compensate.

Whiskey felt her ears burning. She forced herself not
to focus her superior hearing on the different discussions.
Bentoncourt joined Cassadie and she tamped down a rush of
nerves. She reached for Margaurethe's hand, pulling her to her
feet as she stood. "Come on. Let's get this shit over with before
I have a heart attack," she murmured.

A flurry of movement erupted from her security staff as she
moved. She gave Jake an apologetic look, knowing she made
their job more difficult. This was something that had to be done,
however. Two *aga'usi* that had been floating through the crowd
joined the pair already on the floor. They created a loose circle
around her and Margaurethe. Four more positioned themselves
on the dais, giving them a clearer field of fire.

On the floor, Whiskey gave her guests a polite nod and
offered her hand. "Lionel, *Gasan* Francesca." It felt awkward to

use their first names. Bentoncourt was almost as old as Chano, and his wife not that much younger. Margaurethe had said it was normal for a ruler to address her immediate underlings with such familiarity. They would be required to use her royal title when speaking to her. She wondered what response she'd receive in return.

Bentoncourt's dark eyes pierced her as he shook her hand. "Ms. Davis." He bowed politely. "It's good to see you again, *Ki'an Gasan* Margaurethe. It's been some time."

Nice dodge. Whiskey, taking Francesca's hand in greeting, almost heard the sarcastic remark burning the tip of Margaurethe's tongue. She held her breath.

"It certainly has, Lionel." Margaurethe's voice was smooth and hospitable. "And Francesca! It's been many years since I've seen you. How have you been?"

Relieved at Margaurethe's restraint, Whiskey turned to Cassadie. He attempted to kiss her hand, but she was ready for him. It was best if he learned immediately that his glib tricks would be worthless against her. She firmly grasped his hand and pumped it twice, applying enough strength to get her point across. "Thank you for the greeting, Aiden. I wondered if everyone expected me to turn into a three-headed dog up there."

He grinned, an impish flicker in his eyes. "Between you and me, I think it was a valid concern."

She smiled, finding him exactly as Elisibet remembered—quick to adapt but strong in his convictions. Dorst's reports had been quite thorough. Addressing the three of them, she said, "I hope your rooms met with your approval? If not—"

"Oh, I like them very much," Francesca interrupted. "We've a wonderful view of the river. What's it called again?" She looked among them for answers.

"The Willamette." Whiskey recalled Margaurethe's warning about Francesca's air-headed act. Elisibet had no memories of the woman Whiskey could use. By all reports, Francesca had never been to the Sweet Butcher's court and had only married Bentoncourt within the last century. "It's a tributary of the Columbia River north of here."

"I noticed quite a bit of boat traffic, too. Was that a cruise ship I saw just before we came downstairs?"

Margaurethe stepped in to answer, interrupting Francesca's distraction. "Why, yes. There's a lunch and dinner cruise that operates most days." She gave Whiskey a smile and wink. Releasing her arm, Margaurethe took Francesca's and slowly guided her away. "Perhaps one day during your visit we can reserve it for our personal use."

"Oh, that would be brilliant."

"We have a concierge at the lobby desk. They have information on many excursions in the city and surrounding area."

Whiskey didn't know if she should be relieved or worried as Margaurethe disappeared into the mass of people. Now nothing stood between her and two of the most powerful men in the European realm. She didn't think Cassadie was much of a threat, at least not at the moment. The unknown here was Bentoncourt. Regardless of Castillo's insistence that the *Nam Lugal* was loyal to her potential, his manner was more guarded than Elisibet's memories indicated. Debating what to do next, she decided he would prefer a direct approach. She purposely turned to stare him down. "Well, Lionel? What do you see?"

He frowned as he considered a response. Beside them, Cassadie radiated waves of amusement. "I see a replica of a tyrant, though you don't look nearly as perilous as your portrait in the lobby. I see a child playing at being in charge, without knowing the consequences. I see," and he paused, peering closer, "fear."

Whiskey blinked, surprised at his ability. She couldn't afford to let him take over the conversation. Brutal honesty was required. Her voice low, she said, "If you see fear, then you know I'm not Elisibet, for that was an emotion she never revealed to anyone. As for knowing the consequences of my actions, where else could the fear come from but making a catastrophic mistake?"

They studied one another for long moments, oblivious to music and conversation surrounding them.

"Two valid points." Bentoncourt's eyes crinkled. "If I may?"

She felt the nebulous caress of his mind and calculated his motive. Was this a precursor to an attack, or a compelling? In either case, she was confident she could repel him regardless of their difference in age. One of the things she shared with Elisibet was extraordinary mental power. Thanks to the Sweet Butcher, she also had intimate knowledge of these people while they were forced to deal with a stranger. Granted, four hundred years could change a person, but their weaknesses had to still exist, could still be exploited. Even so, Castillo's opinion of Bentoncourt carried a lot of weight with her. He was of the opinion Bentoncourt was on her side.

Beside her, Jake must have sensed the mental request. She silently stepped closer, hovering inches away from Whiskey's right shoulder to stare at Bentoncourt with tucked chin. Whiskey picked up the sensation of soft fleece and the aroma of carnations, Jake's essence reminding Whiskey's guests of her presence. Not for the first time Whiskey marveled at the soft delicacy of Jake's mental touch, knowing how dangerous she could be.

"It'll be fine, Jake." Whiskey waited until her bodyguard tamped down her essence, almost smiling at the way Bentoncourt blinked in surprise at the interruption. "You'll have to excuse, *Zi Agada* Jacobsen. She takes her job seriously."

"As well she should," Cassadie said.

"Lionel?" Whiskey offered him the mental contact, psychically tasting his essence as he did hers. A wash of taste hit the back of her tongue, a well-brewed beer on a hot dusty day. The memory it brought up was distant and musty. Apparently Elisibet had rarely connected with him in her life. It held a hint of familiarity, and she committed the experience to memory. The contact faded and dropped away.

"Thank you."

Whiskey turned to Cassadie. "And you?"

He held up one hand in surrender. "No need to exhaust you, Ms. Davis."

His reason for denial was weak. She wondered if his refusal was because he wasn't who he seemed to be. Cassadie was a fire-starter, a *Tál Izisíg*, and had trained Elisibet in that talent. If any of the *Agrun Nam* would be most familiar to her, it would be him. Considering the last assassin had impersonated someone Elisibet had known in the past, Whiskey frowned. She wondered how she could push the issue without burning any political bridges.

The herald called out over the room, "*Sublugal Sañar* Valmont Strauss and Father James Castillo, The Davis Group Board of Directors."

The interruption derailed her thoughts and eased her frazzled nerves. A welcome smile crossed her face as she saw the padre weaving through the crowd in her direction. Valmont disappeared into the throng. She wondered if she should put security on alert for bloodshed. It would be just like him to goad Nijmege into some sort of public altercation.

"Father Castillo!" Cassadie welcomed the priest into their circle.

"Good evening, *Ninsumgal*." Castillo bowed deep to Whiskey. "*Sabra Sañar* Cassadie," he said by way of greeting as he shook Cassadie's hand. Neatly inserting himself into the gathering, he stood between Whiskey and Bentoncourt, providing a welcome physical barrier.

Bentoncourt smiled, his gruff face lighting. "Father Castillo, well met."

"Thank you, *Sañar*." He turned to gaze at Whiskey, winking slightly. "Is she not everything I told you?"

Whiskey groaned inwardly, feeling her cheeks redden. It was a struggle to not roll her eyes. That was just like the padre to play the proud papa. Good God, what else would he be saying tonight? She suddenly wished she were at Valmont's side, dealing with Nijmege. Potential bloodshed was preferable to this.

"And more." Bentoncourt's grin included her.

Cassadie stopped a waiter, passing out glasses to their small group. Offering one to Jake, he affected amusement when she refused. "So, tell me, Father. How did you find her again?"

"Actually, she found me."

As Castillo regaled them with the tale of seeing the exact replica of the Sweet Butcher wander into his soup kitchen more than a year ago, Whiskey scanned the room. Valmont had latched onto Francesca, irritating Margaurethe no end. Whiskey breathed a sigh of relief. At least he wasn't inciting a riot. *Yet.* Orlaith, McCall and Nijmege had remained near the entrance, watching with calculated expressions. They were talking about her; she needed no superior hearing to see the stares and glares as the three conversed, heads together.

Missing a *sanari*, she scanned the room, wishing she were back up on the dais with a better view. It was several minutes before she located Rosenberg. He had left his place at the rear wall, standing now to one side a few feet away. No doubt he analyzed her every move, observing her profile without her knowledge as she dealt with the common trappings of conversation.

Not willing to allow him anonymity, Whiskey excused herself and approached. Her security entourage shifted with her, creating a bubble of protection that flowed to surround her and Rosenberg. If he was surprised, he didn't show it, his features registering nothing but the general interest they already held.

"Ernst, thank you for coming tonight. I know you've had a tiring day of travel."

He bowed his head. "Ms. Davis, thank you for inviting me." His gaze held a measure of cool calculation as he openly studied her.

Whiskey almost grimaced at his examination, reminding herself it was to be expected. She wondered if it would ever stop. Would she feel like a bug under a microscope for the rest of her long, long life? Not knowing what to say, she resorted to the same question she'd asked Bentoncourt. "What do you see?"

His answer was quick and forthright. "I see *Ninsumgal* Elisibet Vasillas, the Sweet Butcher, reborn as prophesied by Mahar the Oracle."

Her eyebrows rose. She wasn't sure she liked the inclusion of Elisibet's nickname in his pronouncement. "Really? Not everyone agrees with you." She tossed a glance at Nijmege and her cronies.

"Perhaps not."

Well. Not much one for talking. Whiskey struggled to find something to say. "You're in charge of the treasury, right?"

"Yes, I am."

She gave him the once-over, noting his well-muscled frame, thick neck and short hair. His hand was calloused when she had shaken it, the kind of calluses that indicated swordplay. Her hands were beginning to develop the same signs from her work with Pacal and Valmont. "I'm surprised. I'd think you'd be in charge of the military since you're a fighting man."

"It's a matter of timing, Ms. Davis. When I was appointed by the *Ninsumgal*, the sole open position was the Office of Finance."

His words opened a floodgate of memory. Members chosen for the *Agrun Nam* filled the available vacancies. Ideally, a person suited to finance would have risen to Rosenberg's current position. Elisibet had bucked the system, preferring to put ill-prepared people in charge of things they didn't understand. It was easier to keep everyone powerless against her. Nijmege's office was a prime example. Nahib had been *Nam Lugal* and Bentoncourt had led the Judicial Office. When Elisibet murdered Nahib, Bentoncourt had been next in seniority, rising to take over the position of leadership. That was why Nijmege had the Judicial Office now. Elisibet thought it humorous to fill the seat with Nahib's grieving lover.

Considering Rosenberg's obvious military training, she frowned. The European structure separated powers between the *Agrun Nam* and *Ninsumgal's* advisors. Without a monarch, the High and Low Courts had been combined under Nijmege's dominance. To have survived so long, the *Agrun Nam* had to have taken over the military after the Purge, something that had been under Valmont's province as Defender of the Crown. "Which one of you is in charge of the military?"

"Ideally, one of the *ninsumgal's* advisors," Rosenberg explained, not realizing the extent of her knowledge. "However, when Elisibet was assassinated, Lionel took control."

That was a relief. The thought of a Sanguire military trained in covert operations being run by, say, Nijmege was frightening.

"He also assumed control of the knightly orders and our navy," Rosenberg continued without prompting. "The Judicial Office was extended to include Lower Court functions. As there was no more royal household, the palace was abandoned until recently."

"Recently?" Whiskey felt Margaurethe's mind searching for her. She answered by second nature, her ears tuned to Rosenberg.

"When you were discovered, we had it refurbished, and staff and security hired."

She blinked. This was new. "It's still there?" she asked, immediately kicking herself for asking a stupid question.

"Yes. It's ready for the *ninsumgal's* presence now."

Whiskey pondered this as Margaurethe arrived at her elbow. God, it would be awesome to walk the halls of the palace. What memories would a visit prompt? A flash of dinners and dances crossed her mind's eye as Margaurethe and Rosenberg exchanged pleasantries. Margaurethe made their apologies and pulled her away. Whiskey thanked Rosenberg for his candor and said her goodbyes.

Once they were clear, she blew out a breath. "Thanks," she said between her teeth as she smiled at people who bowed or nodded in her passing. "Can I get out of here yet?"

Margaurethe's laugh warmed her. "I think it's time. You've seen and been seen. Now we leave them to their gossip."

"Do I have to make a grand exit?"

Margaurethe took her hand, squeezing it. "Unfortunately. It will be quick, I promise."

They were at the dais, and Whiskey took the steps two at a time, forcing Jake into a trot to keep up. She spun around at the top. Sudden stage fright caused her heart to thunder as all conversation promptly died. She swallowed with a dry mouth before pasting a smile on her face. "Enjoy yourselves, and thank you for coming."

She blushed as her people began a round of applause that forced her visitors to at least make a genteel offering of the same. The *aga'gída* surrounded her, Jake and Margaurethe at either elbow, and guided her out the back of the banquet room. As they quickly made their way through the service corridor back to the elevators, she glanced at Margaurethe.

"I think I'm gonna be sick."

CHAPTER SEVEN

Back in her primary office, Whiskey felt much better for the ginger ale Margaurethe had procured. She sprawled on the leather couch, boots propped up on the coffee table, leather jacket long since discarded and draped on her chair at the desk. Margaurethe sat in a chair across from her, adding a dollop of cream to her tea.

Jake stood at the door, tilting her head as she received a transmission over the radio. "They're here."

Whiskey dropped her feet to the floor. "Let them in." Jake opened the door, revealing The Davis Group board still dressed in their reception finery. As they drifted in, Whiskey said, "Pull up a chair, folks. I don't know about you, but I'm exhausted. Let's make this short."

"At least you got to leave early," Valmont groused. He eschewed a seat, preferring to lean against the bookcase with his arms across his chest. "I had to put up with *Gasan* Bentoncourt's nattering for an hour or more."

"Serves you right. You were only there to annoy Margaurethe." Whiskey gave him a sidelong grin. He lifted his chin in concession, returning a playful smile.

Castillo settled on the couch beside Whiskey. "I spent some time with *Gasan* Bentoncourt. She's a delightful woman, full of questions."

Frowning, Margaurethe leaned forward to pour him tea from the service on the coffee table. "Be careful with her, Father. She'll win into your good graces and pump you for information before you realize what's happening."

Whiskey reached out and patted Castillo's arm. "She's right. Don't get suckered, Padre." She grinned at his consternation as he mentally went over his conversation with Bentoncourt's wife. Turning her attention to Chano, she watched as he slowly lowered himself into an armchair. "How about you, *wicahca*? Have any interesting conversations with our new delegation?"

He grunted in distaste, accepting a cup of tea from Margaurethe with a flash of pleasure that quickly disappeared. "No. That Cassadie speaks like Coyote. He is too smooth, I don't trust him. And the Mayan ambassador monopolized the conversation when I tried to speak with Bentoncourt." He blew on the tea to cool it before taking a sip. "Rosenberg, though. He seems strong of purpose, a soul of deep water. His spirit is that of an Indian, not a white man."

Everything that came from Chano was filtered by his perceptions, including the racial distinctions between Sanguire. Whiskey sighed but didn't say anything. Chano was a wise and just man on the American Indian council, the *Wi Wacipi Wakan*, and his opinion wasn't that different from any other Sanguire in the world be they Mayan or Chinese or European. American Indian Sanguire didn't hate the white man for some distant crime of genocide—Chano had lived through it himself. Their hatred was one of personal immediacy as was their enmity to their southern neighbors, the Mayans. It had taken a lot of work to get the two nations to sit down in talks together. It would take a lot more to get them to come to an agreement, to heal the hostility between them.

"I agree about Rosenberg." Dikeledi had taken one of the chairs at the desk, turning it around to sit tall and straight before the gathered board. "In our dealings with the European Sanguire, Rosenberg has always had a strong presence. He knows his job well and is a shrewd negotiator."

Unlike the American Indian Sanguire, the Africans had long been involved with the Euro Sanguire over the centuries to reasonably positive ends. Whiskey leaned forward, elbows on her knees. "Were you involved in the initial treaties between them and your government?"

It hardly seemed possible, but Dikeledi sat straighter. "I was."

Castillo perked in obvious curiosity. "What can you tell us about them?"

She gave the priest a stern glance. "I cannot reveal confidences."

Whiskey held up her hands. The newest member to the board was prickly. Until she became comfortable with her peers, Dikeledi needed careful handling. "No secrets. I think the padre is just curious about their skills at the treaty table, am I right?"

"Exactly." Castillo nodded. "My apologies, I only meant to ask what your impressions of the *Agrun Nam* were during your dialogues."

Mollified, Dikeledi raised her chin in concession. "They seemed quite knowledgeable and don't appear to have changed. During the African/European negotiations, they were aware of several contingencies that we had thought secret, and bargained well to get what they wanted. In the end, our treaty was mutually beneficial. We've had little cause to revisit it."

A slight *click* drew Whiskey's attention to the door. Dorst smiled at Jake as he closed it, sweeping forward into the room. He paused at the edge of the gathering, an amused look on his face as Dikeledi continued speaking.

"I had not met Samuel McCall before this evening, however. He seemed to be another quiet man, not prone to conversation. Nijmege, as expected, was less than pleasant."

Valmont snorted aloud, shifting to slip his hands into his pockets. "Small wonder that. I saw the storm clouds above her head this afternoon when she arrived." He paused as if an idea had just occurred, his smile widening. "Wait. She always looks like that! Silly me."

"Must you be so flippant?" Margaurethe demanded, her tone indicating annoyance.

"As a matter of fact—"

"Can it!" Whiskey gave Valmont a warning glance. Given the opportunity, he'd poke and prod Margaurethe until she exploded. It was easier to stop him than Margaurethe. His verbal jabs were his way of playing. Before Elisibet's death, Margaurethe had joined in the games as well. Now his pastime infuriated her.

Valmont gave an amiable shrug but remained silent.

The peacekeeper of the group, Castillo smiled at Margaurethe. "I had the pleasure of meeting your mother, Margaurethe. She seems like a delightful woman."

If his goal was to ease Margaurethe's vexation, he failed. Instead, her lips thinned and a line developed between her eyebrows as she scowled. "Yes, she does, doesn't she?"

Castillo paused, realizing he'd made a mistake but uncertain how to rectify it. He glanced quickly around the room, mouth open to speak though he said nothing.

Valmont saved him. "She's much like Francesca Bentoncourt in that respect, Padre. Don't let your guard down with Orlaith O'Toole, either." He bared his teeth in a smile. "The female of our species is most dangerous."

Whiskey couldn't argue his statement. Despite a muscle jumping in Margaurethe's jaw, she didn't seem overly upset with Valmont's summary of the situation. Whiskey reached for Castillo's mind, lightly comforting the dark, bitter chocolate. "One thing I got from Ernst is that the palace is up and running."

The sardonic air disappeared from Valmont's expression. "Really? Now that's interesting. When did they do that?"

Dorst stepped forward, inserting himself into the conversation. "Those contingencies were put into place not long after our dear Father Castillo passed his information on to the *Agrun Nam* a year ago."

"You knew about this?" Margaurethe asked, turning in her seat to look at him.

He bowed deeply, tilting his head to reveal his neck to her. "I most certainly did, *Ki'an Gasan*. My apologies for not having notified you earlier. I didn't think the information pertinent."

After the day she'd had, Margaurethe was on edge and spoiling for a fight. Her chin dropped to her chest, and she drew a breath to speak. Whiskey saw the warning signs and jumped into the conversation to forestall them. "Is it the same palace that I remember?"

Smiling, Dorst rose. "It is! A most delightful place. I'm surprised they kept it up all these centuries."

"I'm surprised it's still standing," Valmont muttered.

Whiskey gave him a commiserating nod of agreement. After Elisibet had been assassinated, the European Sanguire had gone into revolt. The Purge had swept through her city, the violence and destruction killing many of her supporters. Margaurethe had survived only because Dorst had spirited her away hours before the angry mob had reached the palace.

"Well, there was extensive damage." Dorst's long-fingered hands gestured elegant indifference before clasping together. "But the *Agrun Nam* was able to rebuild afterward."

"Why would they do that?" Dikeledi turned to eye Whiskey. "If they hated your predecessor so badly, why would they keep such a reminder of her existence?"

Whiskey shrugged. "I have no idea." She didn't add that she would have preferred it razed to the ground despite her desire to play tourist there.

"You know how it is with Europeans." Dorst's expression was both amused and surreptitious. "They cling to things and places of their past, regardless of how horrid. Very sentimental, they are. No doubt, someone thought they could reseat their government there."

Chano grunted agreement, and Whiskey pursed her lips. She lowered her chin, staring at Dorst.

He gave a subtle lift of his chin in apology. "In any case, not long after your discovery, My *Ninsumgal*, the *Agrun Nam* got it into their heads that you would be returning to rule them. They had the palace renovated and stocked, and a staff brought in to see to your every need. It even has a full complement of royal guards!"

Again the thought of walking through the palace assailed Whiskey. She could almost remember the layout. If she concentrated, she could hear the servants and sycophants, see the livery and royal finery. She remembered her bedchambers, her sitting room, her informal reception room where she'd been murdered. Her eyes flickered to Valmont, briefly catching his glance, then to Margaurethe. Stark emptiness met her gaze. As much as she wanted to explore Elisibet's feelings of nostalgia, Margaurethe's traumatic memories of that time put a halt to the possibility. Besides, Whiskey had other things to consider. "Who hired the guards?"

Dorst grinned like the Cheshire cat. "Why, *Aga Maskim Sañar* Bertrada Nijmege, of course."

Valmont rolled his eyes, his expression grim. "Of course."

Whiskey caressed Margaurethe's essence with her own. "Guess sightseeing will have to wait, huh?" She was pleased to see the warmth return to Margaurethe's emerald eyes and smell the familiar woodsmoke and mulled wine.

Castillo slumped slightly beside Whiskey. "Perhaps in the future."

She snickered, patting Castillo's knee. "You're more than welcome to a vacation, Padre." Looking at the others, she said, "Anybody have anything else they want to add?"

"Just a reminder that we have our first meeting with the *Agrun Nam* tomorrow morning at nine o'clock," Margaurethe said, once more the professional. "This is an initial gathering to begin sounding each other out, so I don't expect it to last more than an hour or two."

Whiskey stood, indicating their get-together was over. "And I'll want to meet everybody in the afternoon to get your overall perceptions." The board members gathered themselves and made their polite exits. Once they'd all left, Whiskey turned to Margaurethe who bustled around the seating area, tidying up the tea service. She intercepted her lover, pointedly taking a dirty cup and placing it back on the table. "Leave it for Helen. She's paid pretty well to take care of these offices."

The corners of Margaurethe's lips curved upward. She didn't argue, instead putting her now free hands around Whiskey's waist. "Shall we retire for the evening?"

Whiskey made a show of checking the time. It was only ten o'clock. "I think I need to head to my apartment. Will you join me? The night is young, *minn'ast.*"

"I'd love to."

"Have a good night, Jake." Whiskey felt a loosening of her shoulders, pleased to have reached her apartment for the evening.

"Thank you, *Ninsumgal.*" Jake bowed her head. "Good night, *Ki'an Gasan.*"

"Good night, Jake." Margaurethe watched the bodyguard disappear into her room off Whiskey's private living area. Jake had taken over the room that the impostor, Andri, had used before he'd kidnapped Margaurethe and been killed by Whiskey. Sithathor, Whiskey's handmaid, also resided in these apartments but was nowhere to be seen. She tended to keep far earlier hours than her mistress; chances were that she was asleep.

"I am starving."

Margaurethe followed Whiskey past the dining room and into the kitchen. She smiled at the Post-it note on the microwave. Despite her dubiety regarding Sithathor, she couldn't deny that the Indian woman took excellent care of her charge. "You're always starving."

Whiskey read the instructions and the microwave hummed into action. "I can't help it. I'm a growing girl." Whiskey turned to grin at her, her hands on the counter.

"You keep eating baklava and you will be a growing girl." Margaurethe slid into Whiskey's personal space, feeling arms wrap about her.

Whiskey nuzzled her ear. "Are you saying I'm getting fat?" Margaurethe made a point of feeling Whiskey's hips and abdomen. "Not yet." She jumped at the sudden sharp nip on her earlobe and laughed. "Don't let your physical training sessions fall by the wayside, *m'cara*."

"Wench!" Whiskey growled.

"Ah, but I'm your wench, love." The aroma of roses and water surrounded Margaurethe. While the essence was similar to Elisibet's, the subtle hint of blood teased Margaurethe's nose, highlighting Whiskey's differences.

"That you are." Whiskey pulled back to look into her eyes. She reached up and brushed a lock of hair away from Margaurethe's temple. "I love you."

"Then we have something in common." Margaurethe tilted her face, eyes closing at Whiskey's tender touch.

"You love you too?"

She smiled playfully, opening her eyes again. "In point of fact...yes." Her smile widened at Whiskey's affected shock. She slid her hands up Whiskey's sides, digging her fingers into the ribcage. As Whiskey jumped and wriggled, unable to escape the tickling, Margaurethe said, "I love you, *m'cara*, and don't you forget it." Whiskey finally succeeded in getting Margaurethe's hands out from beneath her shirt. She held on tight, reminding Margaurethe of the many hours of physical training she'd endured over the past months. Switching tactics, Margaurethe suddenly retreated from her offensive, no longer struggling. Before Whiskey could reciprocate, she pressed forward, capturing Whiskey's lips with her own. The fight instantly drained from Whiskey, her soft lips opening in invitation. Margaurethe accepted, slipping inside both mentally and physically, losing herself to roses and silken touches.

Beep. Beep. Beep. Beep.

They both jumped as the microwave finished its cycle. Breathless, Whiskey chuckled. She rested her head in the crook of Margaurethe's neck. "I really am starving."

"Then you'd best eat, love." Margaurethe leaned her head back to look at the woman in her arms. Whiskey raised her head and they gazed at each other. With a sultry whisper, Margaurethe said, "You'll need your strength tonight." She smiled at the flush that crawled up Whiskey's lighter skin tone. Satisfied she'd kept the tables turned on her lover, she pulled away. She went to a cabinet, fetching glasses to pour juice while Whiskey retrieved her late snack. The next few weeks would be trying in the extreme. Their schedules, already overloaded with business meetings and negotiations, would only become more hectic. This might be the last night they had to truly enjoy each other's company for a while. Feeling the rosewater and blood caress, she glanced over her shoulder, her gaze locking with Whiskey's smoldering black eyes.

She looked forward to making tonight last.

CHAPTER EIGHT

Margaurethe retrieved a cup of tea from the built-in bar of Whiskey's sitting room, the entry area of her apartment that was open to select friends and family. Whiskey sat at the dining table, laughing with Zebediah who was discussing some arcane video game that had recently been released. The young *Ninsumgal* appeared calm and relaxed as she poked a fork through her breakfast. Margaurethe didn't think the others noticed the tightness around Whiskey's eyes, the vague irritation at the new restrictions placed upon her movements, or the fact that her food meandered about her plate without being eaten.

With the *Agrun Nam* in house, Whiskey's movements had become even more restricted than before. A trip to the Residential Lounge for a meal required a squad of *aga'gída* and locking down half the fifteenth floor. Rather than upset the day-to-day schedules of the individuals who lived at The Davis Group, Whiskey had chosen to remain in her apartment for meals. Fortunately, that didn't mean total isolation. Today her American Indian family and the trusted members of her pack had been invited to keep her company until her first meeting with the *Agrun Nam*.

Sithathor had repurposed the bar surface as a breakfast buffet this morning. She and two members of the royal guard had raided the Residential Lounge for the food, the chambermaid augmenting the standard American offerings with steamed rice cakes and condiments from her native India. Whiskey had taken a liking to the spicy foods, endearing herself to Sithathor even more than she already had. Margaurethe peered at the chambermaid as she whisked into the room with a steaming Indian wrap of some sort, placing the plate beside Whiskey. She accepted Whiskey's thanks with a smile, her hands folded before her as she stepped back from the table.

She hailed from the same country as Nahib, the former *Nam Lugal* of the *Agrun Nam*. She claimed to have never met him, but Margaurethe couldn't forget the association. Sithathor had passed all the background checks as well as the physical and mental inquiries before being offered this job. Despite that, her presence remained as a reminder that Margaurethe hadn't made the racial connection between the man Elisibet had murdered and the woman who now served Elisibet's second incarnation so intimately. It didn't help that Sithathor was a *Gidimam Kissane Lá*, a fabled Ghost Walker, long thought lost to the ages and only revealed when it was discovered Whiskey had the same talent.

Margaurethe looked away, forcing herself not to dwell on the matter. Sithathor had been devoted to Whiskey from the beginning, and her attention to every detail of Whiskey's well-being had given Margaurethe cause for respect if not complete trust. She took a moment to dish up fried potatoes, an egg, and some sausage before sitting at the table. Whiskey bestowed her with a sultry look, completely wiping Sithathor's allegiances from her mind.

Across from her, Alphonse and Zebediah ate like they hadn't seen food in weeks. The brothers were young, no more than twenty and twenty-one, making them both older than Whiskey. It was criminal that they'd been allowed to roam the countryside like wild dogs for years. Their parents had been killed when they were youngsters. Not long later, an immature and vicious Sanguire had adopted them into her pack. The brothers sported colorful mohawks and general facial features that indicated a kinship. Alphonse was the elder, tall and thin with blue hair; he was the more thoughtful of the two. The stockier Zebediah had bright red hair and was the most likely to start a brawl. Since coming to Whiskey, they'd settled down, having been recruited by Dorst for their knowledge of electronics and computer hacking.

Beside them, Nupa and Wahca traded words in their native Lakota and Tillamook languages. Nupa's hair was long and free, his normally stoic face animated as he laughed at something the older woman said. Margaurethe decided he had a nice smile when he felt secure enough to reveal it. Whiskey's grandmother, however, always seemed happy and self-assured. She cast a fond grin toward Margaurethe who answered it with the same. Wahca's daughter had been lost to her thirteen years ago; finding her granddaughter alive and well had much to do with her current cheerfulness. Margaurethe spared a moment to look at Whiskey's profile, her heart warming at the sight. Wahca wasn't the only one who had rediscovered someone dear.

Chaniya and Daniel Gleirscher sat at the far end, dark and light, heads together. The sight was odd enough for Margaurethe to make note of it. Daniel was the oldest in the pack, having reached his fifty-second birthday the previous month. He could give Alphonse lessons in silent observation. His was the most level head of the pack regardless of the blond mohawk and multiple tattoos he bore. Chaniya was probably in her midthirties. She was new to the pack, quicksilver competitive and proud, more than willing to dive into a fight and experienced enough to come out on top. Sanguire physical nature being what it was, they both appeared to be in their late teens. Chaniya grinned wide, her teeth flashing against her dark skin. It was answered by a rare smile from Daniel, causing Margaurethe's eyebrows to hike to her hairline. Had the aloof Daniel finally found a paramour?

"That color looks good on you."

Margaurethe smiled at Whiskey's aunt, Zica, who sat beside her. "Thank you." She paused to brush at the cuff of the shirt she'd turned up over the fitted black jacket sleeve. The outfit had come with a pair of black slacks, but she'd chosen to wear a long loose skirt instead. "I've always looked good in green." Zica smiled. "I imagine so." With casual grace, she reached up and brushed the tips of her fingers along Margaurethe's hair. "The red highlights and your green eyes make it a perfect match."

Slightly discomfited at the intimacy, Margaurethe said, "Thank you." It had taken some time for her to become used to Zica's physical familiarity and she still had her moments. Zica was a toucher, seemingly incapable of keeping her hands to herself. She also wasn't shy about voicing her opinions. It was Zica who had suggested that extra security wasn't needed—if Whiskey was who multiple prophecies said she was, she needed no added protection. She would live until she completed her destiny. Margaurethe thought the idea incredibly naive. She was pleased Whiskey hadn't completely fallen for the foolhardy notion, though she occasionally argued that same point when new limitations were imposed upon her.

She felt Whiskey's touch on her thigh, slightly relieved as she turned away. Something about the enigmatic American Indians always unnerved her, even when dealing with Chano. Their culture was so different from her own that it was difficult for her to wrap her mind around their points of view. Instead, she looked into Whiskey's dark eyes, pleased to see the banked fire glowing there, the one they'd ignited last night. Despite the craving, she also saw the fine line of worry between Whiskey's eyebrows. With practiced ease she slipped into Whiskey's mind, blending their essences together in a gesture of support. She stroked the back of Whiskey's hand on her thigh in physical counterpoint. Only rudimentary emotions could be transferred through such contact, despite Whiskey's mental abilities and the growing connection between them. Margaurethe projected love, trust and confidence, watching that slight worry line fade.

"My *Ninsumgal*, your guards are ready." With the moment shattered, Margaurethe schooled her features to professional courtesy, turning to see that Jake had left her position, stepping closer to the table. A flurry of apprehension flew through her connection with Whiskey, and she pulled back, allowing Whiskey her privacy.

CHAPTER NINE

Whiskey's attempt to appease the raging butterflies in her stomach hadn't worked. She'd awakened in a state of trepidation, regardless of Margaurethe's soothing presence and the previous evening's sensual enjoyment. Today was the day for which she'd both been waiting and dreading. Today she would officially face the *Agrun Nam*.

She didn't know whether to laugh or scream.

Apparently, her stomach had become inured to stress since Sithathor's spicy egg and mushroom roll hadn't fully nauseated her. She supposed having met several of the European *sanari* last night had eased her tension. Bentoncourt, Cassadie and Rosenberg all seemed level-headed and willing to work with her. The memory of Nijmege's glare sparked familiar anger and shame, a mishmash of emotion that had become as muddy as the woman's hawk-like eyes. Her breakfast did a slow roll.

"My *Ninsumgal*, your guards are ready," Jake stated.

"Guess I'd better go earn my paycheck." Whiskey pushed to her feet, tossing her napkin onto the table as Margaurethe followed. She pointed a finger at Alphonse and Zebediah. "You two behave yourselves."

Zebediah looked affronted. His brother grinned, shouldering him. "You got it."

Whiskey scanned her guests. "I've got meetings all day, so I'll see you at dinner, okay? Right here at—" She looked at Margaurethe.

"We should be finished with the initial meeting by this afternoon. You have a debriefing scheduled with the board at one o'clock." Margaurethe ran her hand up Whiskey's back, rubbing her shoulder. The touch comforted her. "I doubt we'll get much accomplished today, so you should be finished by five or six."

"Okay. Sithathor, can we have dinner at six thirty, please?"

The chambermaid bowed. "Of course, *Ninsumgal*."

Jake stepped closer, her voice lowering. "*Ninsumgal*."

Whiskey rolled her eyes, ignoring Margaurethe's smothered grin. Whiskey reached out to snag Margaurethe's hand, pulling her toward the door.

"My *Ninsumgal*."

Whiskey paused. Sithathor pressed a small glass into her free hand. She peered at the frothy mixture, feeling Margaurethe stiffen beside her in automatic suspicion. "What is it?"

Sithathor smiled. "Drink. It will help."

Her chambermaid hadn't poisoned her yet. Whiskey took a sip. After one swallow, the flavor of fresh pears bursting upon her tongue, her stomach growled in demand. Whatever it was worked miracles on her constitution. She drained the glass, the skateboarding butterflies mellowing to the point of nonexistence. "Thank you."

"You're most welcome, *Ninsumgal*." Sithathor bowed.

"Knock 'em dead," Alphonse called after them.

"Yeah! Break a leg!"

Nupa snorted. "She's not an actress, Zeb. She's not going onstage."

"Want to bet?" Chaniya asked. "That's exactly what she's doing."

Margaurethe shifted her hand to Whiskey's arm. Chaniya had the right of it; that was what Whisky was preparing to do—put on a show. Hiding her reluctance behind a mask of cheerfulness, she wished everyone well and left the apartment.

In the elevator, surrounded by Jake, Margaurethe and a quartet of *aga'gída*, Whiskey stared at her reflection. She distracted herself from her blanched complexion by dropping her gaze to stare inward. Elisibet had distinctive opinions about the *Agrun Nam*. The trick would be to not let those predispositions get in the way of Whiskey's reality. So far, she'd been able to do so with Dorst, Valmont and Margaurethe, but she'd had months to develop new experiences with them, to learn their strengths and weaknesses from a personal perspective. Other than last night's reception, she'd had nothing but the Sweet Butcher's violent genocidal policies and sentiments upon which to rely.

The elevator opened, spilling its occupants into the lobby. More guards had been stationed here—too many. Whiskey narrowed her eyes, making a note to talk to Sasha about overstaffing. The present number didn't make her safer so much as highlight fear to her enemies. Nijmege had probably taken one look at the amassed forces and felt a smug sense of joy that her unspoken threat had been the cause.

The board awaited her a few paces away. Valmont had chosen an expensive suit today, looking like any high-powered businessman preparing a company merger. He was the only one of the trio who appeared modern despite his dreadlocked hair. Dorst wore his customary gothic leather, a sparkle of glee in his black eyes matching the glint from chrome spikes and snaps. Castillo's cassock flowed to his feet, and he bowed at Whiskey's approach. Chano wore jeans, soft boots and a simple button-up shirt. His concession to the diplomatic importance of this meeting was a red blanket he'd wrapped across his aged shoulders, fringes hanging from its edges and black woven designs showing the stylized artwork of his people. Dikeledi had also brought a dash of color, wearing a long orange boubou with purple and gold designs across the fabric, and large beaded earrings dangling from her lobes. Even Whiskey hadn't dressed for a high-powered corporate meeting—she wore black leather pants and boots, a burgundy button-up shirt and a European-style black leather jacket.

Whiskey's small army stopped. "Good morning." She nodded acknowledgment to her advisors. "Where are they?"

"Already inside, *Ninsumgal*," Jake answered before anyone else.

She felt her heart leap as she glanced at the conference room's double doors a few paces away. The man Margaurethe had hired as a herald stood there, adjusting the sleeves of his shirt. The aroma of mulled wine and woodsmoke warmed her, easing the roar of blood in her ears. She gave Margaurethe a smile. "Let's get this started then."

Jake nodded, leading the way to the conference room. Before Whiskey got there, she had the doors open and two *aga'usi* deployed inside while she halted her charge's advance. After the guards took a quick circuit of the room and its occupants, Jake nodded to the herald who stepped just inside the door.

"*Ninsumgal* Whiskey Davis," he announced, bowing. "President and CEO of The Davis Group."

Whiskey wanted to give in to her desire to flee. Instead, she tucked her chin and entered the room.

The *Agrun Nam* ranged around the nearest end of the oval cherry wood table, leaving the far side available. Three had risen at the herald's announcement. Whiskey expected Nijmege and McCall to show their stubborn disagreement, their seated forms no surprise. Nijmege in particular refused to even look in her direction as Whiskey took her place at the far end. The herald continued to announce everyone until the ample room filled. The new arrivals stood behind their chairs, and six *aga'gída* filed in to take stations on the perimeter. Jake stood at Whiskey's right shoulder. The herald retreated, and the door guards backed out. The door closed with stark finality—it would remain shut until Whiskey called for it to open, whether in the next minute or the next week.

"Thank you for coming," Whiskey said. "Shall we be seated?" Taking her own words to heart, she did so, watching the others follow her lead. She felt markedly better now that she was no longer on shaky knees. Having the table between her and her opponents eased her nerves as well, though she knew it was merely a psychological advantage. If the *Agrun Nam* wanted to attack en masse, a wooden table wouldn't stop them.

Valmont and Margaurethe flanked her, Castillo and Chano on the far side of Valmont, and Dorst and Dikeledi beyond Margaurethe. As expected, Bentoncourt sat opposite, with Cassadie and Rosenberg on one side, Nijmege and McCall on the other.

"Lionel, would you please open the meeting?" Whiskey felt Margaurethe become rigid as she handed the gavel to an *aga'gída* to deliver to the other end of the table. By asking Bentoncourt to start the procedure, Whiskey was allowing him to chair the meeting. This decision gave her visitors power over the proceedings.

Bentoncourt appeared pleased that Whiskey allowed him the honor. He tapped the gavel before him. "I hereby call this meeting of the *Agrun Nam* and The Davis Group Board of Directors to order." His voice was gruff but pleasant. "I believe the *Agrun Nam's* first order of business is whether or not to recognize Ms. Davis as official heir to *Ninsumgal* Elisibet Vasillas."

The already tense atmosphere thickened. There it was, baldly stated, the elephant in the room. Its mention so soon in the caucus surprised Whiskey. None of her talking points had touched on this. Her goal was to negotiate a treaty with the Europeans just as she had with the American Indians and the Africans, not take over as the Euro leader. She glanced at her advisors. Castillo was openly agape at Bentoncourt's audacity. Margaurethe and Valmont hid their astonishment with practiced ease, though both stared with rapt fascination. Dorst smiled in serene pleasure while Chano and Dikeledi calmly watched the proceedings.

Whiskey resisted the urge to jump into the silence. Until this motion was up for debate, she had no place to speak. By yielding control to Bentoncourt, this had become a meeting of the *Agrun Nam*, not The Davis Group. Castillo had pounded Roberts Rules into her head for months, she couldn't interfere until the proper time. The wait was going to kill her.

"I move we vote on the matter," Cassadie said.

"I second the motion," Rosenberg intoned beside him.

Bentoncourt glanced to his right at his two mute companions. "The motion to vote on Ms. Davis's legitimacy has been put forward and seconded. All for?"

Two hands rose into the air. Whiskey didn't need Dorst's intelligence report to have predicted the split. She almost smiled at the faint resignation curling Bentoncourt's lips.

"Those opposed?"

Nijmege and McCall immediately responded. Rosenberg didn't bother to respond to Cassadie's grimace for his abstention.

Bentoncourt sighed. "The floor is open for arguments."

Perching her elbows on the table, Whiskey leaned her chin on joined hands. Most of her directors watched the proceedings with polite interest. Valmont gave an audible groan and leaned back in his chair, preparing for a long haul. McCall shot Valmont a look of distaste. Whiskey intercepted an unruly grin from her friend. She reached out with her mind to rein in Valmont's natural sarcasm, not wanting him to piss off the *Agrun Nam*. Not yet, anyway. In response to her mental tap, he gave a soft snort and looked away.

"Unless there's been some new development," McCall began, "there is no evidence genetically linking *Ninsumgal* Elisibet with Ms. Davis. She cannot be Elisibet's heir if she isn't of the same lineage. In fact," he said, waving in her direction, "her familial background is a complete mystery."

Bentoncourt looked across the room. "Father Castillo, you were involved in that investigation. Have you turned up any new evidence?"

Castillo looked at Whiskey, asking permission to speak. She nodded, and he smiled as he stood. "Yes, *Nam Lugal*, I have. While all formal European inquiries into *Ninsumgal* Whiskey's lineage have met with dead ends, we have discovered she is a member of the American Indians through her mother. We are still searching for information on her father, whom we only know by name."

This appeared to be news to Nijmege. "You mean to say she's half Indian?" Before anyone could respond, she scoffed, a grin doing nothing to soften the hard angles of her face. "Unless her father is a direct descendant of Maximal Vasillas, this motion is out of order."

"What's the matter, Bertrada? Nervous?"

Whiskey frowned and kicked Valmont under the table.

Bentoncourt used the distraction. "We're straying from the issue. Let's stay on topic. I don't want to be here all day and night."

"Hear, hear," Dorst whispered, tapping his fingers together in quiet applause.

Whiskey gave him a significant look, wondering if she'd have to monitor him too. His expression turned contrite though his eyes remained high-spirited.

"Whether or not Ms. Davis is of the same lineage of Elisibet is moot," Rosenberg said. "Had Elisibet announced an heir not of her blood, that person would be leading us now. Genetics have nothing to do with the issue at hand."

"True enough." Cassadie looked across the table. "So, Samuel, Bertrada, your argument is invalidated. Shall we vote again?"

"To what end?" McCall asked. "It will remain the same— two for and two against with an abstention."

"So we come to the meat of the matter," Bentoncourt said. "What will it take to sway your vote?"

"More than you can possibly pay," Nijmege growled.

McCall stopped her words, leaning forward. "I suggest a regent, someone to oversee the ruling of our kingdom until Davis can be legitimized."

Whiskey blinked in surprise and scanned her advisors for their responses. Margaurethe was rapidly angering. She knew that most of the people across this table had ordered Elisibet's death. This political tap-dancing did nothing to change that. To Margaurethe's mind, Whiskey was the embodiment of Elisibet and should be returned to power immediately. She'd worked toward that goal half her adult life. Chano seethed at the implied insult of Nijmege's tone regarding Whiskey's parentage. Castillo remained calm, as did Dorst, though the spy revealed a trickle of amusement at her prying. Valmont simply shook his head, his expression one of pity. Only Dikeledi seemed unperturbed by the *Agrun Nam* conversation.

"A regent?" Cassadie asked, voice incredulous. "We've been in power for centuries, and now you suggest we give control to a third party?"

"It certainly beats giving it to an untried youth whose validity is in question," McCall said.

Whiskey slowly sat back in her seat, frowning. She had called and they had come at her order. Though they argued about her place in their government, they subconsciously believed it was at the head of it. Rather than discuss mutual support and economic growth, obligations toward and equality with other coalition members, or pursuit of the common good for all Sanguire they chose to start off their negotiations with this. Their system was flawed, but they didn't seem to be aware of the schism. They had broken it when they hadn't replaced the Sweet Butcher, limping along as a royal parliament without a monarch.

Bentoncourt hammered the gavel to gain order. "Either she is our *ninsumgal* or not—that is the question we are currently debating. Once the vote is finished we can discuss avenues for the transfer of power."

Nijmege glowered at Whiskey, her hatred palpable without mental project.

Robert's Rules be damned. Whiskey stood up to be recognized. "Chair recognizes Jenna Davis."

"I believe the *Agrun Nam* has misconstrued my reasons for calling them here. I do not seek recognition nor do I wish to become the leader of the European people." Whiskey felt Margaurethe's disgruntlement. Nothing would have pleased her more than to have Whiskey anointed European *Ninsumgal* just to disrupt their lives. Doing that would jeopardize what The

Davis Group was created for, however, and that was to unite the Sanguire peoples worldwide under a single banner.

Cassadie leaned forward, frowning. "You do not seek to reinstitute your monarchy?"

"I do not." Whiskey grinned at his confusion, not pointing out that his words confirmed the European monarchy was hers for the taking. She gestured to her advisors. "We wish to negotiate an agreement between the European Sanguire and The Davis Group, nothing more." Her lips widened into a smile. "And to put an end to the hostilities that have been directed toward me from your esteemed council."

Cassadie's glance flickered toward Nijmege but he said nothing.

"Then I stand corrected." Bentoncourt lifted his chin to Whiskey. "My apologies. We'll postpone this motion indefinitely." He tapped the gavel. "Would you prefer to discuss another topic?"

"I would." She turned to Jake at her shoulder, giving her a stack of papers that Margaurethe had brought. "I move that the European Sanguire and The Davis Group become diplomatic allies."

Dorst again tapped his fingers together in delight. "Oh, I must second that motion!"

"We've taken the liberty of drawing up an agenda, which *Zi Agada* Jacobsen is distributing. It contains the general outline of previous diplomatic arrangements The Davis Group has made with the *Wi Wicipi Wakan* of North America and the Southern African Commonwealth. I thought it would be a good starting point." She resumed her seat, watching as each *sanari* received their agenda. Forcing her shoulders to relax, she focused on the topics at hand. Now maybe they could get some work done.

CHAPTER TEN

Whiskey threw herself into an armchair, scrubbing her face in weariness. Her board of directors trailed in behind her, Jake closing the door and taking position just inside. Helen, Whiskey's receptionist, had arranged a lunch buffet. It filled her office with the aroma of sliced meats, potato salad and the tang of dill pickles. Margaurethe immediately opened the concealed liquor cabinet behind Whiskey's desk to retrieve beverages. Castillo joined her, accepting a chilled bottle of root beer.

Chano sank onto the couch, his bones almost creaking aloud. Long tedious hours of negotiation took so much out of the elderly American Indian. Sometimes Whiskey wondered if she should ask for someone else from the *Wi Wicipi Wakan* to represent their government on the board. Chano had taken the post because of his age and wisdom as well as his physical location—he lived in the Pacific Northwest. She couldn't imagine doing this without him, though. He scowled in her direction, his spirited gaze reminding her about judging books by their cover.

Without invitation, Valmont followed Whiskey's lead, going so far as to drape a long leg over one arm of his chair. "Dear God, I'd forgotten how much I hate these things." Relieved by his diversion, Whiskey looked away from Chano and grinned. "Me too." The amusement they shared muted as Margaurethe set a glass of soda beside her. Displeasure surrounded her lover like a cloud, having been evident from the beginning of the meeting. Whiskey was unsure where it had come from. She'd successfully gotten the *Agrun Nam* onto the right path despite Nijmege's attitude and Bentoncourt's attempt to hijack the proceedings. Why was Margaurethe still angry? Had it been Whiskey initially granting Bentoncourt control of the proceedings or Nijmege's constant nattering that had gotten under her skin?

Valmont also noted Margaurethe's negativity and pulled an apologetic face, though his smile didn't fade. *"Better you than me,"* lay unspoken between them.

Castillo also seemed uncharacteristically solemn where he remained beside the liquor cabinet, not rejoining the others. Whatever was eating at Margaurethe also had a solid bite on him. Whiskey ran through the morning's discussions in her mind. Her initial agenda had covered general topics—nation-states obligations, mutual support and economic growth, and issues of equality and justice. Nothing out of the ordinary, nothing that hadn't been discussed in meetings with the Mayans, Africans or American Indians. It had to have something to do with the European *ninsumgal* motion. The rest had been nothing more than the standard opening salvo of a political dialogue.

Dorst approached the buffet, rubbing his palms together. "If I may, *Ninsumgal*? I find that tedious political maneuverings weaken me beyond endurance. I'm most famished."

"Go ahead, Reynhard." His distraction gave Margaurethe the opportunity to move back to the bar and avoid a quiet word. Whiskey pushed away a stab of irritation, both at Dorst's interruption and Margaurethe's unknown issue.

Valmont pulled himself to his feet. "I'll second that. Do you want anything?" he asked as Dikeledi joined them.

Still frowning, Whiskey waved him away, standing herself. "No, go ahead. I'll get something in a minute." At the cabinet, Margaurethe busied herself with a sweet tea for which Chano had a particular fondness. "You want to tell me what the problem is? You've both been pretty quiet."

Neither spoke. Castillo studied his bottle with interest, and Margaurethe stared over Whiskey's head in thought. The others turned away from the food to watch the proceedings from the corners of their eyes, an ingrained reaction to protect their backs from potential danger.

A hint of anger teased Whiskey's heart, the familiar sensation reminding her that Elisibet's first inclination to the unknown was belligerence. Despite intimate knowledge of her inner emotionalism, her annoyance grew. "Any time now," she said. "We can't work together if we don't discuss things."

Castillo sighed and gave her a direct look. "I find it disappointing that you had the opportunity to make a serious change, yet you threw it away. I believe *Ki'an Gasan* Margaurethe feels the same."

Confusion assailed Whiskey's annoyance. "Change? What are you talking about?" As soon as the words came out of her mouth, she knew to what Castillo referred.

Margaurethe's voice was flat as she explained what Whiskey already knew. "Once a question is brought up for a vote, it must be voted on unless there's a valid argument to table it. I doubt Lionel would have dropped the subject of your European monarchy without your input."

Whiskey almost laughed in relief. "For a second there, I thought this was something serious! All I did was cut through the bullshit. Debating the point won't change our goals." Her humor dissipated when they both remained quiet. "Do I need to remind you of the bigger picture? I know you've been vested in my assuming the European throne for centuries, Margaurethe, but you're getting off track. We're working on something larger, remember, something that will benefit all Sanguire not just the Europeans." Again they didn't respond, and Whiskey's anger freshened. "It's called politics, Padre. You taught me the subject."

His dark eyes were direct. "Perhaps."

She tucked her chin, her internal ire building. No matter how much she learned, no matter how many flowery words of honor and support and caring were blown up her ass, her closest advisors still didn't trust her to lead, not even Margaurethe with whom she shared so much more than politics. They thought she was too young, too stupid and too impetuous. Did Castillo see the same thing Margaurethe did when he looked at her? Did he long for Elisibet's return to right the wrongs of the *Agrun Nam*? It was bad enough having to live down her homeless street kid reputation. Why the hell did she have to live down someone else's notoriety too? The voice of Pacal, her Mayan personal defense instructor, abruptly crashed into her mind. *"Acting is the sign of maturity, reacting the sign of a weak and childish person."* His words doused her anger, reminding her that she was still an infant in the scheme of the world and the Sanguire. Elisibet had been a prepubescent child when she'd taken the European throne but hadn't had the strength of mind to stop herself from striking out with immaturity. Whiskey was older, better than that, and had the wisdom of people who cared for her.

She exhaled roughly, expelling her anger. Castillo's gaze had softened. He opened his mouth to speak, but Whiskey interrupted. "No. Don't begin with regrets and recriminations, Padre. We both know I need all the knowledge you can give me if I'm going to survive…if we're going to create this vision. If you don't like what I do with that information, tough. But skip the guilt routine. It won't do you any good." Margaurethe's mental tendril touched her, but she pushed it away, momentarily needing the distance to gather her emotional balance.

"Whiskey—"

"No." She looked away from Margaurethe, turning back to the others in the room. Jake stood sentinel at the door, ever vigilant, nonjudgmental. Dorst, Valmont and Dikeledi remained paused at the buffet table and Chano watched from his seat on the couch. "Let's be honest. We all know the best that'll ever be said of me is that I didn't turn out like Elisibet."

She heard a bottle being set down behind her, heard the rustle of clothing, felt the displacement of air cool upon her hands as Castillo came into view. He knelt before her, head bowed.

"I offer my most humble apologies, My *Ninsumgal*. I reacted as your tutor, seeing an erring student, not my *Ninsumgal*. The weight of ruling the Sanguire will be heavy on your shoulders. I swore to follow your lead in all things, to offer my body, mind and soul to ease your burden. I've inadvertently added to that weight rather than help lift it from you." He raised his eyes, baring his throat in supplication. "Will you forgive me?"

A mixture of emotion washed through her. The anger was still there, a faint echo of ancient ugliness. Castillo had taken a position in her heart that had been empty since the death of her parents. She loved him as her true father. A flicker of remorse passed through her that she had overreacted to his and Margaurethe's desire to see her at the head of their homeland. It seemed her personal insecurities were as dangerously subtle as Elisibet's. They worked against her as good or better than any outside threat. Despite Castillo's knowledge of Whiskey's mental strength, he had knelt before her, placing himself in peril. It was a risk he knew well; neither of them would forget the last time she'd faced down her wrath and grief, Margaurethe included. Castillo had been witness, and Margaurethe had almost not survived the encounter. Perhaps that was why he had put himself so readily at her mercy now, to remind her of her true power.

She felt the sudden shame of acting like a petulant child, wistfully gripping Castillo's hands. "There's nothing to forgive, Padre. We're all tired and doing the best that we can. Everybody screws up." She didn't voice the fact that her errors would have worldwide repercussions. People died when she made mistakes. "Come on, get up and get something to eat. We're nowhere near done with our briefing."

He stood, a welcome smile on his face, though his eyes displayed sorrow. Taking her hand, he gave it a gentle kiss. "Thank you, My *Gasan*."

She shooed him away, pretending nonchalance. Her mouth tasted like ashes, and her stomach held a solid lump where once it pined for sustenance. All the same, she needed to make an appearance that everything was well, that the misgivings of two of the most important people in her life were nothing but a hiccup, meaningless to her. She forced herself to return to Margaurethe who had remained at the liquor cabinet with a stricken expression. She smiled and caressed an olive-toned cheek. "It's all right, *minn'ast*. I understand." Margaurethe's essence brushed hers. She allowed the casual contact, not giving her lover access to the deeper areas of her mind. Whiskey needed to get a handle on her emotions before opening herself that much. The lack wasn't lost on Margaurethe. Regret fluttered across their bond. In response, Whiskey kissed her. "We'll talk later. After things settle, okay?"

Margaurethe searched her face for truth. Whiskey didn't know whether or not she found what she looked for, but her expression cleared and she nodded once in agreement.

"Let's get some food before we faint away from starvation. We've got a long afternoon ahead of us."

Whiskey escorted Margaurethe to the buffet and proceeded to fill a plate for herself with food she didn't want. She joked with Valmont, treated the others with good humor, and generally jollied most of her advisors back into a positive frame of mind. Margaurethe remained slightly subdued, serving Chano his sweet tea.

Castillo seemed encouraged by Whiskey's acceptance of his apology. He sank onto the couch between Dikeledi and Chano with a plate and napkin. "I think the only thing keeping me awake was the effort to refrain from yawning."

Valmont snorted. "And will you put that into your fine book, Padre?"

"Of course not."

Margaurethe made an effort to smile. "No, our *Ninsumgal's* biographer will no doubt increase the initial tension and hint at the shock and amazement as Whiskey deviated from the *Agrun Nam's* plan."

"That was rather startling, wasn't it?" Dorst tittered behind a hand as he moved closer. He chose one of the chairs by Whiskey's desk and sat. "I knew that Lionel has always supported My *Gasan*, but I had no idea he'd so publicly start the ball rolling."

The dispute with Margaurethe and Castillo still fresh in her mind, Whiskey forced herself to remain upbeat. "Maybe putting that to rest will cool Bertrada's jets."

"That is doubtful," Dikeledi intoned. She held a juice bottle in long-fingered hands. "She seeks to avenge a wrong and has been consumed by her wrath."

Chano nodded, swallowing a sip of tea. "Agreed. Her hate is too strong. She will never allow you to rest."

Whiskey had often intervened between her two newest directors and the Euro Sanguire majority that comprised the board, not wanting Chano's and Dikeledi's opinions to be coerced by their personal sentiments regarding the European Sanguire. She'd lived in foster homes where children were manipulated by the propaganda their caseworkers and care providers spewed about missing or mentally ill parents. Such actions caused nothing but heartache and grief. The last thing Whiskey had wanted was to turn this corporation into a mirror image of a dysfunctional foster home or Elisibet's court. Therefore, this joint sentiment coming from the two directors who weren't involved in the Sweet Butcher's debacle caused Whiskey to blink in surprise.

Valmont pushed out of his chair and went to the buffet for seconds. "Finally! Glad you could join the party." He began making another sandwich.

Margaurethe grimaced faintly at his flippancy. "I'm happy you are able to see past the surface." She glanced at Whiskey, searching for an indication to censor herself and finding none. "As Reynhard has reported several times, Bertrada's goals are to kill Whiskey in any way possible."

"What if she can't succeed?" Castillo asked, staring at his root beer in thought.

Whiskey frowned at him. "What do you mean?"

He looked up at her. "What if Bertrada literally cannot succeed at her goal? What will she do then?"

Since discovering Nijmege's ill will toward her, Whiskey had always assumed she'd be able to reason with the woman.

Spending hours in a closed conference room with her had laid that daydream to rest. Even Chano and Dikeledi understood that Nijmege was irrational in her desire for revenge. It had never occurred to Whiskey that she might fail.

"She'll destroy The Davis Group." Chano's voice was matter-of-fact.

"She will." Valmont nodded, settling down with another sandwich. "She's a malicious bitch who has made it her life's goal to extract revenge from Elisibet's future self for the wrongs done to her." He took a healthy bite of bread and lunchmeat, oblivious to Margaurethe's chin lowering in distaste.

Castillo's mouth pursed. "There has to be some way to reach her, some way to appeal to her common sense."

A frown creased Dikeledi's dark skin. "Everyone has their breaking point, Father." She tilted her head, causing her dangling earrings to sparkle as they shifted with the movement. "I have seen Nijmege in negotiations before. She has never been so... adamant. I do not think the European Sanguire will enter into an agreement with The Davis Group lightly."

The talk continued on, skewing away from Nijmege's irrationality and on to other topics of their initial meeting. Whiskey listened with half an ear. She had accepted that her life would be devoted to picking up one mess after another left by Elisibet. The *Agrun Nam* was the largest tragedy. Elisibet had stripped their power to the bone, and they hadn't yet discovered how to strengthen themselves.

Despite Whiskey's exasperation with living under the Sweet Butcher's shadow, she'd always tried to understand how Elisibet had come into existence, how the political disasters had begun. It was the only way she could shovel through the shit and find the gems and pearls within. Attaining a throne as a child, not being able to trust anyone or anything, it wasn't any wonder Elisibet had become so paranoid and bloodthirsty. What a horrible life. And here Whiskey stood, following a tyrant's footsteps, walking a tightrope between sense and outright futility. She trusted her advisors and her lover with her life. They would be there to help her when able, to guide her where necessary. But they couldn't lead in her stead. They couldn't be responsible for her choices. No matter what The Davis Group did, Whiskey held the ultimate accountability.

She was twenty years old, older than Elisibet had been when she'd been put into power. But in the nature of the Sanguire, Whiskey was a babe in swaddling clothes. She didn't even have the benefit of learning to rule from childhood. This situation had been dropped on her like a ton of bricks and threatened to smother her. She was supposed to be partying right now, maybe getting high, getting drunk, hanging with her friends outside the adult clubs, dancing at Tallulah's, going to bed with some bar pickup. Not this!

"Act, don't react."

Calmness washed over her, and Whiskey let out a huff of amusement. She caught Margaurethe's tentative questioning glance and smiled, reaching out to take her hand and essence. As she felt the mulled wine and woodsmoke caress her, she listened to her advisors chatting on about subjects unrelated to their negotiation. The sky outside had darkened considerably, the occasional raindrop pattering against the large window. Regardless of today's hurdles, Nijmege's menace, or Whiskey's personal epiphanies, time moved on. "I think we're done for today."

The others industriously cleaned up after themselves, placing used cups and plates on the buffet for removal, Whiskey included. Gone were the days when they all assumed servants would follow them around with trays and vacuums. Whiskey refused to make extra work for Helen simply because her people had a superior sense of entitlement and the majority of the service staff were Human.

"Remember," Margaurethe said as they approached the door en masse. "No negotiations tomorrow, but Dikeledi and Castillo are due to meet with the Chinese delegates regarding the feasibility of a communications business venture. And do recall that we have a symphony to attend at the convention center. We'll be leaving from here at about five in the afternoon."

Valmont groaned and rolled his eyes. "Another function? Good God, Margaurethe! How many of these things must I attend?"

Castillo chuckled. "The unfortunate downside to politics."

"At least you don't have to come up with another suit at the last minute, priest," Valmont snarked with a minimum of heat.

With an exaggerated lift of his chin, Dorst quipped, "I'd be most happy to open my wardrobe for you, Valmont."

The thought of Valmont in hard-core black vinyl and leather made Whiskey laugh. Valmont winked at her before gifting Dorst with a scowl. Before the mock argument could continue, Whiskey shooed everyone out the door.

Valmont held back as the others drifted through the reception area of the executive offices. "You're wrong, you know."

Whiskey glanced at him, sobering at his uncharacteristically serious demeanor. "About what?"

"The best thing that will be said about you, young *Ninsumgal*, is that you gathered our people together and created the Sanguire Golden Age."

She gaped after him as he turned and walked away.

CHAPTER ELEVEN

Valmont waited until the elevator doors closed upon Whiskey and her entourage before losing his smile. He hated seeing her like this—the general stress, the day-to-day political hassle of a youngling in her position. The added weight of Elisibet's infamy didn't often show itself as it had this afternoon. He'd seen hints of it, expected the dross to appear with the arrival of the *Agrun Nam*, but he despised its reappearance.

He, Dikeledi and Chano were the only directors who didn't reside on the property, though they each had office space. Whiskey had asked them all to eat in her apartment this evening, but Valmont had declined. Dikeledi had also bowed out, citing the need to jot down notes from today's negotiations and prepare for the next day's meetings. Chano had accepted, leaving Valmont unaccompanied as he glanced around the second-floor foyer.

He wasn't truly alone. The Executive Dining Room was doing brisk business, as expected on a late rainy Monday afternoon. He no longer had a retinue of security traipsing along after him these days. Margaurethe had at least gotten over her suspicions that much. As he stood there, a group from the R&D department left an elevator, their scientific jargon hardly pausing as they gave him a respectful nod in passing. Valmont entered the vacated car, pushing the button for the third floor rather than the lobby. Exiting moments later, he noted the overpopulated cardiovascular room with its treadmills and ellipticals industriously burning away Human fat cells. He nodded as he passed the security station and went out the patio door.

The wind was brisk with a hint of chill mist. Rain was always in the forecast for a Pacific Northwest fall and winter. At least it wasn't pouring buckets this time. He didn't deviate from the main path as it took him around a corner and to a skywalk connecting The Davis Group headquarters with the property next door. Traffic rolled by beneath him on Clay Street as he passed overhead.

Warmth enveloped him when he stepped into the foyer there. He couldn't help his faint shiver as he readjusted his suit jacket. Chuckling at the guard seated at the security station, he said, "It looks like I should have brought an umbrella."

"We have one you can borrow on your way out, *Sublugal Sañar* Valmont."

"Much appreciated." He walked to the desk, signing in on the clipboard. "How's the day been?"

"Slow and steady." The guard took the clipboard to confirm Valmont's signature, initialing beside it.

Valmont turned to eye the elevators behind him. "The *Agrun Nam* are on the…twelfth floor?"

"And the fourteenth."

He leaned against the security desk. "Where would I find *Aga Maskim Sañar* Nijmege?"

The guard checked a roster. "She'll be on the fourteenth, *Nam'en*. Suite 1432."

"Thank you."

Valmont was happy to reach fourteen. His elevator had filled with a handful of Human accountants on a lower floor.

They'd filled his ears with the boring wonders of finance and economic theory during his short exposure. Had they not been employees of Whiskey's, he might have considered taking a bite out of one or two of them just to stir up excitement. Instead, he glared at the numbers on the elevator panel until he was able to make his escape.

A sign on a wall indicated he should turn left to reach suite 1432. It had been months since this building had seen renovations, but the scent of new carpet and paint lingered on the air. Originally an office complex, Margaurethe had converted the upper floors to diplomatic quarters for visitors and opened the lower levels to flesh out the business offices needed for her growing communications empire. With research being conducted next door, a nearby building being restored to serve as a shipping facility, and a factory being built in Beaverton, Valmont had to admit that Margaurethe had done quite well for herself over the decades.

Rounding another corner, he saw two doors with Sanguire guards posted outside. Both had brassards indicating the *Agrun Nam*, but the first one had a strip of aquamarine cord stitched into it—Nijmege's color. Valmont tucked his chin and approached the closest man. "I'm here to see *Aga Maskim Sañar* Nijmege. Please tell her I'm here."

"Do you have an appointment?"

Valmont glanced sharply left and right, empty except for them and the guard down the corridor. "Is there a line?" He reached out with his mind to tap against the man's barriers. The guard was strong, yes, and a few hundred years old, but no match if Valmont really wanted to get in and do harm. "Tell her I'm here while I'm still being polite about it. If she wishes me to go, I'll go."

The guard flushed, glancing at his companion several doors away. It didn't matter that Valmont had spoken quietly, they were all Sanguire and his words had easily carried. With a frown he murmured into his microphone.

While they awaited a response, Valmont eyed the other guard. His brassard had a small gold star rather than the aquamarine cord, indicating that he worked for Bentoncourt. As soon as Valmont was inside, Bentoncourt would know he'd been here. Well, let him wonder, then. Movement drew his attention back as Nijmege's door opened.

A Human servant held the door wide, bowing and gesturing. "My *Gasan* will see you now."

Valmont affected a delighted tone. "Why thank you!" He smirked at the door guard, enjoying the grinding jaw as he stepped past. He was ushered into the sitting room where Nijmege stood glaring at him.

Neither of them spoke until the servant was dismissed. "What are you doing here?" she demanded.

"I wanted to talk to you. Can't old friends sit down and chat anymore?" Valmont moved closer but didn't take a seat without invitation. Annoying his mentor's widow wasn't his goal, no matter how entertaining the prospect.

"We're not friends." Nijmege studied him, a haughty sneer on her face. "You've betrayed me, just as you've betrayed others in the past. I don't think you'd know how to be a friend."

Her words struck him hard, reminding him of the last time he'd sold out a friend, murdering her at the command of this woman and the *Agrun Nam*. It wasn't easy, but he refused the bait. "Perhaps not. But I'll muddle through."

She blinked, unprepared for his refusal to take up her challenge. He couldn't blame her. Normally they'd trade words and insults until one or the other marched off in a huff. Wary, she waved a hand at a chair. "Sit down."

"Thank you." Valmont hovered until she did the same across from him. "I trust you're settling in well?"

She scowled. "I am."

"Good, good." He stared out the window, seeing the river and southwest Portland in the distance. He'd come here to talk to Nijmege yet couldn't find the words to begin. For centuries she'd been ill-humored, ever peevish that her role in Elisibet's death hadn't been more tangible. Now he was reminded of the bitter woman he'd succored, the woman whose grief had driven her to push a treasonous statute against her monarch.

Perhaps spending time with Whiskey wasn't a good thing after all. It seemed her influence had made him overemotional. Compassion was both a strength and a weakness.

"Well?" Nijmege demanded, interrupting his thoughts. "Why are you here? Begging for your little mistress?"

"Actually, she doesn't know I'm here." Valmont gestured toward the door and the guard beyond. "At least until it's reported that I signed in downstairs."

With an unpleasant smile, Nijmege leaned forward. "Won't she be suspicious of your visit, then? Will she think you're scheming behind her back to assassinate her as you've done in the past?"

The words struck him with discomfort, igniting the guilt he'd carried for centuries about his role in Elisibet's death. Tamping down the emotion, he shook his head. "I think she'll understand why I came here once I tell her the reason."

His deflection again confounded her and she straightened in her seat, peering at him imperiously. "Speak up, then. I haven't all day."

"What will it take to convince you to leave this path of retribution, Bertrada?" He scooted forward, settled on the edge of his armchair with his elbows on his knees. "Elisibet is dead and has been for hundreds of years. Whiskey isn't Elisibet."

"How can you say that?" She stood, walking away to put some distance between them. Spinning around, she glared. "Don't you hear that honeyed voice, see her mannerisms? She is Elisibet regardless of her true age! She's proof that Mahar's Prophecy is true."

Valmont rose, taking only one step toward her. "Which gives even more reason why you need to lay this farcical retaliation to rest! If she's proof of Mahar's Prophecy, then she'll live despite anything you do. She has a destiny to fulfill."

Nijmege rewarded him with a nasty grin. "I've heard that the people here bandied about that theory. You assume she's invincible because of her *destiny*." She crooked her fingers in air quotes. Dropping her hands, she cocked her head. "Did it ever occur to you that a dead martyr has far more reach than a living one?"

Whiskey's aunt had brought up the supposition that Whiskey couldn't fail by virtue of the prophecies from various nations. None of them mentioned her dying as a necessary requirement for uniting the Sanguire people, and Whiskey had run with the idea. The significance of Nijmege's threat hit Valmont physically, crystallizing his senses. Though nothing in the myths and legends said such a thing, that didn't mean it wasn't feasible. He shook with a sudden adrenaline rush, his canines automatically unsheathing in his mouth. "You have got to be kidding me."

Pleased she'd surprised him, she bared her fangs with a laugh. "I can't believe that not one of you on that illustrious board of directors considered this."

Valmont tucked his chin, forcing himself to relax, his teeth to sheathe. Killing Nijmege would be a pleasure, but that would leave Whiskey without his experience or skills. If Nijmege's guards didn't kill him before he got out of this suite, he'd be subject to European law and given a death sentence. If The Davis Group fought it, there'd be no treaty with the European Sanguire and possibly even open war. Taking a deep breath, he studied Nijmege, perversely enjoying her confusion when he didn't attack. "Look what happened to Judas Iscariot. Are you willing to go down in history as the woman who killed our hope?"

She tucked her own chin, the smile gone from her face. "Gladly."

There was no talking to her. He knew that now. Shaking his head, he gave her a slight bow. "My apologies for disturbing you, *Aga Maskim Sañar* Nijmege. I'll see myself out." Expressions of confusion and pain flickered across her face, reminding him of the woman he had once known. They quickly disappeared, her hawk-like visage returning to the stoniness it had held since the death of her lover, Nahib. *The Bertrada I once knew died then. How could I have missed that?*

With profound sorrow he left her standing in her suite, quietly closing the door behind him. The guard outside watched with wariness as Valmont paused, glancing down the hall to

Bentoncourt's suite. The guard there was different, indicating the first had gone to report Nijmege's visitor. Valmont couldn't dredge up the interest to wonder what was being said and debated if he should visit Bentoncourt next. *No, Lionel already knows.*

Valmont squared his shoulders and left the floor. At the security desk, he signed out of the building with little fanfare, taking the skywalk back to The Davis Group headquarters and his automobile. There was nothing to be done at this point, nothing that hadn't already been said, no one who needed warning. He had harbored the notion he would be able to convince Nijmege, but finally accepted the fact that such a thing was impossible. Unless Whiskey appointed him Defender of the Crown, he could do nothing to champion her against Nijmege's threat.

By the end of the year, one or the other of them would be dead.

CHAPTER TWELVE

Margaurethe quietly closed the bedroom door, leaning back against it to survey the room and its occupant. The room was large—more a suite than a simple bedroom—as befitted a woman of Whiskey's station. Well appointed, it boasted heavy wood furnishings, plenty of closet space and its own small sitting area. Had there been time during the hasty renovations, Margaurethe would have installed a fireplace as well. Unfortunately, she'd needed a secure base of operations more than the comfort of a crackling fire in the *Ninsumgal's* bedchambers. Perhaps she could arrange to have one installed in the future when the precarious political sessions were over.

Never one to display puritan attitudes in privacy, Whiskey had already shed her silk shirt, tossing it at an armchair. She sank onto a chaise lounge to unlace her boots, still wearing a camisole. Margaurethe watched her from the door, enjoying this moment of vulnerability to which only she was privy. Whiskey's pale hair glowed golden under the nearby lamplight, and her dragons writhed along her arm as she worked the boot off her foot.

She loved watching Whiskey, adored the sight of her as she slept or ate or played with her pack mates. Even when anger twisted her beautiful face, when ire sparked her black eyes, Margaurethe couldn't help but be enamored. At first she thought it was due to Elisibet's long absence from her life, a dysfunctional failing that gave her a predisposition to submit herself to Whiskey. She had yearned for the return of her lover for so long…The internal sound of laughter lilted through her mind. Her relationship with Whiskey could hardly be categorized as "submitting." They'd had some explosive arguments over the months they'd been together, more so than Margaurethe had ever experienced with Elisibet. At first, she had worried that these outbursts would ruin any chance of friendship between them. Their arguments had made them stronger, however, something she'd never taken into account. Would the past have been different if she'd opposed Elisibet more frequently and vehemently?

Whiskey dropped her second boot to the floor and stood. She noted Margaurethe still at the door and cocked her head. "*Minn'ast?*"

Margaurethe set aside useless thoughts of history and smiled, walking toward her future. Strong arms wrapped around her waist as she caressed Whiskey's back. "I love you, *m'cara.*"

"I love you too."

Their difference in height was more pronounced now that Whiskey was barefoot. She leaned into the hug, easily laying her head on Margaurethe's shoulder. They stood still for long moments, savoring their closeness. "I'm sorry for the way I behaved this afternoon."

Whiskey stiffened, leaning back to stare into her eyes. "You don't have to apologize—"

Margaurethe placed a finger upon her lips to hush her. "I do. You were right. I became distracted and lost focus. I've spent so many years preparing for this potential meeting that I'd forgotten our goal." Whiskey looked like she wanted to argue more, but Margaurethe smiled, replacing her finger with her lips. Blood and roses swelled along her senses as the warm lips beneath hers became pliant and accepting.

After several glorious minutes Whiskey sighed and pulled away. "Apology accepted then."

Smiling, Margaurethe brought her hand up to caress the side of Whiskey's face with her knuckles. "Thank you. I realize I made you doubt yourself, doubt my belief in you. I want you to know that no matter what happens, no matter how I might rant or rail or scowl, I do believe in you and your strength and foresight." She ducked in for another kiss. "I'm an old woman. I sometimes forget." The comment did as she intended, causing Whiskey to laugh. Her smile widened.

"Old woman, my ass." Whiskey tucked mahogany hair behind Margaurethe's ear. "You don't look a day over five hundred, *minn'ast*."

Margaurethe chuckled, modestly shrugging her shoulders. "I work out."

They enjoyed the levity, not having many opportunities for playfulness these days. Whiskey held Margaurethe close, one hand burying itself in Margaurethe's hair. "I'm sorry too. Sometimes I can't help but act like a temperamental two-year-old whining about an early bedtime."

"You have nothing to apologize for, *m'cara*," Margaurethe soothed, gently rocking them. "You're a youngling. It's expected."

"I'm *Ninsumgal*."

The pronouncement sent shivers along Margaurethe's spine. It was rare that Whiskey used the term so forcefully in reference to herself. She'd grown into her role as time went on but still had issues regarding her position and Elisibet's past. Margaurethe forced herself to pay attention as Whiskey continued to speak.

"I can't afford the luxury of using my age as an excuse for my mistakes. Elisibet did in the beginning. I remember several times she purposely chose to hide behind her youth to act like an ass, to get what she wanted. I don't want to be like that. I can't make those sorts of mistakes."

Margaurethe stepped back, studying Whiskey with concern. "We all make mistakes, love." She tapped Whiskey's nose as dark eyes rolled in exasperation. "Sometimes they have a significant impact on others, yes, but you can't go into this demanding perfection of yourself. It will destroy you, destroy your soul." Her lover appeared unconvinced, reminding her of the primary difference between Whiskey and Elisibet—Whiskey had a streak of empathy that heightened her insecurities, causing her to castigate herself for her perceived failings, real and imagined. According to Whiskey, Elisibet had held similar insecurities but not the human nature to comprehend them, preferring to tamp her weaknesses down into the depths of her soul where they festered and grew ill-begotten fruit. "Besides, you are far too honorable to use your youth as an excuse. That alone makes you different from Elisibet."

The pronouncement startled Whiskey as Margaurethe had hoped. "You don't often say things like that about her."

"No, I don't." She sighed, closing her eyes to search for the words. "You know I loved her dearly. I have no doubt that she loved me in return. Ours was a passion that burned bright, singeing everything in our hearts and souls. Her death devastated me, and it took me a long time to recover." She peered into Whiskey's face, finding her hand and holding it tight between them. "But what I have with you is so much stronger, it has a depth that Elisibet and I never enjoyed. I don't like hearing ill of her, that will never change, but as I experience our love," and she squeezed Whiskey's hand, "I realize what was missing then. Elisibet lacked something, something that you do not, and it colored her every deed and thought."

Whiskey whispered, "Sympathy."

"Compassion," Margaurethe corrected. Tears stung her eyes at her heart's confession, but she smiled. "Valmont was both right and wrong. You will usher in the Sanguire Golden Age, but it won't be the best thing said of you. You offer so much more than that. You're an example of the heights to which our people can strive. Strong leadership, kind-hearted and level-headed. We should all be so lucky to have you in our lives."

Smiling and misty-eyed, Whiskey kissed the back of Margaurethe's hand still clutching hers. "Thank you," she whispered. After a sniffle, she gave a slight shake of her head. "I know you believe that even though I don't. It still means a lot to me to hear it."

Margaurethe understood that this was merely one battle in the ongoing war with her lover's misgivings. Rather than push onward with another volley, she chose a tactical retreat. Whiskey had an obstinate streak that clashed brilliantly with hers at the most inopportune times. Better to withdraw, sowing a seed of certainty in Whiskey's doubting mind. Changing tactics, she bent in for a kiss, releasing Whiskey's hand to cup her cheek instead. Slow embers of arousal grew higher as their lips parted. With a husky voice, she whispered, "Surprisingly enough, we have another evening to ourselves. Shall we make the best of it while we can?"

Whiskey's smile became provocative, her hands drifting across Margaurethe's back to slide along her sides and hips. "What do you have in mind?"

Margaurethe glanced at the bathroom. "I have it on good authority that the *Ninsumgal* has a glorious whirlpool bathtub."

"I like the way you think." Following her gaze, Whiskey laughed. "Do you think the *Ninsumgal* will mind if we use her bath salts?" She turned back and stole a kiss, promptly moving her lips along Margaurethe's jawline and toward her ear. "I bet she won't."

The gruff whisper combined with a sharp nip at her earlobe made Margaurethe gasp, her desire burning hotter. She reached out with her mind, bathing in the aroma of roses as Whiskey gathered her, body and soul. "*Mmmm, m'cara.* I'm sure she won't mind at all."

As they drifted into the bathroom, Margaurethe counted herself lucky to have found her true love not once, but twice within her lifetime.

* * *

Seated on the edge of the bed, Margaurethe watched the gentle rise and fall of Whiskey's chest. An hour before dawn, the young woman still slept in the carefree manner of youth, her consciousness trusted to Morpheus's realm as she wandered the hinterlands of the dream world. She smelled of warmth and sleep and mortality, causing Margaurethe's heart to ache with a love so deep, she thought she would drown.

She'd never witnessed Elisibet in such a state, even when waking beside her. Her first lover's protective shell had wrapped completely about her soul, no matter her level of awareness. Elisibet hadn't needed protecting, hadn't wanted it. Those rare times, in the beginning, when Margaurethe had given in to her need to wrap Elisibet in a blanket of security had always ended disastrously. It was as if in order to deny her weakness, to prove her strength, the *Ninsumgal* had gone out of her way to contrive insult from one person or another, engineering a reason to punish them in the most drastic way possible. She'd had an uncanny sense of people, always going for their weakest points whether it was as simple an act as public humiliation or as horrible as peeling skin from muscle with excruciating leisure. It hadn't taken long for Margaurethe to cease displaying her protective nature.

Margaurethe had carried the youth in that relationship, those first decades a revelation as she grew in ability and experience. She had come to love Elisibet with fanatical fervor, refusing to see the glaring faults, rejecting the reality of their peoples' plight as the European Sanguire writhed within the unmerciful butcher's grip. When Elisibet had dallied with other women it had never been her fault. Margaurethe knew Elisibet's very blood ran to excess, and women always flirted with her. How could they not with the shroud of authority woven so thoroughly through Elisibet's essence? Elisibet couldn't help but respond to their overtures.

Her lips thinned at the recollections of those youthful delusions. Truth be told, Elisibet could have been monogamous had she tried. Somehow, being with Whiskey seemed to have broken through the idealized view Margaurethe had held of Elisibet for centuries. There had been so many things that occurred, so many hints and portents that should have made her flee the palace, return to the O'Toole estates and save herself not only a broken heart but near insanity. Why had she stayed?

She set aside the question, knowing it would never be answered to completion, not without Elisibet herself standing before her with whom to discuss the issue. Margaurethe had a different puzzle to ponder. With Elisibet, Margaurethe had always been the supplicant. The natural order of the realm had put her lover in charge in all things. Elisibet had been rabid about control, never letting it go, even in intimate play or sleep. A youngling with no prior experience, Margaurethe had assumed such was the way it should be and hadn't fought it. As time passed, she'd noticed other couples, subconsciously picking up the vagaries of power within their relationships, and wondered deep down in a secret place why things weren't the same for her and her lover.

She'd been spirited away from the palace after Elisibet's murder, away from the sight of blood spilling across her dress, spreading upon the cool marbled floor. The Purge had begun as those wronged by the Sweet Butcher had risen up against those who had assisted in her oppression. Margaurethe, safely residing with her mother, had been oblivious. As the *Agrun Nam* had gathered their resources and put down the Purge, she'd lived in a dream world, one where Elisibet still existed.

Margaurethe remembered some of the hallucinations despite the passage of several hundred years. Elisibet had come to her, day and night, and they'd spent hours talking or kissing or playing games—all the things her lover had never had time to do before. She always seemed to leave just before someone walked into the room, and no one had believed Margaurethe when she spoke of these visitations. It wasn't until Mahar had uttered her prophecy that Margaurethe had been able to break the bonds of insanity and return to the world. Only then had she accepted that Elisibet had died in her arms. But she would return—the oracle had said so—and Margaurethe would wait for her.

Whiskey sighed and mumbled in her sleep, rolling over onto her side. Her shoulders were bare, the tattooed arm flung across the sheets where it would have embraced Margaurethe had she still been in bed.

The power structure of this relationship was quite different. Margaurethe had held the upper hand from her first meeting with Whiskey. A small smile pulled at the corner of her lips and her heart thumped in memory of that first sighting, excited by the recognition they'd both experienced across a crowded dance floor. She savored their initial introduction, remembering the smell of Whiskey's hair, the feel of her burgeoning mental abilities, and the scent of the dragon's blood ink she used to write in her journal.

Whiskey never wrote in her journal anymore.

Margaurethe pushed the errant thought away, returning to more pleasant memories.

It had been refreshing to see the youthful exuberance she had missed with Elisibet, the raw emotions, the wonder of seeing new things, the enthusiasm she held for life. Elisibet had been far too jaded to show such weakness to anyone. Margaurethe could see the beginnings of such posturing in Whiskey, remembering the street youth standing in the middle of The Davis Group lobby, struggling to be cool and collected though hopelessly out of place. As Whiskey grew in experience, she became more at ease in her skin, not often acting with the wonder of a child.

The hitch had come after the death of the assassin, Andri, three months ago. Something had happened to Whiskey then. She'd sealed a part of herself away from Margaurethe, a small shell of protection in her mind, guarding her thoughts. No amount of prying had dislodged the containing force. Margaurethe had given up on direct confrontation, instead looking to Castillo for probable answers, not that he'd had them. She knew the specifics of what had occurred during her kidnap and captivity from security reports and interviews with those involved. No one appeared to be hiding anything except Whiskey, which meant it was the internal dialogue of her young lover, a thought or belief, not a cover-up.

After yesterday's board meeting, this mental separation had intensified. Margaurethe's concern was that Whiskey held anxieties that grew with each dispute, each altercation, youthful inexperience and indiscretions fueling her sense of self-deprecation. Had Elisibet started this way? Had she taken in the vile whispers and rumors of court intrigue as a child, planted them in an internal garden of insecurity, nurtured them until they ruled her inner world? The only one Margaurethe could possibly ask was Dorst, and she couldn't trust any answer he'd give. He'd been at Elisibet's side from the beginning, devoted to her from her brutally short childhood and onward. He would never give up her confidences, even to Margaurethe, even despite her death centuries ago. And despite her and Whiskey's conversation last night, Whiskey still appeared to be protecting some thought, some emotion. The shell remained intact, even in her sleep.

Just as Elisibet had always done.

Margaurethe remembered Whiskey's initial fears. Whiskey had experienced visions, memories of Elisibet's time that had confused her during her walk along the Strange Path. Her primary concern had been whether or not she was truly herself or Elisibet's mental and emotional clone. Drawn to Margaurethe because of those alien memories, she hadn't wanted to get lost within them. Her fear had kept their intimacy from evolving for several months as Whiskey and Margaurethe both sorted out their personal confusions with the specter of Elisibet hanging over them. After the initial shock of their first meeting, Margaurethe had almost always seen Whiskey, though there had been the occasional jarring recollection. Whiskey's mental touch was so like Elisibet's it had confused Margaurethe in the beginning. The emotional differences between them, however, staggered her. It helped that Whiskey's eyes, black as night, were no comparison to the glowing pale ice of Elisibet's. Taste and smell were dissimilar to what Margaurethe remembered of her previous lover. Every so often, the odd muted sensation of Elisibet's thought patterns gave Margaurethe a momentary upset but they didn't often occur. Margaurethe hardly gave those rare instances a second thought anymore.

She lightly caressed Whiskey's sleeping mind, finding the shield tightly in place. Her scowl deepened. The shell didn't feel like Elisibet. It was wholly Whiskey. Another lesson from Elisibet's memories bequeathed to her successor? What thoughts did Whiskey defend in her sleep?

Too many questions. Never enough answers.

Whiskey moved again, hand searching the sheets. She inhaled deeply and cracked open one eye, spotting Margaurethe perched on the side of the bed. "You okay?" she asked, her voice a rough burr.

Putting away her fears and depression, Margaurethe smiled. "Couldn't sleep."

She yawned, rolling onto her back. "Come back to bed."

Margaurethe stood and slipped out of her robe. The linens were warm with slumber. Despite her troubled thoughts, she settled into the sheets and Whiskey's arms. Whiskey snuggled close, pillowing her head on Margaurethe's breast, pulling the comforter up over both of them.

"I love you," she whispered, her breath deepening as she drifted back to sleep.

She wrapped her arm around Whiskey's shoulders, holding her close. A gentle caress of Whiskey's mind surprised her. The protective outer shell had receded. Not wanting to risk its abrupt return, Margaurethe barely dipped past the surface, bathing in Whiskey's essence with a sense of relief.

Whiskey remained. Elisibet was a memory. The previous morning's political snafu hadn't sullied Margaurethe's future with her lover. It was a misunderstanding, pure and simple. Whiskey would become a better *ninsumgal* than Elisibet ever had been. They would remain together forever.

"I love you too, Whiskey."

CHAPTER THIRTEEN

"Why are we going again?" Zebediah demanded, tugging fiercely on the cuff of his dress shirt. He'd recently shaved the scalp around his brilliant red mohawk, his head gleaming in the overhead light of Whiskey's sitting room.

"Because I said so." Whiskey grinned as he swore under his breath.

With a grunt of exasperation, he glared at her. The black slacks he'd chosen had sinfully skinny legs, and the bow tie dangled untied about his neck. "This is shit. I don't give a fuck about some stupid symphony."

Whiskey tucked her chin and gave him the evil eye. A quick tap of her essence against his reminded him of who held the power. "Tough. You're going. I don't make you suffer near as much as I do. You can survive three hours."

Alphonse came out of the bathroom, his bow tie resembling a gnarled knot. "At least we don't have to wear a full tux and dress shoes, bro." He glanced down at the motorcycle boots on his large feet.

Zebediah grunted and looked away, flushing. It was rare Whiskey took him to task, so his concession came quickly. "Whatever." Still not pleased with his sleeves, he began rolling them up.

Whiskey clapped him on the back in commiseration. She well understood his reluctance, still feeling like a clown when forced to dress up for these functions. Normally she'd have let her pack sit this one out, but Chaniya and Nupa were already attending because her mother and his grandfather had insisted. Castillo had delicately suggested bringing the rest of Whiskey's pack as a cultural experience, and Margaurethe had thought it an excellent idea. That didn't mean Whiskey was going to insist they go far beyond their comfort levels, hence the motorcycle boots and jackets the brothers planned to wear to the event. If Margaurethe wanted to go toe-to-toe with them, Whiskey was more than happy to stand aside.

Margaurethe looked over the younglings with a faint distasteful sneer but said nothing as she donned her earrings. Emerald chips caught the light, flashing with her eyes. She wore a flowing strapless sheath of dark green that balanced her hair color and skin tone. It had been difficult for Whiskey to keep her hands off her lover when she'd first seen it. "Where's Daniel?"

"Here, *Ki'an Gasan*." Daniel entered the sitting room from the corridor.

Zebediah let out a whistle. "Damn, man! Check you out."

A faint blush caressed Daniel's cheeks, but he kept his expression calm. He wore a full tuxedo with a burgundy cummerbund, and his tie looked crisp and polished. A burgundy handkerchief adorned the front pocket. He hadn't shaved his scalp, dark fuzz visible beneath his relaxed dirty blond mohawk. Brushing at a piece of lint, he said, "Gotta grow up sometime, *ebànda*."

"Smooth." Whiskey circled him, smiling. "Does Chaniya know you clean up this well?"

Unable to keep his composure under the gentle teasing of his *ninsumgal*, Daniel looked away with a grimace. "Not yet. She said her mother's making her wear traditional clothing, so I thought I'd do the same."

"You look wonderful, Daniel." Margaurethe came forward to pat his upper arm, contributing to his discomfort rather than easing it.

Laughing, Whiskey punched his other arm. "Better than these two."

"Hey!" Zebediah frowning at the leather jacket he'd just donned. "This is a Schott vintage cowhide Perfecto, top of the line." Alphonse snickered and nudged him with his shoulder.

"My *Ninsumgal*?"

Whiskey left off teasing her pack mates. Jake stood at the door, looking a vision in an almost identical outfit as hers. She wore black tailored slacks, a dark bottle-green sleeveless shell and a black jacket that was more thigh-length sweater than anything. The front edge and hem were embroidered with golden and emerald threads. Somewhere amidst all that finery was a firearm. Whiskey could smell the gun oil and knew Jake never left her quarters without one.

"Yes?"

Jake tilted her head toward the door. "The cavalcade is in place and the delegates are gathered in the lobby. Security has cleared your movements."

"And the venue?" Margaurethe asked, picking up a black lace shawl and draping it across her bare shoulders.

"The *aga'gída* are in place and ready, *Ki'an Gasan*. Doors are already open and ushers are seating the *ninsumgal's* guests."

"I guess this is it then." Whiskey crooked her arm, smiling as Margaurethe drifted close and slipped a hand around her bicep. Glancing back at her pack, she saw Alphonse had finished primping in front of the mirror by the door, his blue mohawk perfectly in place. "You guys ready?"

Zebediah grunted, too annoyed to speak. Alphonse smirked at his brother and hustled him out into the hallway. Daniel gallantly held the door, giving a slight bow as Whiskey and Margaurethe passed. The express elevator already stood open, called there by security. As Whiskey entered it with her exotic entourage, she sighed and braced herself for the longest night of her life.

* * *

The lobby was awash with conversation as more people congregated in anticipation of the evening's entertainment. Nijmege stared at the sea of black town cars and suits gathered on the front drive of The Davis Group, arms tightly folded across her chest. This little outing was a waste of time. Rather than continue negotiations today, Davis's people had piddled the hours away, letting the *Agrun Nam* stew. Bentoncourt had called a meeting to privately discuss some of the topics that had been raised in their initial meeting with the board of directors, but what difference did it make? If Nijmege was successful, there'd be no treaty to sign; there'd be no Jenna Davis to negotiate with. The Davis Group would cease to exist.

"*Aga Maskim Sañar* Bertrada Nijmege?"

Nijmege turned toward the voice, her scowl easing slightly as she realized she didn't recognize the younger woman at her elbow. "Yes?"

The American Indian woman smiled, her dark eyes alight with pleasure as she held out her hand. "It's a pleasure to finally meet you."

Puzzled, Nijmege automatically clasped her hand in return, relaxing her stance. The woman's grip was strong without being overpowering. She wore a beige Grecian-style gown with a slightly flared skirt, one shoulder bared despite the cool weather outside. Sheer mesh of the same beige material covered her other shoulder, glints of silver from the metallic sequins and beads flashing as she moved. Her dark brown hair was pulled back in a single braid, and silver jewelry adorned her neck and wrists. That she was here in Davis's lair was enough for Nijmege to keep her guard up, though she retained her diplomatic training. "I'm sorry…"

The woman gave a partial laugh as she remembered her manners. "Oh, I'm the one who should apologize! My name is Zica."

Nijmege blinked as she attempted to recollect if she'd ever known who "Zica" was. The name sounded familiar, but she'd waded through a mountain of intelligence information before leaving Europe. Coming up with a blank, she tilted her head in question, a faint grin curling her lips in response to Zica's natural effervescence. "I'm afraid you still have the advantage on me."

Zica reached out, lightly grasping both of Nijmege's hands with a squeeze. "I'm Whiskey's aunt."

"Ah," Nijmege said to gain mental breathing room and process the information. This was Davis's aunt, from her American Indian mother's side of the family. Stiffening, she dropped her chin as she felt the pleasant expression fade from her face. She was glad Zica had released the gentle grip on her hands. It was an effort not to wipe them on the sides of her floor-length gown.

Despite the stern glare, Zica remained bubbly as she peered over her shoulder at the cars outside. "I've never heard Dvorak's Symphony Number Nine, have you?"

"Yes, I have. Multiple times."

Zica wasn't put off by the unrelenting tone. If anything, her smile grew wider. "I imagine you have. Wasn't he Czech? I wouldn't be surprised if you'd attended one of his symphonies personally."

It wasn't any secret that Nijmege hailed from a Slavic nation. The fact that this woman had taken the time to ferret out the information made her uncomfortable. *What's Davis playing at?* She turned and scanned the people loitering about the lobby. Her fellow *sanari* had congregated near the main security desk with their aides and staff, Rosenberg's impassive attention the only one directed Nijmege's way. A colorful knot of Africans stood several meters away, Director Dikeledi surrounded by her people. Elsewhere were smaller assemblages of Asians, Mayans and American Indians. An older woman stood among the last, closely watching Nijmege. Other than Dikeledi, there didn't appear to be anyone from Davis's inner circle to witness this meeting. Bringing her attention back to Zica, she frowned. "What do you want?"

Zica tilted her head, her gregarious smile fading at the acerbic delivery. "To meet you, of course."

"Why?"

"Because everyone seems to believe that you're a danger to my niece, and I wanted to see if that were so."

Taken aback at the blunt response so pleasantly stated, Nijmege almost smiled. She respected political strength, and Zica appeared to have good deal of that. Instead, she looked away, affecting boredom with the conversation. "Why would I be a danger to her? The *Agrun Nam* is here to arrange a treaty with The Davis Group, nothing more." Returning her gaze to Zica, she caught a sympathetic understanding from the other woman's expression, proof that Nijmege's true aim was public knowledge in Davis's camp.

"So you say now." Zica leaned forward, lowering her voice. "But I believe you have unfinished business with who she may have been in another life."

Nijmege swallowed, her only outward indication of discomfort with the conversation. "And what would you know of that?"

"I know that she's not who she used to be." Nijmege was unable to keep a slight sneer from lifting her lip, and Zica's smile widened upon seeing it. "I also know you will fail."

"Are you threatening me?" Nijmege demanded, voice dangerously soft as she felt her fangs partially unsheathe.

Zica appeared startled, a long-fingered hand gracefully rising to pat her sternum. Rather than react to Nijmege's sudden aggressiveness, she gave a light laugh. "Of course not, Bertrada. I'm merely stating a fact. Whiskey cannot die until it is her time, no matter how much you may wish it. Her fate must be completed before that can happen. Any attempt to change the course of her destiny will not succeed."

Another one of those then, just like Valmont. Nijmege had wondered if Davis's friends and family would change their tune after Valmont reported about their meeting the afternoon before. Apparently, they hadn't. Why did they all assume Davis had to live to fulfill her great "destiny"? Misguided idiots, the lot of them.

Inhaling deeply to calm herself, Nijmege forced her fangs to recede. "Thank you for your concern. If you'll excuse me…"

Zica reached out, snagging Nijmege's upper arm for a brief moment. "Your skills and experience can be used for so much good, Bertrada. Don't waste them like this."

Annoyed with the woman's presumption, Nijmege jerked her arm out of her grasp. "Good day." She ignored Zica's fallen expression and the slight trickle of guilt that her actions had caused it. As she moved to join her colleagues, she consoled herself with the knowledge that she was on the right track. Why else would Davis have sent her family to intercede on her behalf?

"What was that about?" McCall asked when she reached him.

Nijmege followed his gaze. Zica had returned to her people, speaking quietly with the older woman who had observed their meeting. Nijmege hadn't seen the elderly man that was a member of Davis's board seated there. Chano leaned on his cane and listened in while a youngling glared over their heads in Nijmege's direction. "Nothing." She shook off her vexation, focusing on McCall. "Nothing of import."

He seemed unconvinced. Before he could question her further there came a sudden influx of security into the lobby. One of the elevators opened and Davis and her party came out, eliciting a rise in excited conversation. Building security approached the *Agrun Nam*. "If you'll follow me, please, I'll escort you to your assigned vehicles."

Nijmege allowed herself to be herded with the others out into the cold night air, ignoring the American Indians huddled nearby. It didn't matter that Elisibet had returned to a family that cared for her. The past wasn't the past to Nijmege; it was an ongoing horror, one that she intended on inflicting upon the Sweet Butcher regardless of who she supposedly was now. Resolve bolstered, she climbed into a car with her peers, refusing to consider that she may be making a mistake.

CHAPTER FOURTEEN

Whiskey leaned forward to peer out the passenger window at the multitude escorted out in small clumps to waiting cars. Jake had insisted she sit in the middle of the backseat as a security precaution, despite Whiskey's preference for shotgun. Jake had taken that position, turning in her seat to look back at her, Margaurethe and Zica. "We'll be ready to roll in a few more moments, *Ninsumgal.*"

Giving her bodyguard an absent nod, Whiskey turned to her aunt seated on her right. Zica was a bit older than Castillo but still held a childlike nature. That affinity was more than apparent now as she bounced in her seat, flashing a grin at her sister's child. "Excited?"

"Oh, yes." Zica laughed, an infectious burble of sound that made Whiskey smile. "I've never had the opportunity to attend a symphony before. It will be educational."

Margaurethe leaned forward to speak across Whiskey. "You might want to talk to your niece about such things." She took Whiskey's hand in her own. "She's less than thrilled with the prospect."

Zica's enthusiasm dampened as she looked askance at Whiskey. "You're not curious? Have you attended one before?"

Whiskey rolled her eyes, gripping Margaurethe's hand in vague warning at her chuckle. "Not really, no. Symphonies are…boring."

"But if you've never been, how do you know?"

Unable to come up with an immediate answer, Whiskey paused. Margaurethe tugged on her hand, laughing. "Yes, Whiskey. How do you know?"

Whiskey resorted to the only logical and mature argument available to her. She stuck her tongue out at Margaurethe.

Jake interrupted their laughter. "*Ninsumgal*, we're ready to roll."

"Then let's hit it." Whiskey gave Zica a fond grin. "My aunt is begging for a new experience." The corners of Jake's mouth curved into a smile as she put out the order over the radio. Looking back at the building, Whiskey saw a bevy of Japanese delegates hustling by on their way to the last car, leaving the lobby empty of all but security personnel. "Tell me Alphonse and Zebediah didn't disappear on us."

After a brief radio discussion, Jake glanced back. "Two cars behind us. They're riding with *Sañur Gasum* Dorst." The driver eased out into the traffic on Naito Parkway, following two others.

Margaurethe snorted in amusement. "No doubt they attempted to sneak away. Reynhard would never have allowed that."

"Nope. Too entertaining to watch them squirm." Surveying the streets outside Zica's window, Whiskey saw construction had barricaded Clay Street. The car cruised up two blocks before turning right onto Harrison. As the vehicle picked up speed, she watched the passing cross streets to glimpse the work. "I wonder how long before they get that water line finished."

Zica turned slightly in her seat, grasping Whiskey's other hand. "I don't know, but it was certainly annoying when they chose to drill in the middle of the night."

"I've delivered our complaints both to the city and to *Saginna* Basco," Margaurethe said, drawing Whiskey's attention toward her. "They've both assured me the disturbances won't happen again. I've been told they're nearly finished at this point, anyway."

Whiskey nodded, scanning scenery out the window beyond Margaurethe, then forward out the windshield. The traffic light ahead turned green upon their approach, and Phineas sped up to keep near the lead automobiles.

"That will be—" Zica's words cut off with a gasp.

Before Whiskey could turn toward her aunt, Jake shouted, "Watch out!" She lunged back toward Whiskey, arms outspread.

A horrendous crescendo of metal and glass blasted Whiskey's ears. The car jolted hard to the left, shaking her like a rag doll. Sharp shooting pain raced through her, blinding white-hot as someone screamed.

Blackness descended over her.

* * *

"Out of the way! Out of the way!"

Margaurethe limped to one side of the ambulance door as The Davis Group's emergency medical crew raced into the garage. They transferred Whiskey from the ambulance gurney to their own with careful precision, mindful of the backboard and neck restraint immobilizing her unconscious form. Still stunned, Margaurethe stared as they wheeled her back the way they had come.

It had taken some argument to get the paramedics to allow this change of routine. Some distant professional part of Margaurethe's mind whispered they should add a private ambulance company to their holdings in the future to forestall such confrontations when lives were in danger. Fortunately, *Saggina* Basco, the local European Sanguire magistrate, had been one of the invited guests, riding in a car behind Whiskey's. He had overridden the medical response team's desire to take the *ninsumgal* to a hospital, using his extensive political clout and taking full responsibility for her health as he insisted she be transported to The Davis Group's emergency clinic rather than the nearest hospital.

"I need someone to sign these waivers," one of paramedics stated, holding up a clipboard.

Whiskey and her entourage disappeared into the building, a bloodstained Jake following, her arm hanging at an odd angle. Margaurethe whirled and snatched the documents from the hapless Human. "Give them to me. I have her power of attorney." After several excruciatingly long moments of paperwork and arrangements for the company's retrieval of their spinal support equipment, the emergency responder gave her copies and returned to his vehicle with his partner. The *aga'gída* directed him back up the ramp and out of the garage.

"*Ki'an Gasan.*" Castillo appeared at her side, putting one arm about her waist to support her as he helped her inside. "You should have let them look at you."

"I'm fine, Father. Just some bruising, a lump or two. It is more important that Whiskey get medical attention." For the most part, her assessment was true. She neglected to mention that the lump was on the left side of her head where it had impacted with and shattered the passenger window. A concussion was the least of her worries right now, her soul remaining with the still body of her lover.

He didn't argue the point, though she saw the desire to do so in his eyes. Before she could demand information, he spoke on his own. "Daniel's already here; he left the accident as soon as the paramedics took over and returned to prep our clinic. The majority of our guests have continued on to the symphony. Dikeledi is representing our interests there. Valmont and Reynhard are still at the crash site with the captain of Whiskey's guard and the local police. It appears to be a simple car accident. The other person ran the red light at the intersection."

"Hardly simple." Margaurethe grimaced at the ache in her right thigh and her pronounced Irish accent as she entered into the lowest level foyer. She wasn't quite seeing double. The area was rife with *aga'usi* guarding every possible entrance and exit point. "I want all information available. Everything!"

"Of course." Castillo directed her toward the clinic, a small set of rooms that had been renovated to include an emergency surgery suite and a blood bank. Until now, it had only been used as a doctor's office where Daniel and a handful of nursing staff saw to the needs of the resident Sanguire. This was the first time it would be used for a true crisis.

The waiting room wasn't any less crowded than the foyer. As Margaurethe was helped inside, one of the nurses rushed forward to help Castillo. "How is she?" Margaurethe demanded, voice harsh.

The nurse raised her chin in supplication. "We're still not sure, *Ki'an Gasan*. Dr. Gleircher is doing a preliminary exam and prepping for surgery now."

Margaurethe pushed her away, grinding her teeth at the stab of sickening pain the exertion caused. "Then find out!"

Castillo nodded to the nurse. "Go. I'll get the *Ki'an Gasan* into the examination room." With a gratified gush of thanks, the nurse abandoned them. He tightened his grip on Margaurethe and moved toward the exam room the nurse had indicated. "Shall we?"

As she was assisted past the windowed door to the operating theater, Margaurethe looked inside to see Daniel, scrubbed and gloved, overseeing Whiskey's surgery. She felt a slight measure of relief, at least it was someone she and Whiskey trusted. Her eyes scanned past the door to see Jake in position, left arm still dangling awkwardly as she pinned it to her side with her right hand. "Jake. Come with me."

Jake's complexion had always been paler than Whiskey's and now appeared even more ashen than normal. "I'll be fine, *Ki'an Gasan.*"

Margaurethe knew that for a lie. She lowered her chin and glared. "That's an order. We have plenty of security officers in place right now. Get in here and let the nurse take care of you so you're able to get back to work."

Blinking hazel eyes, Jake swallowed, glancing at her left shoulder. "Yes, *Ki'an Gasan.*"

It was with relief that Margaurethe eased onto one of two examination tables in the room. She nodded pointedly at the other one and Jake meekly followed her example. Another nurse began fussing over Margaurethe. "No. Take care of Jake first. I'm well enough, but she needs to return to duty." She accepted a nod of gratitude from the bodyguard, turning toward Castillo as he inched away. "Oh, no. You're staying here, Father. You're my eyes and ears until I'm released."

Knowing better than to argue modesty, he acceded.

"Where are Chano and Wahca?" Margaurethe asked.

Castillo watched the nurse examine Jake's arm, poking and prodding at her misshapen shoulder. "Both are back here, though they're waiting upstairs with the rest of their people. We opened one of the function rooms and brought staff down to make coffee and sandwiches." He winced as the nurse expertly twisted Jake's arm. A grating *pop* filled the room as her shoulder was wrenched back into its socket. Turning away, his swarthy skin slightly green, he continued, "A number of others have returned, as well. The pack, of course, several select members of each delegation. I had the *aga'usi* take the pack up to her sitting room to keep them out of everyone's hair."

Blood in the water, her mind whispered. Despite Whiskey's goal of uniting the Sanguire, it was to be expected that a number of delegates would be in attendance here. If something truly happened to Whiskey—Margaurethe's thoughts shied away from the possibility—the various government representatives would scatter to the four corners of the earth in record time. "The *Agrun Nam?*"

"Lionel and Aiden are both here."

Margaurethe nodded absently as a sling immobilized Jake's arm. She forced herself to focus on the political situation to forestall the panic fidgeting on the edge of her nerves. "Do we have any information on the other driver?"

Castillo sighed. "Not yet. The police are involved, so it will take more time to get the information. *Saggina* Basco insists that he will do everything in his power to assist our investigation, but you know how it is with Human government…"

"The Sanguire do not exist, therefore we have to use intel to get what we want, I know." Margaurethe suddenly felt so damned tired. She rubbed the bridge of her nose with one hand, fighting the urge to cry and scream. She'd regained consciousness only moments after the traffic accident, but the sight of Whiskey's unconscious and bloody body had appeared so lifeless that Margaurethe had become instantly nauseous, suddenly seeing Elisibet's pale blue eyes fading in death. Only Dorst's gaudy appearance when he wrenched her door open had reminded her of the current place and time.

"*Ki'an Gasan*, I'm going back to my post."

Margaurethe looked up at Jake, pleased to see a little more color in her wan face. She'd had to remove the long black jacket and stood only in torn slacks and the bottle-green sleeveless shell. The crisp, clean sling highlighted the blood spattering across her clothing. "Do so."

Jake didn't need to be told twice. She gave her a curt nod and hustled out of the room before Margaurethe could change her mind.

Castillo followed Jake's progress, turning back with a troubled expression. "Why didn't Whiskey use her talent? It saved her from the car accident that killed her parents years ago. I would have thought she'd have…blipped out."

Margaurethe had wondered the same. "I can only surmise that she didn't see the oncoming vehicle. She wasn't looking that direction when the accident occurred."

He nodded and pulled away, reaching into his pocket to answer his ringing cell phone.

"*Ki'an Gasan?*" The nurse appeared at her side. "Lay back on the table. Can you tell me where it hurts?"

Margaurethe almost laughed. Where didn't it hurt? Not only was her body bruised and bloodied, but her heart had suffered the most significant damage. It continued to bleed even now as she awaited word from Daniel about Whiskey's condition. After all the security measures and precautions she'd put into place, a simple car accident now threatened to tear her soul asunder.

* * *

McCall attempted to feign interest in the concert despite a number of difficulties. His mind whirled his thoughts into a quagmire of misgiving. He'd only caught the briefest glance of the accident before the cavalcade had passed, but the damage seemed quite dire. The nose of one vehicle had merged with the rear passenger side of the other, leaving savagely twisted metal and glass in its wake. He'd had the benefit of being in one of the forward cars; the procession to the theater hadn't yet been diverted around the accident so he'd gotten ringside seats to the spectacle. Dorst had just ripped open the passenger door opposite the carnage as they'd passed, and McCall had seen the telltale blond hair of Jenna Davis beyond a semiconscious Margaurethe O'Toole. He didn't know whether to be pleased or saddened at the rumor that Davis hadn't survived.

At the theater, the concertgoers had been abuzz with speculation right up until they'd attained their seats and the lights had dimmed. The majority had either arrived on their own from various hotels and residences, or their automobiles had been detoured around the collision to allow emergency personnel into the area. No one seemed to have any concrete knowledge of this state of affairs, not even Director Dikeledi. McCall's gaze slid to the nearly empty balcony seating where the African's brilliant outfit glowed in the low lighting. She sat amid a handful of corporation staff, her daughter equally colorful beside her, the only member of The Davis Group's board in attendance. She was there to put on a show of business-as-usual, a brave front in the wake of potential tragedy. Her presence hadn't stopped the tongues from wagging.

After decades of orchestrating a coup on the *Agrun Nam*, McCall couldn't help but be displeased at Davis's potential loss. He'd so hoped to use her death as a way to implicate Bentoncourt—maybe even Cassadie, as well—and begin the process of becoming the next European *Usumgal*, their next king. Destroy the *Agrun Nam* and nothing stood between him and complete power. Incompetent hirelings had nixed his initial plans, neither completing their missions, both dying at the hands of Davis and her people. His decision to fully back

Nijmege would have at least gotten another *sanari* off the council, though not Bentoncourt. Nijmege might or might not survive a challenge with Davis. In either case, she'd be dead or the target of several nations wishing vengeance, both situations McCall could use to his advantage. With Davis dead of simple bad luck, McCall's scheming would be set back, he'd have to start anew. It was unfortunate that he'd put so much stock into that ridiculous prophecy. *If I have to resort to picking them off, one by one, so be it.*

Beside him, Nijmege shifted, her mouth set in a permanent snarl. McCall almost smiled at her frustration, knowing she felt the same angered dismay at the way fate had played them. This was her sole opportunity to avenge her dead lover's murder. Even if an oracle came forth to spout more drivel about Davis's return from the dead, chances were good that Nijmege would die of old age long before she could gain the retribution she desired. He felt a moment of sympathy for her, understanding more than she would ever know how much alike their goals had been.

The music came to a crescendo and stilled. He returned his attention to the stage as the maestro turned and bowed. The overhead lights brightened, and he checked his watch as the audience applauded. "Intermission," he said, glancing at Nijmege and Rosenberg. "Shall we stretch our legs and get something to drink?"

Rosenberg nodded, standing. "I'll call Lionel." Without another word, he eased out of their aisle and made his way toward the foyer.

McCall rose, surreptitiously stretching his back. He looked at Nijmege who had remained seated. "Bertrada?"

She stared blankly at him, the snarl still curling her lip.

With a sigh he sat again, turning toward her. Taking her hands, he held them tight. "Don't worry. She's Sanguire. She'll be fine."

"You can't know that. I saw as well as you did, Samuel." She seemed to fight with herself, her hands twitching in his before she finally decided to pull them from his grip.

"She's Elisibet reborn, she has to survive at least long enough to unite the Sanguire."

"Martyrs do the work just as well despite being dead."

McCall shook his head, the edge of exasperation easing into his face and voice. "That argument again…did it occur to you that martyrs die for their cause? Being hit by a car running a red light isn't exactly material for noble songs and legends." The perpetual frown on her face almost hid the worry lighting her brown eyes. She wanted to be convinced. He grabbed her hands again, squeezing them hard. "Think about it. She'll survive this because she's Sanguire. She'll be weaker, both physically and mentally. Start digging immediately and you'll likely get her to challenge you with ease."

He watched the idea take hold, the scowl fading as hope struggled to take its place. "Do you think so?"

Scoffing, he shook their hands between them. "Two people were in the backseat with her. You saw Margaurethe."

"Yes, but…"

"No buts. The other was that woman you were talking to in the lobby. That Native American woman."

"Zica? Her aunt?"

The surprise and sorrow flickering across Nijmege's expression were unexpected. Rather than highlight them, McCall nodded. "Yes. There's no way she could have survived the crash. Davis will be emotionally vulnerable. As soon as she's up and moving, you can begin poking the wound. She'll challenge you, I guarantee it."

Nijmege inhaled deeply, straightening in her seat as she became more the *Agrun Nam* council member she was. "Of course." She shook her head, giving McCall a slight smile. "Thank you for clarifying my thoughts, Samuel. I'm fortunate to have you at my side for this." She released one of his hands to pat the other.

"Of course, Bertrada," McCall said, an insincere smile answering hers. "That's what friends are for."

CHAPTER FIFTEEN

Margaurethe shifted uncomfortably in the wheelchair, stifling a yawn. The digital clock on the wall indicated it was well into the wee hours of the morning.

Whiskey had survived her surgery and currently slept in a hospital bed in the clinic, Margaurethe remaining in vigil beside her. Daniel had assured Margaurethe that he didn't expect Whiskey to regain consciousness until midmorning. Various instruments blinked and beeped in counterpoint to each other, indicating she lived and breathed regardless of her deathly stillness and pallor. A nurse remained on duty in the reception area, monitoring the machines and occasionally coming in to check the IV tubes and change the bags providing life-giving blood and fluids.

Rubbing her eyes, Margaurethe moved again in her seat, trying to alleviate the ache in her rear from sitting for so long. Daniel and Castillo had already attempted to send her to her own bed, but she'd refused. She had to be present should Whiskey awake in the night. Besides, memories of Elisibet's death continued to replay themselves every time she dozed, making sleep difficult. She knew she'd get no rest until Whiskey roused and passed Daniel's medical muster. Until that time, she'd remain at her lover's side.

The door eased open again. She ignored it, dropping her hand from her face to the page of the book laying open in her lap. Assuming it was the nurse coming round for another checkup, the quiet voice startled her when she heard it.

"How are you holding up?" Valmont crossed the room and neared the bed, his eyes staring at Whiskey. Jake had entered the room with him, standing at the open doorway.

The emotional upheaval of the situation already overpowering her, Margaurethe couldn't help the cascade of pleasure and relief his presence inspired. Rationally, she reminded herself that she hated him and didn't trust him, but her heart held other opinions. "I'm fine," she answered. She waved Jake away, knowing Valmont wasn't a threat. Jake nodded, a scowl on her face as she left and closed the door softly behind her.

He raised an eyebrow, smirking at her wheelchair. "Doesn't look it."

Unable to help herself, a fleeting grin crossed her face as she glanced down at her chair. Her thigh had suffered a greenstick fracture, the bone not quite breaking cleanly. Daniel had likened it to a green twig that, when broken, tended to peel down the length of it rather than snap in half. Her right leg was currently bound tight with a brace and lay fully extended in the chair, a pointed extremity that put her in mind of a makeshift battering ram. Had she been Human the leg would have been in a cast for weeks, but such wasn't the case for a Sanguire. She'd be confined to the chair or bed for two days and keep the brace on the rest of the week while her superior healing powers took care of the injury. "Could be worse."

"Yes, it could. The car could have been coming from the other direction."

Margaurethe looked away, not liking either the reminder of the accident or the concern in his expression. Her eyes stung with tears, and she took a deep breath to counter the emotional paroxysm. Becoming businesslike, she returned her gaze to him. "What's the word?"

Valmont had stepped closer, coming around the other side of Whiskey's bed to study her unmoving form. "The driver was Sanguire, but no one else was with her in the vehicle." He gave a humorless scoff of laughter. "She works for us, no less. Had just gotten off work and was heading home."

This was indeed news to Margaurethe. She'd been far more concerned with Whiskey than the investigation into the accident. "Who? Who was it?"

"Jewel Pauley. She's been implementing the new shipping protocols in the Columbia Street facility."

The name didn't bring up a face, but these days that was hardly surprising. Portland, Oregon had become a mecca for Sanguire now that Whiskey's existence had become public knowledge among them. Any Sanguire with the right skill set could apply for work, and many did just for the bragging rights of working for the reincarnated *Ninsumgal*, the last known empire-builder. The influx had made the *kizarusi* infrastructure somewhat unstable, which is why a blood bank had recently been added to the clinic to help nourish the growing population.

Still, a Sanguire driving the car that almost killed their last best hope..."Are we sure she was alone in the automobile?"

Valmont nodded, his attention on Whiskey's face. "Yes. Reynhard and I both had a look at the vehicle damage at the scene. She wasn't compelled. No one could have kept her controlled long enough from that distance, nor would they have survived that crash in her passenger seat. It's a wonder Jake did, considering."

Reminded of the bodyguard, Margaurethe glanced toward the door. "Where has she been?"

"Posted outside." Valmont reached out, running his knuckle along Whiskey's cheek. "Like she'd take any time off right now. She did clean up and change clothes, though." His cinnamon-hazel eyes pinned Margaurethe, a sardonic smirk gracing his lips. "You chose well. Maybe she should be named Whiskey's Defender."

She felt the sharp stab of his pain and swallowed against letting it overtake her already turbulent emotions. Valmont had been caught up in retaining his previous title with Whiskey for months, perhaps thinking that such an appointment would somehow negate his past dishonor. Margaurethe had been the most adamant against the idea, unable to let go of her distrust of him. Even Whiskey was against his desire, at least for the present. Rather than snap an irritable rejoinder at him, she sighed and changed the subject. "How are Wahca and the others?"

"In mourning, though hopeful." He sobered. "The padre finally got the old man to get some rest, but the rest of the American Indians are still waiting upstairs. Surprisingly enough, the Mayan delegation showed up for a few moments to tender their condolences. I was afraid there'd be bloodshed, but everyone remained calm."

Considering every negotiation with the Mayans had been fraught with snide remarks and outright shouts between their representatives and Chano, Margaurethe found that bit of news amazing. It was a wonder they'd hammered out as much of a treaty as they'd had with such acrimony between their two races. "I'm sure rumors are about?"

"Oh, yes. Can't have a potential world leader in emergency surgery without that." Valmont chuckled. "There's plenty of gossip about who's responsible, whether she's alive or not, as well as a number of other conspiracy theories. Reynhard would have more information on that count, though."

"I'll ask him when I see him."

A gentle tap on the door paused their conversation. Jake opened it, peering inside. "*Ki'an Gasan*, you have a visitor. *Gasan* Orlaith O'Toole."

Margaurethe felt her heart freeze in midbeat. Why would her mother come here? She turned to see Valmont's equally startled expression. "Of course, Jake."

As the bodyguard stood aside to allow the composed older woman into the room, Valmont swiftly made his way to her. He bowed, taking Orlaith's hand to kiss the back of it. "My apologies, *Gasan*. I must depart. Duty calls."

Orlaith didn't appear particularly upset at his excuse. Her chin had dropped at his approach, and she retrieved her hand from his grasp. "Of course, *Sublugal Sañar*. I'll attempt to refrain from expressing my abject sorrow."

Valmont grinned at the riposte but didn't respond. Instead, he threw a commiserating glance at Margaurethe before exiting the room. Jake closed the door behind him, taking up a post just inside the room.

Orlaith moved closer, studying Whiskey's silent form and the machines attached to her. For a brief moment, Margaurethe wondered if her mother understood the readouts, not entirely liking such knowledge in her hands. Abrupt fear raced through her as she considered her own incapacity—her mother could easily overpower her and kill Whiskey. Such a murder would normally mean death in a European court of law, but Nijmege oversaw the High Court. Would such a charge even be brought against Orlaith?

Margaurethe wasn't the only one feeling concern. Jake countered Orlaith's proximity by gliding across the room and taking up position at the head of Whiskey's bed, opposite Margaurethe. Though still wearing a sling, Jake tucked her chin in threat, the essence of soft fleece and the aroma of carnations obvious to everyone in the room.

Smiling, Orlaith held up a hand, yielding to the flagrant threat. "No worries, youngling. I mean your mistress no harm." She turned, looking for a chair, and found a diagnostic stool, which she retrieved. Sitting beside Margaurethe, she ignored Jake's bristling presence. "I'm here to see my daughter."

"I'm fine, Mother."

Orlaith cast a knowing eye at Margaurethe's leg. "It doesn't look it, *m'cara*."

Margaurethe felt the blush, internally cursing at her overactive excitableness. Once Whiskey was in the clear, and she'd had a chance to get some rest she'd be less inclined toward emotional outbursts. "Daniel says I'll be up and about in a week. Nothing to concern yourself over." A warm hand settled on her forearm, causing her to start.

"You're my only child, Margaurethe. Of course I concern myself when you're almost killed in an accident." Orlaith squeezed Margaurethe's forearm and released it, shifting her weight back. Vague distaste crossed her features as her gaze flickered to and away from the hospital bed. "And her?"

Considering Orlaith was heavy into Nijmege's pockets, Margaurethe stiffened in response. "As I'm sure you've been told, she'll be fine, as well." She ignored her mother's look of askance. "As soon as she awakens and Daniel has had an opportunity to examine her, we'll make another announcement."

"I'm your mother, not a petitioner. Don't give me the party line."

Margaurethe glared, eyes narrowed. "You'll get the same 'line' everyone else gets, Mother. My obligation is to Whiskey, not to you."

Lips pursed, Orlaith returned the glare. "Where was she when you were in my household? When you were a child?" she asked, voice low. "Bedding every harlot that crossed her threshold. And where was she after you announced your undying love for her? Hmmm? Doing the exact same thing with any woman of any station."

"Mother—" Margaurethe warned.

"And when she was dead, who was it who fed you, dressed you, cleaned your soiled nightclothes and bedding? Certainly not her!" Orlaith's accusing finger shot out, pointing at Whiskey. "She only knew how to hate and kill and she nearly destroyed you!"

"She isn't Elisibet, Mother!" Margaurethe growled back, immediately snapping her mouth shut to prevent herself from shouting more invectives.

The door opened and the night nurse entered with two members of Whiskey's personal guard. "Please!" she said quietly as she bustled forward to check her patient. "If you can't keep your voice down, I'm going to have to ask you to leave."

Orlaith suddenly stood, causing Jake and Margaurethe to tense in anticipation of an attack. Two members of Whiskey's *aga'gída* eased closer, flanking the older woman. She ignored their presence, all her attention on her daughter. "Can you survive a repeat of her death? Would you be alive now had others not saved you, cared for you, protected you?"

The nurse, a Human and immune to the mental abilities of the Sanguire surrounding her, clicked her tongue in disgust. "It's time for you to leave, *Gasan* O'Toole."

Before the guards could do more than step forward, Orlaith raised her hand in supplication. "I'm leaving." She gracefully bent down, kissing Margaurethe's temple, ignoring the edgy security people scrutinizing her every move. "Mark my words, Margaurethe, she will be the death of you," she whispered before taking her leave.

Margaurethe sighed, dropping her head to one hand so she could massage the bridge of her nose.

The nurse finished her checks and headed for the door. Pausing there, she turned back. "No more excitement, *Ki'an Gasan*," she said, her sympathetic tone both gratifying and unpleasant to Margaurethe. "You both need your rest."

"Of course, Melissa, thank you." Margaurethe looked over at Jake who had remained at Whiskey's bedside. "You may go as well. We'll be fine."

Jake nodded, not one to argue an order and knowing that Whiskey was safe in Margaurethe's presence.

"Get something to eat, Jake." Margaurethe smiled as the bodyguard paused at the door. "I know better than to order you from your post, but you need sustenance to heal. Take care of yourself. That's an order."

A ghost of a smile crossed Jake's face. "Yes, *Ki'an Gasan*, I'll take care of it." She left the room, quietly closing the door behind her.

Margaurethe wheeled her chair closer to Whiskey's bed, reaching out to take a limp hand in hers. "Don't listen to her, *m'cara*. She doesn't know you as I do. And if I die protecting you, I'll count it as a blessing." She leaned forward to lightly kiss the unmoving fingers. "I love you."

CHAPTER SIXTEEN

Hazy. That was the best way to describe the world around Whiskey. It took several seconds for her to realize that the colors and movement she saw around her were people. Her people. Two wore white lab coats as they puttered around her... bed? Puzzling over the scenery, she blinked, taking stock of the situation. Her exhaustion was such that it was an effort to lift her heavy eyelids again. She felt her brow furrow in confusion. *What happened?* She forced her eyes open wider, lazily scanning the room in which she found herself. This wasn't her bedroom, though the place looked familiar.

Before she could pin down the memory, a face loomed into view. Mahogany hair, green eyes and a worried expression regarded her. "M...Mar..." Her voice sounded rough and phlegmy. Whiskey tried to clear her throat, the numbness dissipating as she came fully awake.

"Hush, *m'cara*. You're in the clinic. You've been hurt."

Whiskey's body ached in response to Margaurethe's words. Something had happened, landing her in the tender hands of the medical personnel she employed. She swallowed, having difficulty with even that simple task. God, she was so dry!

Margaurethe seemed to sense her need. She disappeared from Whiskey's view for a brief moment, returning with a paper cup. "Daniel said you could have ice chips until he's had a chance to look at you."

Blessed icy wetness caressed Whiskey's parched lips. She eagerly pulled the ice into her mouth, allowing it to melt as she swirled it around with her tongue. As she swallowed the liquid, she cleared her throat again. "What happened?" she asked, her voice a weak whisper.

Tears brightened Margaurethe's eyes, and she fed Whiskey another ice chip. "We were on our way to the symphony. You remember?"

Brief flashes of memory crossed Whiskey's mind—Alphonse and Zebediah in bow ties and leather jackets, the bottle-green of Jake's blouse, Reynhard bucking tradition as usual with his full-black leather regalia. She hadn't seen Reynhard until they'd reached the lobby, though she had no recollection of exiting the elevator. "No…We left my apartment."

Margaurethe nodded. "Yes, *m'cara*. Then we got into the cars and drove toward the theater."

Whiskey struggled to remember but came up with nothing but blackness. She gently shook her head, a tremor of apprehension in her mind. "I don't remember."

"That's to be expected, *Ninsumgal*," Daniel said. He'd arrived at the other side of her bed, looking strange with a lab coat over his usual punk clothing. He pulled a flashlight from one pocket of the coat and leaned over her. "You were in a car accident on the way to the theater. Traumatic incidents like that almost always cause short-term memory loss." He played the light across her eyes, monitoring her pupil response and otherwise blinding her. "You suffered some extensive internal injuries, but we were able to operate immediately."

"Daniel saved your life."

Whiskey's gaze flickered from Daniel to Margaurethe and back again. She remembered him standing up to his former pack leader for her, suffering Fiona's wrath when she tortured him as punishment. "It wouldn't be the first time."

A faint smile crossed Daniel's normally grim expression. "You'll be fine, *Ninsumgal*. I want you to stay here one more day, then I'll release you to your apartment. In a week you'll make a full recovery."

Margaurethe captured Whiskey's hand. "Thank you, Daniel. Will there be anything else?"

Something passed between them, a vague discomfort that Whiskey witnessed as they looked at each other. Regardless of her good prognosis, it seemed bad news rumbled upon her immediate horizon.

"No." He pulled a small gray remote closer to Whiskey's free hand. "Push the red button to call a nurse. The television controls are there as well." He turned his attention to Margaurethe. "As soon as you're finished, I have a *kizarus* in the waiting area for her. She needs fresh blood to facilitate her healing."

"I understand. Thank you."

Daniel patted Whiskey's hand and left the room.

Whiskey wished she could remember what the hell had happened. Obviously something more than a simple car accident had occurred. If she'd gotten into a car, both her bodyguard and her driver would have been there. "Where's Jake?" she asked in a moment of panic. "Is Phineas okay?"

"They're fine." Margaurethe pulled away a moment to readjust something, her face coming closer to the bed. "Jake dislocated a shoulder and Phineas came out of it almost without a scratch."

Twisting for a better look at her lover, Whiskey ignored the stretching pain in her abdomen as she noted Margaurethe in a wheelchair. Her fear increased. "You're hurt!"

"I'm fine!" Margaurethe took Whiskey's grasping hand, holding it tightly. "It's a broken leg, nothing more." She rolled her eyes. "Well, that and a slight concussion. I'll be right as rain in a few days, just like you."

Relief eased across Whiskey's terror. "Then what's going on? What happened? Did someone else get hurt?" The expression on Margaurethe's face told the story. Had Valmont been in the car with them? Reynhard? Was that why Whiskey remembered Reynhard so clearly? "Who? Who else?"

"Your aunt, Zica."

Whiskey blinked in confusion, not expecting that answer. As the information filtered through her mind, she frantically attempted to locate a memory of Zica sitting beside her. "Zica?"

"Yes." Margaurethe gripped Whiskey's hand. "She asked to ride with us to the theater. You sat between us, she on the passenger side and I on the driver's. A car ran the light, smashing into the rear passenger side."

Her words echoed in Whiskey's head. The accident had caused serious internal injuries to her and a broken leg for Margaurethe. She could almost see Jake in the front with Phineas driving. A fuzzy image of Jake reaching toward her hovered for a moment in her mind's eye before dissipating. Whiskey felt the tension leave her body as she regarded her lover's sympathetic eyes. "She didn't survive, did she?"

A tear finally spilled onto Margaurethe's cheek as she whispered, "No."

Weariness swept over Whiskey as she turned her head, staring at the ceiling. Another death, another innocent killed because of her. Emotional reserves too depleted to cry, she could only lay there in desiccated mourning.

After several minutes of silence, Margaurethe spoke. "You need your rest. Call the nurse. Once you have some blood in your system you can sleep and heal."

It was a measure of her weakened state that Whiskey didn't bother to argue despite not wanting to deal with a *kizarus* right now. She nodded agreement and pushed the red button. Life would go on. She would live and others would die for her, again and again. Perhaps someday she would be in the right place at the right time and no one else would ever need to be the next sacrifice.

CHAPTER SEVENTEEN

Nijmege exited The Davis Group elevator onto the fifteenth floor Residential Lounge. Before her sat a small oasis. Tables and chairs littered the open area, the room liberally decorated with potted plants and a large wall-mounted television tuned to a national news station; an eternally stocked buffet curved along the far left corner emitting mouth-watering aromas; downtown Portland spread out beyond the large windows, tall brick or white buildings against a backdrop of forested hillsides. A Human attendant puttered about the lounge, refilling the buffet, busing tables as diners completed their breakfasts, and disappearing into a back room for occasional supplies or special orders. A hallway split off into two directions from where Nijmege stood, leading to the private residences on this floor. On the floor above her was Davis's apartment. Unfortunately, Nijmege and her staff were housed in the neighboring building, so she had no point of reference as to the sixteenth-floor layout. It hardly mattered since one needed a special key or code for the elevator to go beyond this floor. No doubt the fire stairwells were equally impassable.

The smell of food called Nijmege from her musing. She wasn't alone here. She studiously ignored a table of guards bearing the maroon and silver scorpion armband of her enemy, marching across the open area to retrieve a heated plate from a stack at the end of the buffet. Castillo and Dorst sat at a corner table near a floor-to-ceiling window, heads together though they'd paused their conversation. They nodded acknowledgment, a recognition she ignored with a disdainful sniff. Another table held a man she recognized, one of Bentoncourt's lackeys, wolfing down his food as he perused a magazine. She recognized none of the other half-dozen diners.

Turning her back on Davis's people, knowing even Dorst himself wasn't a threat in such a public place, Nijmege focused on the food artfully displayed before her. Dorst's preference for playing games was known to her and the priest was a nobody, a child. They were no threat. She picked through the offerings, her stomach grumbling with a different sort of hunger as she dished a selection of fresh fruit onto her plate. It was a good thing she'd brought her own *kizarusi* on this extended jaunt. Human city officials had no doubt begun to feel the weight of so many Sanguire in residence, the police probably baffled by the increase of personal assaults that included biting. Public attacks would worsen as more Sanguire migrated here to attend this "*ninsumgal's*" court. Nijmege found grim humor in the idea, wondering if the increased violence would ever be attributed to The Davis Group.

An announcement had been made that Davis had survived the horrible accident she'd suffered yesterday afternoon. Too bad the delightful young American Indian woman had been killed. Irrespective of Zica's opinion of and relationship to Davis, Nijmege hadn't wished her ill. Nijmege's relief had been absolute at the news of Davis's recovery, however, causing her vague unease as she realized just how much the incident had impacted her. She'd spent so much of her life anticipating this opportunity, this moment in time, that she had nothing else with which to fill her days when she succeeded. For the first time her future was uncertain, and the knowledge unnerved her.

She found a table far from the other diners, disquiet following her with its silent censure, and tucked into her repast. The servant appeared at her elbow. Nijmege gave an order for coffee. Soon a steaming cup sat at hand as she considered the day's workload, a notebook and several files spread out on the table before her. She'd had several messages from Europe regarding both the High and Low Courts. With Davis out of the immediate picture, it looked like Nijmege had time to catch up on *Agrun Nam* business before negotiations proceeded again.

From her position, she saw the elevator door open, expelling Rosenberg. Cassadie the Casanova remained inside, dressed in his health club finest. Why he'd escorted Rosenberg up to this floor was a mystery, considering the spa was on the third. No doubt he'd struck up an "arrangement" with the pretty masseuse working there, a little tryst to sow a few of his many wild oats. Good thing the Sanguire naturally had such difficulty procreating. Had that not been the case, baby Cassadies would have overrun the world centuries ago. She continued reading her files and jotting down notes until a shadow crossed her table. She glanced up to see Rosenberg, plate in hand.

"May I join you?"

Preferring McCall's company to his, Nijmege nevertheless acquiesced. "Please." Perhaps she could pick his brain regarding Davis's injuries and how they could affect their supposed "treaty." As he settled into the chair across from her, and the server approached for his drink order, she examined him. Had he been surprised by Bentoncourt's initial demand to place Davis at the head of the *Agrun Nam*? He'd always been distant from the hierarchal games played during council meetings. How had he felt when Davis had played hard to get? She snorted to herself, hiding her amusement with a swallow of coffee. Whether or not Rosenberg held emotions at all had been a question for as long as she'd known him.

Once he received a glass of juice he began to eat. Past experience kept Nijmege from engaging him in conversation. Rosenberg preferred a silent meal to be followed by discourse. She took his example and finished her breakfast. She'd get more information from him if she waited, though even that would require squeezing wine from a turnip.

They finished their meal, the server appearing from nowhere to gather their plates and offer more coffee. After placing a fresh pot on the table between them, she whisked away, hopefully never to return. Nijmege poured another cup. "I've been meaning to ask your opinion on all of this. I just haven't had the time."

"And I have been meaning to ask your intentions toward *Ninsumgal* Davis."

She soured and looked away. Having chosen a table near the window, she looked out on a parking lot across the way that rapidly filled with cars. Never one to mince words, Rosenberg had gotten right to the meat of the matter. Which would he defend—Davis as his future ruler or Nijmege's right to vengeance? "As I've been told by Aiden, he already has a good idea what I intend. Certainly, you know the same? It was stated as such in council chambers months ago. You're much too intelligent to have missed it."

He appeared unmoved, but then she hadn't expected him to respond to ego stroking. "You wish to avenge Nahib's death by killing the Sweet Butcher. That's been proven."

"Yes." She glared. "Will you stop me?"

Rosenberg's face actually cracked a tiny bit. She realized she had surprised him. As she marveled at seeing this weakness in his emotional equilibrium, he answered, "Why should I? You're quite capable of rational thought. You're able to make decisions on your own." He pondered something deep inside. "If you desire my opinion, I think your attempt is folly."

"Folly?" Nijmege grimaced. "Have you been talking to Aiden?"

"No. Why?"

She snorted. "He believes Elisibet has already been punished for her crimes. If I attempt to inflict punishment on Davis, I will be attacking an innocent."

Rosenberg didn't speak for long moments as he stared at her. His gaze caused her a shiver of discomfort. He didn't attempt to mentally approach but it seemed as if he saw into her soul. "I am not qualified to comment on the moral and ethical repercussions of your actions," he finally said. "The folly I refer to is the death of one or both of you."

"You worry about the death of an upstart?"

"I've not made myself clear. My concern is that you win your goal, depriving us of a much-needed *ninsumgal*. Or, if you lose, stripping the *Agrun Nam* of your centuries of wisdom."

Nijmege blinked. If his words were translated from Rosenberg-speak, did he just say he cared for her? She shook the thought from her mind. Of course not. His issue was the political upheaval that would follow her course of action.

Despite Elisibet's bloody reputation and the Purge that had followed her death, there were those among their people who bought Mahar's Prophecy in totality. They believed Elisibet's return would bring about a Golden Age, that all wrongs would be righted. By now, Davis's ascension to the European throne had all but been publicly announced among the European Sanguire gossips. It hadn't helped that the *Agrun Nam* had prepared the old capitol for occupation last year upon discovering her presence. Soon it and the nearby surviving township would swarm with misguided believers should Davis ever deign to move there. If she died in residence, another Purge might well take place. Considering the delicate nature of national politics, the European Sanguire couldn't survive another such mob action. If by some extreme chance Nijmege died in an attempt on Davis's life, the *Agrun Nam* would go into upheaval. It always happened when a *sanari* died and was replaced.

Rather than give away her current plan to bait Davis into a challenge, Nijmege frowned at her coffee cup. "It's all moot, Ernst. If Lionel has his way, Davis will be accepted as our *Ninsumgal*. I cannot go forward with my plans without being called to my own court for treason."

He tilted his head. "It is true you cannot call challenge. I assume your insulting nature during meetings is designed to cause our liege to make the challenge, thereby relieving you of the burden of treasonous charges."

A slow smile grew on her face. "You're very good. And she's not our liege. I haven't sworn fealty to her, and neither has any of our delegation."

"That will change when negotiations are complete."

Nijmege gave a scoff of disbelief. "You really believe she'll be enthroned as our ruler? She's stated she doesn't want the position."

"It's a foregone conclusion. Our presence here indicates we follow her orders. By that decision alone we've indirectly assigned her power over us." Rosenberg let out a deep breath, his heavy-lidded eyes catching hers. "Our treaty will set her above us, regardless, just as she's been set above the Africans and the American Indians. She need not be invested with the European mantle of rule if she'll be above all nations in the world."

Nijmege leaned back in her chair, sour at his sentiment. "That's the same claptrap Lionel and Aiden have been spouting."

"It doesn't make it any less true."

She shook her head, looking away to keep from snapping at him. Dorst and Castillo were still present, still deep in their talk. Frowning in their direction, she considered how much had been said and gauged whether or not they'd overheard Rosenberg's comments. *It doesn't matter now, does it? My goal is no secret, not even to them.* "What do you think? I've heard from Samuel and Aiden on the matter. What's your opinion? Should I continue on with this 'folly' or give it up?"

His answer was long in coming. "You should see it through. You've waited too long, worked too hard to relinquish your vision of revenge. If you don't follow through with your plans, you will become useless to us. Better to die in the attempt than deny your nature."

Her eyes narrowed. She hadn't expected him to agree with her. For years it had seemed that only McCall was of like mind in most matters coming before the *Agrun Nam*. It occurred to her to wonder if he was a shape-shifter sent by Dorst to gain intelligence information. Without thought, she sent a tendril of her mind to his, verifying his identity. Rosenberg met her essence with his own, proving his validity. "No charges of treason?" she asked, her voice dropping low. "No pleas for common sense?"

"No. I assume you aspire to have Davis challenge you. It's a solid plan. Unless, of course, she names a Champion."

"She hasn't yet."

"No."

"And if she should, I'll go through her Champion first. I will not be stopped, Ernst."

The conversation faded between them, everything having been said. He drained his coffee cup. "If you'll excuse me. I'll see you at our next meeting. I believe Lionel wishes to gather this afternoon."

"Certainly."

Nijmege watched him leave. So. Two for and one against. Two against if she officially polled Bentoncourt. Having the subtle support of two of her comrades made the entire plan feel less unbalanced. She resolved to begin the insults and sniping, perhaps starting with the board members. Word would get to Davis regardless of her convalescence. Eventually Davis would sicken of the remarks, become angry and decide to do something about them. *How does one put a bug in a child's ear about trial by combat?*

CHAPTER EIGHTEEN

Margaurethe shifted in the wheelchair. Her rear was numb. *Except where it hurts.* She sighed, refusing to complain aloud. There were worse things, worse injuries to suffer. She had declined to climb into the second bed that had been brought into the room, stubbornly rejecting the offer though she knew she could use the rest. Her exhaustion was deep enough that she'd be out like a light when she succumbed and she didn't yet want to leave Whiskey's side.

On doctor's orders, Whiskey remained abed. It seemed forever since she'd been rushed into the clinic for surgery, but in reality less than twenty-four hours had passed. Daniel refused to release her to her apartment until tomorrow, though he'd said she was mending quickly and well. She'd partaken of blood not long after regaining consciousness and had fallen promptly into a healing sleep for several hours. Her physical demeanor had improved regardless of the emotional impact of Zica's death. At least she no longer sported that deathly pallor that had graced her skin. The bed had been adjusted to allow her into a slight reclining position, and she currently twirled a spoon in her bland dinner, ignoring a situational comedy that blathered on the television.

Seated across the bed from Margaurethe was Whiskey's grandmother, Wahca. The older woman stared stonily at the screen, unseeing, her dinner unheeded as well. She'd come after Whiskey had awakened and asked for her, remaining at her side ever since. Both she and her granddaughter needed one another's support to endure the tragedy of Zica's demise.

Dropping her spoon with a clatter, Whiskey pushed the rolling tray away and slumped back against the pillows. "I'm done."

Wahca pulled herself from her sorrow to stand. She caressed Whiskey's hair, tucking a strand behind her ear. "Are you certain, *takoja*? You've hardly eaten." She plumped a pillow.

With a light grimace, Whiskey readjusted herself with Wahca's assistance and nodded. "I'm just not hungry, *kunsi*." She glanced at the uneaten plate her grandmother had set aside. "I'll eat more if you will."

Margaurethe smothered a smile as Wahca frowned at the obvious manipulation. Whiskey hurt with the loss of her dwindling family members, but Wahca would now bury her last remaining child, a child she'd had at her side for centuries. She and Whiskey were the only relatives they each had left. This realization sobered Margaurethe as Wahca tucked her chin in burgeoning defiance.

"*Kunsi*," Whiskey said, taking the older woman's hands in her own. "We need to be strong for each other. Please eat."

The soft entreaty reached through the grief. Wahca dropped her gaze to stare at their joined hands before raising it again. A sad smile creased her face, and she shook their hands. "I will. You must do the same." She released Whiskey, pushing the tray table back toward her granddaughter.

Whiskey's pleased expression faded at the realization that she'd been wrangled into a similar corner. With a good-natured sigh, she picked up her spoon, resolved to follow through with their agreement. As Whiskey returned her attention to the bland porridge she'd been given permission to eat, Wahca bestowed a look of such love and caring upon her that Margaurethe's breath caught in her throat. Wahca's face withered into a grief-stricken expression, an abbreviated punctuation of agony that swiftly vanished as Whiskey looked up at her, purposely taking a spoonful of porridge into her mouth to indicate she followed the terms of their agreement. Wahca smiled and nodded, returning to her chair to take up her dinner.

Margaurethe swallowed past the lump in her throat. Here was the difference between Whiskey and Elisibet—the ability to love, to feel, to care for another person more than herself. Elisibet had always loved Margaurethe, but her ability had been finite. She would have moved heaven and earth for Margaurethe or Valmont but never considered doing the same for anyone else. Nor would she have allowed Margaurethe access to her innermost thoughts and feelings. Even Whiskey's recent decision to shield her thoughts from Margaurethe hadn't hidden the depth of her compassion and empathy. Rather she was evolving into a monarch, a sovereign who needed to keep some things close in her heart and mind in order to rule justly and well. Margaurethe felt a lessening of the tightness in her chest, understanding that those moments where Whiskey warded her thoughts against Margaurethe weren't an indication that they were falling away from each other. *How often will I be terrified that she'll take the easy way out, become Elisibet? And why does that scare me?*

A gentle knock on the door interrupted her thoughts. Jake opened it, peering inside. "*Ninsumgal, Sañur Gasum* Dorst is here to see you. The nurse says he can stay for twenty minutes."

"Send him in, Jake." Whiskey shoved the tray away a second time, faint relief coloring her face as Dorst strolled into the sickroom.

"My *Gasan*," he said with overt delight. "You are looking positively radiant this evening!"

Whiskey snorted then grunted at the ache it caused in her abdomen. "I doubt it, Reynhard, but thanks for trying."

He strolled closer, thick boots clomping on the tiled floor as he neared. Behind him, Jake silently closed the door, remaining there to watch as he delivered his best Dorst-patented bow. "I was told you were awake and wishing to speak with me." He straightened, closing the distance between them. "Unfortunately, the nurse on duty wouldn't allow me to see you until you'd had sustenance." He glanced at the half-eaten bowl of porridge, a faint sneer curling his lip. "Which I see you haven't."

"You wouldn't happen to have a cheeseburger in your pocket, would you?" Whiskey asked.

Dorst flashed a grin and winked. "Unfortunately, I was frisked by Nurse Attila before she allowed me entry. I may be able to smuggle some fries in a little later when she's off shift."

"Her name is Alice." Margaurethe smiled despite her lightly disapproving tone.

"Forgive me. I'm getting old. My eyesight isn't what it used to be, *Gasan* Margaurethe. I could have sworn her name tag said something else."

Margaurethe lowered her chin in pretend distaste, enjoying the humor curling Whiskey's lips. As soon as Daniel released her, Margaurethe would see to inviting as many visitors as safely possible to see her. The visitors wouldn't ease the pain of her loss but it might distract her.

"Tell me about the accident." Whiskey glanced at her grandmother. "If you want to go…"

"I'll stay." Wahca set aside her untouched plate. "I wish to know."

Dorst gave Wahca a nod of solemn acknowledgment. "We believe the accident was exactly that—an accident. The other vehicle was driven by Jewel Pauley, a Sanguire who worked for us at the 2nd Street facility. After careful consideration, we've concluded she was alone in the car and too far from any Sanguire to have been compelled. She would have had ample opportunity to brake had she regained control from a compelling. It may have been that she was inattentive—perhaps her dry cleaning slid to the passenger floor, or she received a phone call."

Whiskey frowned in thought. "Were her family supporters of the Sweet Butcher?"

The nickname caused Margaurethe to shiver. "Perhaps indirectly. She went through a thorough background check, as do all people employed by us. Her personnel files don't indicate any undue political affiliations, for or against Elisibet."

"I'm not worried about that." Whiskey scowled. "I just don't want her family thinking there will be repercussions over this."

Margaurethe didn't argue the point. Elisibet had been known to retaliate with extreme force for the slightest insult. If she'd had an immediate family member that had been killed, accident or no, the person responsible would suffer the consequences as well as his or her entire clan. Many influential houses had disappeared from history under Elisibet's reign. "I'll be certain to stress that when we send our condolences."

Whiskey looked at Margaurethe. Her dark gaze stormy, she reached out a hand, not speaking until Margaurethe took it. "Don't shut me out of that. I need to be involved."

Tears stung Margaurethe's eyes. She squeezed Whiskey's fingers as one spilled over her cheek. "Of course, *m'cara*. I understand." As much as she wanted to shield Whiskey from these things, she knew she couldn't. Whiskey's fear of becoming Elisibet and her Human-raised sensitivities had caused some spectacular arguments between them in the past. Yet Margaurethe had come to trust that Whiskey had to make her own way, no matter the amount of pain and sacrifice.

They held each other's hands until Whiskey was positive Margaurethe wouldn't renege on the issue. She released her lover, turning her attention back to a silent Dorst. "And the *Agrun Nam*? How are they handling this?"

"They anxiously await news, as do all the other delegations. At this time, there have been no outright threats of bloodshed from anyone, no dire protestations or dramatic tantrums designed to highlight a withdrawal. Most are content to wait for at least a few more days before making determinations in that regard." Dorst winked, a wide grin on his gaunt face. "I expect they'll be chafing by the third or fourth day, however."

Whiskey exhaled, frowning into her lap. "They need to see me, proof that I'm still alive and kicking."

"Yes, *Ninsumgal*. That's exactly what they need."

The spectacle of a public presentation loomed in Margaurethe's mind, her heart seizing in her chest. Whiskey always went for the brash approach, testament to her youth and inexperience. Margaurethe reached out to caress her lover's mind. "That's not going to be possible, Whiskey. You cannot heal without proper rest, and I doubt Daniel will allow such a circus."

"Margaurethe is right, *takoja*." Rarely one to speak during political discussions, Wahca nevertheless dived into this conversation. "It has only been a day since you were hurt. It will be another before you can leave here. Do not overextend yourself." She cupped Whiskey's cheek. "I have lost both of my daughters. I do not wish to lose my granddaughter as well."

Whiskey's hand cradled Wahca's, and they stared at one another for a timeless moment.

Dorst cleared his throat, garnering everyone's attention. "Perhaps we can do something other than a diplomatic function to exhaust My *Gasan*, yes?" After everyone focused on him, he ran his fingers across the bare skin above his right ear, as if tucking nonexistent hair behind it. "First and foremost, have the members of the various delegations out in the foyer tomorrow when *Ninsumgal* Whiskey is released. They will see her as she is wheeled to the elevator and brought to her apartment."

Margaurethe didn't care for the sound of that. The security setup alone would be a nightmare, but she had to give Dorst credit. The most powerful of the visiting negotiators would see Whiskey had survived her near fatal injuries and report to their superiors that all was, if not well, at least improving.

"Secondly," Dorst held up two fingers, "her sitting room on the sixteenth floor can be opened for a brief period of visitations, perhaps on a daily basis until she's allowed up and about." He stepped toward the foot of Whiskey's bed, running elegant hands back and forth over the metal bar there. "It would be simple to remove the dining table and install a hospital bed there such as this one."

The one thing Margaurethe had been adamant about was not allowing anyone—*anyone*—onto the sixteenth floor that didn't have cause to be there. The layout of the apartments and offices on that floor was entirely different than the majority of other residential floors, making it all the more important to refuse access to strangers. Offering the delegates, especially the *Agrun Nam*, access could endanger Whiskey.

Apparently, Whiskey thought the same as her eyes narrowed. She pursed her lips, an expression of disapproval on her face. "I'm not sure that would be a good idea, Reynhard."

Rather than defend his suggestion, Dorst shrugged.

"Jake?" Whiskey winced as she leaned slightly sideways to see her bodyguard. "What do you think? You're the one whose head will be on the block if something happens."

The woman by the door glided closer, stepping into easier view. "It can be done with a minimum of difficulty. The potential disadvantage of an enemy getting the lay of the land is minimal—none will see beyond your sitting room or much else beside the security desk stationed outside the elevators." She nodded to her security superior. "*Sañur Gasum* Dorst is correct in regard to placement. Additional *aga'gída* can be placed in the corridor and in the room to offset any busybodies."

"And such visitation won't undermine our current security?" Margaurethe asked, still not liking the notion.

"To be honest, *Ki'an Gasan*, there won't be much to see. Four walls and a security desk in the corridor, three doors in the sitting room with no idea what is behind them." Dorst grinned. "It will put the representatives at ease as well as show that you're well prepared for anything they can attempt."

Margaurethe saw nothing she could use to deny the proposition. She glanced at Whiskey, seeing a reflection of her own grudging acceptance of the situation. Having the primary delegates see Whiskey healthy and healing would go a long way toward holding onto the current political atmosphere. This wasn't a decision Margaurethe could make, however. She and Whiskey had bumped heads far too often upon her arrival in Portland. Whiskey was a legal adult in both Human and Sanguire society, and the Sanguire were the less forgiving of the two. Hunters always searched for weakness. If Whiskey were to go into seclusion, it would be assumed by the worst of her detractors that she was weak. Rather than argue for or against the situation, she bolstered Whiskey's essence with her own, savoring the scent of roses and blood as her lover knitted their souls together.

"All right." Whiskey nodded. "Tomorrow morning the padre can announce the time of my release as soon as Daniel confirms it. Reynhard, I need you to coordinate the security for my transfer to my apartment." Dorst nodded, a sleek smile on his face. Whiskey looked at Jake. "I'll need you to organize the *aga'gída* detail on the sixteenth floor."

"Of course, *Ninsumgal*."

Whiskey turned her attention to Margaurethe. "Will you be able to set up a visitation schedule? I could ask the padre if you're not—"

Margaurethe smiled. "I'm fine, Whiskey. Just the broken leg, remember." She tapped the brace on her thigh with one fingernail, reminding everyone of what dwelled beneath the lap blanket artfully draped across her lower extremities. "I can start now and make changes on the fly."

A knock interrupted additional conversation. Jake moved so fast that she was a blur of motion, reaching the door before the visitor could open it. The Human nurse on the other side gasped, hand to her chest as she gaped at the bodyguard.

Dorst smirked. "I believe that Nurse *Alice*," he said with a quick wink at Margaurethe, "has decided my time here is up."

Margaurethe chuckled. "I believe so."

He backed away from Whiskey's bed before bowing. "Until the morrow, My *Ninsumgal*." Not awaiting a response, he spun around and left the room, his physical presence forcing the nurse to step back and out of his way. Jake followed, silently closing the door behind them.

Whenever Dorst left a room, it felt as if a whirlwind had departed. Margaurethe stared after him for a brief moment, regaining her equilibrium.

Wahca took much less time. She pulled the tray table back within Whiskey's reach, drawing everyone's attention. "I believe you need to finish your dinner."

Whiskey stared blankly at the porridge, then looked up at her grandmother. A sly expression crossed her face, and she raised her eyebrow. "As do you, *kunsi*."

A smile grew on Wahca's lips. She raised her chin in capitulation and returned to her chair, dutifully picking up her plate.

CHAPTER NINETEEN

The foyer outside the clinic felt cramped. The room itself wasn't large. It didn't help that a third of the space was dedicated to the double flight of stairs leading down from the more expansive function level, the base of the steps bisecting the room. A low ceiling compounded the matter and the number of bodies pressed into the area to witness Davis's medical release seemed excessive.

Still McCall had come here, as had the rest of the *Agrun Nam* and their immediate aides. At least they'd found fortuitous positions on the steps, garnering a better view than those on the floor. Beside him, Nijmege groused that they'd been moved away from the immediate sidelines as an insult, but he preferred this location. His genetics had cursed him with a small stature. As it was, Rosenberg and Cassadie stood a step below him but occasionally blocked his view. He'd never have been able to see through the throng below.

And throng it was. Though guests had been limited to their immediate delegation members and one aide, the room was packed. Its awkward shape coupled with the inordinate number of guards made the area positively claustrophobic. A two-meter wide path from the clinic to the elevators had been cleared, and an elevator car stood open in preparation of the "great event." The clinic was to McCall's right and a single door stood off in the far left corner leading into staff areas. It was as heavily warded as the elevator. Did they think an assassin would materialize from nowhere during this brief transfer? Anyone idiotic enough to make the attempt would be shredded on the spot. *Perhaps if a Ghost Walker survived.* That would never happen, though. The *Gidimam Kissane Lá* had disappeared centuries ago.

The door to the clinic opened, interrupting his thoughts. A herald called out, "Hear me! Hear me! *Ninsumgal* Whiskey Davis and *Ki'an Gasan* Margaurethe O'Toole!" He stood aside and dropped into a deep bow.

Two *aga'gída* led the procession, sharp eyes examining everyone. Behind them, an American Indian woman pushed a wheelchair carrying a wan Whiskey Davis. Several members of the audience bowed, those who had sworn fealty or wished to ingratiate themselves. McCall studied her as she passed, noting that she seemed well. If she was this healthy after two days, then the rumors of her fading demise had been exaggerated. Someone in the crowd began to slowly clap, inciting others to join. By the time Davis breasted the *Agrun Nam's* position, halfway to the elevators, the applause was strong and loud. McCall found it interesting that Rosenberg didn't join the ovation as Cassadie and Bentoncourt did. He cast a quick glance at Nijmege beside him, catching her sneer of hatred.

Behind Davis was her personal bodyguard, the one that looked so much like her. Her arm was in a sling, but she appeared to be just as dangerous as always. After that came another wheelchair, this one pushed by Castillo. Margaurethe's leg jutted straight out ahead of her.

"So she was injured," Nijmege said. "Sad she survived. It would have made for a wonderful opportunity."

Her voice was loud enough to carry to others around them. McCall glanced about, seeing scowls and calculating expressions directed Nijmege's way. Margaurethe O'Toole was a powerful woman from an affluent family. Her demise would have caused sorrow for many despite her association with Davis. Rosenberg and Bentoncourt didn't deign to react to the crude statement, but Cassadie gave her a withering look. Turning to his companion, McCall saw a wicked gleam in her eye. *And so the insults begin.* He observed as the wheelchairs and guards entered the elevator.

The applause faded as the elevator doors closed. A gentle murmur began to fill the air, cutting off as the herald made another announcement. "Hear me! Hear me! *Ninsumgal* Davis will entertain visitors this afternoon and throughout her convalescence. Please contact the main security desk in the lobby to arrange an appointment." The herald gave a smart bow and ducked back into the clinic to avoid further questioning.

Around McCall the crowd noisily broke ranks. Guards remained stationed at the various doors, but the elevators now began brisk business as representatives standing on the floor headed for the lobby to arrange their appointments. The stairs cleared off with equal alacrity. He shook his head at the delegates' zeal. Chances were that a rudimentary schedule had already been penciled out. All these fools would be doing was confirming an appointment Davis's people had already put into place. Besides, it was doubtful she'd be accepting visitors within the hour.

Bentoncourt seemed to believe the same as he stood aside to allow other more excitable envoys to stampede past. The grim expression he'd held since the accident hadn't changed despite visual evidence that Davis was recuperating from her injuries. Once the last people passed them, he lifted his gaze to stare at Nijmege. "Sad she survived?" he repeated.

Nijmege flushed but tucked her chin in defiance. "I certainly do not wish *Ki'an Gasan* Margaurethe ill, but her demise would have created a wonderful opportunity."

"For what? The pain and suffering of her family would outweigh any 'opportunity' you could have used, don't you think?" Cassadie grunted in disgust. "Aren't the O'Tooles allies of yours? If I recall correctly, you and Tireachan go back several centuries."

"I certainly wouldn't want to cause him or Orlaith such pain, but I can't deny that such a tragedy could have opened up avenues which we could have exploited for our benefit." Nijmege stared down at Cassadie, imperious. "And neither can you."

"Perhaps the Sweet Butcher has returned," he responded with uncharacteristic venom, giving Nijmege a scathing once-over. "You've come to embody everything that was horrible about her."

McCall watched as Nijmege's blush drained from her face, her expression slack with shock before anger twisted it into something more familiar. She bared her teeth, hissing. He briefly wondered if he should intercede when Rosenberg stepped up beside her, grabbing her upper arm.

"Aiden is not your enemy, Bertrada."

She struggled with her fury, visibly trembling with the force of it as she panted. Several long moments passed before she jerked her chin upright in resignation. She looked away, drawing a deep breath to bolster herself, yanking her arm out of Rosenberg's grip. Without another word, she whisked up the stairs and away from her colleagues.

"You're with her, then?"

McCall returned his attention to Cassadie, seeing he was speaking to Rosenberg. Intrigued, he wondered when Rosenberg had changed his stance on Nijmege's plans for revenge.

"This is something she has strived for since Nahib's death. If we do not allow her the opportunity to complete this attempt, she will be worthless as a *sanari*."

Cassadie cursed as McCall's eyebrows rose. "If she completes this attempt, our people may never survive."

Rosenberg remained stoic. "She will go forward with this whether we agree with her or not. I have seen nothing yet that would assure me that Ms. Davis won't become a duplicate of her predecessor. How she handles this personal misfortune will say much about her."

"So this is just a psychological experiment for you? See if Davis can withstand personal loss without reverting to the Sweet Butcher's tactics?" Cassadie took a step backward, putting distance between them. "I have to go before I say or do something I'll regret." Without another word, he spun about and headed for the now clear elevator landing below.

"Remember our meeting tomorrow," Bentoncourt called after him. Cassadie raised a negligent hand, not turning back as he waited for the next conveyance. Bentoncourt turned his attention back to McCall and Rosenberg. "I believe I shall head to the lobby and see to an appointment. I doubt you'll be coming with me…?" At their negative response, he nodded. "Good day. I'll see you tomorrow."

McCall watched him go. A moment later, Rosenberg followed him without a word, leaving McCall alone on the stairs. He turned to scan the foyer below, seeing that the guards had cleared out during the *Agrun Nam's* rather public spat. He replayed the scene in his head as he walked to the base of the steps. The political ramifications of anyone having overheard Cassadie's tantrum would be minimal. He pushed the call button. It was more likely that Rosenberg's stance on the issue would create more havoc than balance. Something like that could stir the pot in some political circles, give McCall some meat and bone upon which to chew, some weapons to use in his ultimate goal.

An elevator car opened for him. In the mirror on the back wall, he thought he saw movement behind his shoulder. Startled, he whirled to look into the presumably empty foyer. The doors began to close and he held out one hand to stop them. Reaching out with his mind, he scanned the area. A number of Sanguire essences could be found—sensations and smells of amber, steel, snow upon the skin, sea air, and a half-dozen others—but none close enough for him to assume they were in the room with him. He jumped when the elevator alarm began to buzz incessantly.

Pulling back, he allowed the door to slowly close, pushing the button for the third floor. Not for the first time he wished he knew what Dorst felt like. For all he knew, Davis's chief spy had been lurking in the shadows under the stairs and had heard the entire argument.

He stared up at the blue numbers changing on the digital readout. Nothing to be done for it now.

CHAPTER TWENTY

Bentoncourt stood as the double doors leading to Davis's apartment opened, his personal guard in position beside him. He'd arrived on the sixteenth floor several minutes ago, making himself comfortable on a padded bench near the security desk. A pair of Mayans emerged from Davis's sanctum, speaking quietly to one another as two of the six guards in the corridor moved into escort positions behind them. Bentoncourt recognized, from previous political functions over the decades, one of the visitors as the Mayan's chief delegate. His companion was also familiar, and it took a moment to place him. Ah, Pacal, Davis's martial arts instructor. Unobtrusive, Bentoncourt studied the most virile of the pair. This was the man in charge of training Davis in hand-to-hand combat. The elevator arrived and they entered without their guards. Bentoncourt mused on the differences between European and Mayan fighting capabilities as the elevator closed on them. The attention of the two guards turned toward him, and he set aside his wandering thoughts.

The double doors had remained open, and Valmont strolled into the hall with a wicked smile on his dark face. "Lionel! Are you ready to see her?"

He nodded. "I am."

Valmont made a show of looking beyond Bentoncourt's shoulder, ignoring the *Agrun Nam* guard standing there. "No one else wished to visit? I thought for certain that Aiden would jump at the chance to fawn. He does love the pretty ladies."

In normal circumstances Valmont would have been correct, though more for the social-political reason rather than romanticism, but Nijmege's ill-spoken words mere hours ago had infuriated Cassadie beyond even his evenhanded ways. Bentoncourt studied Valmont's sardonic grin, unable to discern whether or not Davis's security had picked up the *Agrun Nam's* public disaffection with one another. "Unfortunately, he had prior business."

Clicking his tongue in feigned regret, Valmont attempted a contrite expression. "That's too bad. Perhaps another time." He turned toward the double doors, sweeping his left arm out in a gesture of welcome. "After you."

Bentoncourt indicated his personal guard was to remain behind, the *aga'gída* shifting into the vacated place. Valmont winked as he passed. The double doors opened onto a small vestibule with two doors. Davis's personal bodyguard stood by the open right door, nodding him inside. Bentoncourt followed her instruction and stepped into a shallow but long chamber stretching to his right. Traditional American living room furniture filled this end of it, couches and armchairs clustered before a massive television screen and a cabinet of electronic gear. Several younglings from Davis's pack gathered here, apparently playing a game. Though having not spent any time with them, Bentoncourt knew them on sight from intelligence dossiers. Two were missing, the two volatile and colorful brothers rumored to have perched beneath Dorst's wing.

Valmont passed Bentoncourt, easing around the back of one couch to settle a hip there, arms crossed over his chest and a smug grin upon his lips. The blond bodyguard also walked past, slipping to the far end of the room, and Bentoncourt followed.

Multiple sliding doors on his left displayed a terrace, the glass tinted a deep brown to ward off excessive sunlight. Not that such was a problem here during the winter months with the near constant clouds. An armchair from the gaming area had been positioned to accommodate the American Indian, Chano. He sat with his carved walking stick propped horizontally across its arms, his face a craggy stone. Several wooden chairs lined the patio doors, evidently from an absent dining set. Dikeledi sat in one of these, her back as ramrod straight as her chair, a teacup in one hand. Beside her was the American Indian woman who had wheeled Davis out of the clinic, Davis's grandmother.

"Lionel, thank you for coming." Where a dining table would naturally fit into the floor plan stood a hospital bed. Davis rested there, Margaurethe beside her in a wheelchair with one leg extended. Behind them, Castillo perched on a barstool near another door. The pale bodyguard had taken a position near him.

Bentoncourt finished scanning the room, noting a built-in bar to his right with a guard lurking inside near another door. "Thank you for inviting me, Ms. Davis." He gave a respectful bow, carefully calculated to not offend nor indicate that she held the higher social standing between them. "I'm sure you'd much rather be resting." *And grieving.*

She looked healthier than she had a right to after such a horrible accident. The resilience of youth, he supposed. A day and a half after emergency internal surgery and Davis sat abed without support. Her color was good and her eyes clear as they regarded him. For a brief moment, he entertained the notion that Nijmege was right, that despite apparent evidence to the contrary this youngling held Elisibet Vasillas's barbarous soul and hid it behind a carefully constructed facade of naiveté and sympathy. In that split second, he imagined the flash of pique, the cruel curl of lip, and the narrowing of those eyes in fury before they pronounced bloody judgment upon him. The superimposed image caused his heart to stumble and trip, and he blinked the vision away. Davis's gaze was indeed a narrow one, her brow furrowed with the grief she couldn't publicly express during this dog and pony show.

A faint smile crossed Davis's face. "Eventually I'd go stir-crazy. This might be tiring, but the entertainment factor is pretty high."

He echoed her smile, slightly relaxing as he set aside his nightmare fears. "Such is the burden of leaders, I'm sorry to say. Especially one as prominent as yourself."

She grimaced, indicating her belief regarding her importance. "I wanted to say that I'm sorry our talks will have to be postponed a few days. There's no way Daniel will allow me to continue negotiations." She glanced beyond Bentoncourt to her pack. "It was difficult enough to get him to agree to this."

Bentoncourt lifted his chin in agreement. "You need to recuperate from your injuries." His gaze flickered around the room, catching all the members of Davis's board, ignoring the children with long ears in the conversation area. "As well as observe proper mourning for your family. You have the *Agrun Nam's* condolences, Ms. Davis." This time he bowed much lower than before, including the American Indians in his obeisance.

A bleak expression flickered across Davis's face. "Thank you, Lionel." She glanced away, lifting her chin not to concede a point to him but to prohibit an emotional outburst.

He politely looked elsewhere, allowing her the chance to regain her equilibrium. The adults in the room were more focused on Davis than him with the exception of Valmont who smirked back. When Davis cleared her throat, Bentoncourt returned his attention to her.

"I'm sorry you'll be gone by the time we resume our dialogue."

"Oh, I've made the decision to remain for the time being." He held up both hands in supplication. "With your permission, of course. Aiden and I feel that we should remain available after this tragedy, at least for a few days longer." Castillo, oddly enough, seemed pleased with the statement. He probably understood that Bentoncourt felt too uncomfortable leaving Nijmege behind. Bentoncourt restrained a public sigh and roll of the eyes, once again marveling at his masochistic desire to delve into politics all those centuries ago. All this posing and postulating gave him migraines.

Margaurethe nodded. "We'll be glad to have you here, you need not ask permission."

"Our door is always open to you, Lionel," Davis added.

He studied Davis closely. Was there the slightest inflection on the word "you," or did she refer to the entire *Agrun Nam*? Did her words suggest a hidden meaning beyond the statement? He reminded himself once again that while she might not be the Sweet Butcher he feared in his nightmares, Davis did have Elisibet's depth of political cunning and experience. How much she actually used that information was the question. "Thank you."

There wasn't much else to say. These encounters had been arranged to allay everyone's fears about Whiskey's ability to continue her business and nothing else. She most certainly had dozens more appointments to see to before the end and her much needed respite. Before Bentoncourt could excuse himself, Castillo stood and approached. Taking the hint, Bentoncourt bowed. "If you'll excuse me, Ms. Davis."

"Of course. I'll have Margaurethe contact you when we can resume our negotiations."

"Thank you."

Castillo gestured for Bentoncourt to precede him out of the room, followed by the blond bodyguard. The younglings were still engaged in their digital destruction, but the African and the doctor both had time to scrutinize him as he passed. The young woman was Dikeledi's daughter, and the young man nearing the age when he should set aside childhood. As Bentoncourt stepped out into the vestibule and corridor, he idly wondered how much sway they held over their much younger leader.

Two members of the Chinese delegation stood stiff and proud in the hall. Bentoncourt nodded a greeting and entered the elevator he was shown to, somewhat surprised when Castillo joined him and his personal guard. The doors closed. "Making certain I reach my destination, Father?"

Castillo chuckled. "Nothing so sinister, *Nam Lugal* Bentoncourt. We realized that you may have more questions or comments than would be prudent to bring up in such an informal setting. I'm here to offer any assistance I can."

Bentoncourt arched one eyebrow. "Do you have any further comment, Father?"

The priest seemed to debate a moment, glancing briefly at Bentoncourt's guard. "We are aware of what occurred downstairs this afternoon with the *Agrun Nam*," he finally said. Before Bentoncourt could remark, he held up a hand. "Whiskey is not. She's not yet well enough for this information."

Bentoncourt contemplated their reflection in the mirror-like surface of the elevator doors. Having no witnesses to Nijmege's vicious words had been too much for which to hope. "Then you're the one with the questions."

"Yes."

The door opened on the third floor, but Bentoncourt refrained from stepping out. If anyone knew where in this entire building they could speak without concern for eavesdroppers it would be Castillo. Though Bentoncourt hadn't been able to detect listening devices in his appointed quarters, that didn't mean the sly Dorst hadn't found some way to incorporate them. "Then I am at your disposal, Father."

Castillo lifted a chin in concession and pressed the button for the lobby level. "Thank you." Exiting into the lobby, Castillo turned left, stepping past a security desk to a frosted glass door. "My office is in here, if you don't mind?"

"That will be fine." He ordered his guard to remain posted outside, and was led past an innocuous reception area with the usual accoutrements. There were also six closed doors branching off the foyer, and Castillo went to the first one upon his immediate right.

"Eventually all these offices will be occupied," Castillo explained as he opened the first door. "Right now, only Dikeledi and I are here." He flicked on the light, revealing a long and narrow room crammed with shelves.

Bentoncourt scanned the office as he closed the door behind him. Though there was no window, he didn't feel the usual claustrophobia he might have experienced. The ceiling was at least four-and-a-half meters high. Books filled the entire far wall, a brass rail bisecting it two-thirds of the way up to accommodate a library ladder. He knew from intelligence

reports that Castillo was a history buff and archivist, but he'd
had no idea the extent of the priest's collection. Astonished, he
recognized the Sanguire script on a ribbon protruding from a
pile of scrolls. "You have a copy of the Katsushika Proxy?"

Castillo turned with a delighted smile. "Yes, I do. One of
the original six, I believe. I ran across it at an antique dealer in
Madrid several decades ago. The poor soul had no idea what he
held, and I bought it for a decent price." He sat behind his desk,
gesturing for his guest to sit as well. "I didn't know you were a
connoisseur of ancient history."

"I don't have much time for hobbies, but our ancient
forbears have always intrigued me." He pulled his gaze away
from the artifact, reminding himself why he'd been brought
here.

"Would you like something to drink? I've found myself
addicted to sarsaparilla these days. I've plenty on hand, or I can
call the kitchens if you'd prefer tea."

Bentoncourt raised a hand. "I'm fine. Thank you, Father."

"Then to business." Castillo nodded, leaning back in his
chair to regard his guest. "As I said, your...discussion with the
Agrun Nam was overheard and reported. Don't concern yourself
with rumor. Reynhard was the witness. As far as we know, no
one else did."

"Thank you for that assurance." Though a certain tension
faded at Castillo's information, it galled Bentoncourt that Davis's
chief spy had been the one to eavesdrop on his colleagues'
contention. Airing dirty laundry always chafed, but doing so to
one of the most dangerous Sanguire in the European world went
beyond the pale. He watched the priest, finding his hesitation
of interest. Castillo was the same age as McCall, but it seemed
he was less inclined to hold his emotions as close to the chest.

"We have been...aware...of Bertrada Nijmege's plan for
Whiskey for some time." Castillo waited for an indication from
Bentoncourt, continuing after he received a nod. "We've also
known that Samuel McCall supported her in this endeavor. The
news about Rosenberg, however, concerns us."

Bentoncourt debated with himself. Davis's people seemed to
have evidence that one of the *Agrun Nam* had hired the assassins

that had plagued her since her discovery. He had to admit that even without seeing such information he couldn't discount their opinion as paranoia. Someone had certainly attempted to kill her, using Bentoncourt's name to do so. "You believe Ernst might be the threat?"

"Do you?"

He drew in a breath, eyes scanning the books and scrolls behind Castillo as he searched for the right words. "His intention to support Bertrada can be construed as somewhat suspect, I'll admit. But I don't believe he'd go so far as to hire assassins. He's logical and straightforward, not prone to subterfuge. If he had decided Ms. Davis needed to die, he would have done so under his own name and not in secrecy."

Castillo pursed his lips as he frowned. "You don't think he has designs on your position?"

Bentoncourt released a huff of laughter. "He'd have to get through Aiden and Bertrada first. They have seniority." He noted Castillo's stoic expression. "I realize that his opinion may be rather sudden to you, but he's always been reticent in regard to the matter of Davis's place. To be honest, I'm not certain what tipped the scales with him today. Up until now, he's abstained from every vote on the issue."

"He told Whiskey he saw *Ninsumgal* Elisibet Vasillas at your welcome reception."

Blinking surprise, Bentoncourt's mind raced as he remembered his first meeting with Davis. She must have asked Rosenberg the same question she'd asked him. If such was the case, why had Rosenberg abstained from recognizing Davis as the European *ninsumgal* during their initial negotiations? "I realize that you have no experience with Elisibet, but Ms. Davis's essence is almost identical to hers. It could be that he's decided the similarity doesn't end there."

"So I've been told." Castillo tucked his chin. "Do you believe he may be the person who has sent assassins against us?"

"No," Bentoncourt said with ease. "Ernst is a warrior, a damned good one, and he takes the concept of honor quite seriously. If he had decided Ms. Davis needed to die, he'd have come here himself and challenged her."

They studied one another across the desk for long moments. Castillo raised his chin and smiled. "I appreciate your candor, *Nam Lugal* Bentoncourt."

"Of course." Recognizing their meeting was concluded, he stood, his actions mirrored by Castillo. For being over half Bentoncourt's age and ill-equipped to deal with the higher forms of political scheming, the priest was certainly a fast study. Bentoncourt felt a grudging admiration as Castillo escorted him out of his office. *I could work with a man like this.*

At the threshold of the lobby, Castillo reached out to shake hands. "Thank you, *Nam Lugal* Bentoncourt."

"You're most welcome." He wavered a moment. When he spoke again, his voice lowered. "You realize what Bertrada is attempting, do you not?"

A troubled expression briefly hid Castillo's smile. "We do. Unfortunately, there's only so much we can do to protect Whiskey at this point. Either *Aga Maskim Sañar* Nijmege will come to her senses or the inevitable will occur." He paused. "Are you prepared for the consequences of her actions?"

His words caused Bentoncourt's hackles to rise, and he bit back an immediate retort. Was the priest stooping to threats now? But, no, that wasn't Castillo's style. He merely spoke common sense. Bentoncourt readjusted his perception. The priest only asked whether or not the *Agrun Nam* was aware of the myriad of political possibilities that would occur whether or not Nijmege succeeded. "As a council, we do not support Bertrada's agenda. She is acting as an individual and any consequence of her actions are hers alone."

Castillo flashed him a bright smile. "Thank you. That's what I'd hoped to hear."

In the lobby, his personal guard came to attention. Rather than go back to his apartment, Bentoncourt exited the building by way of the glass doors leading out onto SW 1st Street, his guard following. He needed some fresh air to clear his head and heart.

CHAPTER TWENTY-ONE

The door closed on another petitioner and Whiskey slumped back into the welcome softness of her mattress in slow motion. She'd learned the hard way that sudden movement caused an ache in her abdomen that rivaled the one in her head.

"Almost done, *m'cara*."

She turned her head and smiled at Margaurethe beside her, reaching out to stroke the mind that had cradled hers throughout these interminable encounters. Grasping the fingers that reached for her, she gave them a squeeze. "I can't believe I actually want a nap. I hate naps."

"You need the rest." Daniel arrived at her other side, his fingers automatically finding her pulse.

Whiskey pouted. "I also hate being an invalid." She watched Daniel, his attention on his watch as he checked her vital signs, remembering the first time they'd met. He and his pack had saved her ass from a serious beating or worse. He with his dirty blond mohawk, tattoos and piercings, black leather and vinyl— she'd been annoyed that such a man could enjoy the luxury of an education, become a medical doctor, and throw it away to hang out with rich punks. It wasn't until later that she discovered he was Sanguire, that his lifespan was much longer than any Human she'd ever known, and that he was still considered a child though he'd just reached his fiftieth birthday.

"Better than the alternative." Daniel released her and placed the back of his hand on her forehead.

Her eyes automatically flickered to her grandmother sitting beside Dikeledi. Wahca had lost both her daughters now, both to senseless car accidents too. It was sheer luck that Whiskey, Wahca's only grandchild, had been involved in and survived each of them. It was almost enough to give Whiskey a phobia about ever riding in a vehicle with her grandmother. They said lightning didn't strike twice, but…

Daniel lowered Whiskey's blanket, lifting her baggy shirt to check the surgical wounds on her abdomen. Apparently finding them acceptable, he covered her again. "How many more visitors are scheduled today?"

Margaurethe glanced at an appointment book in her lap. "Three more."

"I suggest you make it quick. No last-minute additions. *Aga Ninna* needs a light snack and a lot of sleep."

The use of the phrase caused Whiskey to shiver, reminding her of the missing pack member who had always called her by it. The Sanguire assassin sent to kill Whiskey had murdered Cora several months ago. At the time, her senseless death had angered Whiskey, but at least she'd had somewhere to vent her fury. Someone had been responsible, someone could pay for the slaughter. Now she had nothing and no one to blame. Zica's death was an accident, and the person responsible dead. No one could be held accountable. Whiskey had been able to contain her ire so far. Her current incapacitation and the painkillers helped. But the part of her that was Elisibet brooded in a vengeful craze, demanding restitution, wanting amends that could never be repaid.

She forcibly set aside her urge for bloodshed. "Who's next?"

Valmont, who had taken to escorting the never-ending parade in and out of her sitting room, hovered at the entryway. "It appears the next one is Orlaith O'Toole."

Margaurethe actually growled, startling Whiskey. She looked at her lover as Margaurethe studied the appointment book. "No, it's not! *Saggina* Basco requested a brief moment of time, and I slipped him in."

"Apparently he decided to forego the pleasure of a visit in favor of your mother," Valmont said, his expression serious.

That alone set off warning bells. Valmont was rarely sober when given the opportunity to tweak Margaurethe's nose and Orlaith O'Toole was a prime opportunity. Whiskey frowned, noting an underlying tension unconsciously radiating from him. Her pack picked it up as well, their attention no longer on the video game but on the other occupants in the room. "What's going on? What happened?"

"Nothing." Whiskey knew it for a lie the moment Margaurethe spoke. She seemed to regret the words as soon as they left her mouth. She lifted her chin, an apologetic look on her face. "We had some words while you were recovering from surgery. It's nothing you need worry about."

Whiskey pushed herself into a sitting position, grimacing at a twinge on her right as the stitches pulled. "What kind of words?"

Margaurethe didn't say, her lips pinched.

"Unpleasant ones, *Ninsumgal*." Jake stepped forward. "They regarded family matters. *Gasan* O'Toole became rather incensed and had to be removed from the clinic."

Whiskey ignored the glower Margaurethe directed at Jake. "Why didn't you say something?"

"What is there to say?" Margaurethe visibly reined in her temper, smoothing her expression. "You're recuperating from an injury that almost killed you. It's nothing you need to deal with now. Once you're better, I'll discuss it."

This nonanswer would have to do. Whiskey was too weak to deal with a confrontation regardless of whether or not it would ease Margaurethe's obvious irritation.

"Shall I allow her in?" Valmont asked from the door.

Dikeledi cocked her head. "If your wish is to avoid a meeting with her at this time, you are free to claim exhaustion. No one would think poorly of you."

Whiskey looked at Jake. "What do you think?"

Jake scanned the room. "I don't believe she'll cause a scene here. There are too many people in attendance. The argument between *Gasan* O'Toole and *Ki'an Gasan* Margaurethe was conducted while you were unconscious and there were no other witnesses."

Chano, having kept silent for the majority of the visitations, spoke up. "You witnessed it."

"I am a servant."

The old man snorted, muttering under his breath about the European tendency toward class structures.

His words made Whiskey smile. He was one of the many constants in her world. Chano could be an opinionated, cantankerous old man upon occasion, but he was also one of the wisest she'd ever met. Valmont raised his eyebrows in silent question. "Let her in."

For a wonder Margaurethe didn't offer immediate complaint, instead grinding her teeth and dropping her chin to her chest with a glare toward the door. As Valmont left the room, Nupa's game character died a loud and inglorious death from his inattentiveness. Chaniya smirked and took the controller from him, beginning another round as Daniel returned to sit beside her. Jake didn't return to her post by the entry into Whiskey's apartment. She stood in the spot Castillo had vacated, a faint smell of carnations about her.

Whiskey tucked her own chin. Whatever had occurred while she was out had riled her *zi agada*. Was Whiskey's future mother-in-law a physical threat? She scanned the room, noting her pack and board of directors, and relaxed. Orlaith O'Toole wasn't an idiot or a suicidal terrorist. Even if she did mean Whiskey personal harm, she'd hardly attempt something here and now.

"*Gasan* Orlaith O'Toole," Valmont announced as he gestured the petite woman forward.

"Thank you for coming, *Gasan* Orlaith." Whiskey smiled. "I appreciate your taking the time, though I thought *Saggina* Basco would be here."

Faint distaste wrinkled Orlaith's nose as she passed the younglings lounging in the sitting area. "My apologies for the subterfuge, Ms. Davis." The expression disappeared as she moved with economical elegance to the foot of the hospital bed, nodding greetings to the others. "I seemed to be having some difficulty in scheduling an appointment of my own, and Alfred offered his. Please do not think ill of him."

Whiskey raised an eyebrow, glancing at Margaurethe who glowered at her mother. "I'm sorry you had trouble with that. I'll make certain the security staff is aware you're as welcome as any other guest we have here."

Blue-gray eyes pierced Whiskey. After a thoughtful pause, Orlaith tilted her head, a gesture that bared her neck for the briefest of moments and also acknowledged the statement with a nod. "Thank you."

"You're welcome." Whiskey cast about in her mind for something to say. Her other visitors had all been political negotiators, intent on confirming her health and the future of their talks. Orlaith had nothing to do with that, only here because her daughter was present. They hadn't spoken since the reception four days ago. "Are you enjoying your stay in Portland?"

"It has been…interesting." Orlaith clasped her hands before her in an easy stance, eyes flickering beyond Whiskey's shoulder at Jake's observation. Turning, she focused on Wahca, blatantly excluding Whiskey from her next statement. "My condolences for your loss."

Wahca, stony-faced, nodded politely. "Thank you."

Whiskey's eyes narrowed. She noted the subtle bristling of everyone in the room at the obvious snub toward her. Had she been at full health, she would have called Orlaith on her discourtesy. As it was, she quickly reached out with her mind to subdue Margaurethe's outrage and gave Valmont a look of warning.

By the time Orlaith returned her attention to the bed, Whiskey had a pleasant expression back upon her face. "I don't wish to take up too much time, Ms. Davis. I know how busy you must be."

"Of course." Whiskey braced herself, knowing from Elisibet's memories that Orlaith O'Toole never walked away from any confrontation without slinging a final barb.

Orlaith nodded and turned away. Valmont eased up from his slouch by the sofa to escort her to the hall. Before he reached her, she turned to regard Whiskey. "Tell me, though, how many more must die before you're satisfied?"

"Mother!" Margaurethe made an automatic move to stand up, hampered by the wheelchair and her leg sticking out at a right angle.

The pack had risen, Nupa taking a step forward only to be blocked by Daniel's hand on his chest. Chano cursed, attempting to creak to his feet, raising his walking stick. Using Sanguire speed, Dikeledi closed the distance between them and grasped his elbow to keep him from toppling over.

"Death follows you with eager hands, Ms. Davis. It's only a matter of time before he takes everything you say you hold dear. Those you keep close are the most in danger; surely you know that."

Jake hustled past Whiskey, drawing near to Orlaith, Valmont taking position beside her. "It's time for you to leave, *Gasan*."

Orlaith held her hands above her head, keeping just out of reach to show they had no cause to touch her. "I'm leaving." She marched to the door, calling back, "How will my daughter die, Elisibet? An accidental victim or another broken heart at your death?"

Whiskey felt light-headed at the rush of adrenaline, the desire to attack coursing through her. It didn't help that Orlaith only said what Whiskey had secretly wondered. She knew some of what had happened to Margaurethe after Elisibet's death, though her lover didn't care to relive that time in either word or bonding. There was always the chance that everyone was wrong, that Whiskey would die and leave Margaurethe alone just as Elisibet had done. She didn't think her lover would survive another breakdown like that.

Daniel returned to her side. It was an effort not to rip her arm out of his hand as he checked her racing pulse. Out in the vestibule, she heard Orlaith's plaintive complaint as either

Valmont or Jake took her arm to hurry her along. Then the double doors to the hallway closed, cutting her off. Daniel released her, turning away to a nearby armoire where he had placed his medical bag.

"What are you doing?"

"I'm going to give you a sedative, *Ninsumgal*. And I think we need to cancel the rest of your meetings for the day." He turned back toward her with a hypodermic needle and a small vial of medicine.

"No."

Margaurethe touched her hand. "Whiskey." She was as flushed as Whiskey felt, her green eyes snapping. "Daniel knows what he's doing. Let him do his job."

Whiskey tucked her chin. "No." She turned to Daniel who held the now prepared needle. "There are only two more appointments. Give me a few minutes to calm down. We'll cut their time, but finish today's schedule." She turned back to Margaurethe, her expression softening. "Please. The next visitors just witnessed her being thrown out of here. I can't let them or her think she has the power to hurt me." She watched her words sink in, observed the slight slump of Margaurethe's shoulders, knowing that her statement made sense. In the beginning, it had been a constant uphill struggle to be in control with Margaurethe, partially due to their cultural and age differences, but also because of Margaurethe's frenzied desire to keep Whiskey safe and secure. The last three months had redefined their working relationship, but Whiskey still occasionally came up against the obstinate wall of Margaurethe's fears.

With a sigh, Margaurethe raised her chin. "Don't make me regret this."

Smiling with relief that she didn't have to fight another battle so soon after the effort to remain calm during Orlaith's attack, Whiskey caressed Margaurethe's mind. She turned back to Daniel. "Doctor?"

He debated a moment. "Two appointments. Five minutes each, maximum."

"Agreed."

Daniel recapped the needle and tucked it and the medicine away again.

The door opened. Jake proceeded to her post with a faint air of satisfaction. Valmont seemed less so, his lips turned into an unpleasant sneer. "She's gone. I took the liberty of removing her from the list of acceptable visitors. And I'm going to have a word or two with Basco."

"Don't." Whiskey shook her head. "Schedule him for his own appointment tomorrow and don't say anything. I'll take care of it."

Valmont gave a disgruntled nod.

A wave of fatigue washed over Whiskey. *Only two more to go.* She straightened, ignoring the twinge in her abdomen as something complained inside. "Let's get this over with. Bring in the next visitor."

CHAPTER TWENTY-TWO

The phone on Margaurethe's desk trilled. "Yes?"

"*Sublugal Sañar* Valmont is here, *Ki'an Gasan*," her receptionist said.

"Send him in." She tugged ineffectively at her jacket hem and then scowled at her desire to fidget. Having spent the better part of two days in a wheelchair, she'd found it impossible to produce the professional image she wanted. Whiskey had fallen into exhausted sleep an hour ago, the political parade having finally ground to a halt for the day. With Sithathor and Jake to watch over her, Margaurethe had decided to come downstairs to the executive offices for this meeting, not wanting to disturb Whiskey with any mental outbursts that may occur. She gave the wrinkled material up for a lost cause, pulling the lap blanket over it and calling out a welcome when she heard a light tap at the door.

Valmont entered with his trademark smirk. "You rang, O High One?"

If there was a way to deepen her frown when he was in her presence, Margaurethe hadn't yet found it. Rather than fall sway to his inane chatter, she gestured to the seating area beneath the long window. "We need to talk."

For once, he didn't offer a flippant response. Somberness stilled his face for the briefest of moments before he grinned, throwing himself in the armchair with casual grace. She wheeled her chair closer. The office of The Davis Group's CEO was a reverse image of its President's next door with the exception that it was slightly smaller. Margaurethe had ordered tea from the kitchen. It sat within reach beside her, and she poured them each a cup. She expertly added a dollop of cream and two cubes of sugar to one, handing it to Valmont.

"I'm surprised you remembered." He flashed her another smile, this one more genuine than his usual fare. "Thank you."

"You're welcome." She refrained from commenting that she'd always paid close attention to her enemies. Much as she hated to admit it, Valmont was no longer her foe no matter their turbulent history. They'd never have the close friendship they'd enjoyed in their youth, but they were no longer so much at odds. He cared for Whiskey—had cared for Elisibet. He and Margaurethe needed to work together now to ensure her safety. She poured tea for herself, adding sweetener and sitting back with a furtive stretch.

Valmont caught it. "It has been a long day, hasn't it?" he asked, rubbing the back of his neck in commiseration.

"Indeed." Margaurethe sipped her drink, eyeing him over the rim of her cup. "What do you think of my mother?"

Valmont chuckled, waggling a finger at her. "Oh, no. I'm not getting into that discussion. I've just gotten in the door, and we're playing ever so nice at the moment. I'd hate to see our burgeoning armistice ruined so quickly."

She grimaced, cradling the cup in her lap. "Trust me, I've had abundant experience with my mother. I doubt you'll say anything about her with which I'll disagree."

He studied her in careful speculation, his sardonic humor fading into that unaccustomed seriousness he'd portrayed increasingly these days. "I think she's acting like a concerned parent. She wants her progeny unharmed, she always has.

I remember her squawks from the isles when I was at court, though I never had the fortune of meeting her until now."

"Misfortune, you mean." Her lips curled at his surprised snicker of amusement. Sobering, she sighed. "I find the timing of her appearance here suspect. Do you think she's involved with the assassination attempts?"

Valmont pursed his lips. "No, not really. Doesn't seem her style." At Margaurethe's look of askance, he shrugged. "If she was the type to hire assassins, wouldn't she have done it centuries ago when Elisibet was a burr under her saddle? Why wait until here and now?"

A distant part of Margaurethe broke, her inner tension easing. She hadn't wanted to believe her mother could be responsible for such a thing but couldn't put the possibility past her. Orlaith had disliked Elisibet long before Margaurethe had met the Sweet Butcher. That dislike had evolved into absolute loathing once Margaurethe had fallen into Elisibet's clutches. "I don't think so either, but I wasn't sure."

His shoulders relaxed, and she realized he'd been waiting for her verbal rejoinder. Scanning their interactions these last few months, she couldn't argue that he had the right to expect it. She'd spent the majority of their interchanges haranguing him for Elisibet's murder, utilizing every opportunity to rub her pain in his face. Even Whiskey's mental intervention hadn't alleviated Margaurethe's hatred, though Margaurethe now had a much better understanding of what had motivated Elisibet's mind and heart. Difficult to take the high road when she had the benefit of a profound mental bond with Whiskey that revealed much of Elisibet's insecurities and exhaustion. Not only had Valmont hurt Margaurethe by killing her lover, but Elisibet had dealt Margaurethe's heart a mortal blow by allowing the situation to occur.

On impulse, Margaurethe set her cup down, reaching out with one hand. Startled, Valmont leaned forward, automatically offering his in return. She grasped his palm, the warmth of his skin against hers a shock as she realized that the last time they'd touched one another was when she'd physically attacked him months ago. "I realize I've been…quite harsh toward you." His cheeks dimpled but he didn't interrupt. Margaurethe fought down her habitual agitation, strengthening her grip in an effort to hold tight to her goal. "I can never forgive you for…what you did." She watched the pleasure drain from his face. "Surely you know that's not possible for me."

Valmont set his tea on the coffee table and cupped their joined hands. "I don't seek forgiveness, Margaurethe. I deserve every word and deed I've received from you and more."

She stared into his cinnamon-brown eyes, so familiar yet so different. There'd been a time when they'd banded together as loving friends, intent on soothing Elisibet's ferocious humors. Valmont had been guilty of spurring much of Elisibet's viciousness, but had matured over the years. The last half-century of Elisibet's life had seen Margaurethe and Valmont working in conjunction to intercept her stabs of fury and violent reactionary tactics. Everything had changed once Valmont's mentor, Nahib, had been executed in such an atrocious manner. Incensed, Valmont had left court, left Margaurethe alone to ineffectually contain Elisibet's anger and feelings of betrayal.

Since meeting and falling in love with Whiskey, Margaurethe had begun to question some of her suppositions, her long held hatreds. Having Castillo as a constant conscience hadn't helped her obstinate desire to clutch every injury and insult Valmont had flung at her, real or imagined, but the strange bond she enjoyed with Whiskey had altered something within her. She'd finally gained access to Elisibet's inner shell of protection, the one she'd never been able to break through during Elisibet's lifetime. She'd witnessed what Elisibet had seen and felt, knew down to her soul how much Elisibet had loved her, the passion she'd felt in Margaurethe's presence.

And the strength of her love for Valmont, her best friend.

"She loved you dearly, you know. Even when you came to her study and fought her."

He blinked, confusion crossing his face. "What?"

"Elisibet loved you to her core, just as she loved me. When she died, she held sorrow for two things—that she left me, and that she'd put you into the position of being responsible for her death."

Valmont pulled sharply away, disrupting their tableau as he stood and strode toward the desk. Whirling around, a bleak anger had taken possession of him. "What are you saying? How could you know that?"

Margaurethe turned her chair toward him. "Whiskey has searched your mind before, hasn't she?" She waited until she received a curt nod of assent. "She has the ability to delve into others' minds, retrieve their thoughts and memories. She can also share her own. By extension—"

"You've seen Elisibet's memories," Valmont finished in a voice of gravel.

"Some of them, yes." Margaurethe slowly stood, not wanting to spook him. His dark skin was ashen with shock, his eyes glassy with potential tears. It startled her to see him so near to losing emotional control. In all the centuries she'd known him, she'd never seen him this close to the edge. "I cannot forgive you for her loss. The pain lies too deep within my soul. But you should know that Elisibet already has."

Jaw twitching as he fought to regain mastery, Valmont half-stumbled to the window, staring hard at the trees and traffic and river beneath his unseeing gaze. Margaurethe turned back to the table, topping off her tea before settling back to drink it. Her throat ached with a need to cry, but she pushed it away. One of them needed a level head at the moment.

Nearly a quarter hour passed as Valmont found a path back from his grief. He'd need more time to process what Margaurethe had told him, but she had no doubt that he'd be back to his nefarious self presently. He muttered an apology and availed himself of the tissue box on her desk, cleaning up his face before returning to his chair.

"Your tea is cold. Shall I pour you another?"

"No." He drew a deep breath, held it a moment and let it go. His eyes remained shiny and slightly red-rimmed, but otherwise he appeared calm. "Why have you told me this?"

"Because you needed to know. You're under the impression that Whiskey hasn't appointed you Defender because of your past actions, that she doesn't trust you. That isn't true."

He scowled. "Then why won't she? If Bertrada challenges her, I can champion her cause. I've more than enough experience in hand-to-hand combat and I think I'm mentally strong enough to take her on."

Margaurethe nibbled her lower lip. "I'm not sure."

Valmont cocked his head, recognizing something within her manner. His eyes narrowed. "But you think you have an idea."

She met his gaze. "I believe she doesn't want you to be killed defending her. I don't think she'll be able to handle it, especially not so soon after Zica's death." She glanced away, unseeing. "Cora's murder affected her deeply. At the time she was able to release her sanguinary urges by challenging Andri."

"And with Zica's death an accident, there's no one upon whom to vent."

"Correct."

Valmont sat back, tapping a finger against the arm of the chair. "Why did you bring me here? Why are you telling me this?"

Margaurethe called up a ghost of a smile. "Foes surround us, and accidents have the misfortune of being blind to what is right and wrong. We cannot go on bickering with each other. It draws our collective attention away from the real threats."

"A truce then, a true one?"

"Yes. And a pact." He raised a questioning eyebrow. "We worked together once before to protect Elisibet. I suggest we do so again for Whiskey. We need to unite as a single front against her enemies."

They looked at one another for long minutes. A slow grin spread across Valmont's face. "One for all, and all for one?"

Recognizing the return of his flippancy, she smiled back. "You read that piffle?"

"You didn't?"

She casually tossed her hair back, reaching once more for her teacup. "Of course not. I preferred *Guy Fawkes*."

Valmont snorted. "Don't tell me you went out for that serialized crap." Seeing the smug turn of her lips, he laughed. "And I suppose you read all of Sir Arthur Conan Doyle's work?"

"Hot off the presses."

"Philistine."

"Heathen."

Their chuckles faded into silence as they regarded each other. Valmont broke the quiet. "You know, I think this is the first time in centuries we've actually had a conversation that didn't end in a desire for bloodshed."

Margaurethe nodded. "I believe you're right." She enjoyed the warmth that had developed between them. It didn't have the depth that their original friendship had enjoyed, but it was preferable to the gut-wrenching pain she'd experienced over recent months. "If you hear of anything from Bertrada, you'll inform me?"

"Of course." He paused. "If she continues maligning you, I might just challenge her myself. That'll take the wind out of her sails."

"And Whiskey's." As much as Margaurethe liked the idea, she knew that Whiskey would be against it. "If anything happens to you as a result, however, Whiskey will be worse off than she is now."

Fierceness briefly tightened the planes of his face. "I'd count it as a debt paid."

"Perhaps, but don't do anything brash. Besides, challenging Bertrada won't change the fact that one of the others has attempted to assassinate Whiskey. Losing you might give that one the edge to succeed."

Valmont's shoulders relaxed as he gave Margaurethe a look of apology. "Of course."

Margaurethe pursed her lips in thought. "No. We need to keep tabs on the lot of them, but I think either Ernst or McCall are the likely culprits."

He leaned forward to take up his now cold cup of tea. Holding it up in toast, he said, "To friendship and Whiskey's continued good health."

Smiling, Margaurethe tapped her cup with his. "Agreed."

CHAPTER TWENTY-THREE

Bentoncourt scowled out the window of his assigned apartment, hands clasped behind his back, not seeing the gray sky and the sluggish river below. Most of the *Agrun Nam* filled the sitting area behind him, quietly availing themselves of a continental breakfast. There came a knock on the door. His senior aide, Baltje, opened it to allow Cassadie inside. Everyone was present.

Still Bentoncourt waited, listening. The emotions from their argument yesterday morning remained fresh between them, and tension crackled in the air. For a change, Cassadie didn't engage anyone in lighthearted frivolity, indicative of his still sour mood. McCall took up the slack, offering to refresh his companions' drinks. Only Rosenberg and Nijmege accepted. Bentoncourt eavesdropped on the general murmur, the sound of silverware on china a light counterpoint to their inconsequential conversation.

Expectant silence eventually settled over them. "Well, we're here as you requested, Lionel," Nijmege stated, her tone as sharp as her tongue. "Shall we get on with it or not? I've plenty of things to do today."

Bentoncourt executed a perfect about-face and regarded his colleagues, his chin tucked to his chest. Cassadie had chosen to sit in an armchair farthest from the others, legs crossed, an air of haughty dismissal cloaking him. Nijmege and Rosenberg shared the couch with McCall beside them in another armchair. Bentoncourt couldn't help but wonder if their seating arrangement signaled that they were as thick as thieves or simply a matter of current circumstance. It pained him to admit that Rosenberg's support of Nijmege had badly startled him. Their neutral member had chosen abstention on every vote associated with Davis to date. Rosenberg looked back at him with the same heavy-lidded eyes, the same calm visage despite his endorsement of Nijmege's plans. "The funeral for Ms. Davis's aunt is tomorrow. I assume we'll all attend?"

McCall nodded. "Wouldn't miss it." He flashed Nijmege a tight smile.

"It would be proper to do so," Rosenberg answered. "I assumed that was why you and Aiden changed your itinerary."

Bentoncourt's smile wasn't pleasant. "About that. I think other changes are in order."

Nijmege dropped her cup to its saucer with a loud *clink*. She raised a finger in warning. "Don't even think it, Lionel."

"As *Nam Lugal*, I decide what is best for the *Agrun Nam*."

"I don't give a tinker's damn."

He ground his teeth. "I think that Samuel, Aiden and myself should remain. You and Ernst shall return home tomorrow."

"*Kutyafasza!*" Nijmege jumped to her feet. "You cannot order me away. You don't have that kind of authority."

"She's right." McCall relaxed, giving Bentoncourt a faint smile. "We're each autonomous and always have been. You might oversee us as a whole, but you can't order us to come or go at a whim."

Cassadie uncrossed his legs, leaning forward with hands on the arms of his chair, his face contorted into a mask of revulsion. "It's hardly a whim! Bertrada's actions will destroy us whether or not she's successful. Can't you see that?"

"Our destruction is equally as imminent if she does nothing," Rosenberg calmly stated.

"You really think that?" Cassadie demanded.

"I do."

Before they could fall to squabbling, Bentoncourt asked, "What evidence do you have, Ernst?"

Rosenberg stood and walked away, putting some distance between he and his companions. Turning, he regarded them with his typical passionless stare. "Neither Bertrada nor Samuel will vote to accept a treaty with The Davis Group. There are no caveats or negotiation points that will alter their positions. Therefore, our presence here is nothing but an indulgence, taking us away from our nation and our people when we must remain vigilant."

Bentoncourt ignored Nijmege's triumphant expression. Rosenberg spoke the truth. Their nation had dwindled over the centuries since the Sweet Butcher's assassination. Dangers lurked at every border these days. "You truly believe we cannot come to agreement with The Davis Group."

"Samuel will vote as Bertrada does in this matter. We all know that Bertrada is irrationally obsessed with her goal. Until she achieves it or dies trying, she remains useless to us."

Nijmege sank back down, giving her thick braid a tug of annoyance at Rosenberg's choice of words but remained silent. Bentoncourt almost found humor at her reaction.

Cassadie swore under his breath. "Then this is the final act. We turn down the treaty now and return home."

Though prescience wasn't one of his gifts, Bentoncourt could see the future of that choice before the ever-logical Rosenberg spoke.

"Which will not deter Bertrada from continuing her path toward that goal. Additionally, the nations around us will grow stronger as they each, in turn, forge alliances with The Davis Group. Eventually, our inaction will put us into the position of having to dissolve our government in favor of allowing our people to make individual choices." Rosenberg looked like a professor lecturing a class of very slow students. "And should Bertrada succeed in her goal during this stage, we will be vilified by the nation-states belonging to their organization. The European Sanguire will be destroyed."

Cassadie cursed aloud, the words sounding foreign. It had been so long since he'd been sincerely incensed about anything that the reappearance of his temper was startling.

Bentoncourt hated to admit it, but Rosenberg's statement felt right. As much as he wanted to curse their initial decision to carry on governing the European Sanguire without a corresponding monarch, he knew that past was past. They'd ridden the broken wagon of their government into stagnation, and he only had himself to blame. Rosenberg remained ever rational, ever stoic—Bentoncourt had to trust his fellow *sanar's* position in the matter. Despite their recent friction over the question of Davis, Rosenberg had always been a stalwart and level-headed man. "Are we doomed to fail then? Fated to lead our people into destruction?"

Rosenberg regarded him. "It is possible to 'arise from the ashes,' so to speak."

McCall frowned. "How? You've said Bertrada's success will destroy our standing on the world stage, whether we support her or not."

As if you hadn't supported her from the beginning. Bentoncourt pushed aside the thought, knowing his indignation had no place in council meetings.

"We remain. We attempt to move past our differences during negotiations—"

"Playact, you mean," Cassadie said, a sneer on his face.

Nijmege scoffed. "Like you've never done the same. That's the nature of your position as ambassador, Aiden. You cannot take the high road now."

Cassadie opened his mouth for a rejoinder, but Bentoncourt spoke sharply. "Silence! Let Ernst finish."

Rosenberg gave a slight nod of thanks. "We continue our negotiations with The Davis Group and allow Bertrada to do what she must." Cassadie harrumphed. "You need not support her, publicly or privately, Aiden. Simply stand aside for the moment."

"How will that ensure our survival?" McCall asked.

"If Bertrada fails, she will die for her cause. We will suffer some consequences but will be able to forge a treaty with The Davis Group regardless. If she succeeds, it will be obvious that she didn't have the *Agrun Nam's* approval for her actions. We may suffer the wrath of our hosts for her decision, but I doubt we'll receive serious repercussions over it. Those will fall upon Bertrada's shoulders."

Cassadie snorted in sardonic humor. "What's the American phrase? 'Throwing her under the bus'?" He winked at Nijmege. "Your supporter has such faith in you."

Bentoncourt carefully considered the ramifications. It was true that Valmont and Margaurethe would become incensed should Nijmege survive a duel with Davis. He studied Nijmege, seeing that Cassadie's barb had done nothing. She'd already made the connections that Rosenberg illustrated now, had already come to the conclusion that she wouldn't live through the encounter. That knowledge hadn't deterred her. The hatred that had burned within her for centuries had used the fuel of her heart and soul. There was nothing left but a husk. *Why haven't I seen that before? How could I have been so blind?*

"Maybe we should wait."

Everyone stared at McCall. He set his coffee down and reached out to pat Nijmege's knee. "Perhaps we can find another way for you to achieve your goal, one that doesn't put you in immediate danger."

With a stern glare and swift movement, she pulled out of reach. "I'm not leaving, Samuel."

"And neither am I," Bentoncourt stated. "If what you say is true, Ernst, I need to remain here to deal with the political backlash, whichever way it goes." He turned to Cassadie. "You need to return home, my friend, in case things don't go well with me."

Cassadie's expression was a mixture of acceptance and rebellion. By seniority, he was next in line as *Nam Lugal*. Should Bentoncourt be killed in the coming folly, he'd need to take control of the council and assign new members. He bared his neck in capitulation.

Bentoncourt mentally sighed. "Ernst, since I doubt Samuel will return, I'd like you to join Aiden."

"Of course."

He succeeded in not growling at Rosenberg. If he hadn't resolved to side with Nijmege in this matter the situation wouldn't have become so dire. Maybe it was the recent accident, the pall of death hanging over everyone's heads that colored everything with despair. "Unless you've something to add, we're done here."

No one seemed inclined to talk, at least not in conference. From the look on McCall's face, he had much to say to Nijmege whose austere glower hinted at a serious argument brewing between them. Rosenberg gave a slight bow and departed, closely followed by McCall and Nijmege.

Cassadie lingered. "This is wrong, Lionel."

"I know. I can't see a way out of it. Can you?"

"Ernst paints a rather dire picture."

"He does." Bentoncourt placed a hand on Cassadie's shoulder. "Whatever comes, know that I've always counted you as a friend and ally."

"And I you." He dredged up a smile, appearing more like the good-natured man he'd always been. "Looks like Samuel may have changed his mind, though. I didn't expect him to try holding Bertrada back."

Bentoncourt smiled, puzzling over McCall's suggestion that Nijmege return home. "Yes, that was odd, wasn't it?"

"I doubt he'll get far. Bertrada has always been overzealous once her teeth finds her prey."

"Indeed." They said their goodbyes.

Bentoncourt stood alone, turning back to the view of eastern Portland. McCall's desire to save Nijmege from certain death could have been rooted in preservation. They'd become tight friends since Davis's appearance on the scene. It was only right to worry for someone you cared about. The problem was that Bentoncourt knew McCall wasn't stupid. The younger man had to have considered long ago that his ally had as much a chance of dying as surviving her indulgent behavior. Why would he backtrack now?

"Baltje told me the meeting has concluded?"

He turned to his wife who had emerged from another room. "Yes."

She saw his distress and closed the distance between them. Draping an arm about his waist she held him close, letting him draw comfort from their embrace. "It didn't go well, I suspect."

Tightening his grip, he hugged her. "Not really, no."

"Can you speak of it?"

He searched for the words. "I hate to say it, but I believe Ernst convinced me that Bertrada must do this."

"Really?" She pulled back to read his expression, her eyebrows raised in surprise. "He must have been quite persuasive."

"He always is." They chuckled in agreement, and she snuggled close once more. "After the funeral tomorrow, I want you to return home with Aiden. Take most of the guards and staff."

"I'm not leaving you, Lionel."

"Francesca—"

"No." She pulled back again, this time reaching up to cover his lips with her index finger. "We're husband and wife. We both swore the same vows, dear heart. I'll not run off to be kept safe and sound while you face danger here. We're united."

He smiled, kissing the finger at his lips. "I had to make the attempt."

"I know. I won't hold it against you."

Bentoncourt held his wife, his happiness vying with the trepidation growing in his heart over what the future would hold for him and his people.

* * *

How many setbacks would he have to endure before he achieved his goal? McCall followed Nijmege down the hall to her apartment, frowning at the back of her head. Rosenberg said a polite farewell and continued on. Cassadie had remained behind, no doubt having his tears wiped by Bentoncourt as he wailed over the unfairness of it all. "May I come in?"

Nijmege's glare pierced him. "Why?"

Exasperation in his expression and voice, he said, "Because we're friends, Bertrada. Allies. You do remember?"

She debated a moment before agreeing with a crisp nod.

Her apartment was similar to Bentoncourt's, similar to McCall's own. Apparently The Davis Group had gone to some lengths to provide quality suites for visiting dignitaries yet had chosen color scheme rather than architectural layout as a means of differentiation. Typical lazy Americans. McCall had become used to the earth tones of his quarters. Nijmege's rooms were predominantly blue and gray but otherwise an exact duplicate of his own. He trailed her into the living room.

She shooed away guards and servants alike until they were alone. "What do you want?"

"I want to know that you're all right." The lie fell easily from his lips. "If you continue on this course, you can't let your anger get the better of you."

Her gaze softened but not by much. "I'm fine, Samuel. Better than fine. This is what I'm meant to do." She sat on a chair, inviting him to do the same.

Instead, he perched on the coffee table across from her, taking her hands in his. "Perhaps it would be best if we took Lionel's suggestion, leave now and—"

"No!" Nijmege shot up and marched away, expression severe.

He studied her stiffness, mind racing. One thing he could count on was Rosenberg's astute summation of a situation. The man was a literal savant in seeing the big picture. If McCall could convince Nijmege to return to Europe, drag this situation out a bit longer, the *Agrun Nam* could fall on its own with no help from him. It would be easier to pick up the pieces and gain total control when surrounded by his countrymen and network of supporters. Staying here, should Nijmege lose her battle with Davis, the others might be able to win through and remain in power. Somehow, he had to get Nijmege to stand aside long enough for the inevitable cascade effect to occur. "I'm not saying give up! You know I support you in this completely. But

Ernst may be right. Should you survive a duel with Davis, you'll still suffer the wrath of her protectors. You'll not live through the day, Bertrada."

A grim smile grew on her lips, one that didn't soothe the ferocity in her eyes or his inner concerns. "I never expected to live, Samuel." Turning to fully face him, she cocked her head. "And to be honest, I don't much care to. Once I've achieved my goal of the Sweet Butcher's demise, I'll gladly accept my fate."

McCall smothered an urge to roll his eyes. Good gods, who knew that a shrewd and cunning political animal such as herself suffered the burden of romantic delusion? "And what? Open your arms, accept death and be reunited with Nahib? What claptrap!"

His scorn drove away her smile. She tucked her chin, glaring at him. "I wouldn't expect you to understand."

"Oh, I understand, all right." He stood, flinging his hands up in the air. "Your childhood was spent daydreaming about princes and castles and magical swords, the knowledge burning in your heart that love would remedy everything wrong in your life. Then you grew up to discover the world was shite, through and through, and that nobody gave a rat's ass other than your own family."

"Be silent!"

"No!" He walked toward her, forcing her back to avoid him. "Then you found a man who treated you well, and you convinced yourself that he was the love of your life. Bollocks! Love doesn't exist." Nijmege's eyes narrowed, but she didn't interrupt, standing toe-to-toe with him. "After he died, you swore revenge. And. Got. It. *Ninsumgal* Elisibet Vasillas is dead, and you had a hand in her assassination. But that wasn't enough for you, was it?"

She snorted. "How could it be if she didn't stay dead?"

He fought the urge to lay hands on her, whirling away to resist the temptation. If he touched her, he might do more than simply attempt to shake sense into her. "I'm not asking you to stop this. If you were born to end her life with your own hands, so be it." He swung back around. "I'm asking you, as a friend, to back off until a later date, to survive, damn it!"

The indignation faded from her hard-planed countenance. She thought he spoke from his heart, as a friend not wanting his companion to commit suicide. He saw the realization on her face and wondered whether or not fostering the belief would get him what he wanted.

"Samuel, you've been a magnificent supporter throughout our time together, a tremendous asset and a dear friend." She came to him, one hand out to grasp his upper arm. "But this is what I'm destined to do, live or die."

The light in her eye was one of fanaticism, a familiar sight to anyone willing to bolster her lust for revenge. He'd seen it often enough through the long nights of scheming in her drawing room. Over the decades, it had banked and smoldered, but upon news of Davis's existence it had flared to a brightness too strong to be extinguished. He'd fanned that flame for months, hoping it would burn their government down so he could rise from the ashes, a proverbial phoenix leading the European Sanguire to the Golden Age.

He needed to come up with another plan. And quickly.

McCall took a deep breath, letting it out slowly as he relaxed his body. Best to let her think she'd gotten through for the time being, at least until he'd had time to throw together an alternative. "I don't have to like it, *lamma*."

She smiled, patting his arm. "If I die in the aftermath, at least I'll have succeeded in my goal."

He refrained from registering his disgust with her beatific expression. "And I can't talk you out of it?"

"No." Her chin dropped, ever so slightly.

With a resigned sigh, he nodded. "I'd best get back to my quarters. I'm sure there are messages to wade through before our next meeting." After carefully extricating himself from her clutches, he saw himself out. In the hall, he glanced back at Bentoncourt's door, wondering if he was still salving Cassadie's wounded ego, and followed Rosenberg's path to the elevators.

This late in the game, he had few alternatives that would remove his fellow *sanari* from power. The *Agrun Nam* seemed to believe it was a foregone conclusion that Nijmege would die in her attempt, win or lose, but what if she survived the altercation? He had no doubt that Davis's supporters would stop at nothing to avenge her. Perhaps it remained necessary to destroy Davis. If he could guarantee Nijmege's win, get her out of the arena and to safety before The Davis Group could retaliate, it might be enough to destabilize their organization, at least until he could come up with an alternative to dealing with the remaining *Agrun Nam*.

It was too bad that luck hadn't put one of their vehicles on the street at just the right time to be smashed. He frowned at his reflection in the elevator door. A prearranged accident would lack in finesse but get the job done. He'd have to put himself in danger, as well, to sell the idea to the masses. He made his way to his apartment as he pondered the possibilities.

CHAPTER TWENTY-FOUR

Castillo exuded a calm he didn't feel, glad for his many hours of prayer and monastic training that gifted him with such talent. He stood in the tiny vestibule of Bentoncourt's apartment, hands clasped before him. There by invitation, he knew to his ecclesiastic bones that this conversation wouldn't be a positive one. A guard hovered at his back, having stepped inside with him, not overtly threatening but making his presence known.

Down the short hall to his left, he heard the aide that had let him inside knock on a door and open it. "*Nam Lugal*, Father Castillo is here."

"Send him in."

"The *Nam Lugal* will see you now."

Castillo smiled appreciation and allowed himself to be escorted by both aide and guard to the office. As he stepped inside, he saw that Bentoncourt had come round the side of his desk and stepped forward to greet him.

"Good morning, Father. Thank you for coming."

"It's an honor, sir." After the pleasantries, Bentoncourt sent the guard away, offering his guest a chair before the desk.

Castillo smothered a sense of surprise as Bentoncourt sat beside him rather than at the desk. Apparently, this was to be an informal meeting. What had changed since yesterday to cause Bentoncourt to request Castillo's visit?

"How is Ms. Davis?"

"Chafing." Castillo smiled as Bentoncourt's puzzled expression gave way to a knowing one. "Despite yesterday's ordeal in her sitting room, she's healed enough to be restless and cranky. It's been difficult."

"And her doctor is forcing her to remain abed." Bentoncourt nodded, an understanding smile on his face. "We've all been there before."

"Yes. Suffice it to say, I'm rather glad I have a reason to be elsewhere right now."

His host barked laughter. "I imagine you are. It doesn't help that she's so young, does it?"

Castillo shook his head. "It does not." They shared a wry chuckle, both sobering at the same time. He wondered if he'd have to ask why he'd been summoned. The request had been passably vague. Since they'd spoken less than a day before, something must have occurred to spur this request for another encounter.

Bentoncourt sensed his mental query and drew a deep breath. "I met with my colleagues this morning."

Ah. Castillo hadn't heard that the *Agrun Nam* had gathered today. It must have been quite volatile for Bentoncourt to request his presence, a bad sign indeed. Despite a sense of dread, Castillo relaxed, clearing his mind to sharpen his focus. He'd need every crumb of information if The Davis Group were to survive the coming engagement.

"We, of course, discussed Bertrada's goal and our official stance." Bentoncourt paused.

"And your official stance is…?" Castillo urged.

Bentoncourt's mouth twisted into a grimace. "We are not involved."

Meaning they were politically disowning the matter. Dorst had suggested this would be the *Agrun Nam's* position should the question come before them. Since the news wasn't a shock, he studied Bentoncourt. There was no reason to have called Castillo here unless there was more to it than reporting plausible deniability over Nijmege's death threats.

"Ernst is of the opinion that the only way our people, our government, will survive is if Bertrada is allowed her way. Whether she lives or dies doesn't matter. She must make the attempt for the *Agrun Nam* to endure."

Castillo carefully considered Bentoncourt's words. Admittedly, he didn't know much about the current political situation of the European Sanguire. He'd been an expatriate from his European homeland for several decades, only recently concentrating on those governments with which The Davis Group had been negotiating. He knew from experience and rumor that his countrymen had floundered since the Purge, but things had been stable for some time. Hearing that his nation might still be faltering unsettled him. "Is our current climate so dire?"

Bentoncourt eyed him, understanding that Castillo asked as a European, not as the representative of The Davis Group. His gaze narrowed in inner debate. "We aren't strong," he finally said, looking away. "We have threats on a number of fronts at this time. A politically supported vendetta against The Davis Group has the potential to destroy us."

Opening his mouth to speak, Castillo closed it again when he couldn't think of what to say. He was a Euro Sanguire and had assumed his country had grown powerful once again. If it was weak enough for a global corporation to be a threat…He gathered his surprise and insecurity together, setting it aside for later perusal. *And a little chat with Reynhard!* "So we are to expect that the *Agrun Nam* will not support or hinder Nijmege's attempt to kill our *Ninsumgal*?"

"Yes." Bentoncourt looked like he'd eaten a lemon. "After the memorial service tomorrow, I'll be sending Ernst and Aiden back to Europe. I'll remain here with Bertrada and Samuel."

The two *sanari* most likely to cause trouble. Castillo nodded in a detached way. Slowly but surely the playing field was narrowing. It seemed more and more likely that McCall had been the one to engineer the multiple assassination attempts against Whiskey, especially given Bentoncourt's opinion of Rosenberg's ethics. He wondered if Bentoncourt realized this. "Thank you for informing me," he said. "I'll notify our board of directors."

Bentoncourt laid his hand on Castillo's forearm. "Bertrada has been quite diligent in her training since news of Davis's discovery." In light of the *Agrun Nam's* position, his words were the closest thing to assistance that he could offer.

Castillo smiled. "Thank you. I'll make certain that information reaches the right ears." Bentoncourt seemed to want to say something else, but they both knew he'd be courting a charge of treason from his own government should he do so. Pushing to his feet, Bentoncourt following suit, Castillo bowed. "I always enjoy our insightful conversations, *Nam Lugal*. Thank you for inviting me."

"And thank you for your acuity, Father." When they shook hands he used both of his, patting their joint grip. "You'll go far in this world."

"I only need to go far enough for God, but I appreciate the sentiment." His host escorted him to the office door where he was passed off to the security officer lingering outside. In moments he stood out in the main corridor, sentries at his back and Nijmege's guards standing a few feet away at her door. No doubt she'd already been apprised of his visit to her adversary. As he passed them on the way to the elevator, he wondered if that was why Bentoncourt had asked to meet in his suite rather than somewhere else. Perhaps he was putting Nijmege on notice regarding whom he supported in this situation.

So, the *Agrun Nam* would survive only if Nijmege was allowed free rein. It was past time to speak to Dorst. If anyone could understand the political intricacies that had caused that decision, it was he. Dorst lived, breathed, and ate complexity on a daily basis. He'd figure out the puzzle and they could develop a plan of action. Unfortunately, that battle plan might result in putting Whiskey into serious danger.

And Margaurethe wasn't going to like that.

CHAPTER TWENTY-FIVE

Whiskey still felt shaky, but was too happy to be out of bed to care. She'd awakened ravenous and polished off both a large farmers breakfast and a small amount of Human blood, both serving to satiate her hunger. Lifting her T-shirt, she studied her reflection in the bathroom mirror. The angry line of Daniel's incision had faded to a dark pink. She ran a finger along it, feeling just a hint of developing scar tissue. It was hard to believe that she'd been fighting for her life just four days ago. *Hooray for superior healing abilities.* She pulled her shirt down and finished her ablutions, relieved to finally be clean after days of bedpans and sponge baths.

Her advisors had gathered in her apartment rather than the more publicly accepted sitting room. That particular area was crowded with her pack as they suffered the same irksome lockdown as their mistress. She felt the bass of their loud music through the floor as she left her bedchambers. The residents assigned to the apartments below her probably weren't pleased, but she doubted they'd complain. Everyone knew the sixteenth floor was the safest place for her pack to gather. She resolved to compensate her downstairs neighbors in some manner as well as talk to her pack when this meeting was finished. Maybe she'd be able to host another rave as soon as this mess with the *Agrun Nam* was over.

As she entered her living room, she saw that Sithathor had played dutiful host and laid out snacks for the meeting. Whiskey scanned the rest of the floor with her mind, not locating her chambermaid. She'd probably made herself scarce to avoid both the board of directors and the rowdy younglings. The only other resident of her apartment, Jake, was present and positioned near the sitting room door. She carried a more easygoing aura than her usual intense stance. She'd developed a level of trust toward the leaders of The Davis Group and no longer saw the need to bristle outwardly in their presence.

Whiskey smiled at the gathering, receiving pleasant greetings from her inner cadre. The accident had put everyone on edge and, for the first time in days, they began to relax. They'd all spent the majority of the last two days at her side while she set the minds of various delegates at ease. "Good morning, everybody. I hope you all had a good night's sleep?"

"Well enough, all things considered," Dikeledi said, lifting a coffee cup in toast. "Welcome back to the land of the living."

"Thanks. Glad to be here." Hobbled by a brace, Margaurethe arrived at Whiskey's side, offering subtle assistance as she placed an arm around Whiskey's waist. Woodsmoke and mulled wine caressed her, reminding her once again how much she loved this woman. Though they'd started out on an adversarial note, Margaurethe had done a wonderful job of stepping back into a more supportive function. This wasn't to say she'd become submissive in any way. Whiskey didn't think Margaurethe was capable of that role after several hundred years of developing into a world business leader. At least she wasn't hovering over Whiskey like she had in the beginning, trusting her young lover to take the reins of authority while she remained a steadfast supporter.

Dorst gave a dramatic exhale, his expression a caricature of victimization. "Alas, I've slaved the night away, *My Gasan*. There's little time for slumber in my business."

Valmont shook his head, a wry grin on his face. "And, oh, how you suffer."

"Indeed!" Dorst flashed them a smile.

Sinking into a chair, Whiskey hoped her rickety knees didn't betray her to the others. Margaurethe sat beside her, right leg extended by virtue of the brace, and offered her coffee, a knowing expression on her face. Rather than call attention to their physical weaknesses, Whiskey winked and accepted the cup with thanks. Scanning the others, she gauged their moods.

Castillo wasn't as cheerful as the others, his dark eyes troubled. Margaurethe had informed Whiskey that he'd met with Bentoncourt the previous morning, though he'd refused to divulge the reason. No doubt he was the cause of Dorst's sleepless night. Whiskey figured the padre had been up just as late with his own research. Chano seemed equally as sober, though he rarely revealed his true emotions in board meetings anyway. Dikeledi was…Dikeledi, cool and professional as always.

"Shall we get started then?" Whiskey asked, looking at Dorst.

He tilted his neck in supplication. "Though quite saddened by your insistence that I not use interception devices—"

"Wiretaps and bugs," Valmont supplied.

Dorst gave him a mock stern glance, but didn't stop speaking, "—We have kept the *Agrun Nam* under constant surveillance when they've been out and about."

Whiskey had recalled their disagreement. "I take it something came to your attention?" Margaurethe's essence strengthened and Whiskey gave her a quizzical look.

"Indeed," Dorst answered.

Her suspicion blossomed as she studied her advisors. Apparently something serious had happened and they were all aware of it. Lowering her chin, she said, "Tell me."

Dorst was all too happy to explain as he preened. "Things are not happy in the European camp, My *Ninsumgal*. Their stressors boiled over the day before yesterday when you were moved from the clinic. After everyone rushed off to gain an audience, they remained behind and had a few heated words."

As he filled her in, Whiskey's mind whirled. Rosenberg had finally made a choice other than abstention. She recalled him telling her at the *Agrun Nam's* welcome reception that he saw Elisibet when he looked at her, not Whiskey. "How sure are you of this information?"

"Oh! Quite!" Dorst chuckled, running a long finger over one of his ears. "I heard it myself."

She blinked, frowning. "I can't imagine the *Agrun Nam* discussing something like this in public, Reynhard. Are we sure it wasn't a setup?" She couldn't figure out what good could come from leaking such information, however.

"I do believe our wonderful priest has the answers you seek, *Ninsumgal*, as it was his knowledge that tipped the scales."

Castillo nodded and cleared his throat. He carefully outlined his two meetings with Bentoncourt, giving a full report to his fellow directors. "So, they won't help her but they won't interfere either."

Valmont snorted. "Bully for them."

"It's not like we expected any different," Margaurethe said. "If they had the wherewithal to do so, we wouldn't be having this discussion now."

"But Rosenberg is returning, not Lionel?" Whiskey asked.

"Yes, that's what he said."

"Why?" She scanned the others. "Rosenberg's support doesn't make or break Bertrada's scheme. Even though he seems to endorse her, he's still sitting on the fence as far as I'm concerned. His approval is based on survival of the *Agrun Nam*, not whether or not she's right."

"I believe Bentoncourt is attempting to show you allegiance." Castillo flushed beneath everyone's sudden attention. "I've always held that he sanctions you, Whiskey. This is just another example in a long chain of evidence. He's remaining as a visible reminder to us that neither he nor the *Agrun Nam* accepts Nijmege's argument or actions."

"Bully for him too," Valmont said, his tone wry.

Rather than let the discussion spiral into quips, Whiskey mentally pinched Valmont. "Given that information, what have you come up with, Reynhard?"

"I've had the most interesting time with our young padre's news." Dorst gave a visible shiver of delight. Valmont rolled his eyes but kept any sarcastic remark to himself. "It seems Ernst Rosenberg may have an excellent appreciation for the finer points of causality. After going over my dossiers of the players involved and the political situation as a whole, I believe he's correct in his assumption. If our wounded wallflower isn't allowed free will to continue upon her path, it could very well destroy the *Agrun Nam*."

Margaurethe gaped at him. "You're joking."

Despite the smile on his gaunt face, Dorst's eyes were stone-cold. "Oh, no, dearest *Ki'an Gasan*. This is no jape. The *Agrun Nam* cannot survive being involved nor can they attempt to stop her. In either case, the world leaders will be led by The Davis Group to destroy them. She must be allowed to continue, live or die, so that the end result is between individual combatants, not governmental bodies."

The thought boggled Whiskey's mind. Had The Davis Group gotten so big already? They'd only been incorporated for less than a year. She reminded herself that much of the capital and principle of the company came from Margaurethe's worldwide corporations, as well as her contacts with the various governments. Her business connections were decades, maybe centuries, old. And if Nijmege were successful, Margaurethe would stop at nothing to see her and all she held dear in ruins.

Castillo raised his hand. "If I may add, I'm also of the opinion that Samuel McCall is the one responsible for the assassination attempts."

Valmont shed his normal devil-may-care demeanor, taking a step forward with ferocious intensity. "What evidence do you have?"

"None, admittedly." Castillo sank back but didn't fully retreat. "For the most part, we've accounted for the motivations of all the *sanari*. Cassadie and Bentoncourt aren't involved. Cassadie, at least, is so adamant that he's turned his back on the lot of them. According to Reynhard, Rosenberg has a valid reason for his position, which doesn't run to murdering Whiskey to achieve his goals. He's stated that if Nijmege is stopped, the *Agrun Nam* will fall. That eliminates him from the list."

"And that leaves McCall." Chano nodded his grizzled head. "It makes sense."

Dikeledi said, "Supposition. Without concrete evidence, there's nothing we can do about it."

"Who says we need to be aboveboard?" Valmont asked, snarling. "McCall certainly wasn't."

Whiskey watched them bicker as she thought. Castillo and Dikeledi were the voice of reason while Valmont and Margaurethe argued to take immediate action against McCall. Dorst sat back with a happy smile on his face, watching the show. Chano frowned at the floor, deep in thought. *Talk about an even split.* When they began to repeat themselves, she cut in. "We can't charge McCall without evidence in any court—theirs or ours. Hell, we don't even have a court. We're a corporation, not a nation."

Valmont grumbled but subsided.

Dikeledi gave a regal nod, calm approval on her face. "But that doesn't mean we do nothing."

Margaurethe had taken a seat beside Whiskey and now touched her hand. "What do you suggest?"

She shrugged. "Right now? Nothing, not toward McCall anyway. If the padre's right, then we at least have someplace to begin looking when we have the ability to do more than make idle accusations. It seems he's backed off, anyway."

"He has thrown himself fully behind Bertrada's claim," Dorst said. "Perhaps he's decided it's the best way to achieve his goals, whatever they may be."

Which begged the question, what was McCall's intent in attempting to kill Whiskey? Her mind worried the situation, uselessly spinning its wheels when nothing emerged to clarify his position. She set aside the thoughts, focusing on the present. "My most prominent threat is Bertrada."

"Yes." Castillo straightened with a deep inhale. "She is the most dire threat you face at the moment. Over the next few days she will become most malicious. She'll try to goad you into challenging her."

Perplexed, Whiskey frowned. "Why? Why not challenge me? Is there some law about international duels I'm not aware of?"

Valmont grimaced. "It could be she's a musty old Euro Sanguire wrapped in her archaic legal system."

Whiskey eyed Valmont. "Says the man who's only a hundred or so years younger than she is."

"Hey! She's old, youngster." His grin was infectious and she fought to keep an answering smile from her face. Their shared sense of humor was one of the things she liked about him, but she needed to keep this meeting on a serious note.

Castillo interrupted. "There actually may be something to that argument, Whiskey." He pulled a small notepad from an inner pocket and flipped through it. "Last night I spent a good deal of time researching not only the Euro Sanguire laws and regulations regarding challenges, but how they've been conducted in other nations."

Margaurethe leaned forward, her expression serious but otherwise unreadable. "And what did you find, Father?"

Castillo must have sensed the razor's edge upon which he walked. Margaurethe was always sensitive to issues that could put Whiskey into life-threatening situations, and no one in the room felt his next words would suggest anything but that. He didn't look at Margaurethe, but spoke calmly as he studied his notes. "In Nijmege's government, no one can challenge the *Ninsumgal*. It is forbidden to even consider such an action."

Flashes of ancient battles cascaded across Whiskey's mind, each one either individual or paired combat with others. "But Elisibet had challenges. I remember them."

"It is a delicate distinction, My *Gasan*," Dorst said. "*Ninsumgal* Elisibet was never challenged by another."

"No." Valmont shook his head. "No one could challenge her, but she could challenge anyone in her realm."

"Ah." Whiskey sank back, thinking. "That still doesn't explain why Bertrada won't challenge me. The *Agrun Nam* refuses to accept who I am, who I was."

"But that doesn't mean her cultural blinders aren't hindering her." Castillo looked up from his pad. "She may not publicly believe your claim, but she does on a more personal level."

"All of them do," Chano said. He thumped his walking stick on the floor. "Why are they here after you demanded their presence if they didn't believe you are their long-lost *ninsumgal* reborn?"

Margaurethe took Whiskey's hand. "So Bertrada's goal is to get Whiskey to challenge her?"

"I believe so." Castillo lifted a submissive chin in response to the hard stare from Margaurethe. "She's working on internalized habits and instincts. While she publicly disclaims Whiskey, she knows Whiskey is who we deem her to be. To circumvent potential complications with Euro law, she's going to attempt to push Whiskey into challenging her."

"It's a reasonable viewpoint," Dikeledi said. "Should she survive a challenge, she will be safe from litigation as she hides beneath the mantle of her country's law."

Dorst shifted in a creak of leather. "Our esteemed compatriot is correct. Dear Bertrada does lead both the High and Low Courts of her people. The last thing she desires is to be accused in her own country's court."

"And you agree with Rosenberg's conjecture about the European Sanguire, Reynhard?"

He bowed low, showing off the three mohawks striping his bald scalp. "I do, *Ninsumgal*."

Whiskey studied the people in the room with her. Castillo cast an apologetic look in Margaurethe's direction, knowing his information hadn't helped their developing trust. It amused Whiskey at times to realize that Castillo was of a generation that Margaurethe couldn't fathom, though he was four hundred years old. She wondered if he would eventually be just as out of touch with her and her pack. Dorst remained ever eager and ever calm as he awaited her words. Jake hovered at the far door, not part of the conversation yet as cognizant of the repercussions as any of the participants. Dikeledi mirrored Jake's aloofness, her emotional distance beginning to become a welcome anchor for Whiskey's volatile emotions. Chano was the eldest in age but the least experienced in dealing with the corporate world or other governments.

She mentally reached for Margaurethe, holding her lover's essence close. Margaurethe was her heart's lifeblood and always would be, no matter what happened. Unfortunately, Whiskey couldn't allow their mutual devotion to get in the way of what she needed to do, not if she were to follow the path laid out before her.

After a deep inhale, she blew out the breath. "Then I guess I need to brush up on my dueling skills. Padre, what can you tell me about challenges?"

"Unlike Human challenge, Sanguire do not usually duel one-on-one," Castillo began.

"What?" Whiskey frowned. "What's the point of challenging her if she can call in reinforcements?"

Dorst smiled. "Human duels are based primarily on weapons skill, My *Gasan*. Sanguire, however, have their mental abilities to account for."

"Abilities that vary with age, not skill or training," Valmont added.

Confused, Whiskey scanned her advisors. "But I've already been involved with two challenges. I've never had help."

"Not for lack of trying," Valmont groused.

Dorst's smile became feral. "If you recall, you were not a full adult when you conquered Fiona Bodwrda. Technically that was not an official challenge."

Whiskey frowned at the memory of her first duel. Fiona had been the first Sanguire to find her on the streets of Seattle, the first to explain Whiskey's Sanguire nature. She'd also been intent on using Whiskey as a puppet to rule the European Sanguire. The remains of Fiona's pack had become the base of Whiskey's, inherited because her strength of will.

"And I was beside you with Andri," Valmont reminded her. "You blocked my assistance until the last minute."

Whiskey's shoulders slumped. "I thought a second was there to keep everything aboveboard. You know, a witness to the event."

"In Human duels, this is so." Castillo leaned his elbows onto his knees. "But because age drives our mental strength, our rules regarding challenges have adapted."

"So...whoever I name as my second will literally be in the arena with me?"

Margaurethe kept her hand on Whiskey's forearm, squeezing to gain her attention. "Yes. The goal is to even the playing field, so to speak. Normally the one challenged is older than his or her second, but not all the time. You'll need to decide who will be your second in this matter."

Whiskey rubbed her face, wishing the weariness away. Valmont fairly vibrated with agitation. She wondered if she'd have to deny his petition for the title of Defender again. He kept grasping for a position she wasn't sure she wanted to resurrect. If age were a factor, then Chano or Dorst would be Whiskey's best choice. Chano was an old man, however. He might have been a force to reckon with when his body was healthy, but no longer. "Is physical prowess a part of it, then? It's not just mental strength?"

"The ability to physically prove one's self is necessary," Dikeledi answered. "In your two previous encounters, did you not attack with your hands or a weapon?"

Whiskey remembered the taste of Fiona's blood and the sensation of a bullet passing through her. "I did."

Dikeledi gave a regal nod. "As it should be."

Valmont paced as he spoke. "Bertrada has always played with swords, something she and Nahib used to do. I'd wager she's kept up her practice sessions. No doubt you'll be drawn into a battle of weapons."

Relieved he didn't push for the chance to champion her, Whiskey considered her current level of skill. "Pacal says I'm fairly good with a machete..." She trailed off, beginning to see the dubiousness of the situation. Andri the assassin had been far older than Nijmege and she'd had a struggle besting him. Adding a sword fight into the mix might distract her too much to succeed.

Mulled wine and woodsmoke stole over Whiskey and she looked at Margaurethe. "And with your mental powers, you can stop her cold regardless of her greater physical skill."

Chano grunted agreement, his craggy expression thoughtful. "The question then is who will Nijmege pick as her second?"

A chortle drew Whiskey's attention to Dorst. "Why, our dear Samuel, of course! Who else has stood beside her all these long months?"

"Perfect!" Valmont laughed aloud.

His exuberance startled a smile from Whiskey. "Checkmate?"

"Yes!" Valmont flopped onto the couch, partially upsetting Castillo who juggled his coffee cup. "It's absolutely perfect."

Whiskey considered her crash course. "But why choose him? He's only about the padre's age, and she's a century older than you and Margaurethe. Wouldn't she want someone older? Say…Lionel?"

"Lionel wouldn't do it anyway." Valmont waved dismissal at Whiskey. "And the only other person in Bertrada's camp that's old enough might be *Gasan* O'Toole."

Shooting a glance at Margaurethe, Whiskey asked, "Do you think she'll—?"

"No, she won't. She despises challenges and duels." Margaurethe used her free hand to adjust her skirt. "Besides, she has as much experience with swords as I—namely, none."

A sense of relief washed over Whiskey. The last thing she wanted was to be mired in the death of Margaurethe's mother, regardless how much Orlaith hated her.

"Whiskey, no one really understands how strong you are," Castillo said, setting his cup down. "Nijmege will have heard you're stronger than normal, but she'd never comprehend the level of your power without firsthand experience." *Like some of us* remained unspoken.

Valmont nodded, radiating good humor. "Absolutely! She'll consider herself strong enough to take you down. Hell, she'll probably pull McCall in simply to legitimize the proceedings, without really thinking it over."

"The key is to pick your second with care," Dikeledi stated. "Someone younger than Nijmege, perhaps, someone with some weapons experience. That will lull her into a sense of complacency."

That also let Dorst out of the running this time. And Margaurethe with her admitted lack of training. Valmont beamed.

CHAPTER TWENTY-SIX

Margaurethe closed the door on the last visitor, pausing a brief moment to gather her emotions. Jake had left with the others to herd the pack off to their apartments. It was time to prepare for the memorial service later this afternoon. The directors were doing the same. It wasn't often she and Whiskey were entirely alone, and she paused to let the knowledge of their solitude set into her heart.

When she turned, her eyes met Whiskey's across the room. A ghost of a frown remained on Whiskey's face, fading as she set aside her opinions of the meeting and focused her full attention on Margaurethe. For the briefest of moments, Margaurethe mentally stumbled, seeing the Elisibet of her memories in this modern setting. A mixture of joy and sorrow, anger and loss, threatened to overwhelm her. Then her synapses made the proper connections, reminding her that this was Whiskey, not Elisibet, not a hallucination. Instances like this had occurred often in the beginning, growing less frequent as her love deepened, as Whiskey's differences from Elisibet became increasingly pronounced. Living so long in the shadow of Elisibet's death had etched a hideous scar into Margaurethe's soul, one that would take time to fully heal.

Providing Whiskey didn't add to that sense of loss.

Roses surrounded Margaurethe, a hint of water and blood subtly winding beneath the flowery scent. She set aside her trepidation as she limped to Whiskey's side. They were both still fettered by healing injuries. Whiskey had enough to worry about without adding Margaurethe's apprehension to the mix. "How are you feeling, *m'cara*? Would you like something to eat or drink?"

Whiskey smiled, holding out her hand. "I want you."

Margaurethe fortified their mental connection, struggling to cage her anxiety lest it affect Whiskey's. She returned to her lover's side. "You have me, love. Never doubt it." They shared their essences for several minutes, fingers entwined almost as closely as their minds. Margaurethe felt the depth of Whiskey's love mixed with a healthy dose of uncertainty and dread. The doubt faded, replaced by determination though ethereal apprehension flowed within it. Their connection was strong, so strong she knew the moment Whiskey inhaled in preparation of speaking, knew what she would say.

"This is something I have to do." Whiskey's tone was lightly defensive, a stubborn set to her jaw and mind as she prepared for Margaurethe's contention.

"I know." Margaurethe kissed Whiskey's knuckles. "But I reserve the right to detest its necessity." She felt Whiskey's anxiety ease. "You expected an argument?"

Whiskey shrugged, suddenly looking very much the insecure young woman people forgot she was. "Yeah. We've had fights about less."

Margaurethe smiled, her heart full. "Maybe in the past, but not anymore. I don't have to like your decisions, but I can see when they're essential to our goals." She squeezed their hands together. "Don't think I'll not rant and rail when there are safer alternatives."

"I won't." Whiskey grinned, pulling their hands toward her to brush Margaurethe's knuckles with her lips this time. "Do you think it'll work?"

"Two birds with one stone, isn't that so?" Margaurethe reflected Whiskey's nod of affirmation. "So be it. When you are successful, you'll not only remove two of your most dangerous enemies but have the *Agrun Nam* at your feet." A tickle of amusement whispered between them at Whiskey's dour grimace.

"I don't want them at my feet, Margaurethe."

"No, you want them to rule their people—rule my people—well beneath the banner of The Davis Group. Not that they haven't done so already, but at least they'll have better resources upon which to draw in the coming centuries."

"Which reminds me, we should probably ask for some other concessions in their treaty, like changing the power structure of their council. If they don't want a *ninsumgal*, they at least need to correct their laws and regulations to account for it." Whiskey stopped speaking. "What are you smiling at?"

"You, *m'cara*. I'm smiling at you. The woman who plans to put herself into mortal peril to remove her enemies is already thinking beyond that danger." She caressed Whiskey's blushing cheek with one finger. No, Whiskey wasn't Elisibet any more than Margaurethe was the Pope. Whiskey was…more. "I love you, Whiskey Davis. Never forget that."

"I won't, but only on the condition that you don't forget that I love you, Margaurethe O'Toole."

"Agreed." She enjoyed the light chuckle between them, the burble of laughter along their bond. The pleasure was marred by the realization that Whiskey's scheme could go terribly, terribly wrong. The knowledge cracked her inner calm, allowing her fears to ripple between them. "But if something…dire… happens, I will go to the ends of the Earth to seek vengeance."

Whiskey sobered. She leaned closer, elbow on the arm of her chair as she stared into Margaurethe's eyes, their mental connection deepening to a level that they only savored upon occasion, one that only Whiskey could initiate. "This will work, Margaurethe."

"Whiskey—" An intimate caress, both on her skin and in her mind, caused Margaurethe's eyes to close.

"But I know you need to hear this. If something happens to me, I fully expect you to send both Bertrada and McCall to Hell where they belong."

A flash of bloody vision crossed Margaurethe's mind, nothing substantial, just a collection of quick images that could only have come from the Sweet Butcher. The emotions accompanying the sight were a combination of Whiskey's and Elisibet's—powerful determination and a yearning for retribution. Margaurethe opened her eyes, seeing Whiskey's face, feeling her extended fangs within her mouth. "If you don't, I will."

"As it should be." Whiskey smiled, showing her own fangs.

The demand soothed Margaurethe, the sight of Whiskey's ferocity close to the surface oddly comforting her. Strange how Margaurethe had spent so many centuries attempting to dissuade Elisibet from committing the same acts that she now contemplated doing herself if their plan failed. Perhaps if she'd been less purposefully naive, cultivated the same viciousness in which Elisibet and Valmont had reveled, she would have fared better when Elisibet had died. In the centuries following, Margaurethe had learned to fend for herself, something she'd never had to do in Elisibet's court. In the distant past, she hadn't had the courage to face her native Sanguire ferocity. Now she had no doubt that she would successfully seek vengeance before following Whiskey into death.

"As it should be," she repeated.

CHAPTER TWENTY-SEVEN

Whiskey stepped out onto the third-floor patio, automatically looking up at the sky. Iron-gray clouds rolled slowly past on a chill breeze. The air held cool dampness, smelling of wet concrete and loam from the flower and tree beds. The rain had let up an hour ago but would return, and she shivered despite the thick leather jacket she wore. She caught a memory of Cora's funeral, dripping umbrellas and icy skin, and released it to the depths of her mind. Now wasn't the time for morbid recollections.

Her mother's family was Lakota, and they preferred a more natural setting for their ceremonies. Not that this was a funeral, by any means. This was a memorial service for those who wished to offer condolences to Zica's family. The choice of venue had been constricted due to Whiskey's need for security and a desire to keep the numbers to a minimum. Had they decided to use one of the ballrooms downstairs, every delegate along with half a dozen personal aides would have demanded access, turning this solemn bereavement for a dynamic woman into a political circus.

Jake walked before her, her graying blond hair stark against the black suit she wore. Margaurethe held Whiskey's hand. She too had dressed in the colors of mourning, a long skirt hiding the brace and a fitted jacket beneath a long leather coat. Behind them were two of Whiskey's *aga'gída*. At least six others were stationed around the patio as well as others located both in offices overlooking the garden and on the roof far above. Though their physical presence here was obvious, not many guests realized that high-powered sniper rifles followed their every move.

The patio was small but had been uniquely designed. Planter beds and pathways had been artfully created to portray a sense of solitude despite its location in the middle of downtown Portland. Jake led the way on the meandering path until a small seating area opened up before them. Rows of chairs had been set out, but no one had been seated yet. They'd all been waiting for her arrival.

Her pack was present, as were her directors. Zica had been of an age just young enough to enjoy the youth that surrounded her niece. They would miss her gentle teasing and intriguing conversation almost as much as her family. Five invitations had been given to each senior representative of the delegations in house; none had turned them down. India, China, Japan, Maya, America and Europe were all here, chattering among themselves. It created a crowded atmosphere. Whiskey hated putting a political slant on such a deeply personal gathering, but there'd be business setbacks if any government felt slighted. The last thing The Davis Group needed was to give inadvertent insult to a government negotiator.

She passed closest to the *Agrun Nam* on her way to the front row of chairs, purposely snubbing them. From the corner of her eye she saw Nijmege and McCall swell with anger at her slight. Orlaith glared with them, having finagled an invitation from somewhere, the third of their affronted triangle. The need to utilize this memorial as a tool was another unfortunate consequence of her position. She could only hope that Zica, wherever she was, would forgive her.

Whiskey reached her grandmother, stepping into a warm embrace. They held each other for long minutes as the others silenced their discussions to watch. Whiskey initiated a connection between them, allowing the sensations that were her grandmother to settle over her—the perception of sun on her skin and reddish loam on her hands, the smell of earth intensifying. She felt the terrifying sadness, shared the sense of utter loss they'd both endured, not just with Zica's death but that of Nahimana, Whiskey's mother, dead for fourteen years. Though Wahca had been by Whiskey's side almost the entire time since the car accident, this was the first opportunity they'd had to connect and share their grief.

Eventually they returned to the present. Wahca wiped Whiskey's tears, a tremulous smile on her face as Whiskey returned the favor. She shakily inhaled, looking around at their audience. No one had interrupted their joining, probably because of the stern expression on her immediate guards' faces. Jake especially didn't look like she'd accept any sort of shenanigans from the others, and they'd taken her unsubtle stance as gospel.

Margaurethe took up Whiskey's hand again and they migrated to their seats. Beyond was a small table draped in black. A fat white pillar candle had been lit, protected from the breeze by hurricane glass. It illuminated a large color photo of Zica. She smiled widely at the camera, her eyes alight with mischief, hair free flowing. It was a portrait shot, and she wore an ochre-colored Western-style shirt with brown embroidery, a bone and bead choker of tan and gold caressing her throat. Behind her was the pale blue sky of the plains, wisps of cloud producing a watercolor wash. Whiskey felt her chest tighten as she looked upon the image of her aunt, forever smiling, forever gone.

The others took their seats and an old Lakota medicine man Whiskey hadn't seen before came forward. He wore traditional buckskins and an elaborate headdress. With careful precision, he pulled various things from a pouch, laying them out on the table and began to chant. Whiskey forced her mind to silence, allowing her heart the freedom to mourn while she had the opportunity.

It would be a long time before she'd have the chance again.

* * *

"Can you believe it?"

Nijmege ground her teeth as Davis passed without bothering to even look at her. She turned to Orlaith. "Believe what?"

"Her attire." Orlaith's expression was a cross between annoyance and repugnance. "I mean, really…this is a memorial service. She looks like she's ready to hop onto a motorcycle and raid a small town."

McCall leaned in, voice low. "She doesn't look that much different than the rest of her clique."

Nijmege scanned the other younglings that socialized with Davis, giving them scathing looks for their disrespectful appearance. Leather, chains, brightly colored hair. Even the African's daughter wore clothes that were more appropriate for a drug-deal shootout than a funeral service.

Orlaith tsked under her breath. "Our future leaders."

"Not if I can help it," Nijmege vowed.

"Really?" Orlaith cocked her head. "And what can you do about it, Bertrada? If the stories are true, she's already survived two assassins." Her gaze regarded the meeting between Davis and the old American Indian woman. "We can only hope that her next accident hits the proper mark."

Nijmege's eyes wandered over the gathering. Most of the invited delegates were enamored with their own false displays of mourning, none having actually known the vital woman who had died. Disgusted, saddened that she herself hadn't had more than the briefest exposure to Zica's personality, she glanced at Bentoncourt and Cassadie, who stood off to one side. She took a minute step closer to Orlaith, lowering her voice to a bare whisper. "No. Davis will be dead soon."

Orlaith gave her a sharp look. She, too, checked their surroundings for eavesdroppers, taking the time to link her arm through Nijmege's. "Explain."

"I plan to engage her in a duel before I leave here."

Shock washed across Orlaith's expression before solidifying into interest. "Do you need any assistance? I have few fighting skills, but I know you're much more adept with centuries of experience. I'll gladly stand as your second."

A faint smile curled Nijmege's lips. "I don't believe your daughter will ever speak to you again if you're involved."

Orlaith emitted a haughty snort. "I don't care. I'd suffer worse to get her away from that woman."

"Perhaps. But it would be better if you were there to help her through her grief. She was so distraught last time."

With grudging comprehension, Orlaith nodded. "True."

Nijmege patted Orlaith's hand on her arm. "Never fear, my friend. We'll see the Sweet Butcher's progeny permanently dead soon." She glared at the back of Davis's head, dreaming of the blood that would shortly splash across her pale hair. "Soon."

CHAPTER TWENTY-EIGHT

"Are you certain you don't want me to stay?"

Bentoncourt smiled at the concerned Cassadie. He placed a hand on Cassadie's shoulder, gripping it tightly and releasing it. "No, Aiden. I'll be fine."

They stood in the lobby of The Davis Group headquarters, morning sunlight brightening the floor-to-ceiling frosted glass windows. The coffee kiosk was closed despite the hour, and the lobby held an ambience of solitude. A handful of aides with briefcases clustered here and there, voices lowered as they chatted, subconsciously supporting the overall sense of veneration. It was almost as if they stood in the nave of a church, except the state portrait of Whiskey Davis looked down upon them rather than the Christ figure. Tragedy had turned a three-day visit into a week. Today was Sunday, and it was past time for two of the *Agrun Nam* delegates to return home.

Cassadie grimaced. "I know you'll be fine, Lionel, I just meant...I feel like I'm abandoning you." He glanced at the small huddle of their *Agrun Nam* associates nearby. Nijmege,

McCall and Rosenberg stood together near a sitting area. *Gasan Orlaith O'Toole* perched on a sofa, listening to their discussion. Leaning closer, he whispered, "What happens if things go sour? Who will be here to aid you?"

After following Cassadie's gaze, Bentoncourt shook his head. "I have faith that I won't need protecting. Unlike two of our colleagues, I don't believe Davis is the Sweet Butcher despite holding Elisibet's memories. I'm counting on her to keep her head, regardless of what happens."

"And I'm counting on you to keep your head, in more ways than one." Cassadie stared at him, a frown knitting his dark eyebrows together. "Don't do anything foolish, Lionel." As Bentoncourt affected innocence, Cassadie tucked his chin into his chest. "You know what I mean. Your sense of honor has gotten you into trouble in the past. I won't be here to pick up the pieces this time."

Two town cars pulled up on the front drive, distracting Bentoncourt as he saw them through the clear glass of the doors. He shook hands with Cassadie. "Thank you, my friend, but it's been several decades since I've allowed my heart to rule over my head. I know when discretion is advisable these days. I'll keep my neck protected."

"Do."

A handful of security entered the main doors, looking expectantly in Bentoncourt's direction. "I believe your transport is ready." Cassadie turned just as a guard arrived at their side.

"*Sabra Sañar* Cassadie, if you'll follow me?"

Bentoncourt scanned the lobby. Surely The Davis Group would send some sort of representative to see them off. As if the thought had called him, the elderly American Indian hobbled out from the offices behind the main security desk. Bentoncourt felt surprise. Up until now, the *Agrun Nam's* dealings had been with the other European Sanguire on Davis's board. They'd had little to do with Chano or Dikeledi.

Cassadie turned on his impressive charm, smiling and closing the distance between himself and the man's halting approach. "Director Chano, I'm so sorry we didn't have more opportunity to spend time together."

Chano peered at Cassadie with a sharp gaze, reminding Bentoncourt that venerable age didn't necessarily equate with mental feebleness. "I agree. You should visit again. I can show you some wonderful fishing on the coast."

"That would be marvelous."

As they nattered on the other *sanari* approached, Orlaith in tow. As soon as Rosenberg was near, Chano turned toward him. "And I'll miss your sensible opinion at the negotiation table, young man."

Until now Chano had always struck Bentoncourt as acerbic, not gregarious. He frowned in suspicion, as did Nijmege and McCall. Though it was rude to prod a single Sanguire, especially one that wasn't a close friend, it wasn't particularly barbaric to generally scan an area. Having people with the ability to shape shift was an ongoing security concern, and the mental rake of a crowd a normal occurrence. Bentoncourt did so now, getting a general feel of the Sanguire nearby, recognizing many as his colleagues and their people. Nothing indicated that Chano was anyone but himself, at least he didn't give off the amber and steel Bentoncourt associated with Dorst.

Chano's expression reflected amusement, obviously aware of the sudden interest, but didn't call attention to their curiosity. "Whiskey wanted to thank you for accepting her invitation to visit. She apologizes for not being here to see you off."

Nijmege sniffed. "Typical. She snaps her fingers and we come running. Now she doesn't bother to show her face. It's to be expected from an undisciplined child."

Cassadie's countenance darkened, and Bentoncourt felt a flush of anger spread up his neck. Even Orlaith seemed appalled at the overt snipe. McCall muffled a snort, turning away for a light cough. Only Rosenberg remained unaffected.

His smile faded and eyes sparked, but Chano refused to be baited into an argument. "Most of your staff has already left for the airport. We have two vehicles here for you and your immediate aides. Have a pleasant journey." He didn't wait for a response, promptly turning away from them.

As much as Bentoncourt wanted to take Nijmege to task, he couldn't, not in a public venue and not with Orlaith as witness.

He could tell Cassadie also wanted to say a few choice words, probably ones not as diplomatic as was his normal vocabulary.

"*Sañars?*" a guard asked. He gestured toward the door. "Shall we?"

Rosenberg accepted the escort, not speaking to any of the others as he was led out the doors, a handful of his staff following. Rather than tempt fate, Nijmege took her coterie with her, McCall and Orlaith trailing behind, not bothering to say farewell as they drifted to the elevators.

Cassadie turned toward Bentoncourt. "I know Ernst thinks we can't do anything, but you have to stop her!"

"I'll do what I can, Aiden. I can't promise anything more than that." His words didn't ease Cassadie's troubled mind. What else could he do? Rosenberg's political analyses had rarely been wrong. He took Cassadie's hand and shook it. "Safe journey, my friend. Take care of our people."

They stared at one another a brief moment, Cassadie's eyes expressing what he couldn't say aloud. With a curt nod, he released Bentoncourt. Turning, he gathered his people with a gesture and went outside to his waiting car.

Bentoncourt trailed after, remaining at the door until the cars pulled out into morning traffic. His depression returned with his last glimpse of taillight. Turning back to The Davis Group lobby, he regarded Davis's life-sized portrait—all leather and rags, a sneer on her beautiful face and dragons writhing from her arm.

"God help us."

CHAPTER TWENTY-NINE

Whiskey's anger simmered as afternoon drew into evening. She sat, elbow on the arm of her chair, her chin resting upon palm with her index finger at her temple. This day of political squabbling was almost finished, and her nerves were sharp. Was it only this morning that Cassadie and Rosenberg had left? It felt like weeks ago. She knew some of her weariness came from her still-healing injuries, but the constant drain of keeping her emotions at bay had exhausted her.

As expected, Nijmege had taken every opening to insult Whiskey and her advisors. The strain showed on everyone, even Nijmege's associates. Bentoncourt had spent most the day fighting a perpetual grimace as Nijmege shot one gibe after another at Whiskey. McCall remained stone-faced, though an air of smug joy clung to him as he backed Nijmege's every counter, ensuring that the hours spent in conference were utterly unproductive.

On this end of the table, Valmont echoed Nijmege's anger for altogether different reasons. He watched her like a hawk, rather apropos considering she resembled the creature, and answered her sniping with remarks of his own. Everything said here was being recorded for posterity, so neither of them were too bloodthirsty in their verbal sparring. Whiskey debated the pros and cons of that as she fumed, remaining silent as she accepted the verbal abuse, occasionally stepping in to squelch Valmont's invective.

Castillo had also received much of Nijmege's contemptuous attention. Her snobbery had much to do with her opinion that he was an outsider, a commoner. He had no family in power and served a Human religion. It seemed that Castillo's return sentiment was on equal level, for the sharp barbs aimed specifically at him fell fruitlessly to the ground, not wounding him. He seemed far more irritated in defense of Whiskey than of himself, huffing in outrage only when Nijmege slung barbs at his *Ninsumgal.*

Chano didn't merit even that much from Nijmege. Her European sensibilities followed the straight and narrow regarding the American aboriginals, namely that his presence in these proceedings was unnecessary. On the rare occasion when he spoke, she ignored him with supercilious calm, leaving Bentoncourt or McCall to answer his questions.

Dikeledi and Dorst were the only two that Nijmege treated with any level of respect—the former because the European and African Sanguire had held political treaties with each other for centuries, and the latter due to a healthy fear of the unknown. Who knew what Dorst would accept as insult before taking offense? His cultivated unpredictability stood him in good stead here as he sat back and watched the sparks fly.

Whiskey could have told Nijmege that she had little to worry about in that area. Dorst remained a pleasurable burble upon Whiskey's psyche, purposefully keeping light mental contact with her. He had found many of the slurs and rude comments humorous, his lips turned upward in a perpetual smile. She didn't know whether he truly felt such or if he transmitted this low-grade levity to prevent her from bursting into fury. Studying the shining black eyes of her chief spy, she decided he truly did enjoy the show.

Then there was Margaurethe, who sat stiffly beside her, glaring at their enemies.

Nijmege's threat had drawn them closer than ever. This was something of a surprise to Whiskey. She'd built a place in her mind to house those desires she attributed only to Elisibet, never allowing Margaurethe full access and not looking too closely at her motives for keeping that part of her back. Their pact over the fate of Nijmege and McCall had caused her to reconsider that mental separation. Last night, after Zica's memorial service, she had joined her mind with Margaurethe's, sharing deeper than ever before. The morning had dawned with the two of them entwined and that place in her mind no longer fettered. Instead, the seeds of ire and despair had rooted and grown bearing the fruit of anger, desire, regret and loss that seemed to emanate from both of them.

On an emotional level, they were so close now that words couldn't even describe the sensation. If she didn't need Margaurethe as backup should she fail, Whiskey would prefer her as her second in the inevitable duel. That piece of her that was Elisibet reveled in the joy of their joint perfection, knowing nothing and no one could withstand them. The sensation was both daunting and exhilarating.

Nijmege turned a page, and everyone dutifully followed her lead with the copies she'd handed out that morning. "That's the last of it."

Castillo flipped back through several pages. "While I can appreciate the time it took to gather this information, *Sañar* Nijmege, I fail to see why we need a laundry list of legal proceedings for which your office is responsible. We requested information on your laws, not your courts." He referred to the paperwork. "You've apparently tried treason cases in the last decade but haven't given us specific data on what comprises a treasonous action."

"I've given you all I have," Nijmege said, spine rigid. She shuffled her papers into some sort of order. "I'm done with it. How we run our nation has nothing to do with this treaty."

"Come now, Bertrada," Valmont said. "You've always been anal retentive. Surely you've got what we need." He flipped the

236 D Jordan Redhawk

stack of papers so they fluttered and settled into a haphazard pile in the center of the conference table.

"I've more important things to be worried about." Nijmege glared at Whiskey rather than Valmont, daring her to argue.

"Treason is a capital offense with the Euro Sanguire, we understand that," Castillo interrupted before Valmont could egg Nijmege into further tantrums. "We're not attempting to undermine that, we'd just like to know what constitutes a treasonous action in the European government. If a treaty is signed, will another member state inadvertently break laws while visiting your country out of ignorance? What will the repercussions be?"

"This is useless! We'll never make a pact anyway."

Valmont chuckled. "Meaning, no, Padre." He pointed a thumb at Dorst sitting across from him. "Maybe Reynhard can give you a hand in that regard."

"I'd be most happy to assist you, Father Castillo." Dorst almost preened, his actions lightening the tense atmosphere in the room.

Castillo, still vaguely irritated, nodded in appreciation. "Thank you, Reynhard. Perhaps we can talk when this meeting is concluded."

"Which would be now," Whiskey said. "We've gotten little done, and I need a break. We'll continue this tomorrow."

Bentoncourt nodded, his tone disgruntled. "I'll have more pertinent documents available first thing in the morning."

Nijmege opened her mouth to snipe but stopped at a sharp look from McCall. Whiskey imagined she'd planned on saying something about the *Nam Lugal* of the *Agrun Nam* doing footwork like an errand boy. Instead, Nijmege's lips pinched closed and she looked away.

Bentoncourt continued. "I expect I can have the data in less than an hour. Do you wish to continue after a brief recess?"

Whiskey turned her attention from McCall's indiscreet interference. "No, Lionel. I think we're done here for now. We'll meet again tomorrow."

"Of course, *Ninsumgal*."

All eyes shot to Bentoncourt at his use of her title. *That's new.* His compatriots didn't seem pleased, but Dorst's pleasure shot off the scale. Whiskey didn't bother to call attention to Bentoncourt's slip—if slip it was. She straightened from her slouch. "This meeting is adjourned for the day. We'll gather again at nine tomorrow morning." She banged the gavel and the rustle of movement filled the air.

"I hadn't expected that," Margaurethe murmured as she gathered papers.

"Me neither." Whiskey tapped her stack of paperwork into some order, watching Nijmege across the table. "Doesn't look like they did, either."

Margaurethe raised her voice. "Lionel, we'll be having a small dinner party this evening downstairs. The *Agrun Nam's* invitations have already been delivered to your quarters."

"Thank you, *Ki'an Gasan.* I've enjoyed your chef during my stay." Bentoncourt patted his abdomen. "Enough so that I believe I've gained ten pounds since I've arrived."

"Matthew is excellent, isn't he?" Margaurethe asked, coming around the table to join Bentoncourt. Her gait was smoother, the heavy brace having been replaced with a lighter version. She placed an arm in Bentoncourt's and escorted him to the door, followed by Castillo and Dikeledi.

Whiskey watched her lover play hostess, her gaze flickering over the others collecting their things. She gave Jake a hand signal as she left the table and her bodyguard returned it, remaining behind to tidy up the table. This wasn't one of her duties, but Whiskey had to make herself approachable by Nijmege. Though Jake didn't like it, they both knew that neither Nijmege nor McCall would attempt assassination. Nijmege had her goal and McCall was content to follow her lead for the moment.

Nijmege's eyes narrowed, jumping over to Jake's physical distance. She glanced at McCall—something passed between them—but didn't approach. Instead, she turned and swept away on the heels of Dikeledi, McCall in tow.

Frowning, Whiskey released her pent-up breath. "Damn."

Dorst's musical tones stopped her from saying more. "Perhaps our darling Bertrada is not as eager as she claims to be."

"Or darling Samuel is holding her back," Valmont agreed, though his voice was sardonic as he gazed at the *Agrun Nam's* retreating backs.

"It could also be that she requires a different audience, *Ninsumgal.*"

Whiskey turned to Jake who had reappeared at her side. "What do you mean?"

"Everyone here knows what she's doing and why. If she were to cause challenge in a private setting, there's the chance that you won't make it a public duel. She needs that publicity, not only to prove to the world that she can and will destroy you, but because it won't offer you an opportunity to sweep her under the rug."

Dorst tapped his fingertips together in overt joy at his protégé's analysis. "Oh, I do love how you think, young woman. You make me proud!" He rolled his eyes heavenward and placed a palm against his chest in paternal bliss.

Both Whiskey and Jake smiled at his theatrics. "Then this dinner party should be where it happens." Whiskey nodded, squaring her shoulders. "I hope so. I'm tired of waiting."

Valmont clapped her on the shoulder. "As am I."

CHAPTER THIRTY

This dinner party was considered small. In reality that meant approximately seventy-five guests rather than three or four hundred milling about. Several round tables sparkled with candles and china place settings, some seats already occupied with delegates. Chano commanded The Davis Group table at the front of the room, chatting with Dikeledi's daughter and Daniel. Dikeledi held conversation with the Mayans at another table, probably working on a clause of their upcoming treaty. As usual, Dorst had made himself scarce. People tended to avoid him due to his reputation and his presence would have put a pall on the evening. That didn't mean he wasn't here, lurking about as one of the servants. Margaurethe counted herself lucky that the remainder of Whiskey's pack held a stunning lack of interest for these types of functions. At last report from security, they were holding an impromptu party in the poolroom, too gratified at the lightening of restrictions to care about a fusty dinner party.

The majority of the dinner guests still hovered just inside the entry where a wine bar was doing brisk business. Tall cabaret tables and servers offering hors d'oeuvres peppered the open space here. A gentle murmur of conversation ebbed and flowed as people mingled, a small lake of formal attire moving with the tide of gossip.

For a wonder, Sithathor and Margaurethe had gotten Whiskey into a stunning black evening gown. Despite adamant argument against the dress, she wore it well. Black satin and backless, it clung in all the proper places, showing off her narrow waist and the swell of her hips, the material flaring at the thigh as it flowed to the floor. Blessed with a natural grace, Whiskey appeared to have often worn such clothing. The muscles of her arms and back spoke of her martial arts training, the dragon tattoos writhing boldly along her right arm. Her blond hair had been pulled back at the sides, the normally straight tresses tumbling down in a wave of curls, which Sithathor had insisted was an integral part of the appearance.

Margaurethe sipped at her wine, admiring the view as Whiskey spoke with three of the Japanese delegates. Elisibet had always preferred men's clothes to women's as well, but even her lofty station hadn't protected her from the cultural norms of her day. Most state functions had required her to dress appropriately for her gender. Whiskey wasn't as socially inclined, preferring pantsuits—the more utilitarian the better. Her attempts to wear cargo pants and leather jackets to formal functions were based on serious consideration, and Margaurethe had used it to their benefit since the *Agrun Nam* had arrived.

Margaurethe wondered if perhaps she should have gotten pictures of Whiskey this evening when she'd had the opportunity. It might take a decade before Whiskey could be cajoled into another outfit like this. She'd conceded to the ensemble only as a means to an end. Hopefully a less androgynous appearance would give Nijmege a sense of power, and she'd push harder to achieve her challenge before the end of the night...providing Margaurethe didn't find cause to kill the witch first.

Valmont sidled up to her, brandy glass in hand. Taking position at her side, he turned to regard their *Ninsumgal*. "She looks spectacular. Your work?"

"And Sithathor's." They shared a smile, and Margaurethe studied the room. Since their private discussion three days ago, she'd found Valmont's presence much less irritating. Somehow they'd reached a state of amity that had been missing since their strained reunion several months ago. The lack of spitefulness oddly relaxed her. She located Nijmege with her knot of delegates near Whiskey's table and became restive once more. Nijmege held court with a handful of guests, including Margaurethe's mother, the group casting sly smiles toward Whiskey upon occasion. Margaurethe wished Orlaith had departed before now but knew such a boon was too much to ask for. "Do you think Bertrada will get this over with?"

"One can hope." Valmont followed her gaze. "Looks like she has quite the following there. McCall, your sainted mother and a couple of the Chinese ambassadors. Is that Singh from the Indian consulate?"

"Yes." Margaurethe lowered her glass, grimacing. "He's been swayed by Bertrada's opinions it appears."

"Huh." Valmont sipped his wine. "I doubt it. He seems to be a fair-weather friend. I find it hard to believe that the Chinese and the Indians are willing to overlook their differences for a situation occurring half a world away."

Margaurethe tilted her head toward Whiskey's interaction with the Japanese contingent. "Which is worse for China? Dealing with the Japanese or the Indians?"

"Excellent point. Six of one, half dozen of the other. It could easily be the Indians conversing with Whiskey and the Japanese by Bertrada." They stood in companionable silence for several moments before he spoke again. "About Whiskey's plans…"

"Yes?"

"Has she discussed the issue of her second with you?"

Margaurethe studied her wine. Though a part of her knew that Valmont would be the best choice among Whiskey's colleagues for the upcoming battle, she dreaded the thought of Valmont at Whiskey's side. She didn't know if it was mere jealousy or the niggling doubt that he'd betray Whiskey once more. "No. She hasn't mentioned who she's considering."

He stood in long silence, before asking, "And are you on board with this plan?"

Margaurethe gave him a slight grimace. "To be honest? Not as much as I should be. I'd much rather you and I sort it out than put her in danger."

He shrugged, regarding his glass. "That's still an option. Bertrada's not the European *Ninsumgal*. I can challenge her if I wish."

"And then what?" Margaurethe looked at him. "If you die, Whiskey will be despondent and still have a price on her head. Bertrada is older than you, remember, she has more power."

"You could join me as my second."

Flabbergasted, Margaurethe knew she probably gaped like a dying fish. Before she could deny his words she snapped her mouth closed and turned away to stare at their dinner guests. Why hadn't that thought occurred to her before? She ran her mind through all the variables, becoming more and more confident that it would work. Neither she nor Valmont could stand up to Nijmege alone, but the two of them together could sway the scales. It was the exact scenario Whiskey planned for only with different individuals involved. Yes, Whiskey would be infuriated, but she didn't have the authority to intercede in a fully Euro Sanguire challenge, not being European. "Are you certain?"

Valmont's dark eyes lit up. "Of course! Bertrada may know swords, but I'm better. She'll probably still choose McCall on the basis of mental equilibrium."

A twinge of uncertainty pierced Margaurethe's hope. "That's more than I have. I've never been one to dabble in the martial sports."

"You've never put yourself into the position of dealing with challenges, either." Valmont chuckled, lightly touching her forearm. "And all our reports say that McCall is even less inclined toward that sort of thing anyway."

Margaurethe scowled. "No, he prefers hirelings to getting his hands dirty."

"What do you say?"

She debated the idea. "Are we certain she'll choose McCall as second?"

He scoffed. "Who else would accept? No one truly knows how powerful Whiskey is. They suspect, yes, but it's not a known element. Bertrada can eat three younglings for breakfast without breaking a sweat. She doesn't need muscle or power to help, even against the two of us."

"She just needs to follow the proper rules for a duel."

Valmont nodded affirmatively. "I'm certain she's already discussed it with him. And I'm certain she's assuming I'll be involved as second anyway. From her point of view, she has a youngling and a younger man as opponents. McCall will simply be there to ensure propriety."

The idea took firm root in her heart. Margaurethe was less than sixty years older than Valmont. Joined together, they would level the playing field if Nijmege chose McCall as her second. "It might work."

"And we might be too late." He stared over her shoulder with a scowl.

Margaurethe turned away, seeing Nijmege and her entourage bearing down upon Whiskey. *Not yet!* She hurried toward them, still awkward from the less restrictive binding on her injured leg, sloshing wine across her hand as she jostled an inconvenient guest. By the time she extricated herself, the incident had cost her several seconds delay. She arrived at Whiskey's side, hearing Nijmege's strident tones.

"—Should consider placing yourself in danger rather than cowering behind your family and friends for protection."

A collective gasp rose from the witnesses, both those Nijmege had brought with her and the ones loitering nearby.

Whiskey's eyes flashed at the invective, but she remained calm. "Is that the best you can do, Bertrada?"

"No, it's not." She closed the distance between them, fangs bared as she glared. That insult alone was cause for attack in polite Sanguire society. "You are a *san-rabarra, sulum*. You're not *ninsumgal. Nu me'en nata.* You're an *unu narra.*"

Margaurethe swelled in fury at Nijmege's abuse. "*You are a slave-bastard, covered in shit. You're not ninsumgal. You do not exist. You're a fraud.*" Beside her, she felt Valmont do the same. She opened her mouth to give challenge herself, damn the consequences, but froze before the words could leave her mouth. Roses and blood caressed her, calmed her, held her still. She slid her eyes toward her lover, realizing that Whiskey also held Valmont silent. She dropped her gaze, knowing the moment was lost, and Whiskey immediately released her hold without retreating. Margaurethe felt her lover's cold fury and determination.

"I challenge you, Bertrada Nijmege, for the affront you've given me now and all previous insults either within or outside of my hearing." Whiskey bared her teeth, snarling at her enemy. "Put your money where your mouth is, bitch."

Nijmege smiled, a flicker of glee glowed within her eyes. "Accepted! Shall we meet tomorrow?"

"No!" Valmont shouldered between them. "She hasn't been released from her doctor yet."

Margaurethe fought back nausea, glad Valmont, at least, was thinking clearer than she. "Only after she's completely healed from her injuries."

Nijmege sneered at the two of them. "Another day? Maybe two? I can wait that long." Fangs still bared, she smiled at Whiskey. "And who shall the child call as her second, hmm?"

Whiskey tucked her chin. "You'll know by the end of tomorrow."

With a snort, Nijmege whirled about and paraded out of the room, Orlaith O'Toole in lockstep with her. McCall seemed a little pale but had a look of satisfaction upon his face as he followed.

Singh and his Chinese comrades suddenly realized they were in each other's company, and awkwardly went their separate ways. This cued the other guests to drift away—the fight was over for the moment.

Margaurethe leaned close, taking Whiskey's hand. "Do you need time?" She saw Jake hovering just behind Valmont and nodded toward the door.

"No." Whiskey smiled, no longer appearing angry or tense. "I'll be fine until later. After all, we have guests." She projected serenity beyond her years.

Margaurethe allowed herself to be escorted to their table, a morass of pride and fear whirling through her. The deed was done, the challenge called, and their goals would soon be realized or ruined. Whiskey had shed the fear and uncertainty in an effort to set her guests at ease. She was no longer the ungainly teenager trying to act mature in circumstances far beyond her abilities. Somehow she had evolved into this refined young Sanguire woman who would eventually rule a world.

As Margaurethe was seated at their table, she wondered when that had happened, and how she could keep up.

CHAPTER THIRTY-ONE

Languid, Whiskey stretched and yawned, relishing the comforting bed warmth and the feel of the sheets as she came awake. Rubbing sleep from her eyes, she opened them, turning her head toward her lover. Margaurethe remained asleep beside her. Whiskey rolled over, propping herself up on one elbow to get a better view.

Tousled mahogany hair splayed about Margaurethe's face, its reddish highlights visible to Whiskey despite the darkness of the room. Though the taller of the two, Margaurethe's delicate features were almost elfin in appearance compared to Whiskey's. Those features were currently relaxed in repose, giving the impression she was only in her midtwenties. Stress and habit created fine lines about her mouth and eyes when she was awake, aging her another decade. Sometimes Whiskey had difficulty believing the woman at her side was in actuality almost seven hundred years old.

She shifted, twining a lock of Margaurethe's hair about her fingers. Gently, she touched her lover's mind, sampling the somnolent sensations there. Her movement or touch roused Margaurethe, and Whiskey traced along Margaurethe's consciousness as it returned. When green eyes opened to look at her, she felt her heart flip in her chest. "I'll never be able to express how much I love you, *minn'ast*," she said, her voice rough from sleep.

A hazy smile teased Margaurethe's lips, creating the expected lines along her mouth. She moved, reaching her arms above her in a lithesome stretch that put Whiskey's mind into a completely different frame. Bringing her arms down, Margaurethe draped one across Whiskey's shoulders. "I'm sure you'll figure out a way, *m'cara*."

Whiskey grinned, leaning in for a quick kiss, her hand stroking Margaurethe's bared shoulder. As much as she wanted more, she knew her breath was probably foul from the alcohol she'd imbibed at the dinner party last night. Rather than subject Margaurethe to the torture, she rolled over onto her back, pulling her lover into the crook of her arm. They lay together, minds and legs entwined as they both came fully awake.

Mornings like these had been unheard of in Whiskey's prior life. Normally, she'd awaken in a youth shelter or under a bridge. Rarely she'd find herself beside a bar pickup, neither she nor her partner inclined to spend much time together, both eager to flee the stiffness of an impromptu dalliance with a stranger. Even when she'd enjoyed sex with people she'd known, a sense of embarrassed awkwardness always followed in the light of day. The intimacy she'd developed with Margaurethe was much richer than she'd ever experienced. She'd spent years longing for something she couldn't name. Now she had it and she'd be damned if she'd let it go.

Margaurethe broke their silence. "Did you sleep well?"

"I did," Whiskey said, somewhat surprised at the revelation. "I hadn't expected to, but I slept like a log." She'd felt an odd serenity envelop her when Nijmege bared her fangs last night. That tranquility hadn't fled in the harsh realization that she'd challenged an eight-hundred-year-old Sanguire woman to a duel. "What about you?"

"I did as well." Margaurethe snuggled closer, her hand stroking along Whiskey's abdomen.

They remained silent several minutes longer. By the sensations coursing across Margaurethe's mind, Whiskey knew the quiet would end soon. As Margaurethe became more and more alert, her emotions turned from comfort to uneasiness.

Margaurethe sighed. "About the challenge…"

Smiling, Whiskey hugged her lover. "Yes, about that…" She received a slight pinch on her side for her droll tone.

"Have you considered who your second shall be?"

Whiskey forced herself to seriousness. "I have." She pulled back to peer at her lover. "Why? Do you have any suggestions?"

"I think Reynhard would be an advantage to have in the arena." She glared at Whiskey's guffaw, though the expression was without true heat.

"He would against anybody else, yeah." Whiskey snickered again. "But I'm trying to ensure that Bertrada uses McCall as her second. If I call for Reynhard, she might look for someone closer to his age to support her—he's at least as old as Chano or Sithathor."

"Then you'll need someone not much younger than she, someone with weapons experience." Margaurethe dropped her gaze, relaxing into Whiskey's embrace.

"That is what Dikeledi suggested the other day." She rested her cheek against Margaurethe's head, deeply inhaling the smell of her shampoo. "I think you already know who I'm considering for the job."

"Valmont."

Whiskey half expected Margaurethe's mood to sharpen into anger and disgust. When it didn't, she frowned. "You're not upset?"

Margaurethe shook her head, her hair tickling Whiskey's face. "Not as much as you expected, I'm sure."

Pulling back again, Whiskey stared at her. "Who are you and what have you done with my fiancée?" She received a stronger pinch in retaliation and pinned the offending hand beneath her arm.

"Valmont and I have had our differences, but we've decided to set them aside for the nonce," Margaurethe crisply informed her. She didn't quite stick her tongue out, but Whiskey got the definite impression the thought had crossed Margaurethe's mind.

She smiled, hugging her lover. "I'm not complaining."

"Why Valmont?" Margaurethe asked, her voice muffled against Whiskey's throat.

Whiskey stared at the ceiling in thought. "He has the weapons experience I'll need. Bertrada does have some skill in that department, more than I do." Margaurethe nodded. "He's of the right age to set Bertrada at ease. If she doesn't think she'll have a chance, she might appoint someone else as her second." Fire erupted in her heart. "And I want McCall," she growled.

Margaurethe mentally soothed her, woodsmoke and mulled wine a fine counterpoint to the banked flames of her rage. "And his petition to be your Champion? Has that changed?"

"No." Whiskey used the change of topic to avoid her anger. "No. I don't need a Defender of the Crown. I'm not the European *Ninsumgal*, regardless of what I might have been in the dark past. That's a Euro Sanguire position, not one within The Davis Group."

"As it should be, though it's unfortunate." Margaurethe turned away to look at the alarm clock on the nightstand. "The modern era certainly could use some of the old ways."

Whiskey smiled, setting aside her contemporary Human sensibilities regarding the aristocracy of the past. "What time is it?"

"Time to get up, My *Ninsumgal*," Margaurethe teased. "Daniel wants to see us this morning and you need to speak with Valmont."

Disappointment washed through Whiskey and she groaned. "I don't want to. Just five more minutes?"

Margaurethe had already sat up, feet over the side of the bed. She looked over her naked shoulder, a glint in her eyes. "And what, pray tell, can you accomplish in just five minutes?"

Not one to decline such a flirtatious invitation, Whiskey reached for her. "It'll be faster if I just show you."

* * *

Valmont stood in the reception area of The Davis Group's executive offices, idling at the window as he watched pedestrians and traffic navigate the wet streets of a Portland autumn. He'd received a message this morning to speak to Whiskey and was in good spirits. There could be only one reason for her to want to see him this day.

"*Sublugal Sañar* Valmont! How glorious to see you!"

Valmont whirled to see Dorst approaching. "Reynhard."

Dorst's eyes glittered with wicked joy. "I presume you're here to see our *Ninsumgal* as well?" Before Valmont could answer, he turned toward the receptionist stationed at the large desk. "I do so hope she has those lemon tea cakes. They grace the palate so delicately."

The receptionist smiled. "If you'd like, *Sañur Gasum*, I can see if the kitchen has any."

"Oh! That would be wonderful, Helen. I'd be forever in your debt."

While Dorst continued to flirt and tease the receptionist, Valmont frowned. He thought he'd been called here as Whiskey's second, but now had doubts. Did she mean to ask Dorst instead? Had Nijmege already announced McCall as her second, thereby allowing Whiskey to utilize someone with more strength despite the board's strategic discussion? Why then would she have asked for Valmont to attend this meeting? Perhaps she wanted to grill him about Nijmege. He'd spent the majority of his childhood and youth in her household. Whiskey probably thought he'd have information she could use in her upcoming duel. His anticipation took a tumble, and he struggled against the rise of self-denigration that had been his constant companion for several centuries.

"Valmont?"

He broke away from his inner thoughts, seeing that Dorst had paused halfway to Whiskey's door. "What?"

"You're coming, aren't you?"

Inhaling deeply, he straightened his shoulders. "Of course."
Inside Whiskey rose from her desk, a smile on her face.
"Have a seat." She gestured to the sitting area rather than her
desk chairs. "Helen's running a quick errand and then we can
get started."

Valmont smoothed the disappointment from his face,
putting on a rakish grin. He dropped onto the couch, crossed his
leg at the knee and stretched one arm along the back. "Where's
Margaurethe?"

"Doing her thing." Whiskey also chose the couch, turning
sideways with her right knee drawn up to accommodate herself.
"She's getting the…venue prepared."

"Really?" Dorst settled in an armchair, his bright eyes avid
with interest. "Do tell. Not the ballroom, I hope."

"The gymnasium." She smiled at Dorst's titter.

"Blood is quite difficult to remove from carpet," Dorst
agreed.

Valmont watched Whiskey pale despite her blasé handling
of the topic. As much as he wanted to hound her regarding her
choice of second, he refrained. She'd had a difficult childhood
and a harsh adjustment period as she came to terms with both
a life and past life so far removed from her normal experience.
Sometimes it was difficult to believe she was still a toddler in
Sanguire terms, not even two decades old. With so much on her
plate already, he didn't want to add to her burden. "I imagine it
would be much easier than to replace carpet or clean it, as well,"
he said, drolly agreeing with Dorst. "Much too expensive."

"Not to mention the awkward questions from the carpet
layers."

Whiskey's smile became more natural at their ribbing. She
opened her mouth to speak but a tap at the door interrupted
her. Helen entered with a plate of lemon tea cakes to add to
the coffee setting, receiving smiles and blessings from Dorst.
Valmont utilized the time to grab a cup of coffee, pouring a
second for Whiskey.

As soon as Dorst had finished his coquetry and Helen had
left the room, Whiskey turned to place both feet on the floor.

"So you know I've called you here because of the challenge. I need to choose a second and I need more information."

Valmont's mood drooped. He'd been right. He was here to fill in any blanks Whiskey might have regarding Nijmege's abilities. He forced himself to pay strict attention to her words. Even if he wasn't her second, he couldn't let her go into the arena without a thorough background and understanding of Nijmege's training and habits. So focused on this task, he didn't quite believe Whiskey's next words.

"Valmont, I'd like you to be my second."

He stuttered, his mind blank for several moments. "Wh-what?"

Whiskey grinned. She reached over to pat his knee. "You. My second. Challenge. Will you?"

The gears in his mind began turning once more, picking up speed as the fuel of delight sped them along. "Yes! Yes! Of course!" While a distant part of his mind tried to concentrate on at least acting somewhat mature, his heart wallowed in pleasure. Whiskey trusted him. She trusted him with her life! Margaurethe had been right. With considerable effort, he turned to the conversation at hand.

"What have you got for us, Reynhard?"

Dorst nibbled delicately at a tea cake. "Not much more than our dear Valmont already knows, I'm sure. Bertrada has always had sword training. In fact, I believe she used to train you, didn't she, Valmont?"

"Um, yes." Valmont recollected his early training sessions in Nahib's household. "She was rather formidable at the time, but didn't apply herself beyond appeasing Nahib's desire that she be capable of defending herself."

"Do you know if she continued her training?" Whiskey asked.

Dorst wiped his mouth with a napkin, pausing in thought. "It's my understanding that she left off for a time after Nahib's execution. Once Mahar's Prophecy was spoken she returned to it, but even that faded off over the centuries. One can only hold fury for so long before it exhausts one."

"And she's had more than enough to keep her busy on the *Agrun Nam*," Valmont said. "That's a full-time job without a *ninsumgal's* advisor to handle the High Court."

Whiskey nodded. "So if we're lucky, she's rusty. If we're extremely lucky, she hasn't trained in years."

"Unfortunately, your luck isn't that good, My *Gasan*." Dorst's face held a measure of sympathy. "Once word of your return reached Europe, she renewed her training."

"Has she been working out here?" Whiskey sat forward.

"Not that I'm aware."

Valmont also leaned forward. "I doubt she would anyway. The last thing she'd want is to show off her skill before her enemies."

Whiskey scowled. "Unlike me. I've had at least two training sessions since the *Agrun Nam* has arrived."

"Be thankful it's only two, *Ninsumgal*." Dorst reached for another tea cake. "That would hardly give her a decent showing of your skills, providing she did witness them."

As they continued to discuss strategy and tactics, Valmont enjoyed an inner tranquility he hadn't known in centuries. He watched as Whiskey flashed smiles, spoke in serious tones, or scowled in annoyance, and all the while his heart sang. She trusted him with her life.

I cannot let her trust be in vain!

* * *

Nijmege listened to the delicate strains of music, eyes closed to catch every audible nuance, ignoring her companions. Modern electronics certainly had improved the quality of recording instruments. She almost couldn't discern the difference between this playback and sitting in the symphony audience itself.

McCall grunted. "I do wish she'd hurry."

Nijmege cracked one eye open to regard her nervous partner. "She called challenge, Samuel. The deed is done. There's nothing to do but wait."

McCall stood with his back to her apartment window, a scowl on his face. He harrumphed, an utterance more suited to a middle-aged visage than his youthful one. "It would be nice to know who she'll choose as her second."

"It hardly matters." Nijmege shut her eye again, trying to pick up the feel of the music. "She'll die, and my goal will have been met."

Orlaith raised a wine glass in toast. "As it should be."

The women's unconcern didn't sit well upon McCall. He paced, disrupting Nijmege's philharmonic concentration. "What if she chooses Dorst? Neither of us can withstand him. And by all reports, she's quite strong in her own right, regardless of her youth."

Perturbed, Nijmege gave up listening to the music, turning her full attention to him. "Reynhard hasn't been seen or heard from in almost four hundred years. Granted, he may have utilized his time keeping his martial skills intact, but he was never one for the dueling field to begin with. Despite his age, his strength has always lain with his covert ability."

"Davis would be a fool to pick him." Orlaith sipped her wine.

Their words didn't soothe him. "Why can't she be a fool? You've chosen me as your second. That's rather foolish, don't you agree?"

"You could have declined," Nijmege reminded him. He grimaced, obviously wondering if he still had the opportunity to do so. She relented. "You'll be fine, Samuel. Trust me. You won't need to physically fight anyone. All I need is for you to be there with me. Your strength will be enough to overcome that *ñalga súp* and anyone ill advised enough to agree to side with her."

Orlaith nodded. "All this talk that she's as powerful as Elisibet ever was is nothing but claptrap. Have you ever heard of a youngling coming through the *Ñíri Kurám* with such strength?" She barely paused to allow either of them to answer. "No. You haven't. It's impossible. Even the Sweet Butcher wasn't as strong as her propaganda claimed."

McCall hardly heeded her words, continuing to pace up and down the span of windows as the light of day faded behind him. Nijmege found it odd that he'd been a staunch supporter over the last months, yet now seemed ready to bolt at the least provocation. His lack of experience and prowess in a fight had him quite apprehensive, the complete opposite of her. For the first time in centuries she felt peace, knowing her path loomed steady, her destiny nearly completed. His agitation rather spoiled her heartsease.

A knock interrupted more conversation, and an aide leaned into the room. "*Aga Maskim Sañar*, *Sublugal Sañar* Valmont is here to see you."

A rush of adrenaline pushed Nijmege out of her chair. Valmont! "Send him in."

McCall stepped forward. "Does this mean he's—"

"Should I leave?" Orlaith asked.

Nijmege waved McCall to silence, shaking her head in the negative as the door reopened and Valmont sauntered into the room. She only had to look at him to know the truth.

"Bertrada, Samuel, *Gasan* Orlaith." Valmont gave them a nod of acknowledgment rather than the slight bow that befitted their rank. "I believe you know why I'm here."

"Stop posturing and spit it out," McCall snarled, his normally cool demeanor breaking under the strain.

Valmont grinned. "My, aren't you the demanding one, Samuel. Really, Bertrada, I know you like them young, but he's hardly a puppy."

McCall bristled but recovered his control.

Nijmege didn't think it would be beneficial to agree with Valmont, especially since her companion actually did resemble a recalcitrant pup at the moment. "Get on with it, Valmont," she stated, her bored tone masking the eagerness beating in her chest.

"I'm here to inform you that *Ninsumgal* Whiskey will meet you tomorrow morning in the gymnasium on the third floor of The Davis Group headquarters. Does half past ten meet your approval?"

"It does." A slow grin broke through her attempt to remain serious. "I choose edged blades as weapons. I assume you're to stand as her second?"

"I am."

She nodded, feeling an unexpected pang at the knowledge. Valmont had been her lover's protégé, had fought against the Sweet Butcher's iron-fisted control during the last years of her life, and had avenged his mentor's execution by assassinating Elisibet. Nahib wouldn't have wanted them to come to blows. *This is necessary.* "Samuel will be mine. We'll be there."

Valmont gazed at her, a wealth of meaning behind his eyes. He understood her position as she understood his. "I'm sorry it has to come to this, Bertrada. Nahib—"

"—Is dead, and I intend to make certain his murderer joins him. Permanently!"

Closing his mouth on what he'd planned to say, he bowed in acknowledgment. The sardonic smile rushed back onto his face as he looked at McCall. "Samuel, ever a pleasure. It's a shame your first duel will be your last."

"Get out!" Nijmege snapped. McCall was already on edge. Valmont's verbal assault would only serve to unsettle him more.

Chuckling, Valmont came to attention and gave her a salute before leaving the room.

"Don't let him upset you," Orlaith said, turning to McCall. "He's just trying to get under your skin, make you lose focus."

Disgruntled, McCall dropped into a chair. He wiped at his face. "Well, it's working."

Nijmege came to kneel beside him. "You have no need to worry. I've been training for months since we heard news of Elisibet's return. You and Valmont will be on the sidelines, offering mental strength—nothing more. He'll only enter the melee if Davis is alive but physically incapacitated, and that's not going to happen."

"You're certain?"

Nijmege smiled, patting his hand in a pacifying manner. "Of course. As soon as I get close enough, I'll have her head. The duel will be over." It seemed Valmont's opinion of McCall held some merit. The younger generations hadn't had as much battlefield experience and it certainly showed now. She wondered how he could be so powerful in council meetings but fainthearted when it came to confrontations. He'd obviously spent too much time using *kizarusi* rather than seeking his own sustenance. Providing she survived this ordeal, she vowed to take McCall hunting when they returned home. He needed to understand his Sanguire nature.

It doesn't matter. Tomorrow morning I'll have achieved my goal. Serene in that knowledge, she continued to reassure her wilting comrade, heart soaring.

CHAPTER THIRTY-TWO

Whiskey stared at the blue digital readout above the elevator panel as it counted down. Just before it reached the recreation floor, she took a deep breath. It did little to quell the butterflies roller coastering through her stomach but did moderately bolster her nerves. When the doors opened onto the third floor, she gave a passable imitation of a confident smile and exited with her entourage.

Valmont and Margaurethe flanked her, Jake leading the way and two *aga'gída* behind, a lethal phalanx protecting her as she walked down the crowded corridor to her possible death. This short span of hallway was lined with well-wishers, most of them employees of The Davis Group, all of them Sanguire. There was none of the happy excitement normally exhibited before a sporting event. As they passed the locker rooms she wondered if that was due to the nature of the dispute or from something more native to the Sanguire. She'd been occasionally surprised by them as a people, especially when they came together in large groups. She'd been raised by Humans and hadn't known she wasn't one herself until she'd fallen in with Fiona's pack of malcontents over a year ago. The Sanguire people's long-lived nature tended to dampen much of the Human hullabaloo with which she'd grown up.

Or maybe they know something about today's outcome I don't.

She pushed away the depressing thought as Jake reached the gymnasium entry. Two security guards stationed there opened the doors, and she preceded Whiskey inside. Whiskey followed, forcing herself to remain calm.

Much like the corridor, the large glass-enclosed room was lined with spectators. These were higher-ranking delegates visiting Portland as well as local dignitaries and supporters of The Davis Group. A dozen or so Humans had been invited to observe the duel, friends or assistants to the Sanguire upper crust, and they peppered the gathering. Whiskey picked out various political leaders, giving them regal nods of recognition. Looking up, she saw that the fourth-floor offices overlooking the gymnasium held a good number of her people, including her pack. They'd have a much better view of the proceedings from their vantage point. She supposed if she'd been more like Elisibet, she would have installed gallery seating around the room for debacles such as this. She faked a confident grin for Zebediah's eager thumbs-up signal.

A number of individuals clustered in the center of the room. They were the Sanguire witnesses, the *lú-inim-ma*, who would join together and shield the combatants. Their purpose wasn't to protect the duelers from outside attack, rather they would keep a mental wall in place to stop outside intervention from the fighters' allies. It wasn't unheard of that a duel without shields resulted in a free-for-all among the witnesses.

Her Mayan trainer broke away from the *lú-inim-ma*. He waved her closer. Her two royal guards stayed back but Jake accompanied the others forward. Pacal took Whiskey by the shoulders, turning her this way and that. Brief embarrassment at being treated like a piece of meat in front of all these high-ranking people disrupted her nerves. Before she could do more than blush, he thumped her in the chest, bringing her attention sharply to him. "You're strong, you're competent, and you'll beat that *malandro* without fuss." He bent forward to stare into her eyes. "And if you don't, I guarantee I'll have you running 'chete drills for the next month."

His rough admonition broke through the fog of fear. Smiling, she said, "If I don't then I won't be here to run those drills."

Scoffing, Pacal straightened. "Always the smart aleck. Do as I say!"

An impertinent grin remained on her face as she bowed. "Yes, teacher."

Satisfied, he patted her shoulders and stepped to the center of the room. He was one of *lú-inim-ma*, overseeing fairness on both sides. His companions were representatives from all other nations here, including Bentoncourt, Chano and Dikeledi. Whiskey found it odd that members of her board were on hand to keep the peace, and wondered if the others felt the same. She guessed that combining that many minds together—she counted a half dozen clustered there—would keep everyone on their toes. Not only would they guard against outside interference but also internal strife between them.

"You heard him, *m'cara*. I know how you detest his machete drills." Margaurethe leaned close, whispering into her ear, "I love you, Whiskey Davis. Finish this and come back to me."

Whiskey swallowed against the lump in her throat. "I will, *minn'ast*. I've only just found you, I have too much to look forward to." She received a blistering kiss that nearly made her forget her place until Valmont whistled softly.

"Perhaps you two should retire to the locker room for a quickie?"

She broke away from Margaurethe and Valmont was treated to their mock glares. He pretended terror, stepping back in a faux cower. Laughing, Whiskey hugged Margaurethe tight. "I'll see you in a few minutes." She reluctantly let her lover go.

"*Ninsumgal*."

Whiskey turned to her bodyguard. "Jake?"

"No insult intended toward *Sublugal Sañar* Valmont, but I would have preferred you choosing me in his stead." Jake glanced over her shoulder at McCall and Nijmege standing with Orlaith O'Toole several meters away. Leaning close, she whispered, "Nijmege's wrists are both thick, indicating she can use a blade in either hand. In the boardroom, however, she predominantly utilizes her right. Be wary."

"Thank you, Jake. I appreciate your experienced eye."

Her bodyguard's returned stare was substantive. She held Whiskey's regard for a long moment before lifting a chin. "Luck, *Ninsumgal*." She turned and trotted away, taking position beside Margaurethe.

"Must we endure further delays?" Nijmege called across the short space between them. "Or can we, as the Americans say, 'get this show on the road'?"

"What's the matter, Bertrada?" Valmont grinned at their opponent. "Can't wait to see the gates of Hell?"

Nijmege pointed a bared sword in his direction. "As you'll be there before I, at least I'll have the benefit of company."

Valmont frowned, tapping a finger against his chin. "I'm sorry. Was that an insult or a compliment?"

Whiskey enjoyed Nijmege's faint confusion before her face jelled into a steely determined expression. Nijmege wore leather for this fight though hers had the benefit of looking much older and more worn than Whiskey's attire. The sword Nijmege carried was a military saber, ninety centimeters of tempered steel with a simple aged gold cross guard. That gave her the reach of Whiskey, but not the strength. Whiskey carried a Mayan machete, the only edged weapon with which she had any experience. It was a sleek black blade of sixty-three centimeters with a wider curved and double-edged point. The lighter weight would give her a speed advantage compared to Nijmege's heavier sword. Whiskey knew from training experience that the heavier tip of her machete could break steel weapons despite its lightness.

McCall looked horribly out of place in sweatpants and a T-shirt. He tried to retain a hard glare, but uncertainty clouded over his face. He, too, had a sword strapped to his waist, a similar version of Nijmege's. She'd probably allowed him to borrow the weapon, which heartened Whiskey. His apparent lack of experience corresponded with Dorst's opinion of his capabilities.

Valmont must have thought the same. "Samuel," he called. "Quite a weapon you have there. How virile! Did you know when you arrived here that your cohort would be calling you to your death?"

Tucking his chin, McCall deigned to answer. His skin held the color of curdled milk. Valmont raised his own sword, a slightly curved cutlass with an intricate basket over the hilt, and saluted him.

"Don't listen to him, Samuel. He's just trying to get a rise out of you." Nijmege glared at the officials. "Will you please take your places and get on with it? I've waited about as long as I care to."

The *lú-inim-ma* peered down their noses at Nijmege, dislike evident on most of their faces. Being chosen for this task didn't make them any more or less superior to her, they were all of the same social standing within their countries. Their conduct suggested she'd suffer the consequences should she survive this encounter. Nevertheless, they broke apart, scattering around the room.

Orlaith took that as her cue, leaving Nijmege's side to take up position along the perimeter of the gymnasium. Whiskey glanced at Margaurethe on the opposite side, knowing that part of her lover's emotional quandary involved her mother's blatant support of Whiskey's enemies. Had Whiskey been the Sweet Butcher, Orlaith wouldn't have been as conspicuous. It was becoming commonplace how often Whiskey suffered the ill will of Elisibet's enemies simply because she wasn't the tyrant that her previous incarnation had been.

Moments later, Whiskey felt a dampening effect on her psyche. She'd become so used to mentally sampling her immediate surroundings that it had become second nature. She glanced around the room, startled as her eyes told her the spectators remained present. The sudden lack of psychogenic connections made her feel almost bereft.

"Takes getting used to, doesn't it?" Valmont asked.

"Yes." She rubbed at her temple with one hand. "I hadn't realized how much I use that part of myself."

Dikeledi's strong voice cut off further conversation. "Are the combatants prepared?"

Nijmege growled, teeth bared at Whiskey. "Yes."

Whiskey set aside her discomfort, searching for the anger in her heart. "Yes, I am."

"As the challenger, *Ninsumgal* Davis, will you withdraw?"

"Hell, no."

Nijmege interrupted Dikeledi's next question. "And no, I won't recant either. Get on with it!"

Dikeledi's expression held intense dislike. "Lay on!"

If Nijmege expected Whiskey to feint and parry around the room, she had a surprise in store. Pacal's training included the benefit of immediate offensive maneuvers. He preferred them to feeling out an opponent, instructing his students that more could be learned from an enemy by prompt and vicious aggression. Whiskey leapt forward, closing the distance with startling speed. Taking Jake's observations to heart, she launched an attack upon Nijmege's left side, hoping to cripple it before Nijmege had an opportunity to surprise her.

Unprepared for the confident onslaught, Nijmege froze a fraction of an instant. Whiskey's machete sliced into Nijmege's upper arm, splitting the leather armor and the skin beneath. Valmont hooted approval behind Whiskey. The rich copper smell of blood ignited her lust, her fangs sprouting from their sheaths. Nijmege recovered quickly, spinning away and bringing her saber up for a slice across Whiskey's abdomen. Being within the weapon's longer reach, Whiskey crow-hopped backward to avoid being skewered. She saw the glittering steel continue its rise as it missed her belly and scarcely turned her head in time to avoid receiving a mortal injury across her throat. Instead, sharp pain lanced along her right cheek, indicating where metal had parted flesh. Warm blood spilled down her neck, intensifying the gory aroma. It was McCall's turn to shout encouragement from the sidelines.

Nijmege ignored his distraction, pressing her attack. With a rattle of steel on steel, Whiskey blocked the saber, sparks shooting up between them as their blades clashed. She glared into Nijmege's eyes, attempting to forge mental contact. The smell of wet autumn leaves flowed around her. She felt their damp texture against her skin as she concentrated. For a brief moment, she thought she'd found entry only to be rebuffed both mentally and physically. Nijmege gave her a mighty shove, dropping her blade with a quick slash that connected before Whiskey could dive out of reach. She stumbled back, faltering as she held her abdomen with her left hand.

Nijmege allowed her to fully break off as she stumbled backward. Whiskey's penetrating mental capabilities had probably made an impression. A quick glance at her belly showed a neat slice that oozed blood. Both leather and skin had parted, but the wound was only a centimeter in depth. Had Whiskey not been pushed away at impact, she would surely have died from the wound. Instead, it pained her but didn't cripple her.

"Whiskey!" Valmont remained in place, not allowed by rules of conduct to approach. She felt him along her mind, bolstering her. "Let me in!"

She forced herself to stand tall, at least as erect as she could given the circumstances of her injury. "Not yet," she growled, scowling at Nijmege. Valmont swore but didn't press.

Her enemy's hawk-like face was twisted into a satisfied smile. "Not as all-powerful as you think you are, eh?" Nijmege flicked her saber, drops of Whiskey's blood splattering to the gymnasium floor. "I thought you had the strength and knowledge of Elisibet somewhere in that pretty little head of yours."

Whiskey scoffed. "This? This is nothing." She tucked her chin. "And I thought you were supposed to be some sort of swords master. I heard Nahib had insisted you learn it. Haven't kept up your lessons, I see."

Nijmege pointed her saber at Whiskey. "Never say his name, *za unu arra.*"

"Why?" Whiskey cocked her head in mock thought. "Oh, yeah! Because Nahib had integrity and honor, and you don't." As Nijmege shook with fury, Whiskey smiled. "I'm not saying Elisibet had those qualities either, but you certainly learned her lessons well."

With a wordless shout, Nijmege rushed forward. Whiskey raised her machete to block the madness-fueled attack, feeling the shock of it up her arms and into her aching torso. Again she engaged Nijmege's mind, searching it for weaknesses, but the woman's fury made one difficult to locate. It had been much easier dealing with the older assassin, Andri, several months ago. At least then she wasn't simultaneously fighting for her life on the physical plane. She felt Valmont's mental touch, used his essence to support her own as she struggled to avoid impalement. Again Nijmege drove the point of her saber toward Whiskey's throat, this time in an overhand strike. Whiskey blocked it with her machete, another shower of sparks occurring as the blades grated along their edges. And again the point pierced Whiskey's right side, not far from the original wound.

She cried out in agony, ignoring the roar of approval from McCall and Nijmege's gloating yell. Stumbling away, she fell into Valmont's arms. He held her up, while she sucked air into her lungs.

"Let me in!" he demanded, his brown skin dark with bloodlust.

Whiskey shook her head, stopping as the room spun for a second. "No. Not yet." Sweat dripped into her eyes. She wiped it away with the back of her weapon hand, a smear of blood accompanying it. It amazed her how much exertion it took to fight. Though she felt like she'd been running a three-hour marathon, their skirmish couldn't have been longer than two or three minutes.

Nijmege returned to McCall's side, taking a leisurely drink from a bottle of water she'd brought into the room. Despite her posturing, she felt the same enervation as she fought to catch her breath.

Valmont used the impromptu break to kneel and peer at Whiskey's injury. "Looks like she got you good that time. Stab wound, maybe four inches deep. Bleeding's sluggish." He looked up at her, concern in his eyes. "At least she hasn't separated the muscle wall. Your guts won't be spilling all over the floor just yet."

A wave of nausea went through Whiskey at the image. She smacked him on the shoulder with her free hand. "Stop that! You're not helping."

He gave her a contrite look. "Sorry."

"Stand up. Let me go."

With reluctance, he did as she bid, stepping aside. "You have other…skills at your disposal, Whiskey! Remember, Andri," he said, reminding her that she was a Ghost Walker. That talent had saved her life when the assassin had attempted to shoot her, his bullet passing through her ethereal belly.

"Easier said than done. With him I had some time to concentrate. It still comes and goes on its own if I don't." She pushed away from his support. The wound had gone from burning agony to a deep throbbing ache. She adjusted her weight, hissing and wincing at the increased pain. As she adapted to its intensity, she tried to tell herself that it wasn't any worse than a running cramp. Valmont added his essence to hers, his efforts drawing away some of the pain as she strutted forward with a slight limp.

Nijmege's eyes narrowed at Whiskey's apparent health. McCall's face was more expressive as he stared, faint alarm washing away the tentative smile. "Not had enough, eh? You do realize this fight is to the death, yes?" she asked as she prepared to join the fray once more.

"It has to be, Bertrada. You won't have it any other way."

"Quite right." They came together again, but neither landed solid blows. Nijmege held the grace of a dancer as her sword flashed, sparking as it met Whiskey's machete repeatedly.

They pulled back after the flurry, panting. Whiskey's side ached abysmally. She knew she was dripping blood down her pants and onto the floor, but couldn't spare the time to check the injury. Any attention drawn to it might let Nijmege know how bad it truly was. "Was that the best you could do?" Whiskey asked as she hunkered into a fighting stance, smiling through her weakened exhaustion. "Nahib must be turning over in his grave."

The use of her old lover's name spurred Nijmege forward in another impulsive charge.

Her uncontrolled emotions gave Whiskey a mental opening. Probing hard at a weakened section of Nijmege's mind, Whiskey put all her considerable power into the psychic attack as she brought up her machete to parry the oncoming saber. The mental stab was just enough to freeze Nijmege at a crucial moment. With vicious glee, Whiskey grabbed Nijmege's sword arm, pulling her forward and off balance as the machete speared Nijmege's left side. They crashed together, chest to chest, and she stared into Nijmege's eyes, seeing the slow realization dawn that Whiskey didn't just have Elisibet's memories but her martial experience and rugged mental power as well.

With a grunt of pain, Nijmege pushed Whiskey away, her mental shield firming up around the point of attack. She staggered backward into McCall's arms, sword out to counter another onslaught.

Valmont's laughter pealed across the open space. "Well, dear Samuel. Shall we play now?"

* * *

Sudden terror flared in McCall's heart at Valmont's invitation. He felt Nijmege scrambling at his essence, demanding both his mental and physical support as he helped her stand. "I thought you said you had this well in hand!" he said, voice squeaking in a shameful way.

"I. Do." Nijmege pushed him away, reeling ever so slightly. "I told you not to listen to him. He's just taunting you! I need you with me one hundred percent. Focus!"

"But you're older than both of them!" He waved a hand at Davis who had remained where she was after Nijmege's retreat. "She's just a child."

Nijmege's gasping for breath lessened as needed oxygen filled her lungs. "Apparently she's a bit more than that, my friend."

"But—"

"Enough! We can't back out now. It's too late." She turned to glare at Davis. "She's going to die at my hand. Today." With that, she limped back into the battle, transferring her sword to her left hand.

McCall tried to concentrate, adding his mental strength to Nijmege's to use as she saw fit. He knew on an academic level that a swordsman who could use both hands equally was someone to be feared. Davis didn't look particularly scared, however. His gaze darted to Valmont. Valmont leered back, winking when he caught McCall's eye. Cold sweat swept over him, and Nijmege faltered as a result before he could center his mind. He resolved not to look at Valmont again until this fiasco was over.

Nijmege gave a war cry and attacked. To his horror, Davis was prepared for her opponent's altered weapons hand. She ducked under Nijmege's longer blade, sliding her machete upward with as much strength as she could muster. McCall stared as the black blade sliced leather and the flesh of Nijmege's upper arm, separating the muscle there. The saber tumbled to the floor, hitting the wood with a *clang*.

"No," he whispered. He took one lurching step forward, concentrating his mind on Nijmege's.

She still lived, still fought, though her conflict now seemed fully mental. Davis had brought her machete up for another downward slash, but Nijmege had intercepted it with her still hale right hand. The machete trembled as they both gripped it at the hilt.

Closing his eyes, he took deep breaths to ground himself. He felt the mental struggle between them, marveling at the strength of Nijmege's opponent. *Roses. Roses and blood.* The air was saturated with it as he offered assistance, shored up areas of her shields as they started to tumble. He could sense nothing else and wondered if Valmont was even assisting. Frantic, he opened his eyes to confirm Valmont wasn't sneaking toward his position, relieved to see him in his place.

Sweat beaded on McCall's forehead, dripping down his face at his exertions. Davis and Nijmege fought for dominance over the machete, but Nijmege appeared to be weakening from the mental attack. *This isn't how it's supposed to go.*

He had plans to take over the European Sanguire, plans that had been put into place a hundred years ago. He only awaited a likely trigger to destabilize their entire governmental structure. Rosenberg had told him it didn't matter whether Nijmege lived or died in her pursuit of this challenge. McCall had tried to distract her from her goal, but the time for that had passed. He'd had hopes of her winning this bout and getting her away from The Davis Group long enough for assassins to be set upon her. That could have stirred things up at home nicely. But Davis seemed to be growing stronger. Her forays into Nijmege's mind stabbed pain behind his eyes and must agonize Nijmege. If she truly were the Sweet Butcher returned, McCall would never have the chance to rule the Euro Sanguire. *Never.* The yawning maw of failure opened before him.

He was moving before he realized it, sword upraised. Davis had to die in this match, no matter what. If she survived, a treaty would be negotiated. She'd become overseer of the *Agrun Nam*. He'd never gain the power he'd worked for his entire life.

In his mind, he felt Nijmege slowly dying. Rather than prolong her death throes, he retracted his help, mentally fleeing as he rushed forward to physically attack. Davis's fangs were bared in a hungry snarl as she felt Nijmege weaken, too busy concentrating on her goal to realize her peril. McCall, too, was entirely fixed upon his objective. With a growl, he brought the borrowed saber back for a downward sweep, putting everything he had into the maneuver.

Steel flashed before him, briefly blinding him as a curved cutlass reflected light from the windows. The shock of impact rattled McCall's teeth, his saber slamming into the blade before him. He staggered back, dazed, grabbing his aching wrist with his other hand.

Valmont stepped past the women in the final throes of conflict, an ugly smile on his face. "I was so hoping you'd try that."

McCall's mind blanked as panic swept over him. He brought his weapon up, using both hands to brandish it before him.

As he backed away, Valmont approached, step for step. "It took us a while to figure out who was sending those assassins. You covered your tracks well, but it really only turned out to be a process of elimination." He tapped the tip of the saber, chuckling as it wildly wavered in McCall's grip. "What did you think would happen when we finally pinpointed you?"

"I don't know what you're talking about!" Though Valmont loomed close, he didn't seem too inclined to attack quite yet. McCall frantically searched for help from the assembled witnesses. His only colleague in attendance was Bentoncourt, and McCall could tell there'd be no assistance from that quarter.

Valmont barked laughter, drawing his attention back.

"You certainly don't think Lionel will help, do you? He suspects you as much as we did." Cocking his head, he stroked McCall's saber with his cutlass, the hiss of steel against steel sickening the less experienced man. "What do you think is going to happen if you get out of this alive? I bet you'll be under investigation before you leave this city. No doubt the order has already been given to ransack your office and home."

McCall felt his eyes widen at the thought. He couldn't seem to catch his breath as he tried to recall if he'd left incriminating evidence anywhere.

Valmont closed the distance between them. "You won't be *Maskim Sañar* for long, will you?"

"No!" Unable to help himself, McCall pulled back just enough to gather momentum for a strike. The move left him defenseless and Valmont utilized the brief opportunity to attack.

Nijmege might have been graceful in her skill, but Valmont was almost beautiful in form using a lethal economy of motion. He bore McCall's blade aside, not even blinking as the saber snapped with a sharp *ting!* to fall musically to the floor. His cutlass arced back, floating across McCall's field of vision, deftly slicing into the meat of his inner right thigh.

McCall stood puzzled a moment, still gripping the broken weapon. Why hadn't Valmont gone for his throat, decapitated him? Lethargy washed through him, counteracting the adrenaline in his bloodstream. *But I've hardly been touched.* He dropped his gaze to see blood gushing from the wound. The color was wrong. Having seen his fair share throughout his life, his blood was a much brighter red than he'd expected. It pooled on the floor beneath him. Repulsed, he attempted to step away from the puddle but stumbled. Vertigo spun the room and he fell to the floor as a bone-deep chill took root within him. He stared up at his opponent.

Valmont watched with idle boredom, pausing to study his fingernails a moment before returning his attention to McCall. "Femoral artery," he explained in matter-of-fact tones. "Quick, of course, but Whiskey needs medical attention more than I need to make an example of you." He looked over his shoulder, checking the progress of the other battle. Squatting down, he lowered his voice. "Interesting point of trivia, Samuel. This is how Elisibet died too. I opened the artery and she bled out within minutes."

McCall slumped backward, unable to gather the necessary energy to do more than shiver as Death drew its black cloak over him. His last sight was Valmont's gaze, his last sound Valmont's voice.

"I have to say I have a much better appreciation for your death than hers."

* * *

Nijmege's consciousness faded beneath Whiskey's onslaught. She hardly noted a flurry of movement beside her, the clash of metal, too intent on her goal to pay attention to the sounds of melee moving away. As darkness enveloped Nijmege's mind, Whiskey set aside her vicious glee of victory. That was an aspect of Elisibet, not of her. "I'm so sorry, Bertrada," she whispered as Nijmege released her grip on the machete, her life snuffed out as her mind collapsed.

Whiskey pulled back from the final spiral, knowing from experience and training that to follow a Sanguire into death meant death itself. She stared at the hawk-like features, slack in release, the final spark of emotion dissipating from the muddy-brown eyes. Slumping, she moved with pained and awkward caution as she gently shifted Nijmege's body to the floor.

No longer concentrated on death, she watched her immediate surroundings come back into slow focus. She heard a voice. Turning, she saw Valmont squatting beside the bleeding form of McCall, distantly recognizing the brilliant crimson color and hearing McCall's last expiration. Her friend looked unaffected by wear as he wiped his cutlass clean on McCall's T-shirt before rising. Whiskey attempted to do the same, but couldn't dredge up the energy quite yet.

A rush of sound and sensation cascaded over her. Wincing, she glared around the gymnasium, realizing that the *lú-inim-ma* must have dropped their protective shield. The witnesses had broken into applause, some more enthusiastic than others. Then Valmont was beside her, helping her to stand. Pacal took up a position on her other side, pride on his face as they both helped her from the battlefield.

Woodsmoke and mulled wine eclipsed all other sensations as she staggered into Margaurethe's embrace. She fought the urge to collapse into tears, pulling herself together for a show of strength. Daniel was there, urging her toward a gurney. "No." She shook her head, stopping when it made the room spin. "I'll walk out." No one argued her order, not even Margaurethe. Instead, a bottle of water was shoved into her hands, and she drank greedily. Pausing, gasping, she looked at Valmont. "If we do this again, remind me to bring in a canteen."

He smiled. "I'll do that."

"*Ninsumgal*, you need medical attention. This can wait."

Whiskey gave Daniel a bare nod, allowing them to usher her out of the gymnasium and away from the mayhem. Despite the blood loss, she remained on her feet until the elevator doors closed. Only then did she allow the darkness to sweep over her as she fainted.

CHAPTER THIRTY-THREE

Whiskey stood near the gymnasium windows, arms crossed over her chest as she stared at the predawn stillness. For the first time in months, she was here without a cadre of *aga'gída* to protect her from constant threats. Though she rejoiced in their absence, a part of her kept stumbling over the lack, her mind continually scanning for mental essences that were no longer there. This morning Jake was her only companion, a pale shadow positioned near the doors. Whiskey had gotten so used to her *zi agada's* presence it seemed silly to fire her from the position. Whiskey might have made a dramatic point yesterday morning with the challenge, but eventually fear of her power would wane among those set on getting retribution for the Sweet Butcher's past deeds. Until Whiskey came fully into her own on a physical level it behooved her to have at least one bodyguard on hand, and she'd become attached to Jake.

"*Ninsumgal.*"

She smiled at the window, sensing cold beer on a hot day. "Let him in." The door opened, and she turned to Bentoncourt, dropping her arms to her side. "Lionel, it's a bit early isn't it?"

He bowed and approached. "I thought it best to acclimate myself to European time before I left, *Ninsumgal*. Less jet lag." Visually scanning her, he said, "I see you're well."

"Yes. Daniel patched me up pretty well." Her hand automatically strayed to her abdomen where the majority of battle damage had occurred. Daniel had released her less than six hours after the duel.

"I'm relieved to hear that." His gaze flickered to the floor a few meters away.

She followed his gaze. Only faint stains marred the wood where Nijmege and McCall had met their ends. The brutal violence caused an odd time dilation. Though the challenge had taken place less than twenty-four hours ago, it felt like weeks had passed. At the same time, the fury and fear hovered too close, making Whiskey loath to discuss it so soon. Rather than be drawn into such a discussion, she changed the subject. "Margaurethe tells me that you're leaving today."

Bentoncourt pulled himself away from his survey of the floor. "In less than an hour, as a matter of fact. I'm pleased I inquired after you."

"As am I." She mentally grimaced at her stilted statement, not liking the formal diplomacy. Talking in such a way smothered her like a straitjacket, fettering easy communication and squeezing the life out of mutual understanding. "Look, I'm not going to act high-and-mighty here, Lionel. It's not my style, and I feel like an ass when I attempt it. Let me apologize in advance for offending you by anything I say."

Bentoncourt grinned, relaxing just a hair. His smile took years off his face, and he bared his neck. "I consider myself duly warned."

"What happens now?"

He accepted her blunt question without qualm. "Now I return home and the *Agrun Nam* calls two new members to serve on the council. When that's completed, we'll have a serious look at your latest proposals. I hope to hammer out an agreement between the European Sanguire and The Davis Group within the year."

She studied him. "Just like that?"

"Just like that."

A grin curled her lips at his flippant repetition. It was a side of him she hadn't seen before. "Do you expect Ernst to give you any problems? He thinks I'm Elisibet."

Bentoncourt paused in brief thought. "I doubt he'll stand against you. He sees the benefits as well as any of us." He shrugged one shoulder. "He didn't stand against you this time, really."

"No, he just took abstention to a whole new level because he thought not supporting Bertrada would destroy your people."

"Isn't that what we're here for?" he asked, his deep voice soft. "To keep all our peoples from destruction? You can hardly blame Ernst for his loyalty to his countrymen."

Whiskey chuckled and took his hand in hers. "Thanks for the reminder. Sometimes I get lost in the details and forget the big picture."

"Considering your youth, I believe you're doing a fine job, *Ninsumgal*." He glanced at his watch. "I have to go. Francesca and Orlaith are downstairs with Baltje and our luggage. I had the majority of my staff leave yesterday afternoon and evening."

"Of course." A wave of relief swept over her as she shook his hand, touching his bicep with the other. "I'm glad I had a chance to say goodbye." *And I'm glad you're taking Orlaith with you.*

"As am I." The stilted language sounded much better when he said it. He grinned, an impertinent flash in his dark eyes bespeaking an impish sense of humor that didn't have much opportunity to present itself. Releasing her, he took three steps backward and formally bowed. "Until next time, *Ninsumgal* Davis. I'll keep in touch."

"Thank you again, Lionel. I'm sorry it had to come to this."

Sorrow flickered across his expression, rapidly replaced with acceptance. "Ernst was right. Nothing I could have done or said would have changed her goal. And as for Samuel..." Disgust briefly curled his lip. They stared at one another a moment before Bentoncourt gave another quick bow and turned away.

He paused at the door. "Would you pass on a message to Father Castillo for me?"

"Sure."

"Tell him that we'll expect him back in Europe sometime next autumn."

Whiskey blinked. "Okay…"

"As I said, a restructure of the *Agrun Nam* is in order. I believe he'll make a fine delegate for our upcoming negotiations with The Davis Group. It helps that he already understands the inner workings of your board—he'll fit right in." He actually winked before leaving the gymnasium.

Delight rippled through Whiskey as Jake closed the door behind Bentoncourt. "Man, the padre's going to be surprised."

Jake didn't answer, seeing something in the corridor beyond. Without asking permission, she opened the door once more, this time admitting a sleepy Margaurethe.

Whiskey's heart tripped as Margaurethe approached. She wore a robe over her nightgown, the material a green so dark it was almost black. Her mahogany hair spilled over her shoulders, red highlights glowing beneath the gymnasium lights. Her bare feet whisked across the floor. Whiskey met the tendrils of Margaurethe's mind, wrapping herself in a cloak of mulled wine and woodsmoke.

Margaurethe slipped into her arms. "I woke and you were gone."

"I slept plenty yesterday afternoon. I couldn't get any more."

"How long have you been down here?"

Whiskey shrugged, enjoying the smell and feel of her lover against her. "Maybe an hour?" It had been more like two, but she didn't want to admit to that long an absence. She crossed her fingers in the hopes that Jake wouldn't spill the beans.

Margaurethe pulled back to peer at her. "I saw Lionel in the hall."

"Yeah, he came to say goodbye. He's got a lot of work ahead of him."

"Indeed."

"Your mother's returning to Europe with him."

Margaurethe remained quiet for several seconds. "That's good. We've always done better with long distance."

They held each other for some time, the sky outside becoming gray with impending dawn. Traffic began picking up on the highways across the river, and Whiskey heard delivery trucks beginning to trundle past the building. Reluctant to speak, she nevertheless felt the sensations of fleece and carnations that indicated Jake had bristled. She looked to see her bodyguard standing sentry, glaring out the door at whoever was in the hallway. "I think it's time we went home. It seems we're monopolizing this room."

"An excellent idea." Margaurethe kissed her. They crossed the room, arm in arm. "We wouldn't want Jake to break any bones over the matter of public space usage."

"Nope, not at all." Whiskey chuckled. "It's okay, Jake. Let them in. We're leaving."

The warning in Jake's expression lessened but didn't abate as she opened the door. Out in the corridor, a half-dozen men stood in shorts and T-shirts, two carrying basketballs. Though Human, as soon as they caught sight of Whiskey they straightened and bowed to her.

"Our apologies," Margaurethe said. "The gymnasium is yours, gentlemen."

Their apparent leader, a man who worked in the marketing department, grinned. "No apology needed, *Ki'an Gasan, Ninsumgal*, but thank you." As soon as Jake cleared the entry, they ducked inside to begin their game.

The cardiovascular room was doing brisk business. Every machine was occupied and three women had gathered on mats for a yoga session. "And so begins another day."

Margaurethe smiled at Whiskey. "As it should be."

Whiskey entered the elevator, Margaurethe on her arm and Jake at her back. Today wasn't just another day, it was new and invigorating. She'd survived the enmity of the man who'd been attempting to kill her for over a year, and personally defended herself against the woman who had lusted for her death centuries before she'd been born. There'd be other threats in the future, just as dire, just as serious. For now, however…

She reached out and punched in the elevator express code and the button for the sixteenth floor. "No place to go but up."

GLOSSARY

Aga Maskim Sañar–Bertrada Nijmege's title, Judiciary of the High Court of the *Agrun Nam*

aga ninna–fearsome crown

aga'us/aga'usi–security, policeman, soldier

aga'gída–the Ninsumgal's personal guard

Agrun Nam–council (literally "inner sanctuary")

Baruñal–midwife to the Ñíri Kurám process

ebànda–younger brother

gasan–lady, mistress, queen

Gidimam Kissane Lá–ghost walker, a talent, able to move through solid objects

Gúnnumu Bargún–shape shifter, a talent, able to change appearance

Ki'an Gasan–Margaurethe O'Toole's title (literally "Beloved Lady Mistress")

kizarus, kizarusi–vessel

kunsi–Lakota–grandmother

kutyafasza–Hungarian–dog's dick–swear word of Nijmege's

lamma–female spirit of good fortune, nickname, term of endearment

lú-inim-ma–witness

lugal–male leader of small household unit

m'cara–beloved, an affectation of Margaurethe O'Toole for Elisibet Vasillas

malandro–Brazillian–tough guy, bad guy

Maskim Sañar–Samuel McCall's title, Judiciary of the Low Court of the *Agrun Nam*

minn'ast–beloved, an affectation of Elisibet Vasillas for Margaurethe O'Toole

ñalga súp–nitwit

nam'en–lord

Nam Lugal–Lionel Bentoncourt's title, leader of the *Agrun Nam*

Ninsumgal–lady of all, sovereign, dragon, monster of composite power, official title of Elisibet

Ñíri Kurám–the change, the turning

nu-me-en-na-ta–you don't exist

puru um–idiot, hillbilly

r-a-bar-ra–bastard

Sabra Sañar–Aiden Cassadie's title, Diplomatic branch of the *Agrun Nam* *saggina*–local magistrate for European Sanguire

Sa'kan Sañar–Ernst Rosenberg's title, Master of the Treasury of the *Agrun Nam*

sañar/sanari–councilor of the *Agrun Nam*

san–slave

Sañur Gasum–Reynhard Dorst's title, Eunich Assassin

Sublugal Sañar–Valmont's title, Defender of the Crown

su-lum–covered in shit

takoja–Lakota, grandchild

Ugula Aga'us–Captain of the Ninsumgal's personal guard, the Aga'us

u-nu-nar-ra–fraud

Usumgal–lord of all, sovereign, dragon, monster of composite power, official title of Elisibet's father

wicahca–Lakota–real man, term of respect

za–you; yourself

Zi Agada–chief bodyguard, Jake Jacobsen's title

Bella Books, Inc.

Women. Books. Even Better Together.

P.O. Box 10543
Tallahassee, FL 32302

Phone: 800-729-4992
www.bellabooks.com